Most of the young men favored ~~killing the~~ Whiteman at once, but some were inclined toward bringing him along in the hope that he might recover sufficiently that they might torture him. When they realized that Acorn Girl proposed to save the White man's life, they shouted their disapproval.

The scattered and mutilated bodies that had lain at Usto-ma village were quite vivid in the minds of the people. Mercy seemed almost beyond their comprehension.

At last Acorn Girl drew both her pistol and her knife, taking a stance between the half-dead *Wawlem* and the Panos. "You are my own people," Acorn Girl said, "but if anyone wishes to fight me over this man, then I will fight!"

A moment of stunned silence followed the speech, and no one stepped forward to accept her challenge.

Into the restored calm, Acorn Girl lowered her voice and said, "I, too, Panos have lost those I loved to the murdering *Wawlems*. But the Bear Spirit has sent this man to me for some purpose. Now, since the Whites have taken away my husband and my babies, I declare this *Wawlem* to be mine. I will own him for as long as he lives."

PEOPLE OF THE SACRED OAK

People of the Sacred Oak

Bill Hotchkiss

BANTAM BOOKS
TORONTO • NEW YORK • LONDON • SYDNEY • AUCKLAND

PEOPLE OF THE SACRED OAK

A Bantam Book / May 1986

ISBN 0-553-25624-6

Published simultaneously in the United States and Canada

Bantam Books are published by Bantam Books, Inc. Its trademark,
consisting of the words "Bantam Books" and the portrayal of a
rooster, is Registered in U.S. Patent and Trademark Office and in
other countries. Marca Registrada. Bantam Books, Inc., 666 Fifth
Avenue, New York, New York 10103.

For my wife, Judith Shears, co-author of *People of the Sacred Oak*, whose insights into the psychology of Ooti have brought the novel to life.

Contents

I
Maidu Interlude

II
Jake's Wife and Bear-who-cannot-see-well

III
Pano-ng-kasi The Grizzly Dance

I

Maidu Interlude

Moloko the Condor has vanished from these skies.
Pano the Grizzly has gone away also.
Much has changed but not everything has changed.
Oleli the Coyote still sings in the night
And when the time has come
He will dance and chant his chant of beginning
And the Ootimtsaa Tree will grow once more
And bear all twelve kinds of acorns.
Then Moloko will fly again
And Pano will stand on the mountains and laugh.

1

Shahwodo Moon

October, 1847

The world has not always been the way we see it now. No, there was an earlier world when everyone was rich and happy, but that was a long time ago. Then fires burned on the mountains, and all the ice melted. Rains fell for many months, and the sky came down close to the earth. The Great Valley was turned into an ocean, and Weebehillen, the Big Fish, swam in the waters. The people tried to swim away, but they were eaten by frogs and salmon.

In the thin space between the inland ocean and the sky, a raft floated. It came down from the north, and on it were Turtle and Peheipe, the Clown. No sun, only a little light in the heavy grayness—and terrible, distant noises, as though the mountains that surrounded the inland ocean were splitting apart.

Then a hole appeared in the grayness, and time started over again. Turtle and Peheipe saw a rope of feathers being lowered to their raft.

The hole in the grayness was bright red—like a wound that did not bleed. And from it, climbing hand over hand down the rope of feathers, came World Maker. He stepped onto the raft with Turtle and Peheipe and said, "I have come from above. I have come from beyond the broken shell of no-time. Soon the sky will turn blue again, and these waters will go away. I will make them do that. Then the sun will once more pass across the sky, and the moon will follow. But first I must sit and think."

Years passed, and still World Maker sat motionless, his eyes closed, his thoughts wandering.

Peheipe made strange faces and obscene gestures. At last Turtle grew impatient and spoke to World Maker.

Ooti, Ooti-du, Acorn, Acorn Girl.

She was different from the other Maidu women, and she had always known this. Nor was it simply in the matter of appearance. It was true that Ooti had never been given the tattoos of dots on breasts and arms and she bore no marking at the root of her nose—for her husband, Pine-nut-eater of the Kolo-ma, had persuaded her not to have her flesh decorated in the traditional fashion. Her mother, Tule Elk, had warned her of the dangers of entering full womanhood unmarked, but Acorn Girl had acceded to the wishes of her husband. No, it was not the absence of tattoo markings that set her apart. It was something else, something inside her head and her heart.

Had she been a man instead of a woman, so her father had always insisted, she would have been a leader of her people—perhaps even a Yomi shaman, a sucking doctor, one who drew the *omeya,* the pain, out of those who had been afflicted. She might have been revered, like Kuksu Man, her father. Of all the Maidu men in Tumeli village, only old Hurt Eagle, the man of many winters who had been his teacher, was more respected.

Ooti spread out the rabbitskin blanket atop the big healing rock that overlooked the river and then removed the loose-fitting tunic of deerskin, the hair side worn next to the flesh, and lay down on her back. She closed her eyes and allowed the good heat of the autumn sunlight to flood over her. She could feel the sun's fingers touching gently at her abdomen.

The life inside could feel it also, and Acorn Girl smiled as she experienced the little kicking sensations within her body.

"It will be soon now," she thought. "I am big with child. I have become very clumsy, and I must take great care when I walk along the river trail. But it is good at night when Pine-nut-eater places his head against my belly and nuzzles softly. He wishes for a son, but it does not matter to me. Only that I want to make him happy if I

am able. If this is a son I bear, he will be blessed—I think
so. I think he will be born very soon, during the burning
time, the cry time, the *Ustu*, when we celebrate those
who have died during the past year and those who have
died long before that as well. Such children have the
goodwill of the Spirits, the *Kakini*. . . ."

She herself had been born during the *Ustu* time, eigh-
teen winters earlier.

"I was seventeen," she thought, "and still not married.
The young men feared me because I could run faster than
they, I was more skilled with bow and arrow and with
spear."

No young men came to her father's lodge to talk, and
none sent presents of deermeat or salmon. The older men
admired her, she knew that. But they had not come to
visit either. Kuksu Man and Tule Elk had grown worried
about their daughter and had spoken to her of the possibility of learning the skills of medicine. Tule Elk, in fact, had
actually spoken to her at some length as to the advantages
of remaining unmarried.

"If you share a lodge with a lazy man, Ooti, or one who
spends too much time playing the guessing game, gambling everything away, then your *hubo* will be empty all
the time, very poor. There are many such men, and one
can never tell ahead of time. Then you would have to
starve or come home to us in disgrace."

Ooti remembered her mother's serious expression,
laughed, and turned to one side on the rabbitskin blanket,
luxuriated in the warmth of sunlight.

Then, at the time of salmon-netting, she had met Pine-
nut-eater, the young Kolo-ma Maidu who looked different
from the others—very different. Pine-nut-eater wore the
clothing of the *Wawlems*, the Whitemen: a broad-brimmed
hat and a fringed jacket, and trousers made of cloth. And
he had both a pistol and a rifle, the powerful weapons of
the *Wawlems*.

Acorn Girl had been astonished when Pine-nut-eater
came, unannounced, to visit the lodge of Kuksu Man and
Tule Elk, though at first it never even occurred to her that
the young man with the strange gray eyes and the *Wawlem*
clothing might be interested in her. But when he contin-

ued to come back, she knew—she knew very certainly even before the day when he had come upon her at the Willow Water, where she and several other girls were leaching acorns. Yes, that was the day when he had asked her if she would consider him as a husband.

Pine-nut-eater, his father had been a *Wawlem*. She had known about this from friends among the Kolo-ma, even before he had told her—his eyes cast down, as though he were revealing something that was possibly shameful.

"I am a wealthy man, Ooti," Pine-nut-eater had told her. "But there are things you must know about me. My father was White, one of those *Wawlems* who camped on our river for a year—more than twenty winters ago. I never knew him, for he left before I was born. Then, when I was in my seventh year, my mother, Cooking Rock, died. After that I was raised by the Kolo-ma. They fed me and tolerated me, but they did not want me because I was half White. Even when I grew bigger and stronger than the other boys, they still did not like me very much. At last I went away and journeyed down to where our river joins with the Big River, where the Whitemen have settled and have built their fort. The leader of the *Wawlems*, Sutter, decided that he liked me—and he hired me to lead him and some of his men back into the High Mountains. I still don't know why he wished to go there—maybe to see where the river begins, I don't know. And he has paid me in Whiteman's money. With that I am able to buy things at the trading post, whatever I want so long as I have earned enough money to do it. And whenever Sutter wishes to go someplace he has not been before, I go with him to find the way. He trusts me, even if I tell him I don't know how to get there any more than he does. He treats me almost like a son, Ooti. But then, when I had a horse and weapons and clothing and many blankets, I returned to the Kolo-ma."

"Do your people accept you now, Pine-nut-eater?" she had asked.

He turned from her then, picked up a pebble, and flung it far across the stream. The stone struck a liveoak limb high up on the wall of the ravine and came bounding back to the water.

"No," he admitted. "They don't. Oh, it's better than before. But now many of them are jealous, especially the shamans. And the village clown likes to follow me about and make faces and gestures. I ignore him."

"You threw that stone much farther than I could have," Acorn Girl said.

"I am very good at throwing stones," he answered.

"Will Kuksu Man accept you, Pine-nut-eater?"

"Yes—I think so. He never rejects the presents I bring him."

"That is true," Acorn Girl said. "We have dined very well since you began visiting us. With your rifle, you are able to take game whenever you wish to."

"I have used only the bow and arrow," he said. And she detected a slight redness in his complexion.

"I knew that," she said. "My father explained that to me. The gift is more valuable if it is taken in the way of the Maidus. You are a very fine hunter, but I think I am better perhaps."

Pine-nut-eater laughed aloud.

"That is what I have heard," he replied. "Will you consider me, Ooti? I will wait for an answer as long as you wish."

She nodded, trying hard to keep from smiling. Suddenly she wished to cry out, to laugh, to run as far and as fast as she could and then to leap into the cold green waters of the river.

"Are you able to give me strong children?" she asked, staring him directly in the eyes.

He did not turn his gaze from hers.

"Of course," he replied. "I will give you as many children as you want. What is it? Do you expect me to let you examine my manhood, or what?"

She laughed then—and half-skipped backward a step or two.

"I will do that later," she said. "First I must make a bed for us in my father's lodge. Come tomorrow night, Pine-nut-eater, and bring my father some fine obsidian arrow points and some of the green pigment used for bow decoration. If you will do that, then I will not make you sit up all night waiting for me. I will lie down with you and let you come into me. But you must promise not to be rough. I have never done this thing before, Pine-nut-eater."

And that was how Acorn Girl had become the wife of the young Kolo-ma who had a *Wawlem* for a father, and after a few weeks, with Hurt Eagle the ancient shaman assisting them, demanding that he be allowed to assist, they built their own lodge, a large *hubo* with strong beams in its ceiling, these hewed out by Pine-nut-eater, with old Hurt Eagle admiringly observing the younger man's skill with the metal-bladed Whiteman's tools, the axe and the adze.

And when all was finished, hides stretched in place and bark and brush heaped over them, a firepit constructed, sleeping pallets and an eating bench set in place, then Hurt Eagle had drawn her apart and had given her these words:

Look at me from above, look at me from these hills.
Look at me from the heaven and bless me.

Eta nik hedeng kawm hipining kawyawnaan.
Eta nik hedem yaman-mantawnaanis.

"These are your words, Ooti, I give them to you, and now they are yours. Sing them whenever you need them. You, too, Pine-nut-eater of the Kolo-mas. Live well, and bring me children. I will be their grandfather."

With that the ancient healing priest turned and strode briskly away—as though numerous years had suddenly been lifted from his wide shoulders and sinewy arms.

That was how it had happened. And now, with the passage of a year, she was great with child—almost too large, as Tule Elk had noted, the woman's hand petting at her daughter's hair.

Ooti turned once more onto her back and basked in the strangely powerful rhythm of the orange-red autumn sunlight. The rabbitskin blanket felt good beneath her—yes, and the comforting hardness of the healing rock beneath that. The sound of water swirling over rocks, the agitated cry of a bluejay, and angry chatter and chirring of a gray squirrel—the two creatures, Ooti realized, holding some sort of debate as to the proper ownership of something, seeds perhaps, or simply the right to occupy a particular branch in a particular tree.

Soft wind, a warm breeze, flowing about her, touching at her nose and eyes, touching at her rounded stomach.

She reached down, held herself, pressed, felt a quick response from the life within her.

And drifted into sleep.

The sun and the full moon were in the sky at once, and they were moving closer together. Ooti watched their progress in a state of both horror and fascination.

What would happen when they met?

Long bandings of cloud, like serpents, like huge green and brown mottled serpents, swam in the air, not like clouds but like streamers of mist that moved along the canyon bottoms after a time of heavy rains. Their heads swung back and forth, and their red tongues darted nervously before them.

Then the sun and the moon collided, each devouring the other, and intense red-orange lights flared everywhere. The standing pines and great liveoaks burst suddenly into flame, and the green waters of the river ceased to run, bubbling and hissing and boiling, finally vanishing upward in trails of steam. Boulders along the river bottom sagged, seemed to come loose from themselves, and melted, turning red-hot and fluid.

Fire in the heavens. The earth on fire also.

But Ooti was not harmed. A cool, protecting flood of air ran about her, blowing her long hair, touching at her eyes and nose and cheeks and mouth.

She felt for her abdomen and realized that she was no longer pregnant.

"When did I give birth?" she cried out. "Where is my child? Pine-nut-eater, my husband, what has happened? Where is our child?"

"You did not have a child," a growling, coughing voice said—but where was the voice coming from?

Now it was night. The air was cool, and a light mist was falling, gently, gently.

"What has happened to my child?" Ooti called out again.

Fire sprang up from the center of the healing rock, a small fire, like a cooking fire.

"Come sit with me," the voice said, "and I will tell you. You did not have a child, Ooti. You had two children. Two children came to you out of the Mystery."

A bear—a huge, silver-speckled grizzly. The beast sat down cross-legged before the flames and scratched with a massive forepaw at one of his ears. He blinked and wrinkled his nose.

"You are a bear, and yet you can speak," she said.

No longer was she frightened, even though she knew she should be. For a moment she feared she might still be unclothed, but she realized the good warmth of the deerskin tunic was about her. She pulled the garment tight about her throat, inexplicably wishing to cover her breasts even though Maidu women commonly went unclothed from the hips upward, and sat down across from the talking bear.

"Of course," he said. "I am Pano. I was there at Estawm Yan, the Middle Hills, at the time when Peheipe Oleli created the People while the rest of us were sleeping. Do not be frightened. I am not a ghost, Ooti, and looking at me will not cause you to die. No, I have come to tell you something."

"Tell me?"

"Yes. It is very complicated—this that I must tell you. Everything that you and your people have always known will change very soon. You are dreaming this, Ooti, Little Acorn Woman. I am part of your vision. Listen now."

"I hear you, Pano the Bear."

"I am afraid to tell you too much."

"You haven't told me anything yet," she said, smiling at the grizzly.

"Of course not. Women never let the men get a word in edgewise. Be quiet now and hear me. I have said that you gave birth to two children, to twins, but that has not happened yet. It will happen very soon. Do not be afraid. The People will not take the twins from you and kill them, even though that is the traditional thing to do. You will

give birth to twin sons, Ooti. After that you will not have
any more children for awhile."

"Are you telling me that Pine-nut-eater will leave me?
That he will go work for the Wawlem again and not
return?"

"Those are your words, Ooti, and not mine. You must
learn to listen. You have always been too impatient with
things—ever since you were a child. Always you wished to
beat the boys when you raced with them or shot arrows at
the hanging cones of the sugar pine."

"And I did win—usually I did win," she said.

"Yes. Oleli the Coyote Man and I have both watched
you, Little Acorn Woman. And a time will come when you
must lead your people, even though not many are left.
This is what I must tell you. You will know pain. You will
know grief. Terrible things will happen, Ooti, and yet you
must be strong. The pathway into the future times is
difficult. You will have to cross mountains and canyons. . . ."

She stared into Pano's eyes. And then the body vanished, and only the eyes remained, suspended against
darkness, like two blue-white glowing stones.

She heard her name.

Awakening, she looked up, saw the sun still in the sky,
but lower now, drifting westward. Below the healing rock,
the green waters of the river continued to flow under the
pleasant warmth of autumn, the season of the *Shahwodo*
Moon. The canyonsides about her were just as they had
been before her vision, the water oaks and the blue oaks
and the black oaks ranging in color from russet to deep
yellow, the maples flaring an even more intense shade of
yellow, the poison oak bushes standing out in little clots of
redness, the leaves of the buckeye pale and dry and brown.

A rat-tat-tatting sound from up the canyonside.

"*Panaak*," she thought. "He's been collecting acorns
also, just as we have. Now he's putting *tsoon* holes in a
dead limb, places to store his acorns. . . ."

"Ooti! Wife, where are you?"

She rose, pulled the deerskin tunic about her, and
looked quickly across the river.

Pine-nut-eater was standing on the white bar of gravel, just at the head of some rapids, close by the pounding rocks.

"I am here," she called out. "I am doing what a woman-with-child must always do if she can. I have been letting the sun touch at our child, Pine-nut-eater."

"I grew worried," he called back. "You had been gone for a long while, and I thought maybe . . ."

"No," she laughed. "My time has not come yet. You are strong, my husband. Come carry me back across the river. I like to be carried."

"I know, I know," she heard him respond, thinking she could not hear him. But the words carried perfectly, even above the soft shushing sound of the river.

For a moment she watched the tall, broad-shouldered man who wore the sombrero and the other *Wawlem* garments as he waded through the knee-deep current that dashed smoothly over the gray and white stones of the riverbed, forming a glittering vee in the afternoon sunlight before stilling once again into the deeper water below.

Then she climbed down from the healing rock, careful not to lose her balance and feeling strangely awkward now in these last few days of her pregnancy, and made her way through the thickets of willow and redbud and young alders to the drifted gray-white sand beside the running water.

For a moment, as Pine-nut-eater emerged from the current, grinning now and rubbing at his nose, Ooti thought he looked very much like Pano the Bear.

And fragments of her vision came back to her.

"You've been sleeping on the medicine rock?" he asked as he enfolded her in his embrace.

"Yes," she answered, looking up at his gray, *Wawlem* eyes. "I am so clumsy now. But soon I will be thin once more, my husband. I am not going to let myself get fat now, the way some of the women do after they have had their first child. No, I am going to be thin again, like always. Then we will race to the big digger pine again, and I'll still be able to win."

Pine-nut-eater laughed—a warm, generous, but perhaps slightly patronizing laugh.

"Do you really think I can't outrun you, Ooti?" he asked and at the same time kissed her hair.

"Only once," she said. "All the other times I won. Are you pretending now that you let me beat you?"

"Kuksu Man and Tule Elk gave you the wrong name," he said, laughing again. "You should have been *Sumi*, the deer, instead of Ooti. Everyone knows that acorns cannot run."

"No," she said, holding tight to him and pressing her face against her husband's chest. "But they can sprout and give birth to *Ootimtsaa*, the great oak tree."

Pine-nut-eater lifted his wife, turned, and waded back into the glittering green vee of the current, clucking his tongue as he did so.

And when they were halfway across, she asked, "Do you think it is possible for one acorn to sprout into two oaks, my husband?"

Hurt Eagle received Ooti's account of her vision of Pano, nodding from time to time as the girl related the story but otherwise allowing his wrinkled visage to reveal nothing of his thoughts. When she had finished speaking, the healing shaman whose winters numbered nearly a hundred reached out to touch the tips of his long fingers to her face.

For an instant it seemed to Ooti as though glowing embers had been pressed against her cheek, and she jerked involuntarily backward—back, back, away from the reality of the vision she had just rendered.

"Pretty One," he said softly, "so pretty and so intense. You must understand that sometimes a dream means nothing at all. Other times we dream out what we fear the most. And sometimes I think the dream spirits are merely playing in our minds. Very few come to us from beyond the broken shell of no-time, from Valley Above. I cannot tell you, Ooti, what sort this dreaming of yours has been. I am old, but for you I will undertake a venture into the spirit world of the *Kakini*. And if I am successful, then I will tell you what I have discovered. I think that Pano will tell me the answers to the questions I ask, if I can find him. Will you be patient a while longer?"

Ooti stared into the shaman's intense eyes—eyes almost like those in her vision.

"Yes, Grandfather," she answered.

Hurt Eagle laughed, his tone both amused and pleased and serving at the same time to break the tension of the moment.

"It is good to hear you call me that," Hurt Eagle said. "It is good even though I am not truly your grandfather in blood. Yet it was I who was your father's teacher, I was *kuksu* to him, and now he is known to all as Kuksu Man, a far greater healer than I. So it should always be with a teacher and his initiate. Even though I was already old and beyond the time of begetting any children of my own, your father became a son to me. And so you are my granddaughter. The man who lives behind this mask of wrinkles loves you, little Ooti. Listen to me now. You have told no one else of your envisioning?"

"No one, Grandfather."

"That is good. Speak to nobody of what you have revealed to me, not even to your husband or to your mother and father. Let me discover what I can first. But remember this much. Those children who come into the world during the time of *Ustu* are protected by the spirits of those who have already gone on into the Valley Above. Often we name our children for those who are dead, but this is always the case for those who are born in the time when we celebrate and mourn our dead, the time of burning, the time of cry. In this way the strength of those who have passed beyond is returned to the Nishinam Maidu, to the people of Tumeli village. And so it is among all the Maidu Peoples. If twins should indeed come to you out of the darkness, it is because *Pano* and *Oleli* and *Yelimi* and *Moloko* and the others have willed it. They would not cause this thing to happen merely to have the children, one or both, put to death. Sleep well this night and rest in your husband's arms, Ooti. I do not think there is anything to fear."

Ooti rose, offered a string of *howok* disc-bead currency to Hurt Eagle. The shaman took the gift, nodded, smiled.

"I have too many beads already," he said. "Many have been sick this year and have come to me to suck out the *itu*, the pain. All have brought me gifts. But it is right for you to pay me, for that is the way it has always been. But I will make these howok a part of the present I give to you and your husband after you have presented me with my new grandchildren. Go now, Ooti, and rest. *Shahwodo* Moon is full, and tomorrow you must once again work with the other women at the preparing of the acorns, leaching them and drawing the bitter *suk* from them. After a time perhaps you will bring me some freshly baked *maat*, acorn bread wrapped in a lining of grape leaves. I have lost some of my teeth, but the *maat* still tastes very good to me. Only when I am no longer able to eat it will I be ready to go to Valley Above."

Acorn Girl left, and Hurt Eagle stooped to lay a handful of dry pine needles and a few sticks of the brushwood he had gathered onto his lodge fire.

When he stood up again, his eyes were watering—half from the smoke and half from the pain that ran in his mind. He let out a long, low cry, pushed a clenched fist to his forehead, and then turned to get his elderwood pipe, glanced at it, laid it back down. Instead he withdrew his pipe of carved stone and filled the bowl with some of the tobacco he had purchased from the Mountain People the previous summer.

He lit the pipe and sat down before his fire.

Lilainma wile lelorochu, loibama wile lelorochu!
Children healthy made, girls healthy made!

Then his head went forward, and the old shaman fell immediately into a deep trance.

A burst of air in through the lodge entryway caused the flames to leap up and then to die down once more.

In a swale on the ridgeback above Tumeli village lay the mourning ground, close by the cemetery where the dead had been interred for as long as anyone could remember—

one of several such sites, each in conjunction with one or
another of the seasonal moves of the village itself.

> *Protect us, Wawim, White Bird,*
> *Yaaw-huy-eni,*
> *Don't go away, just circle around.*

It was no longer certain what kind of bird the *Wawim* or
Hawai was, big white birds that in old days had come from
the south, flying in vees and making no noise. But still the
people of Tumeli called out to them.

The acorn harvest was finished, and the women had
now completed the work of curing the acorns, the shelled
kernels, the *ootim hai*, the work of winnowing basket and
pestle, leaching and pounding and forming the flour, the
ootim bat, into cakes and loaves and mush flavored with
crushed bright red honeysuckle berries, *tawaal* the paddle
and *awntee* the large cooking basket.

> *Ootim yaawn ye-koonai, ye-koonai, ye-koonai,*
> *Acorn flower, soon it be mush that already be cool and*
> *hard, only it wiggle, soon it be. . . .*

The harvest had been plentiful, and the coming winter,
all believed, would not be one of *ka-awk*, hard times. And
the men, working in groups, returned with numerous
deer, the flesh carefully cut into strips, smoked, dried,
and packed away along with the dried salmon and salmon
flour from fish netted out of the river.

Now came the mourning rite, and the people of Tumeli
assembled at the *Ustu* ground. On the first evening the
actual mourners, those who had lost family and loved ones
during the previous year, visited the burning ground just
as the sun flared to crimson in the west, off across the big
hills beyond Kolo-ma. These cried for a time and then
sprinkled acorn meal on the graves.

The following day the enclosure was prepared, and poles
were set up from which dangled strings of woven baskets,
furs, strings of beads and dentalium and woodpecker
scalps—an abundance of things, many of which had been
prepared specifically for the occasion of the *Ustu*. Widows,

having cut their hair, attached this to the poles, whether in a woven basket or hanging free. Larger articles and mounds of food were placed at the foot of the poles.

Kuksu Man, as primary leader of the village, spoke out the traditionalized set of instructions, information hardly needed by the mourners but required by tradition. And when he was finished, just as the sun went down for the second day of the *Ustu*, the fires were lighted, and the basket-hung poles began to blaze, throwing off long trails of sparks into the near-darkness.

The people would cry out and mourn throughout the night, each group remembering its own dead and singing its own songs.

It was at this time that Ooti knew her labor had begun.

The moments had ceased to pass in their familiar way. The moon, approaching full, was already on its track down the western sky, but Ooti was not sure if it had been only a few heartbeats or an eternity since the first great convulsion of pain had gripped her swollen belly just as the evening sky had darkened to violet and the fires of the *Ustu* had begun to blaze up in the gathering twilight. She had waited for the wave of agony to pass, and then she had sought out Tule Elk, her mother, to tell her that it was time to go to the sheltered spot beyond the next ridge, a place that they had already chosen for Ooti's birthing.

"You must walk on ahead," Tule Elk had said, briefly caressing her daughter's hair. "The child might overtake you even before you get to the lean-to. That happens sometimes. I will follow as soon as I have found our helpers."

The older woman had hesitated, then, and just as Ooti was turning to go, she reached out and squeezed the girl's hand.

"Do not be afraid, Little One," Tule Elk added. "Oh, that is a silly thing for me to say. We are all a little bit afraid, but there is no reason for you to be. You are very strong. This is a happy night. Listen to how I ramble on. My daughter . . ."

Tears were visible in the older woman's eyes, small

glintings of redness from the *Ustu* fires. She embraced Ooti and then went running across through the gathered people, her awkward gait made even more so by excitement. Ooti couldn't help smiling as she herself turned to begin her walk toward the birthing place.

But Tule Elk and old Water-strider, a woman who had helped to bring many babies to light in the village, actually caught up to Acorn Girl well before she reached the place in the fold of the hills where the stand of oaks provided shelter, for a second wave of pain took her so that she had to kneel in the path, doubled over and gasping, for some time before she was able to continue. Small Ears, Ooti's friend from childhood, had joined the other three women after they had reached the birthing spot, and Ooti lay wrapped in a soft rabbit blanket within the lean-to beneath the oaks. The two older women worked at getting a fire started, for the evenings were growing chilly in the moon of *Shahwodo*, the time of acorns stored away for winter.

When the next pain came, and Ooti was unable to stifle a groan of agony, Small Ears gripped her friend's hand tightly, her round eyes wide with fear and sympathy—for she had never given birth either, was not yet even married although she had celebrated her *Wulu* dance almost two full years previous. Tule Elk stroked her daughter's forehead with a damp swatch of rabbit fur and murmured sympathetically.

But old Water-strider, Ooti found, was a merciless tyrant.

"Get up, now, you lazy girl. When the pains come, you must get up on your knees and grasp the stake, or else the baby will have to do all the work," she ordered in a harsh voice. Then she pushed at Ooti's shoulders until the young woman complied.

It was after that when time ceased to have meaning. The night wore on in alternating periods. When the pain had passed, she could lie back on her rabbit blanket, exhausted, resting for the next effort, the next unbearable agony that she would somehow come through, Water-strider's eyes fixed on her face, so that with the first renewed grimace she could order the girl to move, to kneel, to pull against the firmly planted stake.

Flicker of firelight, occasional murmurs as the women talked from time to time, and now and again Ooti would realize with a kind of mild surprise that the moon had advanced far beyond its position the last time she had noticed.

Now she was resting again, and the moon was dropping down the western sky toward the shadowed blackness of the hills beyond Kolo-ma. As had happened several times before, Water-strider made her raise her knees, and the old woman's hand probed inside her. This time Water-strider gave a grunt of satisfaction as she withdrew her hand.

"Almost," she said to the others. "The opening is nearly big enough now, and I can feel the baby's head. It has taken a long while, but it will go well now."

Acorn Girl half-heard the words, let her eyes drop shut for a moment before the next convulsion came. The spasms were now almost without letup, and Water-strider would not allow her to lie down again. Ooti knelt, pulling fiercely and automatically at the stake, sweat pouring down her face despite the chill of the night. Water-strider let out an explosive sound of triumph, reached beneath Acorn Girl, and eased something out—as the two other women broke into wide smiles and exclamations of delight. Water-strider held the infant upside down for a moment, at the same time ordering Ooti to push again for the afterbirth.

The child burst into a piercing, thin wail, and Water-strider passed what Ooti could see was a son to its grandmother. Then the midwife received the afterbirth and tied the umbilical cord with a strip of leather.

Ooti smiled dazedly, reaching her arms out for her child—when another convulsion of pain gripped her tired body so that she cried out in surprised anguish. She knew instantly, without thinking, what this meant. Her vision of Pano had been genuine, just as Hurt Eagle had ultimately concluded.

Ooti gripped the heavy branch again, her muscles quivering with exhaustion, and she noted at the same instant the looks of deep concern that passed between Tule Elk and Small Ears. Water-strider's jaw tightened, and she made no move to receive the second child.

"Ahh!" she muttered. "This is very bad luck. There is a shadow-child coming now."

Small Ears pushed the old midwife aside and reached out her own hands to receive the twin, and when it had come, Acorn Girl slumped down exhausted, her vision beginning to go dark. But she saw Water-strider taking the second child from Small Ears and knew that the old woman would bear it out into the night and then would return alone.

With an almost superhuman effort engendered by terror and by a need so deep that it could not be comprehended, Acorn Girl pushed herself up and cried out.

"No!"

The three women turned to her, staring, puzzled.

"Small Ears, Mother, do not let her kill my baby. Hurt Eagle has dreamed . . . please . . ."

And then her vision did darken, and she seemed to be falling endlessly into a black whirlpool, and the roaring around her ears prevented her from hearing anything else.

Then the roaring stopped, and she was aware of nothing.

2

Pano Intervenes

November, 1847

"I cannot fly," said Turtle. "Sometimes I swim in the dark waters, but I must always come up for air. We have been on this raft for a long time now, World Maker, and all you do is sit there. Will nothing else ever happen?"

Peheipe jumped up and down and shouted, "You promised the sky would turn blue and the waters would go away! And all you do is sit there! I can't fly either, and I don't know how to swim. God, I wish I had a woman—it's been so long. . . ."

World Maker looked at the two of them and said, "First we will need some dirt. It's far down under the water, and I don't know how to get at it."

"Is that all?" Turtle asked. "Then I'll go down and get some for you."

Turtle leaped into the dark waters, and World Maker nodded wisely. But Peheipe was crying and pulling at his hair.

It took Turtle another four years to swim to the bottom and then back to the raft. He burst to the surface and climbed onto the raft, but he had lost the earth he had tried to bring up.

World Maker drew a stone knife from out of the folds of his robe and proceeded to scrape bits of mud from under Turtle's horny toenails until finally he had managed to collect a tiny brown ball. This he held in his hand. He gazed at it, gazed hard. And the earthen pebble grew. When he gazed a second time, the ball grew yet larger. A third time and it became larger still. And after the fourth time the ball of earth had become as large as the world is today.

"Now the world is new," he said.

"Look!" Peheipe cried out. "Mountains have come up out of the water—and now there are mountains all around the water as well."

"We must take our raft to the land that rises from the middle of the water," Turtle said, "for that place will be called Estawm Yan, the center of everything."

Morning light slanted in through the smokehole of the women's hut, and Ooti awoke, raising one hand to her forehead to brush away the vague sense of apprehension that still clung from a dream that she, even now, barely remembered—a dream of fire and confusion, a sense of loss. Her movement caused the infant sleeping against her bare breast to stir and flail out with a tiny fist before subsiding back into sleep, the lips making sucking movements as the child dreamed. The remnants of Ooti's vision left her entirely, and she touched at the little mouth with a finger, delighting when her son tried to devour it.

Only now did she sense Pine-nut-eater's gaze upon her, and she looked up to see him grinning broadly as he rested on one elbow, watching her.

Their other son rested on his stomach next to the father, his legs partly bent beneath so that the little rump stuck up in the air. The child's eyes were squeezed tightly shut.

"That one has good instincts," Pine-nut-eater laughed, gesturing to the twin who was still sucking at Acorn Girl's finger. "He is always ready to fight or eat."

"They are both that way," Ooti insisted. "They are always hungry as coyotes. It is good that I have so much milk, but even so I think we will have to start giving them meat broth and acorn gruel very early."

Pine-nut-eater ran a finger across his wife's nipple, and she shivered with an involuntary flash of desire.

"I would like to nurse, too," he teased. "I am much bigger than these two. Perhaps I will just shoulder them aside and . . ."

He squeezed gently at the rounded breasts, noticeably larger now that she was nursing, the nipples redder. He touched at the white drops of fluid that appeared, put his finger to his lips.

"Umm. Yes. You don't need these little coyotes. I will milk you. And then you could milk me. Ooti, it has been such a long time since we have made love. . . ."

"And it will be a long time yet before we can again. It would be very bad luck to make love before my bleeding has stopped, especially when we have already challenged the Spirits by . . ."

She was unable to say the words that were required to finish her thought, but Pine-nut-eater knew what it was she had not spoken.

"It will be all right," the husband assured her. "Hurt Eagle has seen in a vision the same thing you saw, and there is no one more powerful than he is. None of the *kuksu* priests would dare to challenge him. As for the other thing, I will just go out and howl at the moon."

Acorn Girl laughed softly, and Pine-nut-eater caressed her shining hair.

"It is daytime, my husband," she said.

"Then perhaps I will run through the village, screaming like a *Moki*, like a crazy person."

Ooti laughed quickly and then pressed his hand against her cheek, her face becoming serious once more.

"Sometimes I am frightened, though," she said. "I could not have let Water-strider take our son out into the woods and leave him, even if I had not had the vision of Pano the bear. And yet that is the way it has always been done among our people."

"Sometimes things change, Ooti. In Captain Sutter's party there was a pair of twins, and they were both big, healthy men—although they looked so much the same that it took me a long time to tell one from the other. I learned from them that the Whites have always let both twins live, and they seem to be taking over the whole world. Every day there are more of them."

"Yes, but it is probably different for them than for the Nishinam."

"Then you should have faith in your own vision and in Hurt Eagle's vision. Besides, I am half White, and that means our sons are also part White. So maybe it's different for us, too. Ooti, I think you worry too much."

"And you do not worry enough, my husband. Sometimes I think that you don't believe anything."

"I believe that I am hungry," he laughed. "When is your friend going to get here with our breakfast?"

Pine-nut-eater rose and stretched and began pacing back and forth in the small lodge. He and Ooti had been confined to the women's hut for eight days now, since the night of the twins' birth, both husband and wife under constraints not to leave the small, brush-covered *hubo* except briefly to perform necessary physical functions. The time of confinement was for ten days, as was customary.

Acorn Girl sensed that the sharp curtailment of activity and freedom of movement were much more wearing for her husband even than for herself, although now that she had recovered most of her strength after the difficult and exhausting birth, she, too, was becoming increasingly impatient to be outside. Merely to take a walk through the hills had become an almost unimaginable luxury. She was very glad that there were only two days of the ritual confinement left.

The baby lying against Ooti began to stir and whimper, and she put him to her breast quickly to keep him from escalating into a full wail that would wake his brother. As the child began to suckle, his little hands making kneading movements against her breast, she watched her husband as he stood in the shaft of light from the smokehole, still naked, swinging his arms back and forth to loosen sleep-stiff muscles. She admired again the leanness, the hard suppleness of his male body—and felt once more the warm stirrings of desire.

Yes, some of the old rules were very hard to follow.

A cheerful voice sang suddenly from outside the *hubo*. It was Small Ears.

"You'd better get out of bed, you lazy people, and you had better cover your nakedness, Pine-nut-eater, because here is your breakfast."

"You'd better think about who you're calling lazy, Small-Eared Turtle," Pine-nut-eater called back. "The sun is nearly straight up in the sky, and we have been starving to death for hours."

Acorn Girl's husband was still fastening his loincloth when Small Ears' round-cheeked, impertinent face poked through the door. She darted in through the low entryway and made a playful grab at the garment as Pine-nut-eater tucked the front in place.

"Be careful what you uncover, Small Ears," Ooti said. "There's a raging demon under there—*Yohyo*, the big head."

"Never mind about that," Pine-nut-eater ordered. "I want to know what you have brought us to eat."

"Something good."

Small Ears rolled up her eyes and patted her stomach in pantomimed culinary ecstasy before she stooped and reached outside to retrieve the basket of food, presenting it to Pine-nut-eater with a flourish. He looked closely at the steaming mixture in the shallow, leaf-lined vessel, then smelled it, wrinkling his nose in disappointment.

"This is nothing but *waalawm*," he complained. "You never bring us anything but *waalawm* or *maat*. Where is the meat? I want a big piece of roast venison, or some boiled rabbit. Even dried salmon would do, or some nice fat grubs."

"Hush, silly husband," Acorn Girl said. "You know we can't eat meat until the time when we leave the women's lodge."

"I think this whole business of birth should be turned over entirely to the women," Pine-nut-eater growled. "I don't see what good it does that the men should have to starve and be required to stay in the women's hut when their wives give birth. We don't have the babies. . . ."

But he began to scoop up the mixture of acorn mush and berries, eating with good appetite despite his very vocal displeasure.

He sat down on the mat next to Acorn Girl again and ate as his wife suckled the infant. Although she knew that a good wife should wait for her husband to finish before she began eating, she could not resist dipping into the basket of warm, tart-sweet mush.

Small Ears picked up the second twin and bounced him gently to keep him quiet until his brother was finished nursing.

"How does it go in the village?" Ooti asked her friend. "Do you think we'll be able to have the naming ceremony three days from now without everyone in the village tearing us apart?"

Small Ears' moon face grew serious.

"Hurt Eagle has spoken out for you. You know that. He has let everyone know that he has had a vision, but he has not told what it was yet. He will do that at the naming, I guess. But Water-strider has been at work, too, and last night she got a delegation of women together, and they went to Hurt Eagle's lodge to complain of you. They were terrible. They went through the village, wailing and predicting great calamities if both the twins and maybe you, too, weren't killed. I think they frightened many people. You know that Water-strider is a *Netdi* dreaming doctor."

"Hurt Eagle is ten times more powerful than Water-strider, and so is Kuksu Man, my father. No one but the foolish old women she is friends with pays any attention to what she says."

Pine-nut-eater nodded.

"What did Hurt Eagle do then?" Acorn Girl asked.

"He was very angry. He is terrifying when he is truly angry. His face looked like the black hail-clouds, and his voice sounded like thunder. He told Water-strider and all the women so loudly that everyone in Tumeli village could hear that if they didn't stop their foolishness, he would send his *sila* after them, and they would all die."

"He would never do that," Ooti said. "He is not a killing shaman. I know that he has very strong magic in his killing-objects, but he has never used one of them to hurt anybody. That is what my father says."

"I don't know," Small Ears replied. "After I saw how he looked yesterday, I wouldn't want to be Water-strider and test him out."

"Most of the people will do as Hurt Eagle wishes," Pine-nut-eater insisted. "Everyone knows that he is the most powerful shaman the Tumelis have ever had, except for Kuksu Man, maybe. What about Kuksu Man? Has he said anything?"

Small Ears shook her head.

"He has kept silent. He and Tule Elk are both staying pretty much out of sight. Even though he is the leader of our village, everyone knows that whatever he might say would not be objective because you are his daughter, Ooti."

"That's the wise thing to do," Pine-nut-eater agreed.

The child that Small Ears was holding had grown more and more restless, at last breaking into an outraged wail that mere jiggling could not allay, and Acorn Girl rose, gently dislodging the nursing twin, and exchanged babies with her friend, putting the second twin to her other breast. The first twin gave a few cries of protest, but he was comfortably full, and he quickly dropped into the intense sleep of newborns.

"I have not seen my mother since the night of the birth," Acorn Girl mused wistfully after a period of silence. "Do you think she really accepts what I have done? She cannot visit the marriage lodge because the old way forbids it, and she must not speak to Pine-nut-eater any more."

"Tule Elk loves you, Ooti, and she loves her grandchildren. I could not have kept Water-strider from taking your baby that night if Tule Elk had not helped me. I see her every day when I go to get your meals, and she always sends her love to you."

"I know that," Acorn Girl said, dissatisfied. "But does she really think . . . ? Well, never mind, then. What of Kuksu Man?"

"He has not spoken much about it, but last night he told me that sometimes the ways of the Nishinam must change. That the changes are for the good—if *Olelbis*, the One Who Sits Above, wishes these changes. I think he was saying that *Olelbis* wishes the twins to live, since you and Hurt Eagle have both had such strong visions."

"My wife worries too much," Pine-nut-eater said with a smile. "I was just telling her this before you came with our miserable meal."

"If you keep complaining, I will not bring you any food at all," Small Ears retorted.

The fires which had blazed brightly earlier in the great *k-um* were dying down now, and the shadows descended from the top and from the outer edges of the big, earth-covered dance lodge. None of the assembled people of Tumeli village moved from his place, however, and the little murmurs and whispers died to an expectant silence.

Acorn Girl, sitting in the row nearest the fire, along with Pine-nut-eater and her mother and father, could not suppress a slight shiver of anticipation, a curious mixture of excitement and a delicious fear that she always felt at a shaman's gathering. The twins, wrapped in soft rabbitskin blankets and lashed snugly to their willow-basket cradle-boards, slept soundlessly. Very soon now, Ooti knew, Hurt Eagle, who sat motionless and with eyes closed on the other side of the fire, would rise, and the true purpose of this assembly would begin to be revealed.

Not that there was anyone among the Tumeli Maidus who was unaware of the reason Hurt Eagle, the man of many winters, had sent out the formal invitations—strings with two knots to indicate the two days until the gathering, the date obviously coinciding with the day after the new mother and father would be permitted to leave the women's hut. Everyone had also known, of course, that the invitation was actually of the nature of an order, for to stay away would have been to offend the old shaman, and one did not wish to risk a powerful doctor's wrath. Such a one could send a deadly, magical *sila* after the offender, and then there would be no escaping certain death unless the shaman chose to call his instrument back.

Earlier there had been the feasting, with everyone partaking of roasted venison, acorn bread, smoked salmon, and pine nuts—the food having been prepared by Tule Elk and Small Ears and a few other of their women friends. Even those who disapproved of Ooti's action and of Hurt Eagle's defense of that action enjoyed the food and the informal dancing that had come after.

But now, with the fires dying down and the lodge soon to be plunged into total darkness, the evening was reaching its climax, and there were none, not even Waterstrider, who could remain totally unaffected by the anticipation of what was to come.

When the faces of most of the spectators had vanished into the darkness, Hurt Eagle rose. He was dressed simply, as was his custom—wearing, in addition to his loincloth, only a single feathered amulet on a thong about his neck and at his waist a pouch that contained his secret objects of power. Over one forearm hung his sorcerer's cape, its bead and quill designs hypnotic with mystery and power.

Even though nearly a hundred winters had passed through the shaman's eyes, and the weight of the accumulated years had caused him to stoop forward at times when his mind wandered and he was not concerned with the observations of those about him, still, on this night, confident in his powers and with his audience seated before him, Hurt Eagle stood tall—taller even than Pine-nut-eater—and his broad shoulders were held square. Firelight glinted in the sheen of bear grease he had applied to his face, chest, and forearms, accentuating the still considerable masculine power that was his. For this moment he had seemingly thrown off the attrition of time itself.

No one in the room stirred as he began to speak, his voice raised in a chantlike tone and surprisingly strong.

He has taken on the strength of our animal guardians.

"There has been much talk in the village," he said, "and much division. Some foolish people are saying that I did not have a true vision concerning the new little ones who are here tonight. And so I am not going to tell you what I saw in my dream."

Here the old shaman paused, listened to the rustle of surprised whispering among those gathered.

"What I am going to do is to call *Pano*, the Spirit Grizzly. Maybe he will come here himself and tell you what he has already told me."

A sound in the room now like a faint moaning of wind. The people murmured in audible astonishment. Light from the fire was now almost entirely gone—and only the vaguest illumination of the figure of Hurt Eagle. He did not speak or move until the light had disappeared entirely and the dance lodge was heavy with darkness and expectancy. When he spoke next, he allowed his voice to come sharply, in reprimand, out of the blackness.

"Perhaps those who do not believe the words of their shaman will believe the words of Pano himself. . . ."

With that he began a high-pitched, keening chant in a language that none of the others recognized, a language that only powerful shamans and the Spirits knew. The song went on and on, a sound like the voice of a river at times, at other times resembling the cry of a hawk or the wild clamor of geese passing overhead. The people could tell by the faint, rhythmic shuffling sounds that Hurt Eagle had begun a slow dance in time to his chant, and he accompanied himself by pounding with a rattle made from the dried husks of cocoons, striking it against the center post of the lodge.

The singing seemed to go on forever, and Ooti felt as if she were drifting into a trance. Hurt Eagle's voice seemed to quaver strangely, so that sometimes the chant came from his place near the remains of the fire, sometimes it came from behind her, even from far outside, or from everywhere at once. The hair at the back of her neck prickled, and she began to sense that Hurt Eagle was not the only one chanting, that already Spirit Creatures had entered the *k-um* and were singing.

Suddenly the chanting stopped, and in the silence the people heard a whirring, clicking sound that seemed to begin near the smokehole of the lodge and descend to near the fire, and everyone knew that *Ene*, the grasshopper who often acted as a messenger for the other Spirits, had entered. Hurt Eagle addressed the grasshopper in the strange language of the chant, the only understandable word he used being *Pano*, and Ene responded with several chirps. When Hurt Eagle spoke again, it was in a tone of command, and Ene chirped a quick response, after which he departed, the clicking of his wings ascending toward the smokehole and becoming inaudible. Everyone understood that the shaman had sent Ene to seek Pano, the grizzly.

Hurt Eagle resumed his chanting, which was interrupted at intervals by the arrival of various spirits, some of whom the people recognized and some who were strange. *Doritu* the heron came in with a tremendous sound of wings—so that some of the people ducked. And one spirit spoke with a terrifying roar. Several of the children began to weep when this spirit entered. Ooti shivered, but she had confidence in Hurt Eagle's ability to keep things under control. She wondered whether this roaring spirit might be fire, or a river spirit, or perhaps even thunder.

Hurt Eagle spoke to all these Beings, always using the recognizable name of *Pano*, and continuing his chant between visits. At last a heavy shuffling became audible, made its way around the outside of the lodge, and finally approached Hurt Eagle, accompanied by the strong, wild odor of bear. This visitor snuffled and grunted in the manner of grizzlies, and even before the shaman addressed him, everyone knew that Pano had at last entered the dance lodge. Pano spoke in a deep growl, but when Hurt Eagle responded this time, it was in the language of the Nishinam Maidu.

"We are honored by your presence, Grandfather Pano," the shaman said. "I would ask that you speak the language of my people so that these gathered here may understand your words."

"Why have you called me here?" Pano growled. "I have other things to do."

"I know that, and I would not have called you if it were not very important. Many of these people will not believe what I tell them I saw in my vision, and . . ."

With a roar, Pano interrupted the shaman's words. Several women screamed, and the children wailed. But Ooti's twin sons slept soundly through the tumult.

"What kind of people are these who will not heed the words I spoke to my friend Hurt Eagle?" the Bear Spirit demanded. "I was taken away from my business to talk to these foolish ones? Perhaps I will call to the clouds, and they will send so much rain that the earth will be covered again, and these people will all drown. The salmon will chew at their flesh, and the small fish will pick their bones clean."

"Aaiiee!" Hurt Eagle called out. "I would be sorry if you did that, Pano, because I don't think my people are bad. You must not harm the Nishinam Maidu of Tumeli village. No, it's just that what you told me is a new thing for them, and they are afraid. It is important for them to be certain."

"All right, then," the voice of Pano answered, "but I will only tell them this one time, and I will not tell them everything. People of Tumeli village, something very important is happening. Olelbis has waked up from the long dream he has been having, and now he has started a different dream about a different kind of world. That is why everything has changed. For a little while the Nishinam people will not notice this change, but before very many seasons pass, all that you have known will be turned upside down. Some of you will still be here, some of you will be in Valley Above, and some of you will change along with the world. I tell you this: the old ways will come to mean very little. You may think the world is becoming very bad, but it is only what Olelbis dreams. Perhaps someday things will change back to the way they were before. I don't know everything."

Kuksu Man, himself a powerful shaman, had the right to address the Spirit. And so the village leader spoke his first words of the evening.

"Will you tell us, Grandfather Pano, what we may do to prepare ourselves for this new order of things?"

The lodge had once again become hushed, even the children quiet now as the people waited in stunned silence for the next words of the Bear Spirit.

"There is not much you can do," Pano replied calmly. "You can keep the old ways in your hearts, and pass them on to your grandchildren to keep in their hearts, for you may need them again someday, and in any case it is good to remember things. But for now you must be ready to live in different ways, or else you will cease to exist. That is all I will say on this subject, except that it is worse for my people than for yours. The Pano race will soon no longer be in this world at all, and when the last grizzly is gone from the great valley and the mountains that rise to the east and the west, then I will also cross over to the Other Side, and no one on this side will see me again."

There was silence for a long time after that, broken only by the harsh sound of Pano's breathing. Those gathered together in the lodge struggled to assimilate the devastating message, and when Hurt Eagle finally spoke, his voice was very quiet and gentle.

"This is sad news," the ancient shaman said, "for the land will be lonelier without Pano. We fear the grizzlies, but we love them also."

"No, not sad," Pano replied. "That is only the way it seems to you. It is as I said—this is just what Olelbis chooses to dream. Things have changed many times before now, more times than you can imagine. Once the oceans covered the land, and the fish left their bones high up in the mountains. You can see this in the rocks of the Coast Range. But that is a story for another time. Where are the little ones who were born together, for I think that is the real reason you called me here?"

"That is true," Hurt Eagle replied, "for the people do not believe that you wish both of them to live."

Pano roared, and in a sudden flash of light and an explosive thump, the fire blazed up again, and Pano stood in the smoke, erect on his hind legs, towering above the flames. He turned his head slowly, searching first one way and then the other, and then he dropped to all four feet and shambled to where the twins lay in their cradles between Acorn Girl and Pine-nut-eater. Ooti couldn't help shrinking back a little in fear, for although she suspected, as did everyone in the lodge, that Pano was Hurt Eagle wearing the grizzly bear costume, with the great head of a real grizzly towering far above his own head and the whole skin with paws attached covering the man, yet she also knew that in this costume Hurt Eagle *was* Pano, was inhabited by the actual Bear Spirit, and as such inspired awe and fear.

But Pano only touched at first one and then the other with a massive paw. Then he reared back up to his hind legs and addressed the gathering, bellowing and at last waking the twins so that their wails were like an accompaniment to the command Pano was giving.

"These are under my protection. Whoever dares to harm either of these will have me to deal with, and you know that I am not always gentle. They will be named tomorrow at dawn. Hurt Eagle will name them, and their names will remind you that they are my special wards."

The light from the fire died out quickly, and now the assembly was once more plunged into darkness. Pano's voice came, more gently now, out of that darkness.

"I have told you that things are changing," Pano said. "Among my people twins are often born, and they have always been permitted to live. It has not been that way among your people before, but now things are different. I have said what I came to say, and I will leave now."

With that the Maidus heard Pano's shuffling steps as he left the lodge, and after a moment they heard his roar again from outside the *k-um*. Once again the fire blazed up, and Hurt Eagle stood there alone, dressed as he had been before. The people gasped in astonishment, for it did not seem possible that the shaman could have removed his costume so quickly, and they knew that it could not have been Hurt Eagle who shuffled out of the lodge and then bellowed from the hills beyond. Surely, then, they had truly been honored by a visit from the great Spirit Bear himself.

Ooti pondered this matter, still shaken by the experience of the evening. It must be as Pine-nut-eater had said—that she need not be afraid for breaking with the tradition.

The old man stood swaying in the firelight, gazing about himself as if uncertain where he was. His eyes were so wide that the whites showed all around the edges of the irises, glinting orange reflections back from the flames. In a moment the eyes rolled back so that nothing but white was visible. The head slumped forward, and the knees began to buckle.

Kuksu Man, who had been expecting just such a collapse, had risen and was at Hurt Eagle's side in time to catch the old man and ease him to the ground.

The younger shaman examined his mentor and in a moment rose to pronounce his findings.

"Hurt Eagle will be well," he said. "It is as it always is when a healer is visited by a powerful spirit. We will let him lie here by the fire until he has recovered himself. For the rest of us, we may dance and pray, both for Hurt Eagle and for the two new ones, but you must be careful not to touch the one who was my teacher, for it would be very dangerous to anyone who is not a *kuksu* healer. While Hurt Eagle is in this state, he is still full of spirits other than his own."

Kuksu Man led the chanting and danced slowly around the fire and the prostrate form of Hurt Eagle. Some of the people drifted away to their own dwelling places to sleep, but others stayed on to watch and to participate in the chants and dancing.

Toward dawn, with Hurt Eagle having by then recovered his strength, the old shaman assumed the lead position in the dance. By this time, not more than twenty of the people remained, and now these left the dance lodge and made their way up to the crest of a nearby hill, one so situated as to command an unobstructed view of a long stretch of the distant Sierra Nevada.

Acorn Girl and Pine-nut-eater, each carrying one of the twins, walked along with Kuksu Man on one side and Hurt Eagle on the other.

The procession reached the lookout point before sunrise, but at a time when the gray dawn light had first allowed colors to be visible. The sky was perfectly clear, blue-silver except to the east, where a pale-yellow diffusion of light showed where the sun would soon appear. The group stood in silence, but a variety of birds and squirrels barked their cries into the chilly air, a complicated harmony of trills and chitterings. To the east, the high peaks of the great range were blue-white, the winter having arrived long since at the higher elevations.

Hurt Eagle stood at the front of the group, gazing intently eastward, and when the first point of light appeared above the mountains, he turned to Acorn Girl and Pine-nut-eater, the husband now holding both the twins, and asked, "Which is the firstborn?"

"This one, Grandfather," Ooti whispered, gesturing.

She took the child from Pine-nut-eater and handed him to Hurt Eagle, being careful not to look the old shaman directly in the face. For now she found herself in a strange and sudden awe of him, the same Hurt Eagle who had always been like an indulgent grandparent to her, upon whose lap she had once climbed without hesitation, pulling happily at both his clothing and his hair.

The *kuksu* healing priest held the infant out toward the rising sun and called in a high, chanting voice: "*Eta nik hedeng kawm hipining kawyawnaan*, Look at me from above, look at me from these hills. *Eta nik hedem yamanmantawnaanis*, Look at me from the heaven and bless me."

After the traditional words, he called out, "Behold this child, who is protected by Pano, the great bear. Behold Bear-who-comes-before. I name him this because he was the firstborn." Hurt Eagle then took the other twin, and after blessing him in the same way, pronounced, "Behold Bear-who-comes-after. Now these are their names, so that neither they nor anyone else shall forget that they are Pano's special charge."

The days following the naming ceremony were clear, the skies endlessly blue, and almost as warm as midsummer, as often happened in the foothills and river canyons in late autumn. For Acorn Girl, colors seemed more vivid than she could ever remember, and she pursued her old

tasks with a new sense of joy. It was pleasure to sit
streamside in the warm sun and leach acorns in bath after
bath of clear water. It was pleasure to work the strands of
willow and redbud into baskets, to watch the abstract
patterns of red-brown and white form as she talked idly
with Small Ears or Tule Elk, the twins sleeping or making
gurgling sounds in their willow cradles nearby.

Most pleasant of all, perhaps, was to sit in the evening
after the air outside had grown chill, the fire blazing in
their little *hubo* lodge, she and Pine-nut-eater alone with
their sons, and to feel the pull of a small mouth at the
nipple of her breast while she and her husband spoke of
other things, things of importance and things of no
importance.

Apparently the gathering at the dance lodge and the
words spoken by the Bear Spirit through Hurt Eagle had
been effective, for there was no more talk in the village
about the twins—at least according to Small Ears, who
kept very good track of all that went on in Tumeli. It was
true, however, that a great many of the women did not
come to see the new babies during the first days after the
confinement, and this was not as it usually would have
been. Under normal circumstances, everyone would be
eager to see the new arrivals, but in this case there were
many who, although not inclined to dispute the powerful
vision of the shaman, apparently could not bring themselves wholeheartedly to condone an act that they still
half-feared would bring disaster upon them all, and they
dealt with the conflict by pretending it and Ooti and her
children didn't exist.

This avoidance saddened Acorn Girl when she chose to
think about the matter, but her days were full with her
chores and her family, and most of her friends remained
loyal to her. Another small blot upon Ooti's otherwise
cloudless happiness in this time was Water-strider. Although the old midwife had said nothing openly, Ooti was
sure that she was not reconciled to the twins' existence.
She had undoubtedly been humiliated by Hurt Eagle's
public and dramatic refutation of her position, and Ooti
was sure that the woman had been following her about
when she was outside, for although the midwife stayed at

a distance, yet much more often than would be expected in the normal course of events, Ooti had turned to see Water-strider watching her, the stare very fixed and hostile. Ooti was sure that the old woman shaman was trying to cast a spell upon herself and the twins, but she was not very much concerned. Hurt Eagle was much more powerful, as was Kuksu Man, her father. Between them, they would be able to counteract easily any evil Water-strider could effect.

Perhaps the most serious threat to her happiness, or at least the one she took most seriously, was Pine-nut-eater's signs of growing restlessness. He spoke frequently of his time with Sutter and the other *Wawlems*, and she sensed that her husband was perhaps preparing to go off with them again.

One morning after the first meal and after the twins had nursed, and as Ooti was preparing to go out with her leaching basket and another container full of acorn kernels, Pine-nut-eater had said, "Come with me today, my wife. There is something I want to show you. Besides, it is a fine day. Wouldn't you like to go off into the hills the way we used to? We'll take some dried meat and some acorn bread and spend the day."

"What of the Bears?" she asked, referring to the twins in the way they had come to be designated by their parents. "I can't leave them while they're still nursing."

"You will carry one Bear, and I will carry the other," he smiled. "Women always make much of little."

"All right, then, we will do that," she laughed suddenly. "We will go together, carrying bears into the woods."

The prospect of the small adventure pleased Acorn Girl, and she sang a nonsense song and did a dance step as she hastened to wrap some food and place it into a net carrying bag. She packed the twins' bottoms in extra thick layer of tule fluff and wrapped the children and lashed them into their cradles. Then, with both carrying bag and one cradle suspended from bands around her chest, she helped Pine-nut-eater to fasten on the other Bear. With that, the husband and wife set out from Tumeli village.

They walked upstream for a time, and then, following deer trails through manzanita and scrub oak, made their way to the top of a ridge where sugarpines grew. After a time they dropped back down to a creek on the other side of the ridge, coming to a meadow, a relatively level expanse perhaps as wide as an arrow could travel if shot from the bow of a strong hunter. The grass was brittle and yellow, with only a faint hint of new green underneath, for the rains had been late in coming this year.

"We have found a good place," Pine-nut-eater said, somewhat mysteriously, as Ooti thought.

"A very good place," she agreed. "A good place to put down these heavy Bears and rest, I think."

Each helped to unburden the other, and they set the children and the net bag in the shade of a liveoak that grew near the head of the meadow, for the sun was high by now, and the thin frost of the time of the *Yapakto* Moon, *winter divided* in the Maidu reckoning, had vanished. The autumn sunlight, in fact, was quite warm.

The adults rested for a few moments, leaning against one another. Then Acorn Girl suddenly sprang to her feet and ran wildly across the brittle grass, flinging her arms up and shouting, "I'm free, I'm free!"

Pine-nut-eater laughed and ran after her. She glanced back over her shoulder at him and put on a burst of speed. She ran as she had run before the pregnancy, and even as he pursued her, Pine-nut-eater admired the lithe, quick movements. She was already nearly as slim as she had been. Excitement rose in him with the pursuit, and when he caught up with her downstream where the canyon walls narrowed the meadow to a strip, he tackled her gently, rolling so that his body broke her fall.

"I could have outrun you if I wanted to, even now," she gasped, still laughing.

He held her tight against him, his hands gripping her buttocks, and stared into her eyes, smiling faintly, and then slowly rolled her over onto her back and held her pinned against the ground.

"Surely it is time now," he said. "Your woman's bleeding has stopped, and the twins have lost their umbilical cords long ago."

"The moon has not yet . . . ," she began but found his fingers covering her mouth while the other hand moved on her breasts, her belly, at last down to her thighs, making little circles of fire in her flesh until she no longer cared about the moon.

They made love with a hard, fierce urgency that left them gasping, twined in each other's arms and drowsy, still half-hungry after the long months of abstention. They were roused from their lethargy by the furious wailing of first one, and then both of the twins, a chorus clearly audible even from the far end of the meadow.

"The Bears!" Ooti said, starting up. "I forgot about the Bears. Now I will have to nurse them, and they will know what we have done."

She smiled guiltily at Pine-nut-eater.

"It is good that they learn early," the husband shrugged, caressing Acorn Girl's long hair.

When the twins had been fed and their cattail-fluff packing changed, Ooti touched at first one tiny sleeping face and then the other. She looked up at Pine-nut-eater, who sat with his back against the liveoak, his eyes half-closed.

"It is true," she said. "I forgot about them completely. How could I do that? Perhaps I am not a very good mother, after all. I love them so much that it is like an ache in my breast, and yet there have been times when I wanted to leave them behind and go hunting with you, or go running in the woods. I envied you, that you did not have to be burdened every minute."

She paused, looked down, looked up again, her eyes large.

"I should not speak such things," she added uncertainly.

"You will not abandon your babies," Pine-nut-eater said, smiling. "Sometimes you wish to have freedom again. That doesn't seem so bad. When we are older, we will both teach them to hunt. I do not need a woman in my lodge every minute to prove that I am a man."

"No other woman has ever been as lucky as I am."

"No other woman is like you are," he replied. "You

speak of hunting. That is really why I wanted you to come today."

"To hunt? But we didn't bring bows. And the twins . . ."

"I wanted to teach you to hunt with another weapon," Pine-nut-eater replied, drawing his Allen & Wheelock revolver from the holster that he always wore strapped to his side.

Ooti wrinkled her nose.

"I don't want to hunt with that," she said. "It makes so much noise it scares away all the animals, and it smells bad."

"I wasn't really thinking about hunting with it," her husband said. "But I do want you to learn how to use it."

"But why?"

"It is not that I expect anything bad to happen, but my Acorn, you must have noticed that Water-strider and some of the others are less than friendly."

She shrugged.

"I have noticed that Water-strider is always there when I go out, that she stares at me. I think she is trying to put a spell on me. But I am not afraid of her."

Pine-nut-eater nodded.

"So long as it is only incantations and evil looks, I am not afraid for you either. It's just that I'm not entirely sure . . . probably there is nothing to worry about, but I want you to know how to use the pistol. There are times when the magic of the *Wawlem* Maidu, the Whiteman's magic, is more effective than either Hurt Eagle's power or the bow and arrow, that is all."

"But my husband, I will have you to protect me," she began—and then, even as she spoke, she began to realize the full import not of what he had said but of what he hadn't said.

He wanted her to be able to use the pistol to protect herself and the twins. He had spoken more and more frequently of the *Wawlems*, of those downstream who had built a small settlement near the village of Kolo-ma. The *Wawlems* were going to use the river's power, in some way that Pine-nut-eater had tried to explain to her but that she didn't understand, in order to turn trees into flat boards, the boards to be used in making more dwellings

for more *Wawlem* Maidus somewhere. Acorn Girl had not
paid much attention because the matter hadn't seemed
important. And Pine-nut-eater had discussed with her the
words spoken by Pano through Hurt Eagle, that a time of
change was coming. Pine-nut-eater thought that the change
had to do with the *Wawlems*, who he insisted were
coming in greater and greater numbers to the lands of the
Nishinam. He thought that their numbers were endless.
In order to survive, he insisted, it would be necessary to
learn of these strange-colored men, most of who lived
without their women. Pine-nut-eater knew something of
them and spoke of his time among them, of the eventual
necessity of teaching the twins some of the White people's
ways. She had listened, participated in these discussions,
imagining them to be mainly theoretical, directed at some
vague time in the future.

Now Acorn Girl understood, in an unpleasant flash of
illumination, that her husband had not been theorizing at
all.

"You are going away," she said at last, her voice flat,
hopeless, putting the words not as a question but as a
statement of irrevocable fact.

3

Spirit Impersonators

December 1847-January, 1848

*World Maker lifted up his hands, and the sky cleared
and turned blue, and the sun rose in the east.*

*Then the heat was terrible, and Peheipe held his hands
over his eyes and shouted, "You don't know how to do
anything right! Everything will be burned up in the heat
of the sun!"*

World Maker nodded, and after that the sun went down

into the west, and Estawm Yan was covered with pure darkness.

"Is it always one thing or the other?" Turtle cried out. "It is hard for me to move in this cold darkness."

World Maker spoke:

"Look in the east, then. Now my brother the moon is rising."

Cool light gleamed from the spires of Estawm Yan and shimmered on the waters all around.

Then World Maker spread his arms, and stars appeared in the cloak of blackness. He pointed, one by one, and began to name them.

"How long will this take?" Peheipe demanded. "Turtle, you and I will grow old and go into death before he's half finished."

World Maker ceased the naming and turned to face his two companions.

"Neither of you will die," he said. "Perhaps you will change forms after awhile, but you will not die. That is the promise I make you. Now watch. The moon will disappear, but the sun will come up once again. See—there it is now."

Light, more temperate this time, spread out over the waters and fell on the mountain island of Estawm Yan.

"It is lonely here, and there's nothing to do," Turtle sighed.

"I want a woman," Peheipe said, rubbing at his private parts.

"Be patient, little friends," World Maker answered. "The time is near to give this world a purpose. I am going to cause life to grow."

"This god is full of magic," Peheipe said.

And World Maker reached into the folds of his ever-flaming robe and pulled out a shiny green nub.

Turtle and Peheipe stared at it and looked puzzled.

Ooti held the revolver out before her with both hands, aiming the way Pine-nut-eater had taught her to do, sighting along the short barrel, one eye closed, just as one would sight an arrow. She aimed at a small piece of rabbit fur she had fastened to a winter-bare branch on a maple tree some twenty paces distant. She squeezed smoothly on the trigger, reminding herself to be patient, not to jerk, concentrating on keeping the barrel lined up with the target.

As always, the explosion came unexpectedly. The shot went a little wide, gashing the bark perhaps three finger-breadths to the left and above where the rabbitskin hung, and the recoil brought the gun back beside Ooti's head as if by magic.

Small Ears gave a half-suppressed shriek and covered her ears at the noise of the shot, and Acorn Girl turned to laugh at her friend.

"You have been with me at least twenty times when the gun has fired, and every time you do that," she teased. "Surely by now you know what is going to happen."

"That is true, but every time it is such a terrible noise that I can't help myself," Small Ears apologized. "I don't know how you can stand it."

"You are the one who always wants to come with me," Ooti reminded the other girl. "Why don't you try it? It's fun once you get used to it. I'll teach you everything Pine-nut-eater taught me."

As always, Small Ears quickly backed away, holding her hands up protectively in front of herself.

"No! I think you are crazy even to touch it, Ooti. I come along with you because I am afraid you will hurt yourself. I think you have always wanted to be a man. Even when you were a little girl, you would rather play at bows and arrows and running with the boys than make baskets or prepare food."

"That's not true," Acorn Girl returned. "You know I am a very good cook, and everyone says my baskets are as fine as anyone's. I don't see any reason why I can't do both things. I wish I could do this better, though," she added, squinting ruefully at the torn bark all around her target. "I don't think this thing is nearly as accurate as a bow and arrow."

She sighed, raised the pistol again, sighted along the barrel, squeezed slowly, slowly.

* * *

The same night Acorn Girl and Pine-nut-eater had re-turned from their day away from Tumeli village, the rain had begun. She had wakened in the dark to hear the hiss of heavy drops on the ground and on the thatched cover-ing of their *hubo*. The downfall continued unabated through the next day, with only occasional periods when the dull gray sky would break to reveal blue for a time. And for many days after that the weather was dreary, cold and wet.

Acorn Girl felt that the weather fit her own mood, the monotonous gloomy gray, the chill and the damp, for she was depressed and angry that Pine-nut-eater would not change his mind about going to work for Sutter, the *Wawlem* chief who told the Whitemen at Kolo-ma what to do.

Husband and wife had quarreled frequently in the days before he left, something they had never done before. And in between fights, at night when the fire had burned low, they made love with an almost angry urgency. When Pine-nut-eater left, Ooti was repentant, half-convinced that it was as much because of her sharp tongue as for any other reason that he had gone away so soon—even though he assured her of his love before he left and was careful to repeat his insistence that she practice with the pistol when-ever she got the chance.

Acorn Girl moved back into her parents' lodge, for their large, earth-covered *k-um* was much more comfortable in the damp weather than her own thatched *hubo*, and both Kuksu Man and Tule Elk insisted that they were very lonely and had far more space than they knew what to do with. The two grandparents were utterly infatuated with the Bears, as was Hurt Eagle, a frequent visitor. And now that the children were being fed partly upon a mixture of very thin acorn gruel, meat broth, and honey, Ooti had considerably more freedom than she had enjoyed for months. Not that there was a great deal for her to do with such freedom, for the weather continued unpleasant most of the time, but on those few days when the sun came out, or the drizzle even let up for a time, days like this one, she would go away from the village, taking the gun with her. Often Small Ears accompanied her, and sometimes she would take the twins and Tule Elk as well.

Today she had not brought the babies out. The sky was threatening, and, as she squeezed off her last shot, the report of the pistol was taken up and extended in a long rumble of thunder. Acorn Girl glanced at the sky, which had become quite black to the east, hastily uncapped the unfired rounds in the chamber, and wrapped the revolver in a piece of oiled deerskin. Already the first scattered, heavy drops of rain were beginning to fall.

"Aiieee!" Small Ears grumbled. "I knew you would get me wet. I should have had more sense than to come out with you on a day like this."

The two young women threw their deerskin cloaks around themselves, pulling them over their heads, and ran up the trail toward the village—but they had come far enough away so that the noise of the shooting would not disturb anyone, and there was no chance of their reaching home without getting drenched.

Another long, drawn-out roar of thunder overtook them, and before the echoes died away, the hillside to the left of the trail lit up with intense, purple light—and there came a tremendous crash, as if the earth had ripped open beneath them. Rain came then, as if a river in the sky had broken loose.

Small Ears screamed and threw her arms over her head, but Ooti found herself laughing hysterically. She was strangely exhilarated by the violent storm, and she had an impulse to throw off her cloak and dance naked in the downpour.

"Now I know you are crazy," Small Ears shouted over the hiss of the rain. "I think this is your fault, Ooti. I think that the noise of your small thundermaker attracted the storm spirits."

"Never mind," Acorn Girl said, still laughing. "I think I remember a place where we can keep from drowning until the Storm Spirits get tired and ease up."

The shelter that Acorn Girl had in mind was quite close by, up the canyonside but within view of the trail. It was, in truth, nothing more than a lean-to that she and Pine-

nut-eater had put up as a shelter when they were hunting
one day more than a year earlier, with one end of the
brush and branch thatch supported by a huge fallen liveoak.
Even if the lean-to had not survived the year, it could be
built back quickly enough and would afford at least some
protection.

They found that the main support branches of the shelter were still in place, and most of the tangle of covering
brush as well. The girls worked quickly to rearrange the
overlay, and Acorn Girl used her flint skinning knife to cut
fresh fir boughs to place over the top. When they had
finished and crawled inside, both were soaked to the skin.

"Ouf!" Small Ears gasped. "I am so wet that it hardly
seems worth the bother to stay out of the rain now."

"I'll build us a fire," Acorn Girl offered.

"How will you get a fire started, Ooti? Everything is
wet, even in here."

"Some of the things the *Wawlem* Maidu have are good,"
Acorn Girl responded, her voice purposefully mysterious.
"Watch."

With her knife she dug out chunks of the rotten wood
from the oak log, taking them from below the curve of the
trunk where the wood was driest. She made a small pile of
soft wood just inside the front opening of the lean-to,
sprinkled the pile liberally with gunpowder from the horn
flask Pine-nut-eater had left to go along with the gun, and
then struck a spark from the flint-and-steel fire-starter he
had given her as a gift when they were courting. The
powder went off in a flash, and the small pile of wood
caught instantly. Acorn Girl added wood gradually, broken-
off twigs from last year's roof as well as more chunks of
rotten oak, and soon the fire, though small, was burning
brightly enough to make their shelter noticeably warmer.

Most of the smoke from the blaze blew back into the
shelter, making the young women cough and causing their
eyes to water. But they huddled about the small flame
anyway and let the warmth steam the wet from their
clothing and hair. They spread their cloaks against the log
and sat in only their rush skirts, warming the bare skin of
their breasts and arms and backs near the fire. Large
drops of water were still falling into the fire from their hair

when they heard a shout above the hissing of the rain outside.

Acorn Girl peered from the opening but could see nothing.

The shout was repeated from much closer, and in a moment Tied-wing, a young man from the village and Pine-nut-eater's best friend among the Tumeli, crawled past the fire and under the shelter of the lean-to. He grinned at the two surprised girls and shouldered between them to sit next to the little blaze.

"It was kind of you to start this fire for me," he remarked. "A man likes to have a fire when he has been out hunting in the rain."

Ooti stared at the newcomer, speechless for a moment, and then she burst out laughing.

"What are you doing here, Tied-wing? Were you spying on us?"

"No," he answered, his eyes innocently wide. "As I said, I was out hunting. See?"

He held up two dead rabbits, dangling the creatures by their ears.

"The great hunter has caught rabbits?" Small Ears mumbled.

"Yes," Tied-wing continued. "I caught them in my snares. I will give one to each of you for building me a fire."

"Ho," Ooti teased. "I think maybe you were hunting a different kind of rabbit. Maybe a small-eared rabbit."

"I like small-eared rabbits," he admitted, the corners of his eyes creasing with suppressed laughter as he stared at the other girl.

Small Ears felt the blood come to her cheeks, and she refused to look at either of her companions. Yet she could not hide a tiny, embarrassed smile.

"But usually," Acorn Girl continued, unable to resist, "where you hunt such rabbits is in the village, for such a one lives there, and I have noticed that you are frequently at her parents' lodge."

"Stop it!" Small Ears burst out. "Tied-wing only comes to visit my father. They are great friends."

"That is true," Tied-wing agreed. "Your father and I are friends. If I were not an orphan, with so little to offer, then perhaps your father and I would be more than friends. Perhaps we would be related in some way. Maybe I will go with Pine-nut-eater next time and work with the *Wawlems* if they will let me, and I will be able to bring back good things. Ooti, your husband said he would speak to his White friends about me this time."

Small Ears stared in wonder at the handsome young man, her embarrassment forgotten for the moment. She had spoken to Acorn Girl about her attraction to Tied-wing, but, although it was obvious to everyone else in the village that he had been courting her, Small Ears had not allowed herself to believe it.

"This is true?" she whispered, her eyes now fixed on his.

It was Tied-wing's turn to be shy. He cleared his throat self-consciously and then grinned. He suddenly put his arm around the girl's bare waist and whispered something into her ear. She giggled, and then blushed furiously again, glancing up sideways at Acorn Girl.

Ooti began to feel herself to be something of an intruder. It was still raining, but not nearly as heavily as it had been, the downpour having let up to a misty drizzle while the three had been talking. Now Ooti stretched her cramped arms and prepared to rise.

"I think I hear my Bears calling me," she remarked. "If I wait any longer, it will probably start raining hard again."

"Wait. I will come with you," Small Ears said. "My mother will be wondering what happened to me."

"Perhaps you should stay here with Tied-wing until the sky grows clear," Acorn Girl suggested mischievously. "You don't have to worry about babies—yet."

"No," said Small Ears, a note of panic coming into her voice. "It wouldn't be proper."

"No, I suppose not," Acorn Girl agreed. "Still, I think that Tied-wing could probably be trusted to make some nice presents to your father later, so that you could be proud."

"Ooti, no!" she cried out. "Tied-wing, you must let go of me," she added, for the young man held her with his arms around her waist and wouldn't allow her to rise.

After a moment he released her, and she hastened to

wrap her still-damp cloak around herself and scrambled out of the shelter after her friend. Tied-wing followed, and the three of them set out for Tumeli village.

After Small Ears' short display of renewed shyness, she and Tied-wing dropped some distance behind Acorn Girl, who could hear them talking softly together, although she couldn't make out the words.

As they entered the village and passed the *hubo* in which she and Pine-nut-eater had lived, Acorn Girl paused and waited for her friend to catch up. She drew Small Ears away from Tied-wing and whispered to her, "If you ever decide to be improper, here is a lodge which is unoccupied."

With that she hurried away to her parents' dwelling and left the others to do as they chose.

When Acorn Girl entered the *k-um*, both Bears were screaming furiously. Hurt Eagle, who spent much more time in Kuksu Man's lodge than in his own official dwelling place in the medicine lodge, was holding Bear-who-comes-before, while Tule Elk held Bear-who-comes-after. The grandmother was trying to entice the child she held to take some nourishment from the imitation nipple that she had devised from a piece of finely woven netting. Both Hurt Eagle and Kuksu Man were singing a wordless but very vigorous song, a series of *hiyo, hiyo, hiyo*, and Kuksu Man was dancing in place, shaking a rattle, and making a series of comic and grotesque faces for the benefit of the twins.

Ooti stopped and stared at the spectacle for a moment, and then she threw back her head and laughed.

"I don't think my sons are old enough yet to appreciate a medicine dance," she said, "even by two such distinguished doctors."

Hurt Eagle looked up and immediately rose and brought her the red-faced, squalling infant.

"It is not good for children to cry as much as these do. Feed your sons," he commanded. "The poor children have been starving, and their grandfathers were trying to distract them from their aching bellies—while their mother was off playing with Whitemen's toys out in the rain."

"Very well," Acorn Girl agreed, "but let me sit by the fire and dry off while I'm doing it. Here I've run home through the downpour—and have gotten drenched in the process—all so that I could tend to your grandsons. And now all you can do is scold me."

Hurt Eagle, suppressing a grin, arched one eyebrow and glanced at Kuksu Man.

Acorn Girl wrung the water out of her hair and turned to Tule Elk.

"You may as well give me the other Bear, too, Mother. He doesn't seem to want his gruel."

While she nursed the twins, Acorn Girl told the others a little of what had happened in the courtship of Small Ears and Tied-wing. Tule Elk, in particular, listened with interest, for she was very sympathetic to young lovers and had been hoping for the union of which Ooti spoke. For two seasons now she had observed the glances, the visits, the friendship between Tied-wing and Limping Buck, Small Ears' father. So now, at last, something was finally about to happen. . . .

"Tied-wing is a fine young man," the older woman said, nodding wisely. "He will amount to something, even though he is an orphan and will have to work three times as hard as someone with a family to help him. Everyone has seen how those two have been watching each other, and both too shy to say anything openly. I am glad you helped bring them together, Ooti."

"He spoke of going to Kolo-ma to work with Pine-nut-eater and the *Wawlem* Maidus so that he could get gifts for Small Ears' father," Ooti remarked, a trace of wistfulness coming into her voice as she made reference to her absent husband.

"You miss Pine-nut-eater," Kuksu Man said gently.

Tule Elk nodded and glanced at Hurt Eagle.

"I don't think it is any good," she said, "this business of young men running off from their women to get things from the Whitemen. I would not have let Kuksu Man do that when we were young."

"We seldom saw the *Wawlems* in those days," Hurt

Eagle remarked. "It is only since this Sutter has built his fort where the *Yalesumnes* joins *Nem Seyoo*, the Big River. After that many of the Valley Maidus began to work for him, tending his cattle and sheep, and cutting down trees for him to build with. Before that the *Wawlems* only passed through our lands, sometimes camping for a time, but always moving on again. Yes, and one of those first *Wawlems* was Pine-nut-eater's father. Your husband is Maidu, Ooti, but his blood is part White. That is why he gets along with this Sutter, perhaps."

"No matter," Tule Elk said, "I would not have let my husband go."

"Would you now?" Kuksu Man asked his wife, teasing her and moving to slip an arm around her and pinch an ample buttock. "Since I have grown old and ugly, you are no longer interested in me."

"Stop that!" the wife cried out, slapping in feigned indignation at Kuksu Man's hand. "You know that's not what I mean."

Acorn Girl smiled at her parents. Tule Elk had put on weight with her middle years, as most Nishinam women did, but she was still a very good-looking woman, Ooti thought, her large breasts still nearly as firm as a young girl's, and her wide-set, sparkling eyes really beautiful. In the same way, in his daughter's eyes, Kuksu Man had always been one of the handsomest men in Tumeli village. The years had done little to change his body—his shoulders were perhaps more heavily muscled than they had been, and he had just the slightest suggestion of a pot belly. His face was creased with the sun, but still square-jawed and high-cheeked.

"It is good," Ooti thought, "to have grown up in a lodge where the mother and father love each other. Pine-nut-eater and I will be like Kuksu Man and Tule Elk."

The thought was as much an inward prayer for the future as an assertion of fact. For some reason that she didn't understand, a slight chill, a suggestion of darkness passed through her mind with the thought, but she pushed it away quickly.

"Perhaps this would be a good time to go down to Kolo-ma village," Tule Elk was saying. "You have had no message from your husband, and you are worried about him. That is a natural thing."

"I'm not worried. Who would bring a message? Pine-nut-eater will come back when he is ready to come back."

"Perhaps Tule Elk is right," Hurt Eagle said thoughtfully. "I don't trust the *Wawlems*, but I have a sister at Kolo-ma, and I haven't seen her for a long time. It is good to go there. Soon this rain will become snow where we are, but it doesn't snow very much at Kolo-ma."

"Now is a good time to stay inside the lodge and build a big fire," Acorn Girl said. "You know it isn't a good time to travel, especially with two little ones as new as the Bears," she added, nodding at the infants who had fallen asleep on her lap, one still clinging to a breast.

Hurt Eagle drew back his lips and made a soft whistling sound.

"We can wrap the children up so they'll never feel the cold," he insisted. "I will carry them myself."

"There is some other reason why you think we should go to Kolo-ma," Acorn Girl said slowly.

Hurt Eagle glanced again at Kuksu Man and Tule Elk and then turned back to Ooti.

"Very well, then, I'll tell you," he said. "My sister lives with another widow, and this widow, although she is not young, is very healthy."

The old man gestured with his hands cupped in front of his chest at the word *healthy*, so that the others laughed.

"She does not wish to come to Tumeli to live with me," Hurt Eagle continued, "and I do not wish to go to Kolo-ma to live with her, but when I visit my sister, this healthy widow doesn't mind warming my feet. It has been a long time, as I said, and my feet are very cold."

"Men all speak nonsense," Acorn Girl said. "You will tell me the truth, won't you, Mother? Why does everyone suddenly want to go away? Is it because of Water-strider? I know that she has been trying to put a curse on me, but she doesn't frighten me."

Tule Elk glanced nervously at her husband, then turned back to Acorn Girl.

"I will tell you the truth. It is more than that. She has begun to stir people up again. Some have started to forget

the message Hurt Eagle brought to them from Pano, and
bad feelings are growing. Sometimes when I go down to
the river to leach my acorns, a group of women that have
been talking will grow silent, and others tell me what
Water-strider has been saying. And it is not just the
women. Some of the men are starting to side with her,
too. If it were not such a foolish thought, I would believe
that she is getting ready to have a showdown with Hurt
Eagle and Kuksu Man."

"That would be very bad," Ooti said. "She would lose,
of course, but then there would be even more bad feeling.
I should pay more attention to what goes on in the village.
I didn't believe it was anything more than one crazy
woman who hated me."

"Today she has been having some kind of a meeting at
her lodge all afternoon," Kuksu Man nodded. "There have
been at least ten people in and out of there all day long. I
think the midwife is trying to get them worked up to
something, but no one can find out what it is. I think it
would be wiser if we went away for a while, just as Hurt
Eagle suggests. That way the people would remember
who their leaders are, and the witch's words would fade
from their minds."

"I will not let her run us out of our own village," Acorn
Girl snapped.

"You are too hasty, Granddaughter," Hurt Eagle said,
his voice soft and patient. "When people in a village
cannot agree, then one side or the other has to leave so
that the bad feelings won't keep growing. It is not that
those who leave have conceded defeat. No, it is just that
they are wise enough not to want their people torn apart."

"It is my home, my people, too," Acorn Girl said.
"Water-strider is the one who is trying to cause trouble.
Let her leave. If you wish to go to Kolo-ma, Grandfather,
Father, then that is your business, and I can't stop you.
But I will wait here until my husband comes and tells me
he wants me to move."

"I could tie you up and have some of the young men
carry you," said Kuksu Man, his own temper flaring briefly.

Tule Elk shook her head.

"Hush, Husband. You know you would never do a thing

like that. And you, Daughter, I see your eyes beginning to catch fire and something coming to your lips. Do not speak words you will regret later."

Ooti lowered her gaze to the floor of the lodge.

"You are wise, Mother," she murmured, but her stiff-backed posture did not relax. "Still, I will not run away from a bitter old woman—or flee after my husband until he says he wants me."

She lifted her eyes to challenge her father's gaze again.

"Well then," Hurt Eagle said, his voice just above a whisper, "I think it is too early to worry very much, anyway. Water-strider hasn't done anything openly. She won't act until she feels she has enough support to force the issue with us."

"Who knows what a crazy person will do?" asked Kuksu Man. "I am the *Huku* of the Tumeli, the head of the Kuksu Society, and I hold the magic cape that Hurt Eagle gave me when he believed he had become too old to lead any longer. But maybe Water-strider thinks she can become the *Moki*, the highest in rank among the animal impersonators."

"The *Moki* are insane," Hurt Eagle said, "and that is how they receive their power. But Water-strider is only *wut-a*, crazy. She has been humiliated, and my vision of Pano has made her bitter. Her hatred is what is causing her to do what she is doing."

"I don't think she is crazy at all," Kuksu Man said. "I think she wishes to be leader of the village."

"Yes," Hurt Eagle agreed. "She will find some man who will do as she says, one the people can call their *Huku*, but Water-strider would be the actual leader. She has been waiting for a long time to get something that she can use to turn the people against us."

"Have you always known this?" Tule Elk asked, surprised.

"I have suspected it," Hurt Eagle said. "It does no good to speak ill of people until they do something openly."

"It is as I said. She is insane," Kuksu Man insisted.

"Still, there is no real reason to leave right now," the old shaman said, shrugging his shoulders. "I had only thought of avoiding some trouble, but there will be no trouble for some time yet. Most of the people remember that you have been a good leader, Kuksu Man, and they will never side with her. And it is true, as your daughter said, that she should obey her husband now, and not her father. There is no harm in remaining here in Tumeli village until the trouble actually comes, if it does."

"Sometimes I think Ooti obeys no one but Ooti," Kuksu Man grumbled.

Hurt Eagle rose and stretched elaborately.

"I will go out for a little fresh air now," the old shaman said. "My legs get cramped from sitting in one place too long. Shall we go walk around the village, Kuksu Man? Perhaps when we come back, the women will have something cooked that is good to eat. Then I will spread my blanket here for tonight, if that is permissible. I have been away from my own lodge for so long that the fire has gone out by now, and it will be cold there."

"Fresh air?" Acorn Girl giggled. "Grandfather, there's a river coming down from the sky out there."

"Silence, Daughter," Kuksu Man ordered. "We know it is raining. Do you think we are afraid of getting wet?"

Then, with great dignity, he rose. And the two shamans left the *k-um*.

Ooti's eyes came open in the darkness, and she was so wide awake it was as if she hadn't gone to sleep at all. She looked about cautiously. It was completely black inside her father's lodge. No, she realized, not completely. There was a disk of moonlight on the floor, light that came in through the smokehole, and in the faint, reflected radiance she could make out the sleeping forms of the others in the lodge—her parents, and Hurt Eagle, the old shaman's snores competing with the lighter, more nasal tones of Tule Elk.

Acorn Girl tried to remember what had waked her. The twins lay snuggled against her on either side, neither Bear stirring. She told herself that it was nothing, but there remained a strong inner urging that she should not go back to sleep, that something was wrong. She lay utterly still, drawing her breath and releasing it carefully so as not to make the slightest sound, and listened intently.

She heard it again—a tiny crackle, as if a twig had been stepped on, a dry twig—and something else less definable, something like an almost inaudible murmur, perhaps the sound of several people breathing. Whatever it was, it was just outside the lodge.

"Probably nothing but a raccoon or a porcupine," the daytime part of her mind insisted. But there was a darker consciousness that knew differently.

Acorn Girl moved ever so cautiously, slipping by tiny degrees away from the babies, crouching as she moved step by slow step to the entryway. Pine-nut-eater's revolver, which she kept loaded and next to her when she slept, was clutched in her hand.

She knelt and looked out through the round opening, keeping her face within the shadow of the lodge.

Moonlight. Stillness. Tumeli village bathed in silver and shadows, sleeping. Nothing stirred. Moonlight-dappled shade under the cluster of firs beside the lodge, the upright forms of the trunks.

Suddenly she leaped backward into the *k-um*, screaming involuntarily and in wild terror.

In the confusion of voices, the sleepers wakened and calling out, the twins going off into startled shrieks, Ooti tried to recall what she had seen in the shadows of the fir trees. *Shapes. Upright forms, almost as still as the trees. Animal heads, towering, upright animal forms, indistinct in the shadows, sprinkled with vague light.*

"I was dreaming," she thought. But already, before Kuksu Man had fully risen, before she could move, the dark forms were pushing into the lodge and whispering something in near-unison, a kind of hissing chant. She could not make out the words.

Acorn Girl raised the pistol, aimed in panic at the lead figure, did not fire at the last moment.

Don't shoot unless you mean to kill. . . .

Pine-nut-eater had spoken those words so many times they acted like a physical restraint upon the automatic response to raise the pistol and fire.

"It may be someone come with a sick child to be healed," she told herself, "and I only imagined. . . ."

"Who is there?" Kuksu Man called out sharply. "If you have business in my lodge, speak."

"We have business with your daughter, Kuksu Man, and with the evil twins." said an unfamiliar and hissing voice.

Acorn Girl scrambled backward to her sleeping platform where the babies continued to scream.

A hand from one of the forms reached out for her, brushed her.

"We, the Animal Spirits, the Spirits of the wind and water and earth, are very angry that this sacrilege has been committed," another voice hissed. "We will spare the mother, but we want both children."

At once, Ooti understood. She raised the pistol again, shouted, "Stop, Water-strider!"

The ringing tones of her voice caused the advancing shadows to hesitate.

"You know that I have the Whiteman's *death-maker*," she continued. "I will use it before I will let any of you touch my sons."

After a moment's silence, the sibilant whisper that Acorn Girl was now certain belonged to Water-strider spoke again.

"We know Water-strider, but she is not here. We are Angry Spirits."

Acorn Girl was unable to suppress a nervous giggle, and the lead figure and then the others began their slow advance upon her again.

Ooti aimed low, just above the ground, and, with a quick prayer to *Pano*, fired.

Blue-white light flashed and with it came the sharp roar of the Allen & Wheelock revolver. The thick smell of powder smoke.

A scream.

"Aieee! My foot! My foot is broken!"

The voice was quite human.

At that instant the lodge fire, which had been nothing but embers, flared into intense light, and Hurt Eagle stood behind it, his white hair falling wildly around his shoulders and his magic cape held out before him. The figures near the entrance were revealed as human forms,

cloaked and painted and wearing the towering masks used
for the sacred *kuksu* dances.

But one figure was on the ground, the human inhabitant
of an *Oleli* disguise clutching in agony at a bleeding foot.

Hurt Eagle held his hands cupped before his chest now,
his cape across one forearm. And the hands seemed to
have some small object hidden in them.

"Now," the ancient shaman said, "we shall see who
these *Spirits* are. I think they are Nishinam Maidu of
Tumeli who shame us all and profane the sacred rites."

And, without pausing, he began to chant: *I am holding
my sila, now I am praying to it, now I am telling it who
my enemy is. Is this the woman called Water-strider? Is
this the one who pretends to have power? If that is who is
here now, my sila, my sacred killer, the one whose power
I have not called upon before, go and find the witch called
Water-strider. . . .*

He paused briefly, fixing the frozen group before the
entrance with his intense, unwavering stare, and then
abruptly flung his hands apart and outward, and shouted:
"Now!"

With a shriek, the figure in the lead, one wearing a
towering deer's head mask, collapsed, the knees buckling,
the hands clutching at the breast. The other masked ones
moaned and stumbled over each other in the attempt to
get out the exit. The figure in the deer's head costume
pushed itself up and tried to crawl to the outside, but
collapsed again upon its belly, the deer's head coming
loose and falling to one side.

The face revealed belonged to Water-strider.

"Stay, Crooked Knee, you fool!" Hurt Eagle roared, and
the last of the dancers to crawl to the entryway, the one
with the bloody foot, stopped as if instantly paralyzed.

Hurt Eagle strode over and pulled the painted coyote
mask from a young man whom Acorn Girl recognized as
one who had been a novice shaman, one whom both Hurt
Eagle and Kuksu Man had helped through the difficult
period of his initial visions. The young man's eyes were
wide now with fear, and his body trembled.

"Please don't kill me, Hurt Eagle," he begged. "The
witch-woman must have cast a spell on me. I didn't know

what I was doing. She told us that you had fallen from the good ways, that the Spirits would bring disaster upon us if . . ."

"Stop your babbling, Crooked Knee," the master shaman snapped. "You are too silly to kill. Your foot needs tending, and after that I hope never to see you again."

The young man nearly wept with relief and continued to pour out incoherent streams of self-justification and re-crimination against Water-strider, these intermingled with pleas for mercy. Hurt Eagle ignored him and turned to stand over Water-strider, who still lay as if dead.

"Wake up, old woman, you ridiculous old mud hen," he called, kicking at her lightly. "Open your eyes now, or I will tell my *sila* to kill you instantly."

Water-strider did not move, but the eyelids opened cautiously, the pupils sliding to one side to look up at Hurt Eagle, firelight glinting in them.

"Sit up, woman!" the shaman shouted. "I am losing patience with you."

Water-strider scrambled up to a sitting position, still holding one hand curled at her breast.

"Aieee! Hurt Eagle has brought her back from the dead," Crooked Knee shrieked.

"You have killed me certainly," Water-strider was whin-ing at the same time. "Now I will die, and at the hands of my own people."

"Silence!" Kuksu Man thundered from where he stood near the fire. "Neither of you will speak in my lodge until you are asked to speak. Ooti, go see who is standing outside the *k-um*, shivering in the moonlight. The shot from Pine-nut-eater's pistol has awakened everyone. Tell them to come in if there are not too many."

Acorn Girl could hear the murmur of voices outside. With knees still shaking from the aftereffect of the night's happenings, she rose and went to the entrance. A number of Nishinam, having heard the screams and the shot, had gathered—among them Tied-wing, who held one of the masked figures by an arm. Small Ears was standing just behind her lover.

Two other young men restrained a second of the raiding Animal Spirits, the latter having already removed his turtle mask.

Acorn Girl motioned for those gathered to enter the *k-um*, and they came, dragging the reluctant and terrified masqueraders with them.

Small Ears reached for Acorn Girl's hand.

"What has happened?" she whispered. "Are you all right, Ooti?"

Acorn Girl gestured wearily, squeezing Small Ears' hand in reassurance.

Inside, Hurt Eagle still stood over Water-strider, who crouched like a trapped animal, her eyes darting from side to side as if seeking an impossible escape. The group who had just entered buzzed with questions, speculation.

Kuksu Man held up his hand, silencing the guests.

"This woman," Hurt Eagle announced, "entered the lodge of the Tumeli *Huku* in the middle of the night and attempted to do harm to ones I love. These others," he gestured to indicate the masked individuals, "also came at her bidding, along with more who have gotten away but whose names I know. Now Water-strider has my *sila* in her heart for her evil acts, and she will die unless I take my killing-object back. That is why she will tell you all, with her own voice, what vicious things she has planned and done, and what a wicked woman she is. After that, she and these others will leave Tumeli village forever. Perhaps they have relatives among the Molma, the Hembem, or the Kulkumish, I do not know. If not, then they will have to draw the *suk* from their acorns wherever they can."

There was a new commotion at the entryway, and then two more masked figures were propelled into the room. Behind them, holding his prized Hawken percussion rifle, came Pine-nut-eater.

Acorn Girl cried out and ran to embrace her husband, who hugged her tightly, laughing as he did so.

"I just happened to see these people leaving your *k-um* in the middle of the night," he said to Kuksu Man, "and I thought that perhaps they might owe an explanation of what they were doing. I see that you have things under control, however."

Pine-nut-eater stared at Water-strider, still crouched beneath Hurt Eagle's commanding figure. Then he asked, "Where are my two Bears? I have ridden a long way to see them."

4

The Serpent in Eden

January-February, 1848

"This is Ooti, the acorn," World Maker said. "It came from heaven, from the Valley Above—that is where I got it. It is a good thing, and from it will grow Ootimtsaa, the acorn tree, from which all twelve kinds of acorns will come. Ootimtsaa will always grow here on Estawm Yan, but very few of the people will ever be able to find it. Nevertheless, it will be here. And its roots will search down to the center of Earth, while its uppermost branches will net themselves among the stars."

"I don't understand," said Turtle.

"Doesn't make any sense," Peheipe agreed. "I don't think you're World Maker at all. I think you're just a crazy person with a flaming coat and a lot of tricks. In the first place, if the tree's that big, everyone will be able to see it. And in the second place, there aren't any people any more. They all drowned or were eaten by the frogs and the salmon."

For a moment the flames of World Maker's robe flared up, and he smiled at his two lost friends.

"I will plant the tree now," he said. "After that I will explain everything to you. Stand back, now. As soon as I place Ooti into the ground, the shell will crack open—and

*the Ootimtsaa will grow very fast. If you do not watch
carefully, you will not even see it happen.”*

World Maker scooped a hole in the earth, placed the
acorn there, and then nudged the dark grains of soil over
it. He stood up and gazed at the spot where he had
planted the Ooti.

Suddenly rain fell. Lightning flashed across the sky,
and thunder roared so loudly that great pieces of stone fell
down from the jagged peaks of Estawm Yan. Steam hissed
up from the earth and created a dense, warm fog.

Turtle and Peheipe rubbed at their eyes, and when they
opened them, a gigantic tree rose before them, its trunk
the size of a mountain, and its branches far into the sky.

“I told you,” World Maker grumbled. “Now sit down
with me beneath Ootimtsaa. Maybe you will like the words
I speak, I don't know.”

The fire in Kuksu Man's *k-um* still burned brightly,
although the circle of the smokehole showed the vivid
gray-violet of approaching dawn. Most of the participants
in the night's events had departed after Water-strider,
apparently considerably chastened but freed of Hurt Eagle's *sila*, had gone from the lodge with the promise to
leave Tumeli before the day was over.

Following her had gone the captured raiders, all young
men except Round Belly, a longtime unsuccessful rival to
Hurt Eagle, the group obviously relieved to have escaped
the two great shamans' wrath unscathed. Those who had
come merely as curious observers had drifted back to their
own lodges when the excitement was over, and all who
remained now were Tied-wing and Small Ears as well as
Small Ears' father, Limping Buck, and a small group of
other older men of distinction, the informal council that
made most of the decisions that affected the village.

Acorn Girl leaned drowsily against her husband and
listened as these men talked, discussing what had happened and also reviewing Hurt Eagle's banishment of the
troublemakers. Tule Elk sat near the fire, feeding it sticks
of wood from time to time, her back to the group, for
although it was improper for a woman and her daughter's

husband to look at each other, yet she was burning with curiosity to hear what he might have to say about his trip to Kolo-ma village.

"I think it is as you have said, Hurt Eagle," Limping Buck was saying, "that there is no other way to keep peace in Tumeli village than by sending Water-strider and her friends away, and yet I am sorry to see this happen, for there will be many who will go just to remain with their relatives and friends, even though they had nothing to do with the mischief."

He paused, drew thoughtfully at the pipe Kuksu Man had passed to him.

"I miss my friend Burnt Hair already," Limping Buck continued. "He would be sitting with us now if his son Crooked Knee had not gotten involved in this foolishness. Burnt Hair is a wise man, and I value his advice. And yet he will have to leave, for his son has shamed him."

"I am surprised that Crooked Knee would do such a thing," Tied-wing mused. "Do you remember, Small Ears, how sometimes I would have to rescue him from the other boys because he was so small and had that limp? He never seemed bad-intentioned until now."

"He was always too easily led," Small Ears said. "The older boys could usually get him to steal salmon from the drying racks for them, and he would be the one to get caught."

"I guess that's true," Pine-nut-eater sighed. "I am sorry this happened, anyway."

"I think you are waiting to tell us something, son-in-law," Kuksu Man remarked.

"Yes, I have been waiting. Perhaps this message I have will help ease the difficulty, I don't know. But first, I have brought back something for all of you."

Pine-nut-eater turned to the bundle he had brought in earlier, opened it, and distributed good, steel-bladed knives to all the men in the lodge. To Kuksu Man he also gave a rifle, along with a quantity of powder and shot. For Hurt Eagle he added a shiny, round object with a black needle that retained its original direction as the old shaman turned the case first one way and then the other, puzzling.

"What is this good for, Pine-nut-eater?" he asked at last.

"I can see that it has some kind of magic, but perhaps it is only useful to a *Wawlem*."

"The needle always points to the north, Grandfather," Pine-nut-eater explained. "You can find directions with it."

"Ah," Hurt Eagle said. "This is a good thing, I guess, although there is always that star that doesn't move to help us find north, and in the daytime there is the sun, at night the moon."

"It's good for cloudy days," Pine-nut-eater said. "It isn't great magic, but I thought you might like it."

Hurt Eagle grunted politely, turning the compass about some more, trying to get ahead of the needle.

"These are fine gifts, my son," Kuksu Man nodded. "I am pleased to have this good knife and the *Wawlem* death stick. Perhaps my daughter can even teach me to use it. But I think the Whites must want something from us in return."

He smiled at Acorn Girl, winked.

"To tell the truth," Pine-nut-eater explained, "I think these gifts were mainly sent to make the young men want more of the same. I have told you before of Marshall, who is the *Wawlem* leader at the mill near Kolo-ma. He is a good man and can be trusted. He needs more of the young men from Kolo-ma village working for him, and he wants more men to work, that is all. I have been with Marshall these past two moons, and he always treats me well. The men will be able to earn good pay in return for helping Marshall build his sawmill."

Hurt Eagle frowned.

"He cuts down trees and turns them into flat planks with his mill on the river?" he asked. "That is what I have been told the mill is for when it is finished. It is a strange thing to do. I don't see why he wishes to pay our men to help him do that."

"It isn't easy to explain," Pine-nut-eater agreed. "There's a large village downriver which belongs to Sutter, the man I was a guide for. John Sutter has a number of villages. There's another where the Ololopa, Yuma, and Tsaktomo villages are, on the branch of the Big River the Whites call Plumas. And another between Sutter's Fort and Kolo-ma, where the square-faced men are building a mill to grind flour out of the seeds of tallgrass. And he raises the big brown deer he calls cattle. I have been to both these places with Marshall during this last visit."

"Are there still others?" Kuksu Man asked.

"Small ones," Pine-nut-eater replied. "And far down the river, next to the ocean, there is another village as large as the one at Sutter's Fort. I have not seen it, and I do not think it belongs to Sutter. But in all the villages the *Wawlems* build their houses out of flat wooden planks. And that is what the mill at Kolo-ma is for."

"How many trees need to be cut down to build a village?" Hurt Eagle asked. "It doesn't seem like it would take that many men or very long to build three villages."

"That is what I would have thought also, but there are apparently many more, and the *Wawlem* Maidus keep coming into these places and other places. They plant crops and raise animals for meat, and they have many people working for them, and everybody thinks he has to have a house of wooden planks."

"It may not be good to cut down so many trees," Limping Buck suggested. "Don't the people at Kolo-ma object to having these strangers cut down all their trees?"

"Most of the younger men at Kolo-ma work for them already," Pine-nut-eater said. "They get rifles and metal pots and bright-colored cloth for their women. Some of them have moved into wooden houses near the sawmill, and they are planting crops like the *Wawlems*. Things are changing. You said that, Hurt Eagle, or Pano said it through you."

"I had hoped that I would already be in Valley Above before the changes came," the old shaman said. "Pano tells us that these things are only the dream of Olelbis, and they are neither good nor bad, but to me they are bad. I am less objective than Pano or Olelbis, that is my problem."

"I do not think things will change so very much," Kuksu Man said. "These *Wawlems*, they do not have very many women. But they must not be very different from other people. I know they have different things, but they still need shelter and food. Besides, we have known of the

Spanish for years, and they haven't bothered us. They stay in their villages far to the south or over along the ocean. There they raise their big brown deer."

"It is said by some that these new *Wawlems* have no women," Limping Buck remarked.

"That is not so," Pine-nut-eater said. "I have seen some of their women in Sutter's village. Most of the men have left their women in the places they came from, but there are even a few women at the place near Kolo-ma. No, what Kuksu Man says is true. The *Wawlems* are not very different from us, just as I am no different, even though a *Wawlem* was my father. But I think what Hurt Eagle says is also true. I think things will change because of them, and this will happen no matter what we do. You may know that I have come to value many of the ways of the *Wawlems*, and I am not afraid of them because I know them better than you. I think it will be good for as many of the younger men as wish to go to work for Marshall."

"I am not so sure," Hurt Eagle insisted. "I have a bad feeling about all this. Perhaps it is only because I am old and don't like change. . . ."

"It is a way to ease the hurt feelings and the split among our people," Kuksu Man offered. "If many are leaving to work at this mill that Marshall is building, it will not be so difficult for those who don't wish to choose sides. Let Water-strider and her group remain here. It will be much less divisive if those who are loyal to us go visit the Kolo-ma Maidus."

Hurt Eagle half shook, half nodded his head.

"I suppose you are right, Kuksu Man. I cannot stand against the way the world is going. Still, my heart tells me something else."

"What do you see, Grandfather?" Acorn Girl asked suddenly.

She knew she shouldn't speak when the men were in council, and yet something about Hurt Eagle's words, or perhaps the tone of his voice, had caused a shiver to touch at the back of her neck, and she had the same fleeting vision of darkness, the same sense of sadness and fear that she had felt for no apparent reason the previous night.

Kuksu Man sent her a quick frown, but Hurt Eagle spoke as if he hadn't noticed anything unusual.

"I don't know," he said, his voice seeming to come from far away. "I heard screaming . . . I thought I saw . . ." He quickly clapped his hands over his ears, shut his eyes. "Nothing. It is only a foolish old man talking. It is only his fear of change."

"There is not much point in us deciding this, anyway," Kuksu Man said after a respectful pause following Hurt Eagle's words. "The young men will do what they wish, no matter what we say. You will have to ask them, Pine-nut-eater."

"I will go," said Tied-wing eagerly.

"We should decide quickly," Pine-nut-eater nodded. "Tomorrow I will give a feast in the dance lodge and invite all who wish to come. Then I will tell the people of Marshall's offer."

"You will have more men than you know what to do with," Tied-wing predicted. "There are many who wish to get rich like you did, so they don't have to wait forever to get married."

Limping Buck glanced sharply at the young man, a quick flicker of amusement quirking the corner of his mouth. Tied-wing looked embarrassed, and Pine-nut-eater rose, slapping his friend's shoulder.

"Come outside, Tied-wing. I have something out there that you might like to see," he said.

"I will come out also," Limping Buck muttered. "I had better be getting back to my own lodge anyway."

"We will all go out," said Kuksu Man. "Wouldn't you like to see this great thing, whatever it is, Hurt Eagle?"

The old shaman rose stiffly, and Small Ears said, "I would like to see it too. Wouldn't you, Ooti? Is this something that women can see as well as men?"

Tethered a few yards from the lodge, his head hanging nearly to the ground and apparently sleeping, stood a brown animal, as big as an elk but not an elk. Small Ears shrieked at the unnatural-looking creature, and the head came up slowly, an eye opened and looked at her, and then the head dropped back down.

"This is yours, my husband?" Acorn Girl asked, baffled. "What do you do with it?"

"I have seen these before," said Limping Buck.

"Yes," Kuksu Man agreed. "The Spanish have these. They are called *kabayo*. The Spanish use them for carrying things, and they also ride upon their backs. This is another present from the *Wawlem* Maidus?"

"Yes. This is my horse now, and his name is Ranger. Marshall gave him to me."

The older men, all of whom had seen horses before, left. But Tied-wing and Small Ears stayed, circling the wonderful beast, but cautiously. Acorn Girl held back, not at all trusting of this huge, quiet creature whose head was the size of her sons' whole bodies, and more.

"Go ahead, stroke his neck," her husband urged her. "Ranger likes to be petted."

Acorn Girl reached out tentatively, but just then the horse shook its head and rolled one eye at her. She drew back quickly.

Pine-nut-eater laughed at her and took her hand, placing it on the brown, furry forehead. She stroked awkwardly, drawing her hand back again as soon as seemed acceptable.

"When you get used to him," Pine-nut-eater went on, "I will teach you how to ride him."

"He will really allow people to ride on his back?" Small Ears asked. "I would not allow that if I were his size."

Ranger nudged his head against Ooti, nuzzling at her hand. She patted at his long nose again.

"I would like to ride on his back," Tied-wing said. "Will you let me?"

"Of course," Pine-nut-eater agreed. "Are we not blood brothers?"

Tied-wing did not wait for further instructions, but ran at the horse and tried to vault onto its back. Ranger threw his massive head up and jumped sideways, dumping Tied-wing onto the ground.

Acorn Girl screamed and leaped away, and the horse reared from her, fluttering its lips and rolling its eyes.

"I can see that it's not going to be easy—introducing the horse to the Nishinam Maidu," Pine-nut-eater said, laughing. "There is no gentler horse in the world than Ranger. In fact, he's so old that almost nothing interests him anymore, and yet the three of you have him shying and skipping like an unbroken two-year-old in no time."

Tied-wing had picked himself up and was approaching Ranger again, a look of grim determination on his mud-streaked face.

"No, Tied-wing," Pine-nut-eater cautioned. "There's a proper way to do this thing. We will let him calm down now, and then I will teach all of you."

In fact, Ranger was already standing as before, legs straddled lethargically and head hanging. Pine-nut-eater reached into the pocket of his Whiteman's clothing and pulled out several lumps of white stuff. This caught Ranger's attention, and the head came up alertly, reaching toward the man's hand. Pine-nut-eater gave him one small piece of sugar and distributed the other lumps to his friends. He showed Ooti how to hold the lump on the flat of her hand, and the horse lipped it up, tickling her hand with his fluttery mouth.

Acorn Girl laughed with delight.

"I'm afraid he's going to eat my hand, though," she said. "I guess I like this animal, however."

"Of course," her husband agreed. "And he likes you, especially if you keep feeding him sugar."

"Sugar?" asked Small Ears, examining the white substance in her hand. "Is this just for the animals, or can people eat it too?"

"Taste it," Pine-nut-eater suggested. "It is something the *Wawlems* love. They get upset when they run out of it."

Small Ears picked off a few grains, put it to her tongue, smiled.

"This is good," she said. "Like honey, maybe better."

Acorn Girl and Tied-wing also tasted the strange food, Ranger at the same time trying to thrust his muzzle in to get his share.

"I hope you have more of this," Ooti said. "I was wondering how we were going to give a very good feast when all I have is acorn meal and dried salmon, the same things everyone else has this time of the year when it's too wet to go out hunting very much."

"I have more of the sugar, and many other good things, things you will hardly believe. You will like it at Kolo-ma, Ooti. You like seeing new things. And someday soon I will take you down to see the town John Sutter has built."

He stopped, and put his arms around her, and hugged her tightly right there in front of the others.

"It is so good to see you again, my beautiful Acorn, my wife," he whispered. "I missed you. Let's leave these two to be amazed by Ranger and go to our *hubo*."

Ooti brushed a strand of hair out of her face and glanced at the others, a trifle embarrassed, and then smiled and put her arm around her husband's waist. The two walked away, arm in arm, without a backward glance.

The feast was a great success. In addition to the sugar, which was served in a hot black drink called coffee, Pine-nut-eater provided various kinds of canned foods, tomatoes and pickled peaches, neither of which most of the people had ever seen but which they liked immediately, and little oily fish called sardines. There was also a very salty kind of preserved meat which was not so popular.

The host distributed gifts to everyone, knives and strings of beads, brightly colored cloth and mirrors for the women. People danced and ate and sang most of the night, and by morning, many had decided to move down to the *Wawlem* village in order to get more of these exotic items.

The excitement over Water-strider's troublemaking was mostly forgotten in the new excitement of Pine-nut-eater's proposal. Many entire families, parents and cousins as well as wives and children of the men who wished to work for the whites, prepared for the trip, particularly when it was learned that both Kuksu Man and Hurt Eagle would go.

Water-strider herself was gone, as promised, before the feast, but Crooked Knee was still in the village, presumably waiting for his foot to heal before setting off on his own journey. Neither Kuksu Man nor Hurt Eagle chose to push the matter further, preferring to let the bad feelings within the village heal themselves through neglect.

Acorn Girl and her family set off for Kolo-ma two days later, the twins in their cradles as well as as many household goods as could be managed strapped to Ranger's bony back. The day dawned clear for the trip, but the morning was intensely cold, glittering coats of frost covering everything, and ice skimming the standing puddles of water left from the long period of rain. Later, as they made their way down the trail along the side of the great canyon, heading downstream and toward the Big River, wraiths of mist rose from the ground, the trees, the rocks, and for a time the sun shone into and through a luminous, pearl-colored haze.

It was afternoon by the time they reached the Kolo-ma village, set on a broad shelf overlooking the valley between high, rounded, broad-backed hills. From the Indian settlement, one could see the astonishing activity taking place next to the river. There was, as Pine-nut-eater had said, a collection of square, wooden dwellings in various stages of completion, and right beside the stream a huge, ungainly-looking structure of beams and planks, its framing not closed in so that it appeared to be a skeleton of some monstrous animal, perhaps that of *Weebehillen*, the Giant fish. This, as Ooti's husband explained with some pride, was the sawmill where they would actually use a large circular steel blade to cut logs into boards and beams. Once the mill was in operation, it would no longer be necessary to use axes and adzes to form the segments of wood.

The family was welcomed into the *hubo* of Hurt Eagle's sister, Born Early, an ancient, leather-skinned woman who was nonetheless quite active, talking a constant stream as she bustled about to get the guests food, interspersing her chatter with jokes, her eyes gleaming like shiny black beads from her withered face. And, just as Hurt Eagle had said, Born Early lived with another widow, a woman of ample proportions perhaps twenty years younger than her housemate. This woman was called Crane, and Acorn Girl was a little shocked to see the knowing looks, the smiles and winks that passed between Hurt Eagle and the large-breasted widow.

When they had eaten a meal consisting of acorn-meal water biscuits and some mushy brown vegetables that Pine-nut-eater called *beans*, the *hubo* emptied, Kuksu Man and Tule Elk going out to look over their surroundings and to decide upon a place to construct their own lodge, Hurt Eagle and Crane leaving together shortly after that for purposes that they didn't bother to explain. Only Born Early remained in her dwelling with the young couple and the babies.

"And now," Pine-nut-eater said, "it is time that I give my wife her gift. First, though, you must wear this."

With a small flourish he drew out from his bundle a garment made of a soft, woven substance much finer and softer than the tule or bark cloth that Acorn Girl was familiar with, and covered with tiny pictures of white flowers on a blue background. He held it up before her, and she saw that the top part was like the upper body of a person, with the chest and arms and a hole for the neck, while the lower part was a long, flaring skirt.

Acorn Girl looked at the strange clothing for a moment, not sure what to say.

"I saw that some of the young women here at Kolo-ma are wearing these," she said at last. "I thought that they wouldn't be very comfortable, but perhaps I was wrong. These little flowers are pretty," she added, not wanting to hurt her husband's feelings.

"Here," Pine-nut-eater laughed. "I'll help you put it on. You'll have to get used to it. You need to wear this when you are in the *Wawlem* village—because among the White people it is the custom for women to cover their breasts at all times. I have heard that the Whitemen go crazy when they see a pretty woman's breasts. I don't know if that's true, but if it is, you will certainly make them crazy."

"It is true," said Born Early, snickering. "I even saw a *Wawlem* chasing Crane once when she went down to their village with her breasts bare. Of course, she didn't run very fast."

"You mustn't tell Hurt Eagle that," said Pine-nut-eater,

holding the dress above Acorn Girl's head. "Here," he said, speaking to her. "You must put your arms up straight above your head. Good. . . ."

As the soft material was slipped down over Acorn Girl's head, Born Early replied, "Hurt Eagle doesn't mind. He is too old and wise to worry about things that don't make any difference. She can still please him."

"Hurt Eagle is very old and wise," Pine-nut-eater agreed, his fingers working the buttons up the back of Ooti's dress, the material drawing tight against her body as he worked, "but I don't know if there is any man who is that agreeable."

Acorn Girl turned around, her hands on her hips.

Pine-nut-eater clucked his tongue.

"I am afraid you may still make the Whitemen crazy," he concluded.

"I think they must be crazy already," Ooti returned. "Or else you are. Whoever heard of such silliness? You are going to take me down among these insane people now?"

"There's something else you should do," Pine-nut-eater said, "but I'm afraid you won't."

"What are these?" Acorn Girl asked as Pine-nut-eater held up a pair of black leather button-top boots. "Are those supposed to go on my feet? Does the sight of women's feet also make *Wawlem* men go crazy?"

"No, but . . ."

"Then I will not put these on," Acorn Girl said firmly. "I think the Whitemen must make their women wear these so that they can't run away from them."

"Wear your moccasins, then, at least," her husband said, his voice rich with resignation. "I want to introduce you to my friend James Marshall. He's going to make me foreman, leader, of a crew of men. I want him to think you are at least a little civilized."

"*Civilized?*" Ooti asked with exaggerated innocence. "Is that what they call it when they torture their women's feet?"

"Be nice, now," Pine-nut-eater begged. "You'll like Mr. Marshall. And after that I'll show you your special gift."

*   *   *

Acorn Girl and Pine-nut-eater walked down to the White village next to the river, leaving the twins to the care of Born Early. Ooti looked about curiously. The valley was already half in shadow, the sun poised to drop the remainder of the way behind the hills downstream, to the southwest. But men were still at work, filling the air with the sound of hammers and saws as they took advantage of the last usable light on one of the few clear days they'd had in some time.

Many of the men were Nishinam people, she realized, although they wore the strange breeches and shirts of the Whites, just as Pine-nut-eater often did. But the others, she deduced, must be the *Wawlems*. They were not so strange or frightening as she had anticipated, despite the heavy hair on some of their faces. Except for their coloring, they looked like anyone else, she thought, and even the coloring of most of them was not startling. One young man who had his hat off, taking a drink of water, had hair the color of grass in autumn, and Acorn Girl did find that a little unnerving. But most of the *Wawlems* had hair ranging from earth-color to the same black as her own people.

They found Marshall at the sawmill, directing construction and walking nervously from one end of the structure to the other and occasionally calling instructions or advice to the men at work. When he saw Pine-nut-eater, he hurried to him, his rather stern-looking face cracked by a slight smile.

The two men shook hands, and Pine-nut-eater introduced his wife.

"How-do-you-do, I-am-glad-to-meet-you," Acorn Girl said, using the phrases she had rehearsed with her husband, for her knowledge of the English language was as yet quite limited, despite the occasional lessons Pine-nut-eater had given her.

Marshall nodded gravely, spoke polite if solemn greetings, and then turned to talk to Pine-nut-eater, the language flowing so rapidly that Ooti could understand almost none of what was being said.

She observed the *Wawlem* leader with interest, for this was the man her husband had spoken of so often. Marshall had a lean face, one which she could see was not used to smiling very much, and sky-colored eyes which looked directly and steadily at the one to whom he talked. Ooti decided that although he was doubtless as completely honest as Pine-nut-eater claimed, he was probably not a very entertaining person.

"What was he saying to you?" Acorn Girl asked as she and her husband walked away from the mill. "I tried to follow the words, but Marshall spoke too rapidly, and so did you. You are going to have to give me more lessons in this language."

"He was just telling me that he was glad I was back and that I'd managed to bring so many men. They're digging what's called a *tailrace* right now—that's a ditch to bring the water from the river to the mill. Marshall says he can use every man with *shovel, pick, digging-stick, or finger-nails*."

"Oh," Acorn Girl said, not understanding much more than she had. She wondered why they wanted to bring the river to the mill—it was only a few steps away already, but she decided to ask that question later.

"Did he call you some other name, my husband? I thought he kept saying a word like *Jake*."

Pine-nut-eater shrugged.

"*Wawlems* give us *Wawlem* names. I suppose it's easier for them. I don't know what *Jake* means or why he chose that name, but it doesn't matter. Do you like it?"

Acorn Girl thought about the matter.

"It sounds strange," she said. "It is very short and a little harsh. It is something like the sound the ducks make when you startle them from the willows along the river."

She grinned and cried out, "*Jake, Jake, Jake*," imitating the duck call.

Pine-nut-eater laughed, put his arm around her waist, and pulled her to him.

The sun went down, and the sky to the west was fading rapidly from a yellow glow to a dull red. A few faint stars were beginning to appear, and husband and wife walked rapidly through the darkening twilight.

"We'll have to hurry or you won't be able to see your gift," Pine-nut-eater urged. "It is a little way down the river, out of sight of the mill and the bunkhouse."

"What is this thing?" Acorn Girl asked. "Why do we have to go to it? Why didn't you simply bring it to me?"

"You'll see," he said mysteriously, walking more quickly yet.

Around a bend in the stream and behind a slight rise from the site of the sawmill they came to it—a small, square-sided wooden house of the same construction style as other buildings she had seen in this valley, but tiny, not much larger than the *hubo* the two of them had in Tumeli village. It was built of peeled logs, and it had a doorway as tall as a tall man, and two more square openings high up in the walls—whose purpose Ooti could not deduce.

She walked slowly around the outside of the building, looking at it from all sides, not sure what to make of it. At last Pine-nut-eater drew aside a cloth curtain hanging behind the doorway and urged her into the interior darkness.

"Wait," he said, "I'll make a light."

He struck his flint and steel and ignited a twist of paper, applied this to the wick of a candle, setting it back in its holder on a rough-hewn plank table.

Acorn Girl looked about her. In addition to the table, whose function Ooti guessed at, were several stumps placed as chairs, and at one end of the room was a mud-brick fireplace. A raised bed fashioned of saplings and hide straps was against the third wall.

"What is this place?" Acorn Girl asked after a long time. "Is this a lodge for Marshall?"

"Would I call it a gift for you if it were Marshall's?"

"Do you mean we are going to live here?" she asked slowly.

"Yes," he said, smiling. "Do you not like it?"

Because Pine-nut-eater seemed so pleased with what he had done for her, Acorn Girl felt obligated to reply, "Yes. It is wonderful."

But her heart felt like a stone inside her. She did not wish to live here, closer to the *Wawlem* village than to her own people. She felt strange in the square building with its more or less inexplicable furnishings. She thought of Pano's words, about how the world was changing, and she knew without doubt that this was what he had spoken of, this and many, many other things—until all the old, familiar shapes had been transformed. She realized now what she hadn't realized before—that for all her brave words, for all her own breaking with tradition, she wasn't ready for the world to turn upside down.

Not yet, Olelbis, not yet, she prayed silently, but she was sure that He-who-sits-above was not going to give much weight to her request.

The dark vision of before, the one that Hurt Eagle had apparently shared, came upon her again, and she shuddered.

"You don't like it," Pine-nut-eater said, his voice revealing disappointment.

"It's just that I'm not used to it yet," Ooti reassured him. "I have seen so many strange things today my head is spinning. We will move into this fine *hubo* or *k-um* or whatever it is tomorrow. I can see that it is much nicer than a *hubo*."

"Marshall gave me special permission to build this house," Pine-nut-eater said, some of his enthusiasm returning. "He even let me take some of the men to help. He and Sutter both think it will be a good example for the rest of the Nishinam people to see us living in the way of the Whites. They believe that this is the only way our people can survive in this new world, and whether we desire it or not, Ooti, I am afraid they are right."

Acorn Girl suddenly found herself crying. She seemed to have no control over it, and she couldn't stop. Pine-nut-eater took her into his arms and held her for a long time, murmuring soothing words into her hair until the tears ceased to come. Then they left and climbed back up to Kolo-ma village by moonlight.

Acorn Girl did, indeed, adjust to life in the new *Wawlem* house. She found it not so lonely as she had feared, for Kuksu Man and Tule Elk chose to erect their own *hubo* nearby, Hurt Eagle sharing this lodge with them. Most of the others from Tumeli, upon learning where their leaders had elected to live, also moved down to the site near the river, among these Limping Buck and his family and Tied-wing in his solitary small shelter. Life went on much as it had before, and Acorn Girl learned that it didn't really matter much whether a dwelling place was round or square. So long as the *tsakawm tsaa*, the *lawm tsaa*, the *babakam tsaa*, and the *hamsum tsaa*—the white oak, the water oak, the liveoak, and the black oak—continued to bear acorns, the *ootim hai*, the Nishinam people would continue in their old ways of living, even though much was changed because of contact with these Whiteman.

It bothered her, however, that her home was better, warmer, and drier and more spacious than that of her parents, and she offered to trade places. Tule Elk refused the offer, not out of politeness but because she was genuinely unnerved by the notion of living in the square *k-um*.

For her part, Ooti learned to sit upon the tree-stump chairs and eat at the plank table, at least upon those occasions when Marshall came to dinner, which were relatively frequent—since the boss himself shared quarters with his men in the bunkhouse.

She came to like the solemn-faced, decent *Wawlem* as much as her husband did. Marshall spoke to her with the same gravity and seriousness as he did to her husband, and her English improved rapidly through listening to and attempting to participate in the conversations of James Marshall and Jake Pine-nut-eater, although these were usually so exclusively concerned with the business of the sawmill that there was little she could add.

On the occasion of the metal parts for the sawmill coming up from *Nem Seyoo*, the Big River at Sacramento, sawblades and massive gears brought up in great wagons drawn by horses twice the size of Ranger, John Sutter himself came to inspect the mill site, and on that evening both he and Marshall walked to Jake Pine-nut-eater's house for the evening meal. Sutter was much more congenial than his unsmiling mill boss, complimenting Ooti upon both her person and her cooking, and giving her three pocket knives as gifts. He told funny stories about his ventures in this new land that he now considered his own, his New Helvetia. And he spoke as well of the land from whence he had originally come, far across the oceans and, so he said, on the other side of the world, a place called Switzerland, a land of lakes and tall mountains—very much,

Acorn Girl concluded, like the snow-covered *Inyo*, the place from whence all the rivers came.

Acorn Girl found that she liked both the round-faced, pink-cheeked Swiss and his foreman, but still she secretly considered them both quite irrational, Sutter believing that he owned the land, all of it, many days' journey in all directions. It was a harmless enough delusion, the Nishinam believed, since everyone knew that no one could pick up the land and carry it away with him. And Marshall, he was building a huge construction so that he could make flat boards out of trees so that other *Wawlem* Maidus could construct lodges far away instead of using materials closer to their villages. These Whites—they dug little holes in the earth, so they said, to grow vegetables— when Olelbis had provided more acorns than people could eat.

Ooti found it all immensely amusing, but if that was what the *Wawlems* wished to do, and if they wished to give the young men articles that they wanted in exchange for work, then there was no harm in it.

There were things about some of the other Whitemen that Acorn Girl found more disturbing, however. She was aware that whenever she went near where the Whitemen were working their eyes followed her hungrily. She knew that the *Wawlems* had women because Pine-nut-eater had told her so, but they didn't have any here. So she avoided the vicinity of the sawmill as much as possible.

But one day when she had been following along the river, gathering rushes for weaving, she found herself face to face with the Whiteman whose hair was the color of dried grass.

His eyes widened instantly, a small smile coming to his lips, and she saw him glance around quickly to make sure that they were alone. Acorn Girl could hear the sounds of construction from the sawmill, but a thick stand of willows blocked vision. She turned to run, but the *Wawlem* had caught her arm. She screamed once before the yellow-haired man clamped his hand across her mouth. Then she bit hard into the palm and kicked at his groin. He hit her across the face then and began dragging her toward the willows, but she grabbed for a dead limb section and hit him over the head with it.

At that moment a voice shouted something behind them, and both turned to see Marshall standing with his revolver pointed at the man.

"You're fired, Penryn," James Marshall said calmly. "Don't ever let me see you near this place again. You know I don't allow this sort of thing—you think I want an Indian war on my hands?"

The man called Penryn had walked away then, a look of vicious humiliation on his face, and Marshall had escorted Acorn Girl back to her house. She did not speak of the incident to Pine-nut-eater, but from that time onward she never went away from the village without the Allen & Wheelock revolver.

It was in the time when the moon of *Bom-hintsuli*, the narrowed trail, was changing to *Bo-ekman*, the trail breaking open, when Ooti woke gasping from a nightmare. Pine-nut-eater, awakened by her movement, held her tightly and asked what she had seen, but she would not tell him.

The mountains were melting, and the Wawlem Maidus, all of them with hair the color of winter grass and eyes the color of the sky, tramped across the ruins, laughing terribly. As she watched, they trampled underfoot her whole village, and she saw the bodies of Pine-nut-eater and the twins, the bodies of her mother and father, the bodies of many of her people go under the heavy boots, and the Wawlems did not seem to notice, but kept trampling the remains of the mountains, kept laughing.

The dream haunted her through the day, no matter what she did to try to forget it as she worked. In the evening Pine-nut-eater and Marshall came in together, and with them was another Whiteman named Bigler. The three were discussing something in tones of great excitement. Acorn Girl heard the word *gold* repeated over and over.

She turned to Pine-nut-eater for an explanation.

"It is the worthless yellow metal that is in all the streams, the soft metal," he explained in the Nishinam tongue. "It was not until Marshall cried out that he had found *gold* that I made the connection. The Whites are crazy for this metal, I guess. They use it as we use strings of shells or woodpecker scalps, a kind of money. Some of their coins are made of it. They can trade it among themselves for anything. I saw some gold coins once, but I didn't think about the metal in the streams then."

"By God, boys," Marshall laughed, "I don't know for sure if this is really gold, but I'm pretty sure. By heavens, this is something, this is something. We've got a gold mine if we want it."

There was an edge of excitement in the usually sober voice that Acorn Girl had never heard before.

"If it is gold, then you had better be careful," Bigler drawled, "or we'll never get John Sutter's mill built."

"No," Marshall replied. "I promised Cap'n Sutter a mill, and a mill he shall have. If the boys want to go prospecting, they can do that on their own time. I may even do a little hunting myself. But the men will have to work on the mill during the day, just as they agreed to do. Meanwhile, I've got to get some of this stuff down to Sutter so he can take a look at it. He'll know for sure, one way or the other."

"I'm not certain that heaven itself will be able to hold the men," Bigler said, "once it's verified. And if word gets out to Monterey and San Francisco, God knows what will happen."

"Right now," Marshall said, nodding, "you and I are the only ones who believe it *is* gold. I showed the nuggets to the boys, and most of them just laughed at me. . . ."

That night, as Acorn Girl lay in her bed waiting for sleep to come, she wondered about the yellow metal and the strange emotions it had seemed to arouse, even in a man like Marshall. The thought of her dream of the previous night drifted into her mind again, and the two thoughts came to be inextricably tangled—the yellow metal, the *Wawlems* trampling the wreckage of the mountains, the wreckage of her own people. The yellow metal rising like a fierce new sun whose heat would melt even the mysterious *Inyo*.

And she thought of the new machinery that was capable

of cutting up whole trees into slabs and pieces. And she thought of the magic *Ootimtsaa* tree that grew in *Estawm Yan*, the Middle Hills. Could the *Wawlems*, with their axes and saws, cut down the Great Oak that World Maker had long ago planted so as to provide food for the Nishinam people?

She could not make sense of anything, and sleep was a long time coming to her that night.

5

Death at Kolo-ma

February, 1848

Turtle, Peheipe, and World Maker rested with their backs against the great trunk of Ootimtsaa. The sun set, and the moon came up over the high mountains to the east, its light a yellow glow through the mists of nighttime.

Then the god in the flaming robes spoke to his friends.

"I do not know what to do next," he said. "I am very tired tonight. Perhaps it is time for me to leave you now. Perhaps it is even time for me to die. Making a world is harder than you think."

"He does it with magic tricks," Peheipe said, stretching out his legs and putting his hands behind his head.

"Listen to me now," World Maker insisted. "There are things called Good and Evil, and these are opposed to each other. Good is the wisdom of Ootimtsaa. And evil—it is simply ignorance. If ignorance wins, then wisdom will vanish. Ootimtsaa will die, and Turtle and Peheipe will find themselves back on their raft once again, drifting on endless waters."

"It is lonely here," Turtle complained.

"Yes," World Maker agreed. "So I will send the two of you across to the mountains. There you will find all the

Animal People. When you find them, tell them I said to come here, to Estawm Yan. Bring back Kopa the goose, Moloko the condor, Sumi the deer, Ene the grasshopper, Tsamyempi the nuthatch, Kaima the heron, Lali the woodpecker, Weyo the skunk . . ."

"What about Pano the grizzly bear?" Peheipe asked. "What if he doesn't wish to come?"

"You are clever," World Maker said. "You will think of a way. Search all over Kaukati, the Earth. Bring everyone. When all the animals have arrived, they will create the People. I will give the power to you, Peheipe. Use it when the time comes."

"What is my name?" Turtle asked.

"I almost forgot that," World Maker replied. "You will be Yelimi. And as for Peheipe the Clown, he will have to be changed. There. Now you look like a small wolf. You will be Oleli the Coyote, one who plays games and is ever full of tricks and humor, loud and sneaky and cunning. Whatever Peheipe Oleli says, Yelimi, always do the opposite. Now I must leave you."

With that, World Maker's robe flared up about him and became white-hot. And then he was gone.

And when daylight came, Yelimi the Turtle and Peheipe Oleli the Coyote looked out and saw that the waters surrounding Estawm Yan had all disappeared. The floor of the Great Valley was covered with lush green grasses, and birds were everywhere.

For a time it seemed as if both Acorn Girl's premonition of disaster and Bigler's warning about the consequences of the gold find were wrong, for the season of cold moved gradually toward the time of flowers, and nothing very much had changed. The men continued to work on the mill and the diversion canal whose flow would turn the big wooden wheel to power the saws. Some of the men went out on Sundays, the day the *Wawlems* routinely took for a day of no work, and prospected for the yellow metal, but Marshall managed to keep them at their other job during the week.

There was not even very much talk about the discovery,

many of the men being inclined to discount it either as a fluke or even, despite all evidence to the contrary, to view the metal as "fool's gold." Some were of the opinion that the whole thing was a trick arranged by Captain Sutter, with Marshall's help, to draw more people to the area, customers for his crops and cattle, his hides, and flour from the grist mill downstream at Mormon's Bar.

Pine-nut-eater knew better, and he was one of the men who spent his days off quietly collecting gold out of the sands along the river. Acorn Girl accompanied her husband on these prospecting trips, and at times Tied-wing or Marshall himself would come along, the men sharing whatever they took out of the river, digging the larger nuggets from bank and stream bottom with their knives and washing mud in a large, shallow acorn-winnowing basket, a *daw*, to get at the flakes of gold that settled to the bottom.

"I thought it was only the Whitemen who go crazy for the yellow metal," Acorn Girl remarked one day, half-teasing and half-concerned.

"Well," Pine-nut-eater shrugged, "you must remember that I am half White. Besides, this gold works just as well to get anything the *Wawlems* have as the trade vouchers Marshall gives us for working, and I can get the yellow metal easily."

"Then why do you keep on working for Marshall and Sutter?"

He looked at her oddly.

"Jim Marshall is my friend. He has always been honest with me. I promised to do this job for him—the gold is only something extra."

Early in *Sha-Kono*, the moon when flowers first appear, the mill was completed. Ooti had thought that perhaps now Marshall would be happier, but he was not. He was more dour, more apprehensive than before.

"I'm afraid it's only a matter of time, Jake," he said gloomily at dinner one evening. "The Mormons have already stopped work down at the flour mill. Captain Sutter can't find a soul to finish the job, and not a board has gone up since they found their own places to dig gold. We're lucky to have the sawmill finished, but I'm not sure that a log will ever go through it. Now that the men have some free time, they're sure to start working their own placers, and the word will spread."

"Perhaps you should just give in to it, Jim," Pine-nut-eater suggested. "Fill your own pockets with yellow metal and call the project at an end."

"No, by God!" Marshall shouted, smacking the table with the flat of his hand. "James Marshall is not a quitter. I contracted to do a job for the Cap'n, and I shall do it. The men will begin cutting logs when the equipment arrives if I have to put them in chains."

"Then that's what we'll do," Pine-nut-eater agreed. "I don't think there is any great need to worry. Hasn't been much excitement here."

"There will be," Marshall insisted, resting his chin on his fist. "As you probably know, Sutter has secured a twenty-year lease on all this land from the chiefs of your people."

Pine-nut-eater nodded.

"I knew that," he said. "Captain Sutter thought that the chiefs didn't know what they were giving away. He hid all mention of the gold in the midst of talk of trees and grass and building sites for mills."

Marshall glanced up sharply.

"I was there when the document was read to Kuksu Man," Pine-nut-eater explained. "He's my wife's father. It doesn't matter. The Nishinam people have no use for the yellow metal. We've always known about it. It is better if Captain Sutter controls this search for gold than if Whites come rushing in from all directions. I trust Captain Sutter, but there are others of your kind I don't trust."

"Those are blunt words, Jake," Marshall said, looking somewhat offended. "Still, I guess I have to agree. Lot of Whitemen I don't trust either, and one or two Indians. Take that damned fool Bennet. The military government down in Monterey has to put its stamp on our treaty before it means anything, and Bennet told every man and his mule on the way about the gold—and then he handed the damned gold to Colonel Mason, right along with the lease agreement."

"What does this mean?" Pine-nut-eater asked.

"What it means is—I just got word that Governor Mason has dismissed the damned lease—says Indians can't make leases."

Win-uti, the moon when the black oaks tassel, was stormy, day after day of warm rains following one upon another. The snow pack in the mountains melted out more rapidly than usual, and the river rose, leaping out of its banks and becoming a raging torrent. It overflowed the diversion dam that had been built upstream, taking out part of it, and filled the channel with debris and mud. Production at the sawmill came to a standstill only a few days after the first logs milled.

Nothing more could be done until the water began to recede, and so Marshall and Pine-nut-eater, along with Acorn Girl, set out upstream the following day to see what they could find on a small tributary creek, the river itself being far too turbulent to prospect. The day was sunny, with only the puffy remnants of the previous day's rainclouds in the sky, and so Acorn Girl had strapped the twins in the cradles to Ranger's back to take them along on the outing.

By this time a number of strangers had appeared, setting up tents and claim markers at various places along the river and its tributaries. Passing half a dozen such establishments, Marshall commented dolefully at each site that soon there would be no room to breathe and no possibility of further work progressing.

Suddenly he stopped, staring intently at a man who had just emerged from a canvas lean-to, a red-faced man with whitish-yellow hair.

"By heavens, Mrs. Jake," Marshall said to Ooti, "isn't that Penryn, the man who assaulted you?"

Acorn Girl glanced apprehensively at her husband, hesitated a long moment before nodding.

Seeing Pine-nut-eater's eyes harden and his hand go to the knife at his belt, Acorn Girl gripped tightly at his arm.

"Please, my husband, it was nothing. Marshall saw him trying to drag me away from the trail and ran him out of the village. Don't do something foolish," she said rapidly, urgently in her own tongue.

"Penryn!" Marshall called out. "I told you never to show your face around here again. Get out, now, or I'll have some of my men assist you."

"That right, Mister Marshall?" Penryn mocked, drawing his pistol as he spoke and training it directly at Marshall's midsection. "I hear that you and Cap'n Sutter got no more right to be here than me."

He glanced up, saw Acorn Girl still restraining Pine-nut-eater, and grinned.

"See you brought my old girlfriend for me. That her buck, there?"

Pine-nut-eater pulled loose from Ooti's grasp and leaped at the man. Penryn swung the pistol around and fired wildly but then went down, flat on his back, under the unexpected force of Pine-nut-eater's charge.

Ranger danced a couple of steps sideways at the sound of the shot, and Acorn Girl put a hand to his halter to restrain him.

Her husband had the tip of his knife at the other man's throat, and Ooti wondered in horror if he would kill the *Wawlem*. Pine-nut-eater's face was twisted with fury, the face of a man that Acorn Girl did not know at all. But instead of plunging the knife into the Whiteman's neck, Pine-nut-eater merely held the blade pressed against the pulse-point. He spoke, his voice trembling slightly with anger.

"I will add to what Mr. Marshall has said," he hissed. "You have one chance to leave, and that is right now. If you don't, I will assist you into the next world."

"Aw, hell," Penryn answered, his voice pitched unnaturally high, "I was just jokin' you folks a little. I never meant no harm to the squaw or anybody else. . . ."

Pine-nut-eater grunted, eased his weight somewhat, and reached out with his free hand to retrieve the pistol that had fallen from Penryn's hand. Then he stood up, handed the gun to Marshall.

"Afraid you're going to have to find yourself another revolver, Penryn," Pine-nut-eater growled. "You're likely to hurt someone with this one. Jim Marshall can dispose of it as he sees fit."

Marshall returned the weapon to Pine-nut-eater.

"You keep it, Jake. We'll call it reparation for the injury this son-of-a-bitch has done your family."

Pine-nut-eater nodded, thrust the weapon into his own belt.

The trickle of gold hunters continued, but it was still only a trickle, although Marshall reported that the find had by now been written up in both San Francisco newspapers. Marshall and Pine-nut-eater tried to explain to Acorn Girl the function of newspapers, but she had difficulty grasping the concept although she knew that the *Wawlems* had a way of making marks on paper, marks that stood for words, like signs. She did not understand, however, how it was that such marks written in something called *newspapers* could be transmitted simultaneously to hundreds of Whites.

"Suffice it to say that it's true, Mrs. Jake," Marshall shrugged, giving up on the subject. "Perhaps someday your husband will take you to San Francisco, and you'll be able to get a better understanding of how our civilization works. Sutter himself may have a newspaper before long, for that matter."

"Perhaps," Acorn Girl assented, also weary of the in-com-prehensible explanations.

They sat, again, in the little house at evening. Dinner was over, and they had drawn the chairs carved from stumps up closer to the fireplace. For the sake of pleasing her husband, Acorn Girl had learned to tolerate the chairs, but of the others who had come to visit this night, only Kuksu Man, with an instinct for dignity among whatever group he found himself, chose to sit, proudly erect, upon the hard stump. Hurt Eagle, Tule Elk, and Tied-wing squatted near the fire, and from time to time either Pine-nut-eater or Ooti would translate what had been said for these others.

"At any rate," Marshall was explaining now, "the reports in the *Star* and the *Californian* were singularly unenthusiastic. There have been so many rumors of gold in this country that I suppose the editors are reluctant to be made fools of."

"Well, that's a good thing, is it not?" Pine-nut-eater asked.

"I suppose," Marshall agreed. "I'm not sure it matters much anymore. There won't be another board cut at the mill until the damned gold fever has run its course. On the other hand, it's certainly to our advantage to keep the hordes away as long as possible. At least there's the chance of our putting up a substantial nest egg so long as the competition isn't too intense. How much gold do you figure there is, Jake?"

"Much, much of it. I have seen it all my life, we all have. But yes, we must collect what we can—as long as it's like money."

"I fear more for your people than anything else, Jake," Marshall added. "When strangers come in, particularly the drifters, the ones looking for an easy fortune—well, they're likely to be hard men, drinkers and the like. It's impossible to know what will happen."

"What of this newspaperman, Kemble," Pine-nut-eater asked, "the one you say is coming to visit us? He will see with his own eyes what is out there. Perhaps his next report in the newspaper will be more enthusiastic."

"Kemble's pretty much the skeptic, I believe. Still, it wouldn't hurt if he didn't see much gold. We'll go out of our way not to get him excited."

Marshall scratched at his chin whiskers.

When the latter remark was translated into Maidu, Hurt Eagle's eyes began to twinkle.

"Perhaps there is something I can do to help," he said to Pine-nut-eater. "Tell the *Wawlem* leader that."

Young Edward Kemble, only nineteen and editor of the *California Star*, had described his desire to *ruralize among the rustics*, and so, escorted by Captain Sutter, he arrived on muleback. He tried his hand at panning gold at several sites suggested by Marshall, but without the slightest show of color, and his tongue-in-cheek response to the situation grew.

Marshall did not suggest dinner at "Jake's house," but rather had his *chef* prepare a thoroughly rustic cookout of beans and roast venison, the men lingering over the campfire afterward.

"It is the truth that we've got a bonanza here, Mr. Kemble," Marshall was saying to the young San Francisco editor when Acorn Girl and Pine-nut-eater arrived to squat companionably near the fire. "It's certainly a fluke that you didn't get a showing at those spots you tried. I've got a surefire place where we'll go tomorrow, though, and we'll make a believer out of you yet."

None of the Whitemen paid any mind to the Nishinams who began to drift in now, and there were perhaps a dozen of Acorn Girl's people gathered when Hurt Eagle, impressive with feather ornaments and his magic cape, made an appearance. He waited for a pause in the conversation and then stood, drawing himself very erect and spreading his arms in the firelight.

Kemble looked up at the ancient man, a smile playing around his lips, and reached instinctively for his notebook.

"Hear me, *Wawlem* Maidu," Hurt Eagle began. "Beware of the yellow metal . . ."

Pine-nut-eater quickly translated the words into English, and Hurt Eagle paused frequently to allow the translation.

"We've always known about this metal," the old shaman continued. "Our ancestors knew that it was evil, that it made men crazy. It belongs to a very bad spirit who lives in a lake, and he will devour anyone who tries to take his gold. I will sing a song to him, for I am a shaman, and he will listen to me, perhaps."

Hurt Eagle went into a chant now, which Pine-nut-eater explained that he couldn't translate, the chant being in the secret language of the shamans.

Kemble was scribbling furiously in his notebook, the twist of amusement around his mouth obviously becoming harder and harder to control.

Hurt Eagle finished the chant, and then he said, "I will tell you a story now. This happened in my own time. A young man went out looking for gold. I don't know why, because my people think it isn't worth anything. Perhaps this man wished to trade it to the Spanish. He gathered up bags and bags of gold, and he went farther and farther away from home looking for this gold. One night everybody in the village heard a terrible screaming and pleading, and a roaring noise. We were all too scared to go outside that night, but the next morning we found this young man's body. It had been half-eaten, and the only way we knew who it was was by the tattoo marks on the chest, because we never did find his head. The demon probably took that to hang up in his lodge down under the lake."

With that Hurt Eagle wrapped his cape around himself and seemed to disappear into the darkness beyond the firelight.

Kemble was unable to control his amusement any longer, bellowing with laughter and rolling on the ground.

"By Jove!" he gasped, wiping tears from his eyes, "was that your idea, Captain Sutter? The ancient Indian curse?"

The journalist scratched something in large letters across the top of his notebook, Marshall smiling slightly when he read it.

"Ah," the reporter said, "this is rich, gentlemen. I truly thank you. I'll recommend to all my readers that they visit the Great Valley of California—for its climate."

Later, Marshall stepped into Pine-nut-eater's house, where Hurt Eagle and the others were gathered, and shook the old shaman's hand.

"Tell your grandfather that I don't think his curse scared Kemble off, but it all worked even better than that. He's heading out for Frisco in the morning to tell the world what he scratched across his notebook."

"What was that word?" Pine-nut-eater asked.

"My good friend Jake, the word was HUMBUG!"

Marshall thought for a moment and then added, "For my own part, I think Hurt Eagle's tale had more of truth than fiction in it, but it served its purpose nonetheless. My apologies if he was offended by Kemble's response."

When this was translated, Hurt Eagle replied, with an enigmatic smile, "How could I be offended by the response of a child? And tell Marshall that the story is true, every word."

Tem-diyoko, the moon of new fawns, brought a prolonged stretch of warm, sunny days, and the beautiful valley along the river that the Whites called the American was lush with grass, riotous with golden poppies and blue stalks of lupine, the delicate leaves on willow and maple a tender, aching green, and the redbuds an intense crimson-violet.

And a new kind of blossoming, a city of tents that seemed to emerge overnight, the dwellings of hundreds of gold-seekers from the Sacramento and San Joaquin valleys, from San Francisco and Monterey, an influx from all parts of the country called Alta California.

"That cursed Sam Brannan has done it," Marshall grumbled. "He selected places to set up his stores here and in Sutter's town and at the Mormons' mill downstream, and then he stood on the pier in San Francisco and waved a bottle full of nuggets and shouted '*Gold! There's gold on the American River!*' And all the fools who had paid no attention to other reports have flocked to Coloma."

It was true that Brannan's store, operating out of a tent itself, was indeed already doing a brisk business in shovels and pans, salted beef and dried beans, the items selling for exorbitant prices in either United States coin or gold dust.

The mood of the settlement had changed, as well. It was raucous, generally roughly good-natured, but inclining to quick eruptions of violence in disputes over claims or suspicions of robbery. Acorn Girl observed that Penryn was back, this time in company with another pair of *Wawlems*, the three of them staking claims contiguous to one another. And a considerable group of the rowdiest of the newcomers gravitated to these three, and often the sounds of drunken revelry, singing, and loud arguments, coarse laughter and cursing, would drift from their campsites at night.

"I think it would be best if we returned to Tumeli now," Ooti begged her husband one day—when it had become

evident that Marshall no longer had any authority over the
inhabitants of the valley that the Whites had come to call
Coloma after the Nishinam village above.

"We will return to Tumeli when it is time," Pine-nut-
eater had replied, his face going hard and stubborn. "The
yellow-haired *Wawlem* is not going to chase me away from
this place."

"There will be trouble, my husband. I have had visions
that I cannot speak of, and these are wild, dangerous men.
You humiliated the Yellow-hair, and now he has a small
army with him. He will seek us out sooner or later."

"Don't talk of foolishness. If Penryn bothers us, I will
kill him, that is all. Come, get the twins ready, and we'll
go up the river."

Acorn Girl complied, but there was a sensation of heavi-
ness in her chest that wouldn't abate. They were going to
guard Marshall's claim a few miles upstream while the
head man was gone—and to work on their own placer, just
above Marshall's. Marshall himself would be away, confer-
ring with Sutter, for several days. He had stopped by that
morning to make the request of Pine-nut-eater.

They made ready supplies for their stay and set out,
leading Ranger with the twins strapped to his back, as
usual. Pine-nut-eater did allow a concession to Acorn Girl's
fears to the extent of skirting Penryn's campsite by a wide
margin, and they reached the claim upstream without
incident.

On the morning of the second day, however, they were
awakened by the sound of gunshots close by, and they
emerged from Marshall's tent to find themselves surrounded
by Penryn and his two associates.

Penryn was grinning and bleary-eyed, the smell of li-
quor strong on his breath as he spoke.

"Hey, Injun Jake, you ready to finish off that little
contest you started? Now that the odds are a bit more
even?"

He gestured to his companions, both armed with drawn
revolvers.

"You're drunk," Pine-nut-eater said. "Go sober up."

"Injun Jake, these here gentlemen are Ezra Johnson

and Milton Lindley. Mr. Johnson and Mr. Lindley, meet Injun Jake. An', of course, the lovely Mrs. Injun."

Johnson, the tallest of the three men, was the only one who did not grin foolishly. His hair was dark and greasy-looking, and his eyes an odd amber color, the eyelids completely veiled by the fold of flesh above them, giving him the coldly unblinking aspect of a reptile.

The other man was short, his face round, almost cheru-bic, his scalp visible through a thin frizz of sandy-red hair.

Acorn Girl, who was still crouched in the entrance to the tent, quickly ducked back inside and grabbed the Allen & Wheelock revolver from her blankets. But as she came out again, Lindley was standing there, still grinning and blinking down benevolently at her. His pepperbox was aimed directly at her head. With his other hand he reached over and grabbed Ooti's wrist and twisted her arm around behind her until the pain forced her to drop her own weapon.

The other two men now had Pine-nut-eater, one hold-ing either arm. Even though he struggled furiously, he could not break their grip.

Lindley, still holding Acorn Girl's arm behind her, bent and picked up her revolver and put it under his own belt.

"Now, Miss," he said quietly, "what we're going to do is just secure you here with this little bit of rope—you do understand English, don't you, Miss?"

"She understands all right," Penryn called out.

"Good. If you struggle, one of these other gentlemen will quickly put a bullet through your husband's head."

"I not struggle," Acorn Girl replied.

"Fine."

Lindley took a coil of rope that he had fastened at his belt and tied Acorn Girl's wrists together behind her back, talking as he did so.

"Now what we're going to do is just take a cord from these loops at your wrists and fasten them to another loop at your ankles, so you're going to have to lie down on your side, like so. . . ."

He shoved her roughly, and she fell down. Lindley looped the rope about her ankles, drawing them up so that her knees were bent and her heels were nearly at her wrists.

Pine-nut-eater cried out incoherently in fury and nearly pulled loose from Johnson and Penryn. Johnson hit him hard across the temple with a pistol barrel, and Pine-nut-eater sagged, shaking his head back and forth.

Lindley finished his trussing.

Penryn laughed.

"Now tell her what we're goin' to do, Milt. You talk so good."

"Well," Lindley said, taking a deep breath, "what we're going to do now is let you watch while Mr. Penryn and your husband work out their differences."

"Ha!" Penryn cried. "God, I love the way you put things, Miltie, I swear I do."

"And then, I think we'll let your lord and master observe as we all pleasure you."

"That means we're goin' to fuck you, squaw. You savvy?" Penryn added.

"Yes," Milton Lindley said. "And then perhaps we'll give you both the gift of eternal bliss."

"He means we're goin' to blow both your goddamn, thievin' Injun brains to jelly an' then drown your squallin' whelps."

"That's another way of putting it," Lindley said. "Now, Mr. Penryn, I'll just subdue our male savage a little, and then I will take your place."

He brought the heavy barrel of his pepperbox down viciously on the struggling Nishinam's forehead, and Pine-nut-eater's head sagged to one side again, a gash opening up above his right eye.

Lindley replaced Penryn, holding the captive's left arm behind him, and Penryn stepped in front of Pine-nut-eater, slapping his face until the eyes cleared. Then he drew back his fist and threw a heavy blow to the solar plexus, following with a kick to the groin.

Acorn Girl's mind seemed to be working much faster than usual, so that what was happening seemed to take a long time. She tested her bonds and realized they were too well tied for her to slip out of them quickly.

The blond man continued to beat her helpless husband.

She could hear each blow and the painful expulsion of breath that followed. Beyond that, she could also hear the squawking of an angry bluejay and the whisper of wind through the grass near her face. Her senses seemed ten times as acute as normal.

She made these observations at the same time that she was thinking with extreme clarity of what she would do. She always carried her skinning knife in the pocket of her dress, and she knew that it was still there. She could feel it pressing against her thigh.

She watched the men carefully, trying not to let her husband's grunts of pain distract her. She needed all her resources focused on one task now. The *Wawlems* were intent on their game and not paying any attention to her. With her fingers she pulled at the folds of material in her skirt, edging the front with its pocket around to where she could reach it with her bound hands. She had to raise her weight off the skirt to pull it all the way around, and she did this by degrees.

When the pocket was at her fingers, she worked the knife out and began sawing at the rope, feeling the painful prick of the knifepoint against her skin more than once. It did not take long to get the rope cut, but felt like an eternity. With her hands loose, it took only one quick movement hidden by the voluminous material of the skirt. She thought, inconsequentially, that perhaps White women's clothes had an advantage, after all.

Very carefully she gathered herself into position so that she could move quickly, pulling her knees up and rolling slowly toward a crouch.

Johnson noticed her.

"The squaw!" he shouted to Penryn. "She's got loose!"

Penryn started to turn, and Pine-nut-eater, in a last, desperate surge of strength, aimed a powerful kick, catching the White full in the groin. Penryn doubled over, and Acorn Girl was upon him in one leap, pulling his pistol from his belt.

She danced back two steps, leveled the weapon, and fired.

Penryn dropped, blood oozing from a hole in the forehead.

Johnson had released Pine-nut-eater's arm in the attempt to reach Acorn Girl, and now he stood frozen as she aimed the four-shot pepperbox at him. He raised his hands slowly.

The moment Ooti had fired, Pine-nut-eater swung back with his elbow, catching Milton Lindley in the throat. In an instant he had pulled both pistols from the round-faced man's belt.

"Look, folks," Ezra Johnson said, seeing immediately how things stood, "we didn't mean you any personal harm. We was just helping out a friend. I'm sorry old Penryn's gone under, but I can't say I'd have done different if I was in your shoes, no sir. So you let me an' Milton go, and no hard feelings, huh? We'll be out of Coloma before you even get there."

"Absolutely," added Milton Lindley. "And we'll leave you half of our gold dust for your trouble."

He was having a bit of difficulty in speaking.

"Do you see any reason to let these men live, my husband?" Ooti asked, surprised within herself to hear the calmness of her voice as she spoke in English. "I have just killed a man, and I feel nothing about it."

This is not right, she thought. But the part of her that was thinking so objectively about these matters was very distant.

Pine-nut-eater's breathing was labored, but he continued to stand on his feet, struggled for balance.

"My wife asks if there is any reason to let you remain alive," he said to Johnson and Lindley. "I cannot think of a good one, except that we are not killers for pleasure."

As he spoke, he slid Johnson's weapon from its holster and handed the gun to Acorn Girl.

"I will leave this matter for my wife to decide," he finished.

Ooti watched the men silently for some moments. She found that, despite her husband's proclamation, she would not have minded killing the two men at all. Her hatred for them for what they had done to Pine-nut-eater seemed to seep up from the soles of her feet and to fill and change her entire being. For a moment she felt as if she were pure hatred, a pillar of hate standing in the guise of a woman. She found her finger tightening involuntarily upon the trigger, and that was when she drew a deep breath and spoke.

"You do not go back to Coloma. If we find you there, I promise I will kill both of you. If I find that you have been there, I will follow you and kill you, just as I killed your friend. You will not leave half your gold. You will leave everything. I will not even allow you to return to your campsite. Marshall will distribute your goods as he sees fit. You may go now, but be sure that we will trace your footsteps when we follow. I hope that you will go to Coloma, because I would like to kill you both."

"My wife speaks well," Pine-nut-eater said, smiling out of his bruised and bloody face.

When the two men had stumbled out of sight, away from the river, Pine-nut-eater slumped to the ground, his back against a tree. Acorn Girl tried to minister to him, using the hem of her skirt to wipe gently at his face. But her husband waved her away.

"We have no time," he said. "They will go back to Coloma, of course. We have to warn our people."

"Our people?" Ooti asked. "I don't understand."

"We have killed a *Wawlem*. There is no time to explain. The two Whites will go somewhere else first, maybe to Sutter's Fort or to the Mormon camp. They will get weapons and as many other Whites as they can rouse to murder. That is when they will come back."

Ooti said nothing more. The twins were still crying, and she tended to them, giving them a twist of fabric dipped in honey to quiet them. She would nurse them later, but now there was no time. Pine-nut-eater's sense of urgency had communicated itself to her, and she had the babies strapped to Ranger within moments. She insisted that her husband also ride, and she prepared a cushion of folded blankets for him on the saddle.

The rest of their belongings she left in Marshall's tent.

When Acorn Girl and Pine-nut-eater arrived at Coloma, there was no hint of any excitement.

Gold-seekers lined the banks of the river, washing out

their sand and mud in pans and baskets. There was no gathering at Brannan's tent store, nor anywhere else. Penryn's camp was undisturbed, the ashes from the previous night's fire cold. Away from the river, where the vegetation had not been trampled into mud, flowers still bloomed under the warm spring sun. Already the grass was beginning to turn yellow, for it had been several weeks since the last rain.

Acorn Girl was vaguely shocked to notice the beauty of the day, the calm of sunshine spread over the valley and canyonsides, and somewhere the unutterably sweet call of a redwing blackbird. Their morning had been a paroxysm of sudden violence, of hate and brutality, and yet the flowers bloomed, the sun shone, and the world went on in its unfathomable mask of peace.

The council of older men that was called to meet in Pine-nut-eater's house agreed that the best thing to do would be to move away from the village of the Whites as quickly as possible.

"They will probably not be back for several days," Kuksu Man said, "and that will give us time to get far away from here."

"This one," said Hurt Eagle, gesturing to Pine-nut-eater where he lay on his bed, "should not be moved. He has broken ribs, as well as other injuries."

"I am well enough," Pine-nut-eater mumbled through his puffed lips. "Kuksu Man is right."

It was painful for Ooti to look at her husband. His face had swollen more in the hours since the beating, and it was a purplish mass of flesh now. He seemed to drop off into a doze from time to time, and then to wake up and speak alertly. She worried about his condition, but she knew that the others were right, that it was necessary to travel immediately.

It was decided that they would leave after the moon, in its first quarter and growing, had set, for by that time the *Wawlems* should be sleeping and would not notice the departure.

Acorn Girl did not load much upon the horse, but she did fasten on the keg of gunpowder and the lead, and she packed the two extra pistols into the saddlebags. The other two she kept out, one in the holster at her waist, the other for Pine-nut-eater. The rifle she put in its scabbard attached to the saddle. She tied Ranger to the post by the front door and hoped that no inquiring White would notice this hint of impending departure.

She kept close watch upon the settlement of gold-hunters in the hours before sunset, saw no unusual activity and no signs of the two Whites who had accosted them. Penryn's camp remained deserted.

Pine-nut-eater slept most of the afternoon, Hurt Eagle sitting beside him and chanting softly. Acorn Girl prayed that sleep would give her husband the strength he would need for the journey later on.

By the time the half-circle of the moon dropped behind the ridges, the campfires along the river had died down to embers, and there was no sign of movement in the *Wawlem* camps. Very quietly the Nishinam in the nameless village by the river moved out of their *hubos*, with no more sound than the occasional sleepy question of a child, quickly hushed by its mother.

With Kuksu Man supporting him on one side and Ooti on the other, Pine-nut-eater was helped to mount Ranger, where he sat, as before, upon a cushion of blankets and slumped against the horse's neck. Acorn Girl carried one twin upon her back, Tule Elk the other. The daughter stepped around the horse to take the reins.

The night was silent, although crickets sang, and the little tree frogs filled the air with their joyous disharmony. Below that, Ooti sensed a deeper silence, a terrible, hushed expectancy. She felt the little hairs on the back of her neck prickle, and a moment later, when she heard the dreadful, demon's shriek that arose in first one place and then another, until they were surrounded by the terrifying, high-pitched ululation, she was not really surprised.

The shrieking was followed by the sounds of galloping hooves, from downstream, coming along the rise behind the village, and a moment later lights bloomed in one place and another as men on foot set fire to pitchpine torches.

For a long moment she was stunned, unable to move,

thinking idiotically over and over, "Where did they come from? How could I not have seen?"

The first crack of a rifle echoed through the canyon, and Acorn Girl watched in horror as her mother pitched forward. More rifle fire followed, a quick volley, and others fell, Kuksu Man among them as he attempted vainly to shield his already dead wife.

People were screaming, milling about and trying to find shelter from the bullets, but there was none. The *Wawlems* were on all sides of the village.

The light grew, and Acorn Girl saw that a *hubo* was on fire, the dry brush and leaves of the shelter crackling instantly into flames.

"That's the bastard, there on the horse!" someone shouted in English, and Ooti saw that it was Ezra Johnson, his hard eyes glinting in the flickering orange light.

She came out of her paralysis now, drew her revolver, and tried to sight in on Johnson. Pine-nut-eater pulled his rifle from its scabbard, put it to his shoulder, aimed. Johnson's hat flew off. Ranger bolted forward, and Ooti grabbed at the reins. Pine-nut-eater tumbled from the horse's back and stood beside her. Ranger reared, and then ran into the night.

Too many things began to happen at once, and Ooti had the sense of being in a curiously slow-moving nightmare. She saw her father half-rise, the infant in his arms screaming, saw a man hit him in the face with a rifle butt. Acorn Girl cried out, tried to get to her father and her baby, was yanked back by her long hair. She turned, saw a fat face gleaming with sweat, the lips grinning in excitement. She thrust her pistol into the midsection of the man, fired the trigger. With a surprised grunt, her would-be captor sank slowly to a sitting posture.

The man who had clubbed Kuksu Man with the rifle butt now put the muzzle of a pistol to his head and fired. Bear-who-comes-before, still in the Tumeli leader's arms, screamed—and the man put his pistol-barrel into the open mouth, pulled the trigger.

Acorn Girl felt herself about to slip from consciousness, forced the blackness away, drew on a *Wawlem* and fired.

He fell, but she felt no satisfaction, nothing but a dull emptiness.

Pine-nut-eater was surrounded by a group of men, Ezra Johnson and Milton Lindley among them. Pine-nut-eater was being held, and Lindley was ripping open the front of his pants with a hunting knife. Ooti knew with a shudder of new horror what the men intended to do. She pulled the trigger of her revolver, but nothing happened.

"No!" she screamed, "no!"

She leaped upon Lindley's back, forcing him down with her weight, and pulled her own knife, stabbing into muscle. She could not tell whether she had struck anything vital.

A quick explosion of light and pain in her head, and then everything went dark for a time. When she awoke, she saw that Pine-nut-eater was dead, his throat slit and a gaping wound between his legs. She knew what it was that had been stuffed into his open mouth, and she vomited.

Laughter, harsh male laughter.

Johnson was sitting astride her, pinning her arms to the ground. All around, *hubos* were blazing now, and the sound of screaming had subsided to the moans of the dying.

Acorn Girl kicked, struggled, tried to rise—but Johnson only laughed again.

"Real hellcat, ain't you?" he said. "Just hold on here for a few more minutes while we mop up, and we'll put that to good use."

A man, not much more than a boy, stood over her, kicked at the side of her head.

"Remember your old friend Penryn?" Johnson asked. "This here's his brother, you murdering little bitch. Too bad you didn't get to see what he done to your kid. Took 'im by the heels and swung 'im against a goddamn tree until his head cracked open like an egg. . . ."

The blond teenager held up a small, bloody form by one leg, grinned.

Again Acorn Girl struggled to rise, and then the blackness returned.

6

Grizzlies

Summer and Autumn, 1848

Then the world was just the way it should be except that the Maidu People did not yet exist.

But Ootimtsaa grew even greater, and it bore twelve different kinds of acorns, just as World Maker had said it would. And these twelve kinds of acorns reproduced in their own fashion, creating all the different kinds of oaks that grow even to this day on the floor of the Great Valley and among the Coast Mountains and among the hills and canyons that lie beneath the Great Mountains where the snow stays even in summer and on the slopes of the Sacred Mountains of Estawm Yan as well, the Middle Hills.

Yelimi the Turtle and Peheipe Oleli the Coyote Clown set out to find all the Animal People. They called in Hawai and Wawim, the big white birds, Akkan the fishes, Panaak, the red-headed woodpecker, Waima the duck, Sumi the deer, K-aima the goose, Ene the grasshopper, Moloko the great-winged condor, Wakwak the crane, Doritu the heron, Pano the grizzly—yes, and all the snakes and raccoons and beavers and wolverines and antelopes and elk, the bluejays and robins and hawks and eagles, the great and lesser cats. They spoke to Piim Hinim Bak the wild grape leaves, to Aw the rock, to Yati the cloud. They spoke to Tukung Kayaw the fast-moving clouds, and sent Toomwey prayers everywhere over Koyo the land, all along Nem Seyoo and Yalesumnes the large rivers. Even in Hipining Kawyaw the Valley Above their cries were heard.

And all the Animal People came in to Estawm Yan and began to debate about what kind of a creature the Nishinam Maidu should be.

Elk thought the Human People should have wide antlers.

Mountain Lion thought they should have long tails and sharp claws.

Salmon thought they should be able to swim up waterfalls.

Rattlesnake could see no reason for arms and legs.

Condor was certain they should have great wings like his so that they could soar about, looking for food.

Frog thought they should have big lungs so they could roar all night.

For a long time the arguing went on. Finally Yelimi got tired of listening and crawled away to a creek.

Peheipe Oleli chewed at his paws and was bored.

Finally all the other Animal People grew tired of arguing and fell asleep.

That was when Peheipe Oleli made the Nishinam Maidus to look as they do now. And when the Animal People awoke, they were not angry at Peheipe Oleli, for he had not made the Humans to look the way he did.

Peheipe Oleli grinned and said nothing. For he knew that he had given the Human Beings a quick and cunning brain, just like his own.

And when Pano the grizzly praised the Nishinam People for resembling a bear, though not so strong, Peheipe Oleli agreed with him and said he had made the People like the greatest of the Animals, only with no fur and smaller.

Since then the coyote and the grizzly have always been friends.

Pain. She became conscious first of the pain in her body, as if she had no body but pain. She saw nothing, only blackness with erratic swirls and sparks of color. Gradually the pain resolved itself into jogging movements, steady, jarring her so that the swirls of color developed a discernible rhythm—blackness, sharp agony translated into a burst of light. The phenomenon interested her for a short time, and then she drifted into oblivion again.

Pano the grizzly and Oleli the coyote sat together near a big fire. Pano had a huge basket of something, and into it he kept dropping hot stones, so that the mixture inside boiled and bubbled. The odor that drifted from the cooking-basket was delicious, and Oleli sniffed the air, his pink tongue flickering out to lick his lips.

Ooti moved nearer to this pair, even though she was a little afraid, because the stew smelled so good, and she was very hungry.

Pano looked up from his cooking and smiled at her, and then he ladled some of the mixture into a small basket and passed it to her. She took it—and then saw that Coyote was watching her very closely, and she didn't like the glitter in his eyes.

"What is this you have given me, Grandfather Bear?" Acorn Girl asked.

"Eat, Ooti. It is very good," said Oleli, answering in Pano's place. Then he bent his head and scratched at an ear with his hind leg.

"I must know what is in this cup before I take it," Ooti insisted.

Pano moved a forepaw and gestured behind him, and Acorn Girl became aware of a pile of bones, on top of the pile human skulls with wisps of hair attached, blond hair and red and brown. She understood then that these were *Wawlem* bones.

"No," she said then. "I can't drink this. There has been enough death for now."

"As you wish," said Pano. "You will be hungry for a long time, then. By the way, your grandfather, Hurt Eagle, is looking for you. He says it is time for you to go back."

"Yes. I will go back, but it's a long way and very painful. I will stay here with you a little longer. Is there anything else to eat?"

"Nothing," Pano said. "But if you will not drink, then I will show you a little picture."

Milton Lindley and Ezra Johnson and the teenage boy who was Penryn's brother, their faces lit by a big campfire. They sat near the fire and drank something out of tin cups and laughed, telling their companions about their exploits in the Nishinam village.

"No!" Ooti cried out. "Please stop this, Pano. I don't want to hear, I don't want to see. . . ."

"It actually happened," Pano replied, and the vision

returned to the fire where Pano and Oleli sat, their stew-pot next to them.

"No," she said, "it did not happen that way at all. That was a dream, and this is also a dream."

Acorn Girl opened her eyes to a dazzle of light, winced, and closed them again. The jogging movement had stopped, but the pain in her body still raged. She waited a time and opened her eyes again, cautiously. The light was difficult to bear, and she kept her eyes narrowed to slits until things began to come into focus.

She was lying on a pile of blankets on the ground.

Overhead the branches of trees interlocked, and a small stream sang through the ravine that she realized they were in. Near her, sitting cross-legged with his eyes shut as in a trance, sat Hurt Eagle. As she watched, his eyes also came open, and he smiled at her, moved nearer and took her hand. She saw tears in his eyes even though he smiled.

"Granddaughter," he whispered, "welcome back. I asked Pano to find your spirit, but I was afraid you would leave me also. You have been wandering in the other land for a long time."

"I don't remember much," Acorn Girl murmured, her eyes growing heavy once more. "I remember Pano. He and Oleli were at a fire, and they told me that you wished to see me. He gave me something to eat, but I am still hungry. . . ."

She drifted back into sleep, and when she awoke again, it was much later, for the sky was dark and stars shone through the branches overhead.

Hurt Eagle was calling her name, over and over.

This time she attempted to sit up, and Hurt Eagle said, "Yes, that's right, you must try to bring yourself back into the world."

He held out a basket of acorn gruel with bits of dried meat and berries in it.

"Here," he added. "Try to eat, my little Ooti. It's been many days since you have eaten. Soon we must leave this place."

Acorn Girl instinctively drew back from the proffered food, the dream of Pano and Oleli returning to her. But she realized what was in the basket and ate a little. It was good on her tongue, but her stomach had shrunk, and she was quickly full.

She sat up further, and someone large and solid quickly moved to help support her from behind. She turned her head then, recognized Crane.

"Why are you here?" Ooti asked, puzzled. "This is not Kolo-ma village. Where are we?"

She looked around her. A short distance away a small fire burned. Perhaps fifteen people were gathered around eating.

From somewhere Small Ears appeared, knelt beside Acorn Girl, and took her hand. Tied-wing stood behind her.

"You will be well now," whispered her friend. "We were afraid that your heart had gone on with the others."

"The others?" Ooti asked slowly. "I remember something. I think it was a bad dream."

She turned toward Hurt Eagle, her eyes wide and pleading.

The old shaman closed his own eyes, his face knotted hard against something. Tears squeezed out of his clenched eyelids.

"It was a bad dream, a very bad one," he whispered. "Don't try to remember too much just yet."

"Where is Pine-nut-eater?" she asked Small Ears. "Where are my Bears and my mother and father?"

Small Ears stared helplessly at her friend, but Crane spoke.

"They are not with us right now," she said gently. "Hush, and don't worry about it, little one."

Something stirred at the edges of memory, and Ooti tried to catch it, touched at it, withdrew. Darkness swirled around the vague pictures in her mind, and she let it take her again.

Pine-nut-eater was with her, and they were in the meadow, making love. She was unaccountably happy to be with him, as if he had been away for a long time.

Pano the bear lumbered into the clearing, Oleli follow-
ing and carrying a basket in his mouth.

"You keep running away and hiding in the strangest
places," Pano said. "Sooner or later you will have to drink
this."

He took the basket from Oleli and offered it again to
Ooti, the same delicious odor touching her nostrils.

Pine-nut-eater rose, then, and she saw that where his
manhood should have been there was nothing but a bloody
wound.

She awoke screaming as Pine-nut-eater moved back-
ward away from her, smiling sadly, and two bear cubs
scampered at his feet.

The jogging motion had resumed, and she realized that
she was upon Ranger's back, trussed over the saddle face
down. Small sounds of movement surrounded her. They
were going somewhere, then, and she was tied like a dead
person to the horse's back.

Small Ears hurried to her side.

"Are you awake, now?" she asked. "I thought I heard
you cry out."

"I am awake," she said, her voice yet thick with sleep.
"I will walk now, like everyone else."

The motion of the horse ceased, and Hurt Eagle came
back and untied her, but she found that when she tried to
stand, her legs collapsed beneath her. Tied-wing and Small
Ears helped her to climb upon Ranger's back once more,
but she rode sitting upright on the cushion of blankets,
leaning against the horse's rough, warm neck.

It was painful to sit up. The place between her legs
ached unbearably, and she knew there was a reason for
the pain.

She had waked, dimly aware of the fires burning down,
and the Wawlem Ezra Johnson forced her legs open, was
thrusting himself inside her. He smelled of blood and the
rotten-egg odor of gunpowder. She dug her fingernails
into his face and cried out. He hit her, a blow that twisted
her head to one side, and the darkness had come again.

There were more wakings, more men inside her, all of it

confused, intermixed with horrible dreams, the violation going on forever, and she at last sank into darkness again with someone tearing at her insides, someone slimed with blood and sweat, and she had prayed, she remembered, that she would not awaken any more.

"It was not a dream," Acorn Girl said aloud, and then all of the memory returned, the broken bodies of her babies, her mother and father lying dead beneath the guns of the *Wawlems*, Pine-nut-eater, his throat gaping like an obscene mouth.

A cry came up in her from some unfathomable depth, rose and rose and emerged from her mouth so that she heard the deep, strange wailing of anguish and did not know that it was her own voice. She could not stop the cry, it possessed her.

The movement of the horse stopped again, and Hurt Eagle and Crane were beside her, Crane taking her into her big arms and lifting her, sliding her down from the back of the horse, then holding her, rocking her as if she were an infant, and saying over and over, "Hush, now, hush. You have remembered, and the pain is more than you think you can bear. I know, little one, I know."

The cry went on and on. Acorn Girl hardly heard the words Crane spoke, was only dimly aware of her as a large, warm presence, a presence that hardly mattered to the shattering, the burning of images in her mind.

At last the cry exhausted her, and she bent double.

Hurt Eagle gave her something bitter to drink, and the oblivion swam in, and she was vaguely aware that she had been put over Ranger's back once more. And the journey continued.

The small band of survivors made their temporary village in a basin high up in the mountains, near the headwaters of the American River, the Yalesumnes. The site was on a bench of one of the high peaks, a small lake at the center, and evergreen forest surrounding them on all sides, so that they were both hidden from accidental discovery at the same time that they commanded a wide view of the surrounding country.

Above the forest, the bare stone of a peak rose over them like a great guardian spirit. And although it had been springtime in Kolo-ma village, in this high country the nights were very cold, a skim of ice appearing at the edges of the lake each morning, and deep drifts of snow lingering in the shade of the white-barked pines and hemlocks.

Ooti's body gradually healed so that she no longer felt intolerable pain when she moved, but something inside her seemed to have gone away forever. She watched the work of building, the others erecting *hubos* of brush and saplings just as they had always done. She observed the beauty of the high country, country she had never seen before—great vistas of sheer granite and basalt, aromatic evergreens and chinquapin, thin, singing air, the soaring peaks patched with white. But none of it truly touched her.

Small Ears came and talked to her. The girl had also suffered, for her father had died in the raid, but her sorrow was mixed with the joy of her new love, for she and Tied-wing were building their *hubo* together and would now live as man and wife. In fact, they had been away from the village the afternoon of the slaughter, making secret love in a secluded place, and Tied-wing would have spent the night in her father's lodge had the disaster not occurred.

Her friend tried not to inflict her happiness on Acorn Girl, but the radiance of new love did not offend the sorrowing woman. She remembered vividly her own pleasure with her husband and, at some level that was strangely distant from her, she was glad for Small Ears.

But this gladness, also, did not really concern her deeply.

Hurt Eagle told her of how he had found her, after the Whites, sated at last with killing and raping, had gone off to celebrate their victory over the savages, apparently leaving her for dead.

"I found just a tiny flame of life in you," the shaman said, his eyes filling with tears again, "and I was terribly afraid that little flame would go out. But I had to get you out of there, and so I carried you for a time until I came to where the horse was standing. Then I put you on his back, and he carried you."

"Ranger ran away," Acorn Girl said. "He was frightened. . . ."

"I don't know," Hurt Eagle went on. "It was not far to where I found him waiting. I think he was confused and was hoping that somebody would return to life, just like I was. Anyway, I kept trying to bring that little flame of life back, and I kept heading up toward the mountains because I wanted to get someplace where the *Wawlems* would never find us. Then others of our people found us, the ones who didn't get killed."

"What of Crane—and the ones from Kolo-ma village?"

"When they learned what had happened to our village, these Kolo-mas decided that they didn't wish to stay there so close to the *Wawlems*."

"And perhaps Crane had one other reason for coming with us?" Acorn Girl asked.

"I don't know about that, Ooti," Hurt Eagle said. But his glance turned toward where the woman tended a cooking fire, and he could not hide the twinkle in his eye.

Acorn Girl took the old man's hands and held them tightly for a moment.

"Grandfather, I am glad you have found each other at last, you and Crane. And Tied-wing and Small Ears, they have also found a reason to be glad."

She paused, not speaking for a moment.

"And you do not have a reason to be glad," Hurt Eagle finished for her. "You are wondering if you have a reason to be alive."

Ooti did not know how to reply.

"I was so afraid that your little flame would die out," Hurt Eagle said, his voice breaking once more.

Acorn Girl felt the mass of ice that seemed to be her insides shift, as if it were about to melt, and she turned away, frightened at what might break through.

"Granddaughter," Hurt Eagle said now, "you have been through a terrible time. We have all suffered and lost dear ones, but perhaps you have suffered most. There is a reason why you didn't go to Valley Above with your husband and your little ones and your parents."

"I do not know what the reason might be," she replied, keeping her voice even.

"I think you have been troubled with visions. Is that not so?"

"Yes," she answered reluctantly.

After a long silence, in which he kept his eyes fixed upon her so that she had no choice but to speak at last, she told him of the first vision—of Pano offering her the food from the pot, and of the *Wawlem* bones. Hurt Eagle did not reply, so Acorn Girl told him of the second vision, of how Pano had pursued her to the meadow where she made love to her dead husband and how Pano and Oleli offered her the basket again.

"Is that all?" Hurt Eagle asked.

"Yes. No. There were two little bear cubs dancing around my husband's feet when he went away."

"Yes," Hurt Eagle nodded. "Those must have been Bear-who-comes-before and Bear-who-comes-after. They were saying good-bye to you. It is good that they have their father to care for them in the Other World. Now I will tell you something that you already know. It is not good to dwell upon the memories of those who have crossed over. If you grieve all the time, they cannot get any peace, and they might come back here, and that would be very bad."

"I cannot help myself, Grandfather," Acorn Girl said. "I do not even know what happened to their bodies. Perhaps they are still lying there on the earth for the animals. . . ."

Her voice broke, then, and the tears came. She couldn't stop them, and she cried for a long time.

"Now you have wept for your loved ones, and you must put your mourning away until the proper time, the Burning Time," Hurt Eagle counseled. "I will give you something to work on. These visions you have had are important ones. The Spirits are telling you something you have to do, and until you understand them, they will make you sick. This is how it is with people who are beginning to be shamans, and until they understand the message of the Spirits, they are very sick. You are sick in your soul, Ooti."

Acorn Girl stared at Hurt Eagle, trying to make sense of his words.

"Are you saying that I will turn into a shaman?" she asked.

"I am saying that you already are one. You just don't realize it yet. I have always known that your spirit was different, that you were born to do something no one has ever done. Now you must go away to a place where the Spirits can find you and tell you what they want, and I will stay here and fast and pray for you, to help you to be strong."

It was the moon of *Tem-simi*, the time when acorns ripen, but high in the mountains there were no oaks at all. And where Ooti was, there were not even any trees.

She climbed upward through the fields of broken stone, up beyond where even the tiny, earth-clinging plants bloomed pink flowers. The sky overhead was deep blue, much darker than it was at lower elevations, and when she stared into the depths, the color seemed to dissolve into minute black specks.

She had not eaten the past day, and hunger and the elevation made things drift from dream-perception to ordinary perception. Stones about her feet took on a strange, hard-edged clarity, but she felt that she, herself, was becoming more and more tenuous, that she was dissolving into the thin, singing air.

She stopped, looked back down the way she had come.

Far below, in the endless folds of dark green of pine and hemlock and juniper, she saw the small, silver gleam of the lake, a nearly indiscernible film of smoke from the cooking fires. Below her, a red-tailed hawk floated in lazy circles.

She resumed her climb.

Reaching the summit before sunset, Acorn Girl found a ledge where she could spread the blanket she had brought with her. She had no food or water, but although she felt the burning of thirst in her throat, the sensation seemed distant, had not much to do with her. In all directions the high back of the great range spread out, the peaks rising individually from what, at this point of perspective, seemed a vast field of more level ground. She had the sensation that she could step from this peak to the next, could go on forever striding from mountaintop to mountaintop. She had the sensation that she had no body at all.

To the west, the sun still rode well above the high ridges, but Acorn Girl spread her blanket on the rocks and lay down, naked, and closed her eyes. She was, she realized with faint surprise, exhausted from her climb. With the sense of fatigue came an intense awareness of her body, of the heat of the sun burning upon her skin, of her nakedness and the deep sky like a weight above her.

"Eta nik hedem yaman-mantawnaanis," she murmured, "Look at me from above and bless me."

She was not afraid, as she had heard most are who go out to seek the words of Spirits. Perhaps it was because she did not feel Spirits around her, but only a vast emptiness that was strangely soothing.

She had thought that she would sleep, but she remained awake. She felt the heat of the sun go away suddenly, so that her skin was cold, and when she opened her eyes she saw that clouds had come up, very quickly as they do in the high country. She closed her eyes again, but the mountain no longer seemed to be empty. In a moment she heard the rumbling of thunder, and the air was suddenly filled with presences, tiny creatures who beat upon her skin and seemed to be trying to tell her something.

Raindrops. Millions of drops of water, and Acorn Girl perceived them as so many separate beings, each with its own soul, busy little people. She laughed at the thought of so many urgent, hurrying consciousnesses.

"Do not rush so, rain-people," she said to them. "You will only end up in the ocean, no matter what."

The raindrops paid no attention to her, but went about their business with as much fervor as ever, the tempo increasing. She realized that she was getting very cold, but she did not seem able to muster the initiative to move.

"Wake up, Ooti," a voice said suddenly from beside her head, and she turned, opening her eyes.

Peheipe Oleli sat there, grinning at her. He stood out sharply from the grayness of his surroundings, as if he glowed from within.

Ooti sat up and drew her blanket around her shoulders.

"I will show you something," Coyote said.

Suddenly the raindrops came down in a flood, and the water rose and rose, even above the mountain peak they sat on. Acorn Girl felt herself drowning, and then *Yelimi* the Turtle swam up beneath them and lifted them upon his back and carried them to the surface. Acorn Girl could see nothing in any direction except water.

"This is as it was in the beginning," she whispered.

"Things are made new again," Coyote said. "Olelbis keeps changing his dream. I am beginning to get tired of it, quite frankly."

In the distance, Acorn Girl began to see something sticking up out of the water. As they drew closer, she realized that it was the same mountain peak she had started on, and that all around them new peaks were showing. They reached the ledge where they had sat before just as the water was receding, except that now the ledge was no longer empty. Pano sat there with his large cooking basket and his little basket.

He held out the small basket to Ooti as before, but this time he kept staring into her eyes. His eyes seemed to grow large, to swirl like thunderclouds, and this time she found herself unable to resist the odor that drifted from the basket, and she took it from him and devoured the contents.

Suddenly *Peheipe Oleli* began to laugh, his canine mouth stretched wide and the laughter coming as yaps that turned to the roaring of thunder.

"I don't like the way he's behaving," she said to Pano the Grizzly. "Do you know why he's laughing?"

"Yes, I know," said Pano. "Do you know what you have just accepted?"

"It was the flesh and blood of the Wawlems," she said. "I have accepted the task of revenge."

"The flesh and blood of the Nishinam people is in there, too," Oleli trilled, and then he went into further fits of wild laughter.

Pano said something more, then the words were drowned in the thunder of Coyote's laughter, and then it seemed that the lightning blazed into her own flesh, and she felt as if she were transformed into pure light.

"I am dying," she thought. "I am becoming Moki the Insane One, the Crazed One. So must it be. . . ."

When she awoke what seemed to be only a few seconds later, it was morning, the sun a white bead above the saddle of a peak to the east. Acorn Girl shivered with the cold and pulled her blanket around her, for she had apparently lain exposed all night. The cloak was damp, the rabbit fur slick, so she knew that it had indeed rained.

Her dreams troubled her deeply. There was much about them that she didn't understand. Why had Oleli laughed, and why had he said that the flesh and blood of her own people was also in the basket? Why had she seen the vision of the beginning of things?

She was certain she would have no further dreams, for this one, disturbing as it was, had the feeling of being a major vision. It was time, then, to return to the encampment in the basin and discuss this matter with Hurt Eagle.

She was still above timberline but approaching a bench where a few stunted and wind-tortured hemlocks grew when she heard the sounds. At first she thought it was someone crying, but as she drew closer, investigating the noises which seemed to issue from the other side of a rockslide, she recognized the non-human quality of the bleating wails.

She approached cautiously, feeling her scalp tighten. Could it be that she was still dreaming, and that Pano and Oleli had yet more in store for her?

She saw first the large, brown, furry hump of the mother grizzly lying on the rocky slope above timberline, and next noticed the two smaller furry forms crawling about and over the larger one.

She froze.

A mother grizzly with young was the most dangerous animal alive.

As she watched, there was no movement at all from the

adult bear, but the two cubs continued to paw frantically at the inert form, every now and then pausing to point their noses at the sky and bleat out several syllables of protest.

Acorn Girl became convinced that the mother was dead, and she moved closer. The cubs paid no attention to the human, so frenzied were they in their attempts to make the mother bear respond, and Ooti gradually came close enough to smell the odor of burned hair and to see the blaze of singed fur on the mother grizzly's side, the white skin showing through. The animal's mouth was open, the lips drawn back in a snarl of pain, the tongue thickened and dried.

"Struck by lightning? Why would she have come up here?" Acorn Girl wondered, and she suddenly remembered what had come after Oleli's laughter in her dream, remembered the sense of her own body shattered and transformed to light by the thunderbolt.

At her words, the cubs turned to look at her, still not afraid, their baby eyes blurry and moist. Something in their animal pain, their incomprehension, their grief like her own grief, touched Acorn Girl in a way that she hadn't been touched in the long moons since the slaughter of those she loved, and she fell to her knees and wept, her face resting on the rough, odorous fur of the mother bear.

Something cold and wet poked at her cheek, and she lifted her head to see the face of one cub, the eyes watching her hopefully.

She stroked the silky forehead.

"You are hungry, are you not, little one?" she said gently. "I would nurse you myself if I had any milk left."

The other little face nudged at her from the opposite side now, and Acorn Girl rose.

"I will come back, babies," she said to the cubs. "You are too heavy for me to carry both of you, but I will bring Small Ears or Crane with me, and we will take you back to the village and feed you."

The cubs watched curiously as she spoke, one tilting its head to the side as if straining to understand.

She left and walked quickly down toward the village, but a sound of sliding rocks made her look back.

Skidding and tumbling downslope, one after the other, came the two cubs.

Hurt Eagle was waiting for her outside the *hubo* that Ooti shared with the old shaman and Crane. He grinned broadly when he saw the two cubs following her as if he had been expecting them.

Ooti and her new set of bears went inside, and she and Crane fed the cubs some cold stew of venison, letting them lick the meat boiled so long that it was like mush.

"You have had a very strong dream," Hurt Eagle said. "I can see that. You look to me as if you have lightning playing around your hair and your fingertips."

Acorn Girl stared at the old man, startled at what he had said.

The shaman nodded and held out his hands.

"Pano gave me a vision too," he said, smiling slightly. "But tell me yours first."

Acorn Girl recounted what she had seen up on the mountain, finishing with her discovery of the dead mother grizzly and the cubs.

Hurt Eagle listened, stroked both cubs at once, nodded, and did not speak for such a long time that Ooti thought he might have gone to sleep.

"Sometimes," he said at last, "we see things in dreams which we don't fully understand for years. The basket that Pano gave to you was not just the basket of revenge, but also the basket of leadership. My vision helps me to see this. Because all people, both Nishinam and *Wawlem*, are in there, you must not be careless in your revenge-taking. This is a sacred thing, Granddaughter. You have in your hands the lives of many people."

"I do not have the lives of anyone in my hands," Acorn Girl protested. "Someday I will kill the *Wawlems* who killed my family, that is all."

"Don't you know that it is more than what you have just said? We have never had a woman as leader before, but everything has changed now. I will tell our people that, and they will realize I speak the truth."

"I do not wish to be leader," Acorn Girl said. "I never agreed to that."

"You accepted Pano's gift," Hurt Eagle replied. "You didn't ask first what was in it."

Hurt Eagle called the people together for a meeting the next evening, and they gathered around a fire in the center of their little cluster of lodges.

He did not dress in any ceremonial garb, nor did he produce any dramatic effects as he had in the past. Instead, he merely sat in the circle and spoke quietly in the tones of ordinary speech, pausing often and for long periods of time as if considering deeply what to say next.

He told them Ooti had had a powerful dream, although he did not reveal what it contained in great detail. He then recounted his own vision, in which Pano had also appeared and told him that Acorn Girl's twins would come back to her in a different form, and that would be a sign.

The two grizzly cubs tumbled over one another among and through the small assembly, and Hurt Eagle picked up first one, and then the other.

"Bear-who-comes-before," he said as he raised the first, and "Bear-who-comes-after," as the second squirming creature was lifted.

Acorn Girl found tears streaming down her face. She closed her eyes and wiped at them with her hand.

"It is not right for the leader to cry in front of the people," she thought, and the next instant, "I did not say I would be the leader. . . ."

One bear cub leaped across her lap, the oversized paws thumping her on the thigh.

She realized that the gathering had become utterly silent. Hurt Eagle was finished talking, and the others were looking at her to see what she would say.

"I did not ask for this," she said slowly. "Tied-wing, you are a strong young man. I think it must be your task to lead the people."

Tied-wing folded his arms across his chest and then, in a hushed voice, said, "I follow Ooti, daughter to Kuksu Man."

Acorn Girl studied the firelit faces before her.

"Do you all say this?" she asked.

There was a general murmur of assent.

"Hear me, then," she said. "My path is the way of revenge. It has been three moons since the *Wawlems* killed our loved ones, and I have not found peace. Pano and Peheipe Oleli have given me the task of revenge, but it will not be an easy path. I do not wish to kill *Wawlems*, but only those *Wawlems* whose faces are burnt into my memory from a night in the moon of new fawns. And I do not wish to take any on my path who do not wish to go."

Again there was a murmur of assent.

"Hurt Eagle says that Pano has sent back my little ones in the forms of these young grizzlies. Hurt Eagle has never lied to me, and it is true that my little ones were under Pano's protection. We have all heard of the grizzly bear shamans, the ones who kill their enemies and leave the marks of bears upon them, but who turn back into human beings in the daytime. That is the kind of shaman I have become, my people. And the spirit of *Moki* the Crazed One guides me."

She saw fear in the faces of some and smiled fiercely to herself.

"All who choose my path," she continued, "will be Grizzly Bear People. We are the *Pano Maidus*, and the *Wawlems* will be sorry for what they have done. They will not go to Valley Above but to whatever place is suited to them."

"Our new leader has spoken well," Hurt Eagle said. "I am one of the Pano Maidus."

"And I," said Tied-wing.

One by one the others added their voices in agreement.

Before the first snows came to the high country, the small band that called themselves the Pano Maidus moved down to the lower elevations. Acorn Girl had been planning how to pursue their purpose. In Ranger's saddlebags was the little store of gold that Pine-nut-eater had collected, as well as the guns and ammunition. She had taught Tied-wing and the other two young men in the

group, Elk's Tooth and Kingfisher, how to shoot—as well
as Crane and Small Ears and old Hurt Eagle. They would
have to approach the White settlements closely while
remaining obscure. Much information could be gained
from the villages of the Nishinam people near the *Wawlem*
camps, but someone would have to buy weapons. And
Acorn Girl decided that she herself was probably the best
choice, since she could speak English.

She obtained another rifle and an old single-shot pistol
from a dealer at Mormon's Bar, observing carefully ahead
of time so as to feel confident that she wouldn't be
recognized.

From another man she bought a horse and a mule,
thinking that they could move much more quickly from
place to place if they had such animals.

The Pano Maidus travelled from village to village, not
staying long in any one place but gathering such information as was to be had and following their leads. They soon
found that their reputation was beginning to precede them,
and they were regarded with something like awe among
the Maidu peoples, even though they had not done
anything.

In a village to the north they were approached by
Crooked Knee, who had been living there for some time
but who had not really been accepted, since it was known
he had been banished from Tumeli village.

Crooked Knee begged Acorn Girl's forgiveness for his
participation in the raid upon her parents' *k-um*, his voice
shaking as he asked, and very nearly in tears.

In Ooti's mind, the whole incident, for which Water-
strider had been primarily to blame in any case, seemed
to have happened so long ago that it was as something that
had taken place in another lifetime, and she felt nothing
but pity and even an obscure affection for the slight,
limping young man whom she had wounded in the foot.

"It is forgotten, Crooked Knee, my friend," she said.

He asked then if he might join her group, and she
assented. After that, he stuck to her nearly as closely as
did the cubs.

*   *   *

It was purely by accident that they happened upon their first victim.

Tied-wing discovered a camp of half a dozen men along a small tributary of the North Fork of the American River, and Acorn Girl, returning with the warrior, made careful observation. With shock she recognized the heavy, sunken-eyed face of the man who had smashed her father's face with a rifle butt and then had shot him in the head.

The group that called itself the Pano Maidus circled wide around the encampment, as was their habit, but they halted a short distance away at Ooti's command, and she herself then watched the camp activities throughout the afternoon.

At last the man she was seeking moved away upstream and out of sight of his companions.

Acorn Girl approached him alone, and he looked up and grinned.

"Do you remember me, *Wawlem?*" she asked.

"I'd be sure to remember you if I'd met yuh," he said, walking slowly toward her.

She slipped back, into the brush, and he followed.

"Do you still not remember me?" she called out. "I remember you."

"That right?" he asked, pushing a clump of young willow brush out of his way with one arm. "Mebbe we can make some new memories, little honey. Why don't you stay still?"

"I was in the village at Coloma, in the spring," she said, almost singing the words.

"Yeah?" he asked, looking a little uncertain.

"Yes," she said. "You are very handsome. Come here, *Wawlem.*"

He took another step toward her and suddenly found that Crooked Knee was behind him, smiling, and Tied-wing was to one side.

"In the village at Coloma," she said, "you killed my father and my baby, and then you raped me. I wanted you to know why you are going to die."

The next instant she plunged her knife into his heart. A wild, strange joy sang through her as she drew the knife down over his face, his clothing, ripping flesh and fabric as a grizzly bear might.

Remembering Kuksu Man as he fell in the dirt, remembering the body of her child. . . .

It was only later, as she sat by a fire miles upstream and petted the cub in her lap, that it occurred to her to wonder at the joy, and to wonder what she had become.

II

Jake's Wife and Bear-who-cannot-see-well

I heard of gold at Sutter's Mill,
　At Michigan Bluff and Iowa Hill,
But never thought it was rich until
　I started off to prospect.

At Yankee Jim's I bought a purse,
　Inquired for Iowa Hill, of course,
And traveled on—but what was worse,
　Fetched up in Shirt-tail Canyon!

When I got there the mining ground
　Was staked and claimed for miles around,
And not a bed was to be found,
　When I went off to prospect.

7

This Land of Eldorado

December, 1849

The typical miner was young, ambitious, capable of overmastering his fear of the unknown, and planning to return to his home in the East when he had made his pile. However, genuinely rich strikes were awarded by the whim of geological happenstance only to a few, and a majority of the miners worked hard and made little. Some stayed on in California simply because they lacked sufficient funds, for all their labors, to return to their homes.

And the Californians expected statehood, immediately if not sooner. In Congress, meanwhile, the slavery question continued to bar direct action, with some senators calling for the Missouri Compromise to be extended west to the Pacific Ocean, thus dividing California at Monterey.

The men of Eldorado, however, were having nothing to do with slavery—had already settled the matter to their own satisfaction. And their "Legislature of a Thousand Drunks" had convened in the town of San Jose.

The site of a permanent state capital? They'd get around to choosing one eventually. In the interim, Peter Burnett was sworn in as the first civil governor, apparently with the blessings of General and Military Governor Bennett Riley, who, in fact, had himself called for the constitutional convention that met in Monterey on the first of September and had ultimately established the illegal pseudostate government, designing nonetheless an admirable constitution, one that would prove the model for the nation of Argentina, four years later. Juan Bautista Alberdi, the Argentinian Founding Father, would write: "Without universities, without academies or law colleges, the newly

124

*organized people of California have drawn up a constitution
full of foresight, of common sense and of opportunity."*

*But the state legislature, once in session, was described
by a San Francisco journalist as "an infamous, ignorant,
drunken, rowdy, perjured and traitorous body of men."*

*And among the Nishinam Maidu peoples, the myth
emerged that Whitemen, the Wawlem Maidus, had found
the Ootimtsaa tree on Estawm Yan, and had cut it down
for firewood.*

The huge, bespectacled individual astride a plough horse
named Old Blue moved ahead, following the Rio de las
Plumas, just as Bully O'Bragh had instructed. Clad in
mountain buckskins, the man appeared almost a caricature
of himself—though less so in this land of Eldorado, where,
by all civilized methods of accounting, the norm was gro-
tesquely abnormal. Even by California standards, however, the former professor of literary Puritanism at Yale
embodied an essentially one-of-the-kind prototype—a Connecticut Yankee turned Don Quixote, his mind full of all
manner of books, with a penchant for memorizing long
passages and appropriate critical commentary as well. He
was six and a half feet tall, weighed in at approximately
three hundred pounds, brute strong and traditionally frail
of health, and formerly given to allergic reactions to everything from ragweed to the odor of blueberry cobbler.

Benjamin Goffe was a man descended from old Judge
William Goffe, a signatory to the death warrant of the
King of England during the days of Cromwell and the
Grand Revolution. The Judge had fled incognito to Massachusetts Colony, leaving behind his family in the process
but marrying an Indian woman and so producing a new
lineage, one that was inevitably guilt-ridden, much given
to minute analysis of sundry matters of questionable importance, and yet, in some fashion or another, uniquely
American.

At the moment, Ben Goffe was a long way indeed from
his Yale classrooms, his East Haven estate, and his beautiful but faithless wife, Etta, whom he had discovered, so to
speak, *post coitum* with a young Catholic priest. It was

even possible, Ben reflected, that his wife's secularization of the man of the cloth was the real reason Goffe had precipitantly left Connecticut, proceeding by stage, canal boat, lake steamer, and river craft to St. Louis and a wrist-wrestling match with a Missouri River scalawag named Hivernan, and a fateful meeting with old mountain man Bully O'Bragh, the latter half coyote, half legend, and half tobacco smoke and bad nature, veteran of the fur trade and every other grand adventure from Christopher Columbus onward.

Goffe found himself humming the words to a ditty he'd picked up along the overland trail to California—one of many such ballads current among *Argonauts* on their way to the goldfields of the Sierra Nevada Mountains:

> O, what was your name in the state?
> Was it Thompson or Johnson or Bates?
> Did you murder your wife
> And run for your life?
> O, what was you name in the states?

"Perhaps I did at that," Benjamin Goffe mused. "In some fashion or another, maybe that's precisely what I did do. A man's a fool to take on a lovely young wife, an man like me at least. Why did I ever suppose the striking Miss Quarrls would ultimately find it in her heart to be faithful to an overaged bookworm and pedant? *Mea culpa, mea culpa. . . .*

The whole thing, he reflected (hardly for the first time), had been a mistake. For years he'd been a bachelor. As a young college professor, he assumed no woman in her right mind could find him attractive. Later, upon discovering his previous assumption was simply not correct, Goffe indeed enjoyed the company of the Fair Sex, though gradually he came to the conclusion that the favors of Professional Ladies entailed far fewer inevitable complications, and so he'd turned to these "dark Angels" at such times as the lure of his books was at a low ebb.

Then he'd met the urbane and cosmopolitan Miss Quarrls, who at first toyed with him and then decided to possess him, his profession and social position apparently the determining factors.

Goffe had no children—indeed, he'd always considered offspring "hostages to fortune," just as Bacon said long ago. Having clearly perceived the nature of that particular *trap*, what need had a man for a wife?

For a moment he toyed with the image of Etta the Spider, crouched in the middle of her web, one foreleg tapping gently at a silken strand. He grinned, shrugged.

Bully O'Bragh, his guide overland from Missouri, managed to live life quite satisfactorily in nearly all ways, in the process forming more or less temporary laisons with Indian women who bore him children and raised them after O'Bragh moved on, plunging ahead to yet another of his interminable adventures.

Then, across the frozen Humboldt River out in the desert, O'Bragh had seen an old Te-moa woman, alone, gathering firewood. Inexplicable! Bully O'Bragh, ancient fox of the mountains, fell in love—and so their trek westward came to a halt while the mountain man went through his ritual of courtship and Ben huddled about a campfire and waited, somewhat impatiently, for the three days it took Bully to accomplish his purpose.

"O' course this child's *in love*, ye dunghead idjit. Necessary to the male constitution, it is, every so often. Benny, me lad, ye might of gone sour on the ladies, but this coon hasn't. Could be I can understand about those Eastern primped-up phonies, but Injun women is different, sure as buffler chips. Find ye the right Injun gal, ye'll change yore tune quick enough. An' that's gospel, friend."

Benjamin Goffe nodded.

"An amazing man is Farnsworth O'Bragh," he told Old Blue as they rode along the trail beside the swirling waters of Feather River. "One day he's courting an Indian widow, and the next he's *pullin' our bacon out o' the fire* when we get into it with those thieves in Truckee Meadows. Match up that old scoundrel against the Federal Army, and even then the outcome would be in serious doubt. A positive genius for getting out of scrapes, and an instinct for *freedom* in its most meaningful sense. . . ."

Here and there along the Rio de las Plumas, Goffe encountered groups of men ranging from a dozen or more to two or three, all engaged in worrying the rocks with

pick, hammer, shovel, and knife—or panning the sands of
the riverbands, using either metal dishes designed for this
specific purpose or frying pans or woven Indian baskets,
the latter wide and low-lipped.

Those who worked the river, Ben came to realize, were
an oddly assorted lot, ranging from well-bred Easterners
like himself, some of them educated and pitifully out of
place, to down-home Southerners, to military personnel
that had apparently deserted ship or garrison in San Francisco or Monterey to come to the goldfields, to Mexican
Spanish and South Americans, to escaped slaves from
Georgia and Louisiana, to refugees from the former fur
trade, younger versions of Bully O'Bragh. And Indians,
there were many Indians engaged in the gold mining,
nearly half of those along the river, by Goffe's informal
census, being Maidu or Wintun or Yana peoples native to
the California hills.

Most of the men were armed, and more than a few were
belligerent in protecting their claims, the few square feet
of earth that local tradition had established as a miner's
own, so long as he continued to work it.

Several times Ben was ordered to be on his way, at
gunpoint.

One party of four had formed a partnership and con-
jointly worked four contiguous claims. One man was Indian, one was a blond fellow of Scandinavian extraction,
the third was a dark-haired, dark-eyed Mexican, and the
fourth was a woman, a finely featured Negress dressed in
men's clothing and apparently quite as adept as her three
partners in the arts of panning or operating a riffles box.

Merchants running strings of mules brought supplies to
those who labored along the river, and the prices charged,
Ben discovered, were outrageously high.

"Plenty of gold, though," one of the mule-runners told
him. "Think what you want, mister, but if I wasn't doin'
this, I could be takin' gold myself. Think upon it. No
reason these dogs should be gettin' rich if I'm not. Tell
you, I've *seen* nuggets up to fifteen pounds, fifteen pounds,
by God! And one of the Goddamn Peruvians came in to
Marysville with a nugget that weighed out at twenty-two

pounds and some ounces. It was in the newspaper, by God."

"Most of the miners I've seen don't look all that prosperous," Ben said, doubting much of what the mule-runner had told him. "The fact is, those I've seen appear to be the most wretched, abused, and impoverished of men. I don't . . ."

"Believe what you want, Greenhorn. But I'll grant you this much. Don't guess your *average* river-hog is making more than four, five dollars a day. And a day's from sunup until sundown. Rain, snow, ice, mudslides, and dysentery—that's their lot. The river comes up, and sometimes a man's claim is completely washed away. Then he's got to wait for the water to go down, or else he just moves on. But the gold's there, it's just a matter of finding it. Come summer, there'll be new strikes all over the region, the Mother Lode, men call it. Up in them mountains somewhere, that's where it all comes from, by God. When the snows melt back, I'm going to sell these mules and go look for it, maybe. Just thinking about it gets into a man's blood. . . ."

At length the huge, twisting canyon of the Rio de las Plumas ended, as the big green river poured out into the Central Valley near a small village called Oroville, a place whose citizens were engaged either in the beginnings of agricultural pursuits or in mining the broad alluvial bars along the river. John Sutter's North Ranch, the so-called Hoch Farm, was nearby, as Goffe learned, but great portions of Sutter's land had been appropriated by the emigrants of 1849.

The village afforded no genuine accommodations, and so Ben, astride the tireless and ever-patient Old Blue, continued his journey southward, through open, grassy lands inhabited by numerous long-horned Spanish cattle as well as by herds of deer and tule elk. Herons, cranes, egrets, and bitterns were seemingly everywhere, and the land itself, as Ben concluded, resembled the terrestrial paradise as much as any place he could imagine on the planet Earth. Even as the year drew to its close, with the

time of Christ's nativity approaching, the spring season
appeared already to have either begun or to be about to
do so. Fresh, green grass was up everywhere and in places
had already become luxuriant, much to Old Blue's delight.

To the south and west of Oroville, rising from the floor
of the wide, level valley like a dream-vision or a desert
mirage, was a small range of mountains, quite steep and
rugged, composed of two major peaks and several lesser,
the entire formation reaching a height of more than two
thousand feet above the level plain, as Goffe calculated
the matter. On the summits was a trace of snow, very
faint, the result, Ben guessed, of the previous night's
gentle rain, a light snowfall at the higher elevation.

Several times he passed near to Indian villages, cousins
to the Maidu people he had seen in American Valley, but
these still living in something that approximated their
ancient ways, with brush- and hide-covered lodgings placed
over shallow pits in the ground, the villages, Ben approximated, consisting of no more than a hundred or perhaps a
hundred and a half souls.

He was astonished to discover a group of half a dozen
girls and young women actually bathing in a stream, quite
naked and unconcerned that he might be watching them—
like gentle, curious animals, he concluded.

Emboldened, he approached their village, which was no
more than a few hundred yards distant. Naked children
came running out to meet him, but then stayed at a
respectful distance, waving and laughing. Ben drew Old
Blue to a halt and observed the activity within the village
itself, the men preparing the carcasses of two deer for
roasting, a large fire already blazing. Women sat outside
the lodges, some of them weaving, some scraping hides,
some preparing to bake a kind of bread. Their usual costume, Ben observed, seemed to be a short skirt of braided
tules or grass and little else. Of the women he saw, all
were bare-breasted except for one old woman who had a
fur blanket drawn about her shoulders, probably of sewn
rabbitskins, such as the one O'Bragh's new wife had.

"Here we have Milton's Adam and Eve," he thought,
"prelapsarian in consciousness and tending to their garden—
no, not even that. This Eden requires no pruning. It runs

to bountiful riot. The people hunt and gather, their simple needs easily satisfied. And they live apparently unashamed of their bodies—astounding! Even with American villages not far away, they go about life just as they have since the Creator put them here. . . ."

Ben reflected on those Indians he had seen engaged in mining, and wondered why they had become obsessed by the lure of gold—why they were so eager to adapt to the Whiteman's ways.

"This won't last long," he thought. "It can't. If a hundred thousand have made their way to California in this past year alone, how many more will come next year? And the next? And on and on, until this land is as completely populated and civilized as Connecticut and Massachusetts and New York—a land where winter never comes. . . ."

But the clouds were rolling in from across the far western mountains, and before dark a heavy, chilling rain had begun to fall—rain blown on the wind, soaking through Ben's leather coat and reducing him to teeth-chattering misery.

He took shelter beneath some huge oaks, an evergreen variety but clearly oaks from the numbers of acorn hulls that were scattered beneath, wrapped a rope about the bole of one of the smaller trees, and lashed a blanket in place, pegging the ends so as to form a makeshift tent.

With twists of damp yellow grass and some black powder, he managed to get a fire going and used his Green River knife to shave off sections of dead creek willow wood into the flames. It took some while before he had managed to create a truly respectable fire, one that was sufficient to warm him through. And even then the smoke kept drifting back under his blanket-tent until his eyes were watering miserably and his lungs stung. Mist formed on the lenses of his glasses, and finally he removed them, preferring to sit in the small, blurry ring of firelight without benefit of anything being in clear focus.

Still damp and uncomfortable, and not bothering to prepare an evening meal for himself, Benjamin Goffe fell asleep with the words of Hobbes rather than those of Rousseau drifting through his mind.

When he awoke in the morning, after an interminable and utterly miserable night, Ben could not help wondering how those in the Maidu villages had passed the time and its chilling rainstorm. In particular, he wondered how watertight the brush and hide lodges were.

He reached Marysville, grinned at a hand-painted sign advertising the town as *metropolis of the northern mines*, rode through the little frontier city of perhaps three thousand souls, observed rough-hewn wooden buildings punctuated here and there by an edifice with a bricked-up facade, observed that the wide streets were little more than quagmires after the heavy rainfall, and concluded that any extended periods of rainfall or the rapid melting of the snows high in the mountains would inundate the town totally, for it was situated precisely at the confluence of the Rio de las Plumas and another large green river coming in from the east—the Yuba, Ben learned, its name a corruption of the Spanish term for grape, *uva*. Indeed, wild grapevines grew in profusion along nearly every watercourse he had seen, with the wrist-thick vines extending far up into the crowns of cedars and creek alders and oaks, this time of the year appearing to be randomly strung bindings of heavy rope. Goffe could almost imagine one great tree or another to be a Lemuel Gulliver, bound in standing position by sundry Lilliputians.

The image once more in mind, a saying of Swift's emerged also: *The reason why so few marriages are happy is because young ladies spend their time making nets, and not in making cages. . . .*

With that, the image of Etta, beautiful Etta, came to mind, and Ben wondered if, indeed, the proper thing might not be to write her. Now, with the distance of a full continent, of three thousand miles between them, a certain part of his nature was beginning to miss her. Whatever Etta's faults, had he not his own faults to match them twice over? In truth, he had never been the attentive and loving husband that she both needed and desired. And hence she had contrived to lay a net for the most harmless of persons, a young Catholic priest, one who, despite an occasional afternoon of sinful lovemaking, must forever remain beyond her possessing fully. The significance of the net rather than the cage. But if he himself had been warmer in his own nature, more . . . passionate?

Perhaps, he concluded, he would write to her. Perhaps there was indeed still a chance that the two of them might eventually be reconciled.

Ben put Old Blue and the two pack mules into the livery stable and then shambled over to the Yuba Hotel, a flimsily constructed two-story building of wood planking, its upper floor suspended on cedar poles above the recessed main floor. He took a room for the night and, feeling extravagant as he neared the conclusion of his long journey across the West Lands, he arranged both to have roast duck and a bottle of wine, the latter a product of the coastal valleys of California and, in fact, quite bad, brought to his room—and to have a bathing tub and quantities of hot water delivered as well.

It was all an outrageously expensive indulgence, of course, but then the hot water was brought up by two serving girls, both of them relatively attractive, Spanish Indians from their appearance. One of these, whose name was Rosita and who spoke a smattering of English, he persuaded to scrub his back for him, something she did both hesitantly and at the same time looking away from him, over her shoulder.

Afterward he somewhat sadly folded his buckskin outfit and put it away, donning once more such civilized garb as he had brought with him. He had been of a mind to go out, to visit one or two of the local taverns, and perhaps even to secure some professional female company, if that were possible.

Instead, however, he lay back on the inexpressible luxury of a genuine wire-coil-spring bed, complete with mattress and freshly laundered bedding, and, closing his eyes for what he intended to be just a few minutes, fell blissfully asleep and passed a dreamless night.

*   *   *

First light found him up and about, and he made his way to what passed for the local restaurant, where he was obliged to pay six dollars for a breakfast of eggs and bacon and coffee.

The establishment, surprisingly enough, was doing a brisk business, and most of the customers were apparently miners, down from the hills. At a table in one corner of the dining area sat a cluster of businessmen, local merchants or perhaps land speculators or lawyers, Ben assumed.

The miners paid for their meals with the appropriate number of pinches from their dustbags, while the business types employed coin of the realm.

Ben ate quickly, washed the meal down with several cups of coffee, paid, and walked to the livery stable to retrieve his mules and Old Blue. The leather suitcase he had carried with him to the Yuba Hotel once more strapped in place, Goffe paid the stable-keeper and rode on out of town, rousted the ferryman from his slumbers, eliciting a stream of the most colorful profanity—phrasings, Ben grinned, that would have done Bully O'Bragh himself proud—and was rafted across the deep green current of the Yuba River.

He paid a dollar for the service, considered the fact that he was rapidly exhausting his supply of cash money, and directed Old Blue southward toward Sacramento City, where John Sutter, the Swiss who had formerly been sole proprietor of the inland empire of New Helvetia, maintained both a fort and an extensive mercantile.

The sun shone brilliantly, and the sky was cloudless. On numerous occasions Ben was certain he could detect the odor of some kind of wildflowers, but he was never able to find them. Thousands of ducks swarmed through the air, and numerous bands of elk and deer, after allowing him to approach within a hundred yards or less, spun into motion and glided away.

After having to ford a fairly considerable river, something he had not anticipated, Goffe came upon something else he had not anticipated. In a clearing on a rise some short distance from the river, Ben pulled his horse to a sudden halt, felt a chill run through him.

Two monstrous bears, golden-coated grizzlies, had killed a cow and were in the process of gorging themselves upon its flesh, perfectly content to dine together, utterly oblivious to Ben's presence. One of the animals sidled about, gave a warning cough, and then returned to its meal. The other monster, the larger of the two, didn't even bother to look up.

Ben turned Blue and his mules back, made a great detour around the area occupied by the hungry bears, and continued his ride southward.

He had seen several huge bears as he and O'Bragh had made their way upcountry toward South Pass, but after that he had seen none. In camp on Cassia Creek he had asked Bully about the absence of bears, and the old scout had said, "Hibernatin' of course, ye dunghead idjit. What would ye do if ye was a b'ar, an' the temperature was hittin' twenty below every night?"

But in the milder climate of the Big Valley of California, Ben reflected, there was little *need* for a bear or anything else to sleep the winter away, not in a land of green grass and plentiful game and herds of slow-witted Spanish cattle.

A few miles further on Goffe detected smoke rising above the horizon, and he knew he was within reach of Sacramento City, the onetime capital of New Helvetia.

He reached the crude but bustling little town of some six thousand souls by late afternoon, having first to pay another fee to another ferryman who, with a more sizable craft, took him across a river nearly the size of the Sacramento, into which it flowed—the Yalesumnes or American River, within the great loop of which the city of Sacramento had been built.

Ben proceeded through the grids of houses, some of them permanent and almost respectable-looking, others mere platforms of planking upon which canvas tents with wooden walls had been raised.

He dismounted in front of Sam Brannan's Restaurant and Monte House, tethered his animals to the hitching rail, slapped Old Blue across the flanks, and said, "My friend, this Connecticut Yankee has got a *powerful dry*. I think it's time to have a drink or two."

Sutter's Fort
Sacramento City, California
Tenth December, 1849

Dear Etta,
Your wandering husband (for I presume that the
bond of man to wife yet applies to our relationship)
has at length arrived in the near vicinity of the
goldmines, and, having done so, realizes perhaps too
late that he misses most keenly the birdsong of your
laughter and your enchanting presence which, in the
best of times, both filled our home and created in one
whose life had too long been empty a sense of fulfilled
completion.

Now we are a continent and indeed an entire
world apart, for the civilizations of New England and
California, if the latter may properly be called a civilization at all, are as nearly unlike as perhaps any two
places on earth. Many times you and I have discussed
the differences, subtle and yet nonetheless real, between America and Europe. But only now, having
ridden horseback through lands that are vast and
largely empty, being inhabited only by a sparse indig-
enous population of savages, have I come to realize
the vastly greater qualitative differences which exist
within the limits of this ever-growing empire nation
of ours.

But enough of that matter. Suffice it to say that I
have arrived safely after a somewhat arduous journey
and that my thinning scalplock is still in its appointed
place.

I know that in our many and sometimes heated
discussions concerning my desire to travel to the West
I spoke always of wishing to write a book dealing with
the times, places, various characters, etc. But it now
appears that I shall be doing, at least for a time, a
different sort of writing, for I have, through a stroke
of fortune, come into the possession of sufficient printing equipment to enable me to establish a small
newspaper, which I should be able to do, God willing, shortly after the first of the year. In this I feel I

am but making a detour, not a basic shift of purpose or direction—for, in gathering and relaying news within a community of miners, I shall certainly lay away both sufficient recollections as well as actual bits of writing as will form the basis for the volume that I have long proposed to myself.

Etta, I do not know how long I will remain in California, but I do not believe the interval will exceed one year. At the end of that time, I would like to return to our home. And I would wish for you to remain my wife.

I have given this matter much thought and have concluded that it is agreeable to me for you to have such friendships outside of our marriage as you wish, providing only that these liaisons are handled discreetly and are kept out of the purview of the community in which we live. The fifteen years' difference in our ages, perhaps, would seem to require some such arrangement.

What happened before I left, and more significantly the *way* it transpired, was most unfortunate. And, of course, I acted badly and played too typically the role of the cuckolded husband. But I anticipate, a year hence, with my having spent this interval of time in a semicivilized condition, it may be more possible for me to act in a manner befitting a learned and sophisticated man.

Perhaps the influence of some of my Mormon kin has, in its way, rubbed off on me—so that I now view both a modified form of polygamy and a modified form of polyandry as being acceptable to normative values and as falling beneath the umbrella of Grace, to so speak, that our Triune God affords us.

What I am saying, my dearest one, is that I think it possible for us to arbitrate our differences and so to arrive at a set of conditions and circumstances that will be agreeable to both of us.

I wish you could read this letter now and not have to wait for its transmission to you, whether by sea or by the even more uncertain mode of overland courier via the Los Angeles Pueblo and Santa Fe.

However, if our respective futures are fated to the pattern of continued and/or renewed companionship, then that fate will surely guide this missive to you.

Your loving husband,
Benjamin

Grass Valley (formerly Boston Ravine), California
#113 Main Street
Thirtieth December, 1849

Dear Sister Elizabeth and Brother Thomas,

Much has transpired since my last letter, which, if my memory serves me, was penned on the third of last month and posted in the city of Marysville the first week in December. I was, as I wrote, awaiting my guide's pleasure and huddling over a fire along the banks of a frozen river in the desert.

Needless to say, I have now reached Eldorado itself and indeed have been in this soon-to-be state (if local rumors may be trusted) for over a month.

But let me, since I have leisure, approach things in some sort of rational order.

First, my letters of credit have now been transferred from the bank at San Francisco to the interior, with accounts established in Sacramento City, at John Sutter's Fort, and here in Grass Valley, at the newly opened banking facility. And for attending to the main portion of this matter financial, Thomas, I thank you most sincerely. The establishment of my funds here in the area where I have taken up residence required less than a week, via a sealed letter countersigned by Sutter himself and dispatched to San Francisco by means of mounted courier.

This man Sutter, a former captain in the Swiss military as I gather, is a very fine and obliging gentleman, most civilized and most generous. At one time he had, by means of a Spanish land grant whose validity is still to be ruled upon, title to an enormous area, one perhaps the size of the state of Connecticut.

But now that empire has shrunk drastically, owing to the influx of emigrants from the East and for that matter from abroad as well, from England, France, Germany, Holland, from Mexico and from South America, even from the Hawaiian Islands and from the Orient. For such is the eclectic mix of humanity here in the mines of the Mother Lode area. And these men, by and large, have not been respecters of previous land claims, Spanish, American, or otherwise.

Once away from the towns, the only significant properties are judged to be mining claims on river bar or canyonside, and these defended with gun and knife. Great fortunes, Liz and Tom, have been extracted from areas no more than fifteen feet on a side.

But to return to the subject at hand. . . .

I arrived in Sacramento City on the fifth of December and made my way directly to Sutter's post. There I was welcomed as though I were an old friend—by none other than the proprietor himself— and was treated to some excellent meals prepared by Sutter's staff of Spanish Indians.

I have also met Jim Marshall, the man who originally discovered the gold—Marshall being one of Sutter's most trusted subordinates. And I have met Sam Brannan, the corrupt but genial leader of the local Mormon population, a fairly considerable group in all, and most of them engaged in mining and I think having fallen away somewhat from the strict morality espoused by Brigham Young, whose primary settlements are far to the east of here, in the vicinity of Salt Lake.

In any case, this Brannan operates a general store which is in competition with Sutter's own, as well as a restaurant and gambling house and other trading posts near Coloma, the original discovery site, and at Mormon Island, yet another important mining area. Furthermore, Brannan owns newspapers both in San Francisco and in Sacramento City. Whatever his original mission, as assigned by Brigham Young, Brannan is now clearly engaged in the mission of attending to his own fortune by means of diverse business operations and some land speculation, for he seems to believe that the greatest bonanza lies not in the earth but in the hands of those who undertake to supply the miners with food and equipment.

There is a vile canard going the rounds that the aforementioned Mr. Brannan collects a proper tithe from all his local Mormon constituents and that the money so collected goes not to Brigham Young's treasury but remains in Sam Brannan's pockets.

I should not speak ill of Brannan, for it is through his offices and those of John Sutter, who dreamily hopes that the United States Government may one day repay him at least a portion of what he has lost to some proportion or another of the nearly one hundred thousand people who have poured into California during the year past, that I have gained possession of a newspaper, with myself as editor and publisher!

Sutter had given credit to a Virginia gentleman, one who was shot to death during a card game several months ago, and so laid claim to a lever-action press, numerous fonts of type, and all other equipment necessary to a journalistic publication, including a considerable stock of paper and inks. Jim Marshall told me about the equipment, languishing at the time in a shed on one of Sutter's docks on the Sacramento River, and of the great successes reported for news sheets in several of the outlying mining towns. Once I had expressed my interest, Sam Brannan came to my assistance and, for a fee, transported the equipment here to Grass Valley, where I have purchased a plank and lath building designed originally as a tavern. The building's former owner, one Horace Belcher, has removed his operation to the nearby tent city of You Bet, a site more convenient to the majority of thirsty miners.

I have already hung my hand-lettered shingle on the front of the building, *The Del Oro Star*, and I must say my enterprise, though I have not as yet issued a single paper, has stirred up quite a bit of interest. I have one competitor in this apparently permanent city of more than three thousand souls and already a number of reasonably constructed buildings of both stone and brick, but the hunger for news and gossip is such that I may reasonably hope to see *The Del Oro Star* as a great success before very long.

I am still sorting through type and learning how to compose from the cases, lock up the cases, ink the rollers and plate, and so forth. And I can see that the operation will require some capable assistance, though I have not as yet discovered a trustworthy person to employ.

No, Tom and Liz, I have not forgotten that my primary purpose in coming West was that of writing a book of some significance. But running the newspaper should prove as sufficient a means as any.

I have learned, though I do not know how reliable the information is, that our esteemed poet and story writer, Edgar Allan Poe, is dead—presumably through his use of alcohol and drugs, if, indeed, those reports were ever to be believed. In any case, if it is true, then America has certainly lost one of her greatest writers, whatever the various critics so-called may have thought of his work. We three in particular have long admired the man's art and have shared magazines and so forth containing his tales of the darkness and complexity of the human spirit. Poe, more than any other writer with whose work I'm knowledgeable, understood the lingering and progressively disintegrating effects of guilt to the point where emotional collapse or psychic explosion is required of the sufferer. Among contemporaries, certainly, only Hawthorne emerges as a serious rival, with such collections (I believe his only ones) as *Twice-Told Tales* and *Mosses*. For myself, I looked to each of these authors to have his greatest work still ahead of him, and now the period has been placed, as I gather, at the conclusion of Poe's sentence.

My information, actually, came from a most singular man whom I met at Sam Brannan's gambling house—one Jean Baptiste Charbonneau, a man of about my age, one who was actually born during the expedition of Lewis and Clark, son of the French guide and the Indian woman, Sacajawea. As a child, Jean Baptiste was sent to school in St. Louis, sponsored and supported by Clark himself, and later on to Europe, where he studied in various places and so became a cultured gentleman. Ultimately, however, the call of his wild homeland became too great, and by 1834 he was back in the mountains in the company of one Nathaniel Wyeth, an enterprising New England fur trader.

The life of this man, Charbonneau, would in itself be a fit subject of a fine book. Consider it, Liz and Tom—a half-breed born on the first expedition across our continent, born in the savage wilderness, and going on to meet with some of the best and most cultured minds in Europe—and then rejecting his new life and returning to the wilderness which bore him.

At present he is, of all things, running a small inn at a place called Cold Springs (or Murderer's Bar) perhaps sixty miles or so south of Grass Valley. His friends include John Greenwood (whom I have also met), the son of Caleb Greenwood the well-known scout and trapper (whom I have not met), and James Beckwourth, the well-known and perhaps infamous Mulatto trapper, Indian chief, and horse thief (neither have I met Beckwourth). Of the latter, Charbonneau speaks very highly of the man, so perhaps some of the reports that we in the East have devoured in our own newspapers have been, in fact, somewhat distorted.

John Greenwood has told me that both his father and Beckwourth know my erstwhile guide, Farnsworth O'Bragh, though neither he nor Jean Baptiste has ever met the man. I come to realize that the mountain men of twenty-five and thirty years ago must have formed, in one way or another, a fairly close fraternity.

I have learned from Charbonneau, Greenwood, Marshall, Sutter, and others some fairly disturbing things about the Indians of this region—which are the Miwoks to the south, the Maidus in this area, and the Yanas and Wintuns to the north, close by a great mountain called Shasta, reported to be one of the very highest in the United States and its territories.

Many of these California Indians have taken to mining, having put behind them what appears to be a fairly idyllic and peaceful mode of existence, a wood and flint culture I would say. Nearly half of all those engaged in mining at present would seem to be Indians. But as a whole they are treated very badly. Those who have adapted to the Whiteman's ways are hardly dealt with equally when it comes to matters of claim-holding, the ownership of property, or in any other matter. For this reason, many simply work for Whitemen or have fully adopted White dress and White ways, often taking on White partners for protection, though even this mode of procedure often does not work out to the Indian's benefit.

But for those Indians who have retained their traditional way, things are far worse. Liz and Tom, you will not believe this—but the killing of an Indian is not considered murder here. The laws are irregular at best in the mining areas, but there are *no laws against killing Indians*. As a result there have been frequent and senseless bloody massacres. Furthermore, it is considered sport by all too many Whites *to go hunting for Indians*, just as one would go hunting for deer or bears or lions.

What recourse or protection do these innocent peoples have? None, apparently. And the mining process pollutes their streams so that it is no longer possible to fish for salmon and so forth in the old way. The Whites cut down the oaks, in many areas laying whole forests bare—for oakwood is the primary fuel hereabouts. And the Indians, who depend upon acorns for food, turning them, I'm told, into a kind of flour or mush that may be stored for winter use, are obliged to go hungry. Hence, rather than starve, they sometimes resort to killing a cow or two. And the consequence of that is, invariably, an Indian roundup, with the Indians being slain upon capture.

Few seem even to think about fighting back,

according to my reports; and most attempt simply to exist by means of avoiding the Whites insofar as is possible.

I have heard rumors of one small band, a group that styles itself the Grizzly Cult, that occasionally lashes out and has proven, thus far, most adept in finding refuge afterward, retreating, it is believed, high up into the mountains—though how anyone can live among the deep snows of the Sierra Nevada during winter is beyond me. I passed through those snows six weeks since but was not obliged to enter into high passes where, I'm told, there are actually glaciers.

James Marshall was present shortly after one of the first of the massacres of Indians, and he believes that those who managed to escape with their lives are among the Indians who have formed this Grizzly Cult. Marshall himself had a close Indian friend killed at this massacre, shortly after the initial discovery of gold, a man he called Jake. It is Jake's widow, he believes, who has become the leader of the Grizzlies.

Another fascinating story, is it not? A warrior woman leading a band of renegade Indians who, the rumor has it, strike quickly and effectively but never without provocation.

Because of the laxity of law enforcement here in the mines, the citizens have, for their own protection, resorted to a well-organized vigilante movement—one that is generally feared by thieves, murderers, and other *villainsdire* far more than a local sheriff or constable. And the Indians, perhaps out of a similar need, have in effect formed their own vigilante group.

I hope to do some investigation into the Indian problem and perhaps even write up a formal recommendation to the Bureau of Indian Affairs. But I fear nothing will be done in the way of establishing reservations and the like until after California has achieved statehood. Rumor, our basic news source hereabouts, suggests that statehood is likely within six months or a year.

I have rambled on at great length now and so

will close. I will send copies of the first few editions of *The Del Oro Star* when they become available.

You may write to me now at the address given at the head of this letter, as I anticipate remaining here for the duration of my stay in California.

Incidentally, I have written to Etta—about three weeks since. While suffering through one of my weaker moments, I found myself actually suggesting reconciliation upon my return to Connecticut. At present I'm not so certain how I feel about the matter. In any case, however, it is possible that she may be in contact with you. But then, I suppose, she is anyway.

With the uncertainty of the mails, it's possible that this missive may reach you before the other reaches her. Or perhaps neither will ever reach its destination.

From the Land of Eldorado, I am
Your Most Devoted Brother
Ben

The last day of the year, the last day of the decade, the last day of the first half of the century.

Ben Goffe saddled Old Blue and rode out of town, up the steep wagon trail that led to Ophir Hill and ultimately across to Illinois Town, beyond Bear River.

From the small settlement at Ophir, complete with half a dozen ragged Maidu lodges at the far end, Ben directed the big Percheron southward, away from the road. He was of a mind to do a bit of exploring this winter day, clear after a period of intense rains, clear and strangely warm, as though spring were about to burst forth.

To the south the land dropped away, a maze of canyon and ridge lying between Osborn Hill to the west and Screwball Hill to the east—a drainage where no more than the most tentative prospecting had ever gone on, though Red Collins at the General Store & Hardware had told Ben that a nugget of nearly twenty pounds had been found near the source of South Wolf Creek, just down from the head of Woodpecker Canyon. The find had been made in late '48, according to Collins, and after that the entire watercourse had been thoroughly gone over though without success.

"Damn crick's down on bedrock," Collins had said. "Where's no gravel, there's no gold. As simple as that. Mebbe down in the rocks somewhere, but that takes a whole different kind of mining. Shafts, tunnels, blastin'. No point to 'er as long as surface gold's around for the pickin'."

Ben worked his way down into the green folds of the canyon, a dense forest of pine and fir and cedar, liveoaks and blackoaks and maples. He passed through a broad meadow where a pair of Maidu lodges of brush and hide squatted over their holes in the earth, lodges that appeared to be unoccupied. He gave them a wide berth and urged Old Blue ahead, toward the mouth of a thickly wooded ravine into which the streamlet from the meadow flowed.

At length he reached a fair-sized creek that ran between twin rows of alders.

"Bottom of the canyon," he told Blue and he drew the big horse to a halt.

Steam was rising from the boles of maple and liveoak, the filaments of moisture curling upward at the urging of the sun's rays and creating a phantasmagoria of half-forms that were instantly created and then dissolved again by the sunlight.

Ben nudged his mount ahead, working him through the thick undergrowth and beneath cedars and alders from which mats of red-gray vines were suspended, the wild grapes that seemed inevitably to grow wherever water was near.

At length he pulled Old Blue once more to a halt, dismounted, left the horse untethered, and walked a few yards further down the canyon. Then he climbed onto a great, flat-topped boulder that had apparently come crashing down the canyon wall due to earthquake or saturating rains a few years earlier, sat down, dangled his legs, adjusted his glasses, and stared into the clear, fast-moving water that hissed and splashed about the base of the rock.

A stick moved in the water.

No, a trout, a big one, light catching from the smooth scales along its gray-green back. Then the fish nosed into the current where it splashed down across smooth rocks, worked its tail and body, and almost effortlessly mastered the flow and disappeared into the glittering stream above, the current pouring along under a haze of shining mist.

What was your name in the States?

Benjamin Goffe laughed.

"Damned if I know," he told the creek.

8

Marshall's Curse

January, 1850

Land of mountains and forests and canyons and twisting green rivers. Land of the Modocs, Shastas, Yanas, Maidus, Miwoks, Monos, Yokuts, Wintuns, Paiutes, Washos.

Grizzly and black bear, mountain lion, wolverine, fisher and badger, wolf and coyote, raccoon and marmot, squirrel, civet, skunk, pica, chipmunk, bobcat, pine marten, fox, possum, mule deer and blacktail, tule elk and wapiti, bighorn. . . .

Skies where the condor wings, turkey vulture, bald eagle and golden eagle, redtail hawk and Swainson's and Cooper's, raven, Sierra gray owl, horned owl, barn owl, screech owl—whistling swan and trumpeter, blue heron and sandhill crane, egret, geese in long vees overhead marking the turning of seasons, ducks and mudhens, loons, pileated woodpeckers and flickers, ouzels darting along streams and kingfishers perched above, waiting. . . .

Salmon and steelhead and trout and pike and perch and catfish, turtles and salamanders. . . .

Trinity Alps, double-crowned Shasta, Lassen, Sierra Buttes, Tallac and Pyramid and Freel's Peak, Round Top

*and Matterhorn, Conness and Dana and Ritter, Humphries,
the Palisade Peaks, Whitney and Olancha—Evolution Basin, Great Western Divide, glacial basins and valleys,
Yosemite, King's Canyon, Mokelumne, Desolation Valley,
the snow-fed brine of Mono Lake, clear blue depths of
Tahoe, Eagle Lake reaching from pine forests to desert. . . .*

*And along the western slope of the Sierra Nevada a
zone of auriferous gravels, tertiary marine deposition whose
source and age are mere speculations, overcapped by volcanic mudflow and tufa.*

*Call it the Mother Lode—if not this, then what? Where
had the gold come from?*

*Men dreamed of pure ledges of yellow high on the backs
of the mountains, while others pondered immense riches
that lay in the deep seams of quartz mysteriously layering
diorite and andesite—it had to be there somewhere.*

*This was the land, still largely unknown and unnamed.
La Veta Madre. Mother Lode. Soft yellow metal that
drives men crazy. . . .*

Ooti walked in the moon-speckled darkness beneath the
towering forms of ancient sugarpines, the tops of many of
the giants soaring higher into the air than those of the
sequoias in the grove further up on the plateau, *toommin*,
high land where sugarpines grow, an area that lay behind
the rocky out-thrust of canyon headwall that the Whites
referred to as End of the World. She did not hurry, both
because her way was frequently blocked by fallen branches
or even the downed body of one of the great trees, and
because she had no particular destination in mind. Even
though two *Ustu*, two times of mourning had come and
gone since the massacre of her loved ones, she still had
trouble sleeping without Pine-nut-eater beside her, and so
she often walked about at night to avoid lying in the
darkness of her hut and seeing again the pictures that
continued to haunt her mind.

She emerged from beneath the trees at a point where
the canyon dropped away nearly vertically, two thousand
feet above the river that she could see glinting at places in
the light of the full moon, which was near its apex. Acorn

Girl paused here, and after a time sank to a crouch, her knees drawn up to her chest. There was very little wind, but the air was bitter cold, even colder at the edge of the canyon than among the trees. She pulled her robe more tightly about her but still could not entirely control the chattering of her teeth. Frost glittered on the ground, and the leaves of the manzanita bushes burned silver.

Despite the chill, Acorn Girl made no move to return even to the comparative warmth of the trees, but rather sat for a time gazing out over the vast stretch of canyon, upstream the wedged hump of a divide and two shadowed clefts where a side stream, with its own canyon, joined the Middle Fork. Downstream were the long reach and complexity of turnings and ridges, the wall opposite bristling with sugarpine and fir near the top, and further down live-oak growing at times almost parallel to the steep wall, manzanita and chaparral like a dark fur, and in places the bare white of sheer rock faces.

The moonlight was almost a tangible thing, filling the canyon with a strange flood, a faint haze that caused the very air to shimmer. The beauty and the vast, inhuman scale of the place drove thought from Ooti's mind and gave her a sense of peace that she rarely found in other ways. Although in the course of the year and a half that had passed since the massacre she had come to accept the tragedy as final and irrevocable, an emptiness that she carried with her like a weight, she had very few moments when the sadness receded, when she was not conscious of pain.

Other things had changed in the intervening time as well. She had become truly leader of the little band of Nishinam, the Pano Maidus. By now the people instinctively looked to her for guidance rather than merely calling her leader. They had faith in her visions, and she had come to expect them to follow her. She felt the responsibility of her position keenly and at times wished she could simply pursue her purpose without having to consider the lives of so many other people, but she realized that this was part of the burden that Pano had seen fit to entrust her with.

Seven of the *Wawlems* who had taken the lives of her

people at Kolo-ma were now dead, either at her own hands or at those of Tied-wing or old Hurt Eagle himself. But the need for retribution was still there, unsated, and the revenge-taking would have to continue. How many others? Twenty or more, Whitemen whose names neither she nor the other Pano Maidus even knew but whose faces there in the half-light of the burning lodges were deeply imprinted in memory. And among these *Wawlems* were two whom she did know and toward whom Pano's vengeance was particularly directed—Pano's and her own. The Whitemen called Milton Lindley and Ezra Johnson. Not until these two were dead, their bodies mangled as though by Pano himself, would her obligation be fulfilled.

Yes. And one other, the smiling, blond man with the face of a child, the one who had held up the small bloody thing that Acorn Girl did not wish to remember. Penryn's younger brother.

She had almost killed that one, in fact, but a trembling that had taken her at the sight of him sent her shot wild, and he had escaped to come after the Pano Maidus with a posse, a group of perhaps twenty miners, most of them drunk, whom Ooti's band had managed quite easily to elude. It had happened in late summer, and both Hurt Eagle and Tied-wing had thought best for the little tribe to retire for a time to some location unfrequented by the *Wawlems*. And when she asked Hurt Eagle if he knew of such a place, he remembered the *toommin*.

The reputation of the Grizzly Cult had by this time grown to wild proportions, the band being at times credited with as many as two hundred cold-blooded murders of Whites. And even among their own people, these rumors had considerable currency. When the Panos entered one Nishinam village or another, they found themselves treated with a deference that was noticeably tinged with fear. And, of course, it was never possible to stay anywhere for very long—not even among friends. For if a Maidu village were discovered to have harbored the Panos, the people would be put in grave danger.

Among the Whites, a price had been put on all their heads—except that, of course, the Whites had almost no information about the people they were looking for.

And so the Panos had come shortly before the time of the Burning ceremony to this high plateau above the Middle Fork of the American, beyond the headland the miners called End of the World, an area rich in game and watered by numerous springs that gathered into three creeks, the latter eventually plunging over the canyon wall and, through a long series of cascades, reaching the river itself. Here the Panos were far above where any of the hordes of gold-seekers who had come to the Maidu lands had as yet reached in their explorations.

Ooti rose, now, sighing. Even in this beautiful spot, peace did not remain with her long. She unwrapped her cloak briefly from her shoulders, shook it out to remove the dirt and pine needles. Moonlight spread a faint blue sheen on the curve of breasts and shoulders, the long hair trailing like a shadow along one arm.

The sight of her own body triggered a curiously objective thought:

"This is flesh that is made to give a man pleasure, and to take pleasure from a man. It is sad. . . ."

The thought was followed immediately by a wave of longing for Pine-nut-eater, a keen, physical sense of loss and emptiness, and she had to gather herself, tighten her muscles and close her eyes briefly to keep from weeping.

At that moment she heard a stirring among the trees behind her, a distinctly human sound and one that could only be produced by an extraordinarily clumsy person or one who wished to signal his presence to another. Acorn Girl turned, and in a moment a figure emerged into the moonlight, the stocky, confident figure of Crane.

"Have you been there all along, then, Grandmother Crane?" Ooti asked, smiling a little.

"I am up often at night, too, Acorn Woman," Crane explained, not really answering. "My bones are getting old despite all this healthy flesh, and sometimes they ache so at night that I can't do anything but get up and walk around a little. I saw you sitting there, and I thought, 'Maybe she's waiting for a vision, so I won't disturb her, but maybe she would like to talk, too,' so I sat down for a while to see what you would do."

Acorn Girl, of course, knew that the woman wouldn't have seen her without following her from the camp.

"I am glad to have someone to talk to, Crane," Ooti replied. "I thought everyone except me and Hurt Eagle was afraid to come out at night. Don't you worry about the Spirits that wander around in the dark?"

Crane nodded.

"I used those stories to scare my children with so many times when they were little that the Spirits lost their power over me. They became my allies, I guess, since they helped make my small ones behave."

Acorn Girl laughed at the originality of Crane's explanation. She did not laugh often, but Crane, like the two bear cubs who had now grown into great, shambling, inquisitive beasts that still thought of her as their mother, seldom failed to bring a flicker of warm amusement to the Pano leader's usually solemn expression.

"I think you should tell me the truth, Grandmother Crane," Acorn Girl said. "I think you followed me here because you had something you wanted to talk about. Why don't you tell me what it is?"

"No, no," the older woman said, her eyes round with extreme innocence. "It was nothing special. It just gets lonesome, being awake when everyone else is asleep. Of course, I have Hurt Eagle, but once he falls asleep, that one is like a dead person all night long, except that he snores like a Thunder Being, and so I know he's still alive."

Acorn Girl smiled.

"Sometimes I can hear him from my own *hubo*, even with the bears snuffling and groaning as they do."

"I know it," said Crane solemnly. "One time Small Ears said she and Tied-wing woke up in their lodge at the far side of the camp because they thought we were having an earthquake. But still, it is a good thing to have a man to snuggle up to on cold nights."

Ooti didn't respond to this obvious opening, but rather sat down again and gazed off across the moonlight-filled canyon. Crane hunched down beside her, and after a moment's silence, went on exactly as Acorn Girl had been expecting.

"You must get terribly lonely, Ooti. I think that is why you are always up wandering around in the night.' "

"Yes, I get lonely . . . ," the young leader said, her eyes still fixed on the canyon wall opposite to them.

"There! That is a terrible thing, especially for a woman who has seen as few winters as you have."

"Crane, you must stop matchmaking for me. I have told you before that I do not wish to marry again."

"I saw you standing there in the moonlight when you took off your cloak," Crane went on as if Ooti hadn't spoken at all. "I said to myself, 'How sad for a beautiful young woman, with a body made to give and take pleasure, that she should lie alone every night.' "

Acorn Girl glanced up, startled that Crane should have said almost exactly the thought that had come to her at the moment of which Crane spoke.

"I know how much you loved your husband," the older woman continued, "but it is time to put sadness behind you. There have been two Burning times since he went to Valley Above, and there is a fine young man who wants you, and you know he will make you a good husband."

"You are speaking of Tied-wing, but he is the husband of my best friend."

"Small Ears loves you also. She has spoken to me about this thing. She would be glad if you would share their *hubo*," Crane insisted. "Perhaps you have not noticed the little signs he has made, how he is always bringing you presents of game, how he so often is there to help you carry wood or water. . . ."

"Has Tied-wing asked you to speak to me?" Acorn Girl interrupted.

Crane did not reply, but she looked away from the younger woman, so Ooti went on.

"I have noticed these signs, Crane. I have not done anything about them because I did not wish to shame him. I love Tied-wing. I have known him since we were tiny children, and he has always been my friend. If he has asked you to speak for him, you must tell him how proud I am that he has wished me to be his wife, and that Pine-nut-eater would also be proud. But I will never marry again, not only because I love my first husband, but because I have been given this burden of leadership. Tied-wing would not truly like being married to a leader."

"He would not mind. I asked him that very thing."

Acorn Girl smiled slightly, but she tactfully ignored the inadvertent confession that Crane had made.

"I could not put that burden upon Tied-wing. Nor do I think Small Ears really wishes to share her husband. I never would have wished such a thing. . . ."

Crane made a low, coughing sound.

"Perhaps you know what is best for you, Ooti. Still, it is a sad thing. Perhaps Kingfisher then? Or Elk's Tooth?"

Acorn Girl laughed.

"Come, Grandmother Crane. I am as stubborn as you are. Let's speak of something different. I am thinking that soon it will be time for our people to move down lower. We have been lucky so far, but it is already the moon of *Bom-hintsuli*, the narrowed trail, and the big snows cannot hold off much longer."

Acorn Girl's prediction proved to be quite accurate, for the following day, by midmorning, the brilliant blue of the winter sky had been obscured by dull clouds which grew increasingly darker as the day progressed. By afternoon the sky to the east had become ominously black, and lightning began to dance along the hills. The sudden downpour of rain quickly turned to sleet, and by evening the gray stillness that followed the thunderstorms began to spit small, wet flakes of snow.

Everyone instinctively felt that this might be the beginning of a snowstorm that would blanket everything in heavy drifts and stay on the ground for months, growing deeper with each successive snowfall until movement would become impossible before spring, and so the little band made its preparations to leave *toommin* that night before they went to sleep.

In the morning they awoke to snow perhaps a foot deep, and the big, soft flakes still falling with no sign of letting up. Acorn Girl thought it best that they depart for lower altitudes immediately, before the going down through treacherous canyon country became impossible, and Hurt

Eagle, although personally loath to set out into such bad
weather, agreed.

The camp was on the move within a remarkably short
time, their few possessions loaded upon the string of horses
and mules they had managed to acquire, along with a fair
supply of firearms and ammunition—items garnered through
trade or theft. The Pano Maidus traveled light, and, with
the aid of their livestock, much more quickly than any
other Indian group.

But the people moved on foot, leading the laden animals, with the exception of Hurt Eagle, who rode on
Ranger because Acorn Girl insisted that he must. Ooti had
attempted to teach the people to ride, but most were still
distrustful of the notion, and only the young men would
consent to get on horseback except in the most dire of
emergencies, when the demand for speed outweighed the
desire for security.

They traveled northward across drainages for which Ooti's
band had no names, although the Whites had already
come to call them Screwauger and Secret Canyon and
Eldorado Canyon, and thence down Humbug Canyon to
the North Fork of the American, moving out of and then
back into snow zones as they traversed the series of canyons and ridges, and then passing out of it permanently as
they dropped down Humbug. The Panos emerged at a
widening of the North Fork Canyon, a place called Green
Valley by the Whites, a site Hurt Eagle remembered from
years earlier. Here oak and pine forest grew on the
canyonsides, and in the bottom there was grass, verdant
from the winter rains, to support the ponies.

Acorn Girl grew increasingly uneasy as they traveled
down to these lower elevations along the river drainages,
for although her people could not stay up high with the
winter snows settling in, yet she was not entirely confident that these gentler areas had not been occupied by
the *Wawlem* gold-seekers. Accordingly, as their path led
down to the valley, she left the band and the animals
secreted in a ravine where a creek poured toward the
main stream and went ahead on foot, taking Tied-wing,
Elk's Tooth, and Kingfisher with her, to reconnoiter the
area. Crooked Knee insisted on following as well, and

when she saw that no amount of argument would persuade him to stay behind with the others, she consented to his company.

The scouting party moved forward, staying to the cover of the trees and those areas of high ground where they could get the widest view of the little valley without being seen by any who might inhabit it. As they made their cautious way over a great pile of boulders tumbled from the canyonside some previous winter and creating an obstruction all the way to the water's edge, they heard loud voices from somewhere ahead.

Acorn Girl and Tied-wing exchanged glances, and then she signaled the others, who were farther behind, to remain where they were while she crept cautiously among the rocks, screening herself as best she could among the willow-brush, bare of leaves this time of year, until she had reached a point where she could see the source of the human sounds.

She lay flat among the brush, her head barely visible over the rocks, and watched. A man was sitting upon a horse beneath overhanging branches of a huge *babakam tsaa*, liveoak. Other men, three on horseback, several standing about, their mounts not far away. The voices were raised, and the *Wawlems* seemed to be arguing heatedly, but Acorn Girl could not make out the words above the roaring of the stream.

Something odd about the posture of the man upon the horse. . . .

Her first instinct was to go back to where her four scouts waited and then to return to her people and lead them away from this place as quickly as possible, but something made her irresistibly curious to understand the situation of those gathered under the liveoak, and so Ooti slithered back among the rocks until she was out of sight. When she reached her four friends, she related what she had seen.

"Perhaps you should return—warn the others that we must get out of here," she said. "I'll come along as soon as I've found out what they're up to. Don't argue. It would be foolish for all of us to risk being seen."

"I will not leave you," Crooked Knee whispered fervently. "The only way you will get me to stay behind is if you cut my throat right now."

Tied-wing scowled in faint annoyance at the young man who had followed Ooti about like a tame raccoon since she had accepted him back into the tribe.

"I won't go either," he said in a tone which would not be denied.

Acorn Girl shrugged.

"Someone must warn the others," she insisted. "Elk's Tooth?"

But Elk's Tooth glanced at Kingfisher, his best friend. He broke a twig into two uneven parts and held the fragments out in one hand, his closed fist concealing all but the ends.

"Our leader wishes one of us to go," he said. "Short stick goes back."

Kingfisher drew the longer twig, and Elk's Tooth started back without another word.

Acorn Girl and her three remaining male companions then worked their way to the upper end of the slide, for in this way it would be possible to approach closer to the gathering of Whitemen, down from the canyonside, where a dense growth of brush and many tumbled rocks provided a means of concealment.

When they had crept close enough to see the men's features, Acorn Girl felt a little start of surprise. The man on the horse, stoop-shouldered beneath the liveoak, was James Marshall, Pine-nut-eater's friend.

One of the other *Wawlems* had by this time climbed into the tree and was crouched on the branch above Marshall, reaching down with one arm to receive the end of a rope which another man was throwing up to him. Acorn Girl saw with a shock that the rope was looped about Marshall's throat, and the oddity of his posture upon the horse was due to the fact that his hands were tied behind him.

"I have heard of something like this," whispered Tied-wing. "They call it *lynching*. They will tie the other end of the rope, and then they will drive the horse out from beneath the man, and he will hang there with the rope around his neck until he is dead."

"No!" Ooti gasped. "We must find a way to stop them."

"Let the *Wawlems* kill each other if they wish," Kingfisher suggested.

"Don't you recognize the man on the horse?" Acorn
Girl demanded. "That one is James Marshall. He was our
friend. He was always kind to all of us."

"You wish to save his life?" Crooked Knee asked, puzzled.

"That is what I am going to do," Acorn Girl said, shushing the others as she watched and listened intently to the
little drama being played out in the meadow below.

"I say we go ahead and hang the son-of-a-bitch," the
one holding the rope was saying. "He ain't never gonna
take us to his real rich places, and that's sure as hawg
dung."

Another man strolled into sight from behind the trunk
of the liveoak, and Ooti recognized the short, stocky form
and the round, babyish face of Milton Lindley.

"Gentlemen, gentlemen," Lindley called out in his mel-
low voice, "a dead man will certainly not lead us to riches.
There are other methods one can use to encourage James
Marshall's appropriate loquacity."

"What Milt's sayin'," the man in the tree called out, "is
maybe we'll try somethin' like cuttin' you up a bit at a
time."

"Correct, correct," Lindley grinned. "We could start
with your toes and fingers, perhaps, and work from there
if you're still not disposed toward generosity. Or perhaps
we might hoist you over the branch, oh very gently, and
allow you to dangle for a time until your eyeballs burst—
then see what you might tell us."

"Boys," Marshall cried out, his voice strained with des-
peration, "I've told you a hundred times since yesterday
that I ain't got no more idea than the rest of you as to
where there's lead. You damned fools, don't you think I'd
of been there digging the gold if I knew where it was?"

Acorn Girl scanned the faces of the others, looking for
the blond teenager, young Penryn, but he was not one of
the group of half a dozen gathered around the unfortunate
Marshall. Upon recognizing Lindley, she had felt her pulse
quicken—could sense that the major portion of her revenge-
taking might be swiftly accomplished. And the big man,

Johnson, he was not present either. But Lindley, at least, was present—and the fierce need to take his life was added to the desire to assist her old friend Jim Marshall.

Pano does not provide everything at once. . . .

"You see the round-faced one," she hissed to Tied-wing, "the short man with red hair? He must die first."

"He was at the massacre?" Tied-wing asked, but he really didn't need a reply. "Very well, Ooti, but if we shoot now, the horse will bolt, and Marshall will strangle to death before we can cut him down."

The four Nishinams conferred briefly on the dilemma, and Acorn Girl hit upon a plan that she believed might have some possibility of working. In a pouch that she carried with her at all times she kept whatever supply of gold she had managed to accumulate, at first that acquired when Pine-nut-eater had been her husband, and after that when she could spare the time she had also searched on her own, for the worthless yellow metal provided the easiest means of acquiring such things as horses and guns from the *Wawlems*. In this pouch was a good-sized nugget she had discovered at the foot of a gravel bank up on the *toommin*, next to a stream. The chunk of gold was the size of a newborn infant's fist, and this lump she gave to Crooked Knee, along with hurried instructions and a few words in English.

As the others drew and aimed their weapons from their place of concealment, Crooked Knee ran out wildly into the sight of the Whitemen, waving the large nugget and shouting, "Gold! Much gold! I show you!"

Milton Lindley and the others turned, saw the unarmed Indian, glanced at one another.

As instructed, Crooked Knee stayed well out of pistol range, and the three men who were still mounted spurred their ponies toward him.

"It's a trap, you blind fools!" Lindley shouted, but the mounted men did not heed him, and the end of the lynch rope, which one of these had been holding, dangled free.

Acorn Girl sighted down on the rider in the lead, squeezed, saw the man fall backward out of the saddle. Simultaneously, Tied-wing fired at another rider, missed. The horses reared and tried to turn back, lunging in confusion. And Marshall's horse also lunged, throwing its bound rider to one side.

Acorn Girl and Tied-wing and Kingfisher now used their revolvers to fire off several shots at the retreating riders, leaping out of cover as they did so and charging toward the *Wawlems*. But the range was too great for accuracy, and none of the shots did any damage.

Milt Lindley had grabbed the reins of his pony and had leaped into the saddle, his fellows struggling to do likewise. Then, in the wake of more wild pistol fire, all the Whites were mounted and urging their horses off down-canyon.

Only two remained. One lay dead, and the other, Jim Marshall, stumbling to his feet, falling, sought vainly for some kind of protection.

Acorn Girl gazed after the rapidly vanishing Whites, her eyes blurred with tears of rage and frustration.

Pano takes too long. I have missed the chance to kill the round-faced man. . . .

She turned back to where her friends, having caught the fleeing Marshall, were now unbinding him.

Acorn Girl stared down at the dead Whiteman, could not remember the face, and shrugged. Then she approached Marshall, who was now attempting to struggle free from the embraces of Kingfisher and Crooked Knee.

Marshall stood suddenly still and stared at her face.

"Mrs. Jake?" he asked. "By God, it is you, isn't it? I knew you must have gotten away back there at Coloma. . . ."

"Let go of him," she said. "Yes, it is me, Jim Marshall. I am Ooti, Pine-nut-eater's wife."

Marshall took a deep breath, exhaled slowly, and tested the movement of his left arm.

"Nothing busted, I guess," he said. "You figuring to kill me too, Mrs. Jake? I didn't have nothing to do with what happened to your village—I want you to know that. You and Jake were my friends. . . ."

"I know that, Jim Marshall," Acorn Girl replied. "You are safe now, but we must all move away quickly. In a little while your friends will realize what has happened, and then they will come looking for us."

"Thomas out there," Marshall asked, pointing, "he's dead?"

"His spirit wanders now," Kingfisher said, speaking in English.

James Marshall shook his head.

"Wasn't a bad man, Mrs. Jake. Just spent too much time with that slick-talking Lindley. Milton, he was one of the ones at Coloma."

"I know that," Acorn Girl answered. "We have killed the wrong man today."

"By heavens, Mrs. Jake, that was the finest meal I've had in days, and I want to thank you for it," Marshall sighed, leaning back away from the fire and filling his pipe, offering the tobacco pouch around to the men in the group before replacing it inside his heavy winter coat.

"You never catch any rabbits for dinner?" Acorn Girl asked, surprised.

"Fresh game of any kind along the rivers this year is a far sight scarcer than prospectors. Besides, I haven't been a free man the last couple of days, and Milton and his boys weren't much interested in feeding me."

It was dark now, and the firelight glinted off eyes and teeth, painted the Maidu faces a deep copper-color, and cast strange, flickering shadows back into the grove of Douglas firs the group was camped within. A fine drizzle of rain fell around them, and although they had erected the best lean-to shelters they were capable of making within a short time, everyone knew the night ahead would be a cold and damp one, and so the people were willing to sit as late around the fire as long as the last member wanted to talk.

As soon as Marshall had recovered himself enough to ride that afternoon, the reassembled band of Pano Maidus had fled from Green Valley, knowing it was only a matter of time until Lindley and the others reappeared, perhaps with reinforcements. The Panos climbed onto the high, semidome of Moody Ridge, above the river, and made camp there, in a place easily defended, just below the snow line.

The man Marshall had identified as Thomas, Acorn Girl's rifle ball having pierced his heart, presented a minor problem, inasmuch as Marshall, from some baffling notion of civilized propriety, argued for staying long enough to give the body a decent burial—while Acorn Girl had been in favor of carrying the corpse along with them so that they might disfigure it at leisure. Finally they compromised by leaving the dead man where he lay, and the fierce Nishinam leader had contented herself with thinking of the great-winged vultures, the *moloko* birds, that might fly down to peck out the eyes before the other *Wawlems* returned. Only when Marshall assured her once again that Thomas had not been at Coloma and had not even been in California at the time did Ooti relent.

Now that they had set up their temporary camp and had eaten, Jim Marshall was inclined to tell his story.

Hurt Eagle suggested more tobacco, and Jim once again fished the pouch out of his coat. Then he began.

"I swear, this gold has become a curse, both to Cap'n Sutter and myself. So many miners have come into the area, maybe fifty thousand or more of 'em, and they've squatted on everything the Cap'n has. They've cut down his orchards for firewood, and they've killed and eaten his cattle and sheep. You haven't been there to see it, Mrs. Jake, but it's God-awful astonishing. Sutter, he just keeps smiling and giving credit to any of the boys as needs it. Nobody wants to work for him any more, and the prospectors are like crazy men. Because of their own greed, they ignore everybody's rights. Sutter's land is overrun, and he's ruined, for certain."

Acorn Girl and old Hurt Eagle, to a lesser extent, both knew English, and yet much of what Marshall was saying was beyond their comprehension. Hurt Eagle translated as best he could for the others, then shook his head and made the gesture of ignorance.

"As for me," Jim continued, "it would have cost me my life for sure if you hadn't been there, Mrs. Jake. I still don't quite believe it all happened. How *did* you happen to be there?"

"It does not matter," Acorn Girl replied evasively. "We spent the summer and fall up high. Now we have to come down because of the snow."

Marshall studied her face, then glanced at the two hulk-

ing young bears who had nosed their way to a spot near
Acorn Girl's feet and close to the fire, one of the beasts
carelessly shouldering Small Ears aside in the process.

Acorn Girl guessed that Marshall had at least heard
rumors of the Pano Maidu, but he didn't press his question further.

"By God!" he laughed. "Those two just sort of walk
right through things, don't they? Must weigh three, four
hundred pounds apiece. They're grizzlies, ain't they? Well,
it was deuced lucky for me that you did whatever you did.
You know, maybe this isn't the right time, but I've wished
I could see you ever since that night when everything
went crazy, and the gold-hunters killed Jake and all the
others. I've wanted to tell you how sorry I was. And to
apologize for my kind, I guess."

"Those men were not your kind, Jim Marshall," Acorn
Girl said quickly. "You were always my friend, friend to
Pine-nut-eater, these others."

"Never thought of Jake as *Pine-nut-eater*, though I knew
that was his right name. Maybe you don't like me callin'
you *Mrs. Jake?*"

"That name is fine," Acorn Girl replied. "It says what I
was to you, and that's what a name is for."

Tied-wing, who spoke a little English, added his voice
in assent and then translated to the others, who also
murmured agreement.

"Well, I thank you," Marshall said, his voice shaking a
bit. "I've got a lot to thank your people for. Will you tell
them that, Mrs. Jake?"

Acorn Girl translated the words, and then Marshall
went on with his story.

"Well, there's not a whole lot to tell, I suppose. Ever
since word got out that I was the first one to find gold
there at the mill, the boys seem to think I must have a
special talent for finding the stuff. I can't get away to do a
little quiet prospecting of my own for the life of me. Every
time I try to slip away, pretty soon I've got myself a
whole damned escort. It's like a plague on me."

The Whiteman paused, drew on his pipe, continued.

"I left Sutter's Fort maybe two weeks ago to do a little
prospecting. Figured I'd got away clear when I found

those six skunks on my trail. They kept their distance for a time, just followin', but then, two days ago, when we'd got further upriver than any of the other gold-hunters, Milton an' his boys jumped me an' told me they'd kill me if I didn't lead them to the gold. I kept going, one place an' then another, thinking sooner or later I'd get my chance and give them the slip."

He paused, rubbed at his nose, and looked into the fire.

"They believe you are *kuksu* for gold," Hurt Eagle nodded. "Perhaps they believe you are able to suck the gold out of the ground, just as a shaman is able to suck out *omeya*, pain."

"Sometimes I think the gold is sucking me right back into the earth," Marshall said. "But hell, I don't know any better than the next man where to find the stuff. If I did, I'd be a wealthy man, and I'd be living in a big house on the Hudson River by now, I guess. That's far over the mountains, to the east—place where I come from. But the boys wouldn't take my word for it, an' after a while I suppose they got tired of my leadin' them to dry holes, and—well, that's where you found me, Mrs. Jake."

The group of Maidus sat in silence after Acorn Girl had translated Marshall's story for them.

"We know now for certain that *Wawlems* murder each other as well as the Nishinam Maidus," Hurt Eagle said at length.

James Marshall laughed bitterly.

"My friends," he said, "we have murdered each other for thousands of years—long before we ever knew there were any Nishinam people."

"Perhaps it would be best if we drove them all out of our country," Crooked Knee whispered, his eyes large with fear.

"Do you say this because no Nishinam you know of has ever tried to murder one of *his* own kind?" Acorn Girl asked, not bothering to translate the remark for Marshall.

Crooked Knee dropped his eyes, remembering the night when he, along with Water-strider and the others, had broken into Kuksu Man's lodge to take Ooti's babies, a night he would always feel shame for. But Acorn Girl saw the look that came over his face and was immediately sorry for her sharp words.

"Some people are only fools, and some people are vicious," Marshall went on. "It's important to know the difference."

Acorn Girl stared into his eyes, wondering how much of what had been said he understood. Marshall smiled slightly, but he added no more to this train of thought.

"It is time for sleep, perhaps," Hurt Eagle said. "I have lived more than a hundred winters, and now I am ready to sleep all the time. When I was younger, I always wished to do something else in bed."

Crane looked away from him, made a soft whistling sound.

"Yes," Hurt Eagle went on, "and now we must dream that no new snow will fall so that our journey northward to the next river will be easier. After that, I do not know where we will go. Perhaps Ooti will have a dream vision that will tell us what to do."

Hurt Eagle had spoken in English, and Jim Marshall nodded.

"Bear River," he said. "But there are gold miners all up and down it. Maybe that's not the kind of place you're looking for, Mrs. Jake."

"Everywhere we go there are miners," she said. "Crooked Knee would like to drive the *Wawlems* away, and yet there are far more of them now than all of the Nishinams in all of the villages. Maybe you should live with us, Jim Marshall. Together, we would always have to stay away from the Whitemen."

They slept then and moved out with the first light of the following day.

James Marshall rode with Ooti's people for a time, and then he left them near the mining camp called Gold Run.

The Pano Maidus continued on their trek toward the stream the Whites called Bear River, for Hurt Eagle remembered a good place on the little northern branch of the river whose canyon lay between that of the American and that of the Yuba.

9

·················

Editor of the *Del Oro Star*

February, 1850

An *Englishman named Hutchings, one who may not have come down from Sinai, provided "The Miner's Ten Commandments":*

A MAN SPAKE THESE WORDS AND SAID: I am a miner who wandered from "Away Down East," and came to sojourn in a strange land and "See the Elephant." And behold I saw him, and bear witness that, from the key of his trunk to the end of his tail, his whole body has passed before me; and I followed him until his huge feet stood still before a clapboard shanty; then, with his trunk extended, he pointed to a candle-card tacked upon a shingle, as though he would say "READ!"

ONE: Thou shalt have no other claim than one.

TWO: Thou shalt not make unto thyself any false claim, nor any likeness to a mean man by jumping one. [Whatever thou findest, on the top above, or on the rock beneath, or in a crevice underneath the rock, or I will visit the miners around to invite them on my side; and when they decide against thee,] thou shalt take thy pick, thy pan, thy shovel, and thy blankets, with all that thou hast, and go prospecting to seek good diggings; but thou shalt find that thine old claim is worked out, and yet no pile made thee to hide in the ground or in an old boot beneath thy bunk, or in buckskin or in bottle underneath thy cabin; but has paid all that was in thy purse away, worn out thy boots and thy garments, so that there is nothing good about them but the pockets, and thy patience is likened unto thy garments; and at last thou shalt hire thy body out to make thy board and save thy bacon.

*   *   *

A month had passed, a time during which Benjamin Goffe became literally obsessed with the problems involved in mastering the art of applying ink to paper. Once the press itself was in working order, Ben set about rebuilding the interior of his former tavern and now printshop and editorial office. Building materials were both difficult to obtain and dearly expensive. Rough pine and cedar planking, fortunately, could be bought locally—a small mill having been constructed a few months earlier to the west of Grass Valley, down where the pine belt ended, at a settlement called Penn Valley. But the nearest source for iron work—nails, bolts, hinges, and the like—lay thirty-five miles to the west, in the town of Marysville. The only alternative was Sacramento City, where prices were somewhat lower. But that metropolis, California-scale, was distant some sixty miles.

Ben took a chance that he would be able to find what he needed in Marysville. With a pair of newly acquired pack mules trailing behind, Ben mounted Old Blue and set off, down through the mining villages of Rough and Ready, Penn Valley, and Smartville. A few inches of snow had fallen in Grass Valley two days earlier, turning the town streets into quagmires—for despite the snow, temperatures remained slightly above freezing. Winter in California, Ben had already concluded, was quite a different matter than in Connecticut. Here torrential rains alternated with periods of clear skies and often a disarming warmth that seemed to signal the momentary beginnings of spring. He'd said as much to Red Collins, the proprietor of the Boston Ravine General Store & Hardware, and the young Ohioan laughed.

"Showed up here last May, just as the town was getting lined-out," he said, "and by God if we didn't get a foot and a half of snow—the thirteenth of May, it was. Then on July Fourth, right in the middle of a big celebration and all, down come the hail. Two hours of it, Professor, until everything was as white as my grandpa's beard, rest his soul. Four inches of hail on the ground, and in July. Before I left Lima, I'd heard that there wasn't no winter in

California. Guess I was reading the same damned lies we all read. Truth is, Big Ben, it's just that winter never makes up its mind in California."

Ben nodded.

A small party had recently crossed the Sierra on snow-shoes, had come in half-blind and frostbitten, with tales of having encountered forty-foot drifts through the Donner Pass.

But a few miles below Grass Valley the final traces of snow had vanished, and Old Blue and the two mules moved ahead with renewed vigor.

A board and beam toll bridge, Ben discovered, had been half completed across the Yuba River, and already a large hand-lettered sign had been prominently posted:

Passage 75 cents

But the big green river was running high, and no work-ers were in sight—not so much as a single caretaker. The half dozen platform tents and the single log cabin were equally deserted.

A long hawser was stretched from one bank to the other, fastened to an oak on one side and a digger pine on the other. It wasn't much to work with, but Ben was determined, despite his animals' sudden loss of eagerness. He urged Old Blue ahead, cursed at the mules, and yanked at their lead lines.

Two hours later, and still wet despite the clear sky and warm day, he was in Marysville, only to discover that no one in town had so much as a pound of nails of any variety.

Cursing silently, Ben turned his animals toward Sacra-mento, made note that the ferry operator did not seem to remember him in the slightest, and once across pushed on toward Sacramento, making camp on the south bank of Bear River, this stream also running high and affording a difficult though not dangerous crossing.

"My friend," he told Old Blue, "there's simply no chance for civilization to develop out here until we get some bridges in."

The Percheron wagged his head and fluttered his lips in apparent agreement.

*   *   *

As Goffe approached Sacramento, the impact of the recent heavy rains became ever more apparent, for the river had overtopped its banks in numerous places, inundating broad areas and stranding animals on islands of higher ground. Deer, tule elk, and long-horned cattle stood about on these isolated rises, mingling together or standing, heads down, as if dazed. And in the shallow waters, beginning to recede now, lay the bloating corpses of numerous cattle and deer, dead bobcats, skunks, possums.

Just north of the city itself, the newly constructed levees, built as protection against such a flood, had ruptured and slid away, allowing the turbulence of the American River to pour into the city. Even the more solidly impacted bulwarks against the Sacramento River had given way, and the entire low-lying area of the fledgling metropolis was flooded, the streets three feet deep in water. Houses set upon less than substantial foundations were tilted in one direction or another, and the human population waded about thigh-deep, plodding ahead stoically or cursing the brown, silty waters.

The ferry master alone was in his element, and his price for passage across the American had risen to two dollars.

Ben and Old Blue and the mules slogged forward, crossed the devastated area, and pressed on toward Sutter's Fort.

Here he was able to purchase the things he had need of and then made his way to Brannan's Restaurant & Tavern, where he found both the owner and John Sutter at a corner table in the company of half a dozen attractive Indian women who appeared, Ben thought, somewhat bored by the intense discussion the two Whitemen were engaged in.

At Goffe's appearance, the discussion lapsed, and the two Lords of Sacramento clapped Ben on the shoulders and bade him join them.

"It's good, God-fearing rum that we're drinking, Benjamin," Brannan laughed. "Cure what ails you and expunge your sins as well. That true or not, Cap'n?"

"Ja, ja, it is good rum, very good. Sit down, Professor Goffe. Sit down. Have you brought us copies of your newspaper?"

Two of the Indian women moved over, and Ben sat down.

"Not as yet, gentlemen," he said. "Apparently there's more to producing a news sheet than merely wishing to do it. I've been getting set up and giving myself an education in printing at the same time. Soon, though, soon."

"I've got recent copies of the *Star* and the *Californian*," Sam Brannan laughed. "That's where I get half the news for my own paper. You might as well, too. Selective plagiarism is half the genius of publishing, as I take it."

"Much obliged," Ben nodded, sipping from the mug of rum that one of the Indian women had poured for him. "But I'll tell you what I really need, gents, and that's a printer. Either one of you happen to have one of those in stock?"

Sutter made an inexplicable gesture toward Brannan, drank off his rum, and grinned.

"*Jawohl, mein Herr*," he said. "I just happen to have one of those. A fine young man he is, Thomas Elkins, who was a printer's devil in Pittsburgh before he came here to make his fortune. If you offer him work, he will take it, I believe."

"Tom knows printing?" Brannan asked. "Why didn't you tell me about that, Herr Sutter, my friend?"

"Ahh!" Sutter chuckled, "because you would not pay him fairly, Samuel. You would not pay him fairly. But Benjamin here, he is a man of honor."

Goffe began to wonder if he was being set up.

"Thomas Elkins?" he said. "If he came to California for gold, why isn't he out digging?"

"He's a mite lame just now," Brannan said, refilling his mug and passing it to the Indian women, who sipped and laughed delightedly.

"*Ja*, yes," Sutter continued. "Thomas was working for me, a gold mine I have over on the Cosumnes River. The others, they steal from me and then demand their pay. But Thomas was a good worker. Unfortunately he broke his leg last summer—fell from some high rocks and ended up in the river. . . ."

"Apparently the water was shallow," Brannan shrugged.

"Now he is a bit crippled," Sutter said. "He gets around well enough, but he cannot stand the cold water. Benjamin, Tom has worked with a printer before. That is what he says, and I believe him. Why should he wish to lie to me? He is an honest young man. Treat him right, and he will be your friend forever. *Mein Gott*, he follows me about like a great puppy dog, and so I have to find work for him to do. Otherwise I fear he would starve. But to you he would be a valuable man. Perhaps you would even be able to start publishing your paper."

"You got a name for 'er yet?" Brannan asked.

"*Del Oro Star*," Ben replied. "When can I meet Tom Elkins?"

Thomas Elkins, however poor a miner he may have been, proved to be not only a tireless worker but a very bright young man as well. He was hardly a master printer, but he knew far more of the business than Ben did and was able to instruct his employer as to the proper preparation of the ink plate, the craft of handsetting type, of the use of wooden furniture about the type, methods of leading, the use of key quoins, and the like.

Within a few days of working together, the *Del Oro Star* printing establishment was in order and ready for business. To this end both Ben and Tom spent time moving about Grass Valley and the outlying areas—Deer Creek Dry Diggings, You Bet, Red Dog, Chicago Park, and Sandy Bar—gathering names, taking notes, talking with any miner who was willing to put down his pick and shovel or to leave his riffles or long-tom unattended in the hope that he might soon be able to point to his own name in print or to read a few of his own quoted words back to his tentmate or partner.

By the first week in February a sufficient collection of local lore and gossip had been gathered, and these items, along with news of the world "Down East," gleaned from the San Francisco publications Sam Brannan had provided, were typeset and locked in place in the chase of the flatbed press.

Ben had initially conceived of a single sheet, printed on just one face, twenty-four by thirty-six inches. But the wealth of quaint sayings and various theories as to the origin of the gold that seemed to be found, in greater or

lesser quantities, along every stream with sand and gravel
in its bed and along ravines leading down from gravel
deposits higher on the ridges—all this led Ben to decide
upon a second page, printed on the verso of the first.

Finally, with a bit of space left over, he put together
some commonsense reflections, whimsically phrased, on
the general business of gold mining, of the problems with
drinking to excess, of the apparent contribution of bad
water and unclean food and general lack of hygiene to the
ever-present cholera and other diseases endemic within
the mining camps. To all of this he added some remarks
on the need for some sort of genuine government and
legal justice beyond that of vigilante operations, kangaroo
courts, and lynch rope.

All was phrased and spelled phonetically in the manner
of an old mountain man and presented under Bully
O'Bragh's byline.

"Is this someone you've invented, Mr. Goffe?" Tom
Elkins asked, looking puzzled.

"You might say so," Ben nodded. "Actually, he's the old
mountain *coon* that rode west with me—madman, guide,
and instructor in all matters pertaining to the trail."

"Oh," Tom said, his voice trailing off. "But won't O'Bragh
mind? I mean—look at the way you've spelled things, Mr.
Goffe."

"Mind?" Ben chuckled. "If the paper finds its way to
American Valley, I have a feeling my good friend Farnsworth
O'Bragh will be paying us a visit. Then we'll get him
talking and sit back and take notes. In four or five hours,
Thomas, we'll have enough material for a year's worth of
columns."

"But are these things you remember O'Bragh saying?"

Ben took off his glasses, wiped the lenses with a hand-
kerchief, repositioned the spectacles on his nose.

"No," he admitted. "But he *might* have said all of it.
I've never known a man with more absolute opinions on
everything—if the old codger exists at all. Hell, Tom, he
might just be a figment of my imagination. Memory, my
young friend, is an extremely complicated phenomenon.
In the first place, it's quite treacherous. And in the second
place, it's highly selective. And finally there's the problem

of memory converting itself into dream—exaggerating, condensing, disguising, rearranging, and so forth. And after we've dreamed a thing, I doubt that our memories of the original happening are ever precisely what they were before the dream occurred. So maybe there actually was a Bully O'Bragh, and then again maybe there wasn't. Great God, I think the lecturer in me is beginning to come back to life. Thomas, let's print us a newspaper. Cinch up the quoins and apply your magic brayer to the plate. . . ."

The first edition of the *Del Oro Star* came out, a laboriously produced run of three hundred copies. Within a matter of hours the copies were all gone, and Ben and Tom were elated.

Citizen after citizen of the boomtown of Grass Valley appeared at the *Star* offices, first to purchase copies of the paper and then, when the edition was history, to demand to know when they might expect a new one.

"Will you look at that!" Tom blurted, staring transfixedly out through the one window whose glass had not been replaced by double thicknesses of waxed paper.

Ben glanced up from his ledger of accounts.

The door opened, ringing the cowbell he had attached to the top of it, and in stepped a vision in yellow taffeta, full skirts with petticoats beneath, thin waist with crisscrossed white lacings, full bosom, with cleavage exposed beneath a white ruff. The red-haired woman's coif was elaborately arranged, with a turquoise-studded tiara set just behind tightly curled bangs. Only the somewhat too thin lips marred an otherwise faultlessly formed face, the cheeks touched with rouge, the makeup perfectly accentuating jade-green eyes.

About the waist, in utterly incongruous fashion, the lady wore a slim silver belt from which was suspended an intricately tooled holster, itself studded with turquoises, that contained a menacing-looking long-barreled black pistol.

Ben rose to his feet and adjusted his glasses. He recognized the new visitor immediately.

Anastasia Atwood, the Rose of You Bet.

"Miss Atwood . . . ," Ben said, bowing slightly, in his best Yale fashion.

"Don't get stuffy, Big Guy," the Rose of You Bet replied. "Look now. I've just read your paper, Goffe, and there's not so much as a mention of the Ophir Hill Palace and Gaming Hall. If my place ain't news enough for you, then you've got no business even pretending to run a paper. You've insulted me and the girls."

Ben glanced down at the pistol, caught himself, and determinedly stared into the Vision's eyes.

"Perhaps I should have mentioned your place in the O'Bragh column," he said. "Look, Miss Atwood, it's just that . . ."

"Hogwash, Goffe. You're a damned professor from what I hear, stiff-backed and proper as hell. Probably haven't shot off your rocks in a year or more. Does this paper of yours sell advertising space, or what? I want to take out a full-page ad in the next issue, in case you get around to printing one."

"You want *what*?"

The Rose of You Bet laughed, at the same time covering her mouth with one hand. And the eyes, Ben noted, had been distinctly narrowed.

"That's what comes of not getting your rocks off, Professor. You get hard of hearing."

"Is that a fact, Miss Atwood?"

"As *facty* as anything else. Now then, you going to sell me some ad space?"

Ben took off his glasses for a moment and squinted at the woman.

"We're not selling advertising until the fourth issue. Company policy," he said. "But maybe you've got a point. It certainly wouldn't do for all the miners in the area to be going deaf, would it?"

"You bet it wouldn't, Professor. So what are you saying?"

"I'm saying," Ben answered, "that I've just decided to do a feature story about you and your . . . establishment. Do you have time for an in-depth interview just now?"

The Rose of You Bet laughed.

"Never been . . . interviewed . . . by a man your size before. Sure, this gal's up to it."

Ben put his glasses back on, felt a ridiculous urge to grin like a schoolboy, and suppressed it.

"Thomas," he said, turning to his wide-eyed assistant, "get a notepad and accompany Miss Atwood into the back room, if you will. This will be your byline."

Elkins started to speak. His mouth opened, but no words came out.

"Back room, hell," the Rose of You Bet said. "Listen, now. Maybe I like you after all, Professor. You and your young man come on up to the Ophir Hill Palace this evening. Me and the girls will give the both of you something to write about. When you get there, tell my barkeep you want to speak to Rose—tell him that in case you don't see me right off."

She turned suddenly toward Elkins, who inadvertently took half a step backward.

"You're the one they call Limping Tom, aren't you? Some of the boys said you were working for the Professor. The rest of you's all right, isn't it? Other than the bad leg, I mean?"

Then, with a dazzling smile, the Rose of You Bet had turned on her heel and was out through the door, the cowbell clanking disconsolately behind her.

Benjamin Goffe roared with laughter.

Thomas Elkins was still shaking his head.

"Well, I've seen the Elephant now," the young man mumbled.

Before leaving for the Ophir Hill Palace, Ben had dressed carefully in his New Haven duds, as he had come to think of them: top hat, somewhat the worse for having been transported across the continent but still serviceable, shoes properly shined, striped trousers, tweed jacket, red and white checkered vest, and broad bow tie. Tom Elkins, in his leather coat and flat-topped sombrero, was impressed with his employer's appearance, and so were the girls at Rose's establishment—for while civilized Eastern clothing was not unknown in the mining areas, neither was it common.

Clarita, Dolores, and Sandy Sue all vied for the Professor's attentions, and Ben, in an expansive mood after the grand initial success of the *Del Oro Star*, lit a cigar, bought drinks for those around him, and held court, delivering a humorous discourse on the Puritan Revolution in Old England, sprinkled with anecdotes concerning such worthies as Oliver Cromwell, John Milton, Andrew Marvell, John Donne, Vane, Hampden, Whalley, and a number of others. Once again Pembroke Castle fell to the conquering Cromwell, as did Preston and Edinburgh. Thereafter the High Court of Justice tried Charles I for treason, and the King's death warrant was duly signed. Scotland and the Protestant part of Ireland were once more brought into legislative union with England. The Rump Parliament sat and was disbanded by Cromwell himself.

But no portion of the discourse aroused so much absolute attention as Ben's account of Cromwell's death and subsequent burial with great pomp in the Tomb of the Kings itself, in Westminster Abbey. And then, once again, the great hero's body, following the Restoration, was disinterred, the pitiful bones and leathery skin, where anything at all remained, to be exposed upon the gallows at Tyburn and ultimately buried beneath that symbol of Divinely Ordained Justice.

Clarita and Dolores wept openly, while Sandy Sue placed her head against Tom Elkins' shoulder and ran one hand down his side until it was out of sight beneath the table.

The barkeep swore and shook his head, mumbling something to the effect that *They all get it in the end*, by *heaven*, waving several would-be customers away while he considered the matter.

Only the Rose of You Bet appeared unmoved, either by Ben's skills as raconteur or by his New Haven costume. Instead, the flame-haired Anastasia Atwood suggested strongly that several customers of her establishment were in need of medical attention to their aural nerves and that, if Ben or his young man did not intend to give her the promised interview, she had various other matters to attend to.

Ben glanced at Tom over the rims of his glasses, and the assistant publisher of the *Del Oro Star* withdrew his notepad and began asking the flamboyant proprietress a series of well-rehearsed questions.

"You going to let a boy do a man's job, Professor?" the Rose of You Bet asked.

"It's the reporter's job," Ben assured her, rising, bowing, and walking toward the bar, the dark-haired Clarita clinging dutifully to one of his arms.

Goffe nodded to a group of hard-faced miners, the men sitting at one of the tables and engaged in a game of poker. One of the miners, a fellow in a crushed black felt, stared at him for a moment and then returned his attention to the playing cards cupped carefully against his chest.

"We have a few more drinks, and then you make love to me?" Clarita asked, pressing herself against Ben's side.

Goffe studied the raven-haired girl with wide-set brown eyes, noted the hint of down over her upper lip, and wondered how old she was.

"Fifteen," he thought, "or perhaps a year or two older—and yet those lips have kissed a thousand men. . . ."

The barkeep placed down two sherry cobblers and stuck paper straws into each.

Clarita sipped hers, and Ben removed the straw and drank his off, thinking as he did so that he himself was hardly following the sage advice of Bully O'Bragh, as recounted in his own newspaper.

"*Sí Senorita, Clarita linda, mi alma.* I would like that very much, *sí, sí.* And yet I am too old for you. My girl, I'm easily old enough to be your father, easily that."

Clarita pursed her lips about the straw in her sherry cobbler, batted her lashes, and smiled prettily.

"My boyfriend killed my *padre*, and then he left me and went into *Baja*. I have no father, and now I will let you be my father. But first buy Clarita another drink, *por favor*."

Goffe laughed and shook his head.

"You will get very drunk, pretty one."

Clarita shook her head, smiled, and winked.

"My drink, it has mostly water, little *vino*. Miss Atwood, that is what she orders the bartender to do."

"Ah yes," Ben nodded, "I begin to get the picture."

At this point the miner in the crumpled black hat strode to the bar, sized up the somewhat taller Goffe, and grunted his disapproval of the fancy clothing.

"Ye're the Professor, huh? The same dude as printed the *Del Oro?*"

"Yes," Ben responded. "The *Del Oro Star*. Benjamin Goffe at your service, sir."

Ben extended his hand, but the miner chose to ignore it.

"Name's Ez Johnson," the miner said. "What I want to know is how come you didn't have nothin' to say about the thievin' Goddamn Injuns—how the greasy little bastards is always stealin' a man's tools an' killin' his dog and eatin' it, if he's got one. Just last week my partner's mule got took—probably ended up in a Goddamn Digger's stewpot. We ought to shoot every one of the greasy bastards, that's what I say. There's lots of 'em workin' crick bottoms just like they was Whitemen, for Christ's sake. They hang around an' watch what a man's doin', an' then they steal his pick an' shovel an' go set up a claim, just like they had a right to do 'er. What's your paper goin' to say about that?"

Ben fiddled with his glasses for a moment and then offered the bearded miner a cigar. Johnson took it, stuck it without comment into his coat pocket, and called to the barkeep for a shot of sour mash.

Ben felt a wave of anger beginning to pass over him, but he resisted the feeling and attempted to remain friendly.

"According to John Sutter," Ben replied, "the Maidus and Miwoks don't eat dogs. Dog meat is taboo to them."

Johnson gulped his whiskey and tapped the shot glass on the polished surface of the bar.

"I know Sutter," he said. "The old bastard's so full of horse dung that the whites of his eyes have gone brown. You're new here, Professor. Me, I been in the mines since before they was any mines. Truth is, I come down from Oregon in '46. I was there when the boys hoisted the Bear Flag, by God. An' I was in Coloma in '48 when we found gold. Worked for John Sutter at that damned mill of his, in fact. Any case, I been here long enough to know the Diggers eat dogs *for a fact*. An' I know that we'd all be better off if the devils was wiped out complete, before California starts bein' a state. After that the Down East bunch will be tellin' us we ought to treat 'em just like they was human, which they ain't."

"And so they've stolen your friend's mule and have

eaten that too?" Ben asked, at the same time removing his top hat and placing it on the bar.

Clarita had slipped away while Goffe and Johnson were talking, and now she returned, the Rose of You Bet with her.

"Ezra," the Rose said, her voice pleasant but at the same time pregnant with proprietary authority, "you're not getting into one of your *moods*, are you? Mr. Goffe is my guest tonight—he's promised to write about me in his paper."

"Aw shit, Anastasia," Johnson shrugged, "I was just tellin' the Professor how the Diggers stole Sonny Penryn's mule an' ate it, is all. Tell 'im it's true. We all heard about it, by God."

Ben was astounded at how easily the Rose had exerted control over the bad-natured miner—gathering, at the same time, that Johnson enjoyed the status of a familiar and valued customer in the Ophir Hill Palace and Gaming Hall. Nonetheless, Goffe's anger was up, and he could feel himself starting to get red in the face. That Miss Atwood should feel it necessary to intervene in his behalf against such an antagonist was more than he was presently able to deal with. Ben glanced down at Johnson's side, noted that the man was not wearing a weapon, remembered seeing the twenty or more gunbelts hanging from pegs in the foyer, and realized that Anastasia Atwood had business sense enough to require *no guns* as a house rule.

"That was the story," the Rose of You Bet agreed. "Don't think anyone saw the Diggers cooking the beast, but that was the story, all right. You looking for female companionship tonight, Ez, or you just come in to drink and play cards?"

Several other miners had now begun to gravitate toward the bar, and Tom Elkins was making silent gestures toward Ben.

"Mr. Johnson," Ben said loudly enough so that all might hear, "has just challenged me to a wrist-wrestling contest— and the loser buys drinks for the house. Good clean fun, that's all, Miss Atwood. Are you ready Mr. Johnson? This is a new sport for me, but I'm willing to try anything once. Is this how it's done?"

Ben turned around sideways and planted his elbow on the corner of the bar.

The miners whooped and yelled, and within moments the entire clientele of the Ophir Hill Palace and Gaming Hall had crowded about. The newspaper editor, the men generally agreed, was certainly big enough, and he might even be as strong as his size suggested. Still, most of those present quickly concluded that Ez Johnson, a man known widely as the hard-driving boss of the Chalk Bluff Long-Toms, quick of temper and fast with his fists, his Bowie knife, and his pistol, was likely to be more than a match for the lumbering dandy from New Haven, Connecticut.

Johnson took another shot of whiskey, held one hand high in a gesture of confidence, shrugged toward the Rose of You Bet, and proceeded to place his elbow alongside Goffe's.

"Rose, you count three," he said, settling himself around and adjusting his body for position.

The two men locked hands, and Ben leaned forward, squinting at Johnson.

The Rose said, *"Three!"*

Ben roared and drove Johnson's clenched fist hard to the polished oak of the bar.

The three or four present who had been foolish enough to place a bet on the Professor whooped with delight, and Ben, remembering clearly enough his contest with Jean-Claire Hivernan at the *El Sombrero Saloon & Watering Hole* in St. Louis, stood up immediately, readying himself for whatever might transpire.

"The Professor won fair and square," the Rose of You Bet declared. "We're all witness to it. And that, gentlemen, will be the end of wrist-wrestling contests for the night. Drinks are on Ez Johnson here, as I remember, and I'll go for another round on the house. Move back, boys. If one of you half-deaf bastards starts something and busts one of my mirrors, I swear by grandma's crotch-hair I'll put a forty-five slug in his mouth."

Anastasia Atwood had her pistol leveled at the group of men, and they, immediately perceiving an authority greater than their own, did as they were bade.

Bravo, bravo!

The dude in the top hat's bull of the mines, by Gawd!

Pay up, ye pizzen-livered bastard!

Hooray for the mines! Ol' Ez is buyin' the mash!

In the face of the apparent sudden shift of sympathies, Ezra Johnson grinned, flexed his hand, and declared, "Boys, I been taken. Fucked by a grizzly in a top hat, I was. All right now, I'm buyin', then. Damned if you didn't jump the gun on me, Professor. But there'll be a rematch by-and-by. You can count on 'er."

The following morning found Ben and Tom hard at work putting together material for a second run of the *Del Oro Star*, for using a shortage of space had precluded them from using in the first edition. With Tom's interview with Anastasia Atwood, under Ben's tutelage, coming together, the two novice newsmen already had nearly enough material to accomplish their purpose. Goffe, secretly pleased with his quick victory of the night before, undertook to do a short piece on *the gentlemanly art of wrist-wrestling*, complete with instructions as to positioning and method and with a certain sly suggestion that men from Connecticut were known throughout the civilized world for their prowess at the sport. Even Bridgeport schoolboys, Ben contended, would prove to be more than a match for all but the most powerful of the miners, owing to superior diet as well as to the debilitating effects upon arm and wrist tendons brought about by working long hours with pick and shovel.

Tom Elkins read the piece and shook his head.

"By the time our edition's out, everyone in the area's going to know about you and Johnson," he said. "And if Ezra doesn't look at the paper, his friends will show it to him and have a laugh. Mr. Goffe, I'm not sure it's such a good idea to antagonize that man any more than you already have."

"Old Ez is a good sport," Ben chuckled. "Likely he'll get a kick out of it."

"It's more likely that he'll wait his chance and then put a rifle ball in your tail, from what I hear. Back in '48, Ez Johnson and some of his friends wiped out a whole Yalesumnes village—just went in and butchered the lot of them. Mr. Sutter told me the story when I first started working for him up at the mine. You'd have been better off if you'd let him beat you, sir. That's what I think."

Ben put down his pencil, adjusted his glasses, and leaned back in his chair.

"Begins to make sense," he said. "That's what we were having our initial disagreement about. It seems Mr. Johnson's in favor of exterminating the local Indian population. Is there more to the story? Anything else you know about our friend Ezra Johnson?"

"No, sir, that's about it. Mr. Sutter told us all to keep an eye out for any strange Indians—and not to trust 'em, other than the ones that were working with us for pay. Word had it that the Indians had already taken revenge on two or three of the fellows that helped Johnson wipe out that village."

"The Grizzly Cult!" Ben exclaimed. "Yes, I know about them. What I don't know is whether they really exist or whether it's just one of those rumors that get carried all over the mining areas. Tom, I'd guess that every time someone's found dead, it's convenient to blame the thing on the Indians. Could be that bears are partly responsible for the stories, too. I came face to face with a pair of grizzlies a couple of months ago. Fearsome looking beasties, there's no question about that. I've read accounts, Tom, and perhaps you have too, about men who were torn up by bears. And these presumed vigilante Indians are called the Grizzlies. . . ."

"Bears are one thing, sir, but I talked to a fellow over in Hangtown. He'd seen a body brought in—all slashed up, as though a bear had done it. But there was also a bullet hole in the forehead, and I don't think any of the bears are using guns yet."

Goffe scratched at his chin whiskers.

"Point well taken," he said. "Point well taken. Possibly the Grizzly Indians will get to Ez Johnson before he's had a chance to read our next edition."

"Then you're going to use the article?"

"Of course, Thomas me lad, of course. An' I'll be signin' Bully O'Bragh's name to 'er, by the Great Blue Jesus. Ol' mountain nigger like Bully, he's bound to have some opinions on wrist-wrastlin'. An' not even Ez Johnson can blame this child for it. *Wagh!*"

Tom Elkins grinned, surprised that his employer could speak so easily in the same species of language he rendered phonetically for the O'Bragh column. But he still doubted the wisdom of the thing.

It was just before quitting time, and Ben and Tom were engaged in hand setting their type. The cowbell over the door rang, and both men looked up.

A lean-faced, blue-eyed, solemn individual had entered the *Del Oro Star* offices.

"For God's sake," Ben said, rising. "Thomas, it's Jim Marshall! You know the man, don't you? Jim, it's good to see you. I was down to Sutter's place a few weeks back, and I guess I missed you."

"Ben," Marshall said, extending his hand. "And young Tom—how's that leg getting along, son?"

"Still limping, Jim. Might even be permanent, but I'm getting along all right. Mr. Goffe's made me his assistant."

"So I hear, so I hear. Well, Benjamin, I guess I've got a story for you, if you want it. Stake me to supper, bunk, and breakfast, and by God, I'll tell you everything that's happened to me. Kidnapped, I was, and damned near hung. Would have been, like as not, if it hadn't been for Mrs. Jake."

"Slow down, man," Ben laughed, clapping Marshall across the shoulders. "There's time enough for talk—by heavens, it's good to see you. Hung? You been stealing horses, Jim, or what? Sutter's not here in Grass Valley, is he?"

"Just me," Jim Marshall said. "I tell you, fate's after me, Benjamin. You'll put it in your paper, maybe? I would have told Brannan, but he's sixty miles from here, and I'm heading north. Am if I can get rid of shadows, that is. I want you to tell the boys I ain't got no more magic for finding lead than they do, which ain't much. If I can just get that word out, then maybe I can have some peace. I tell you, it's a damned curse that keeps following me. I wish to God somebody else had picked up that first nugget."

"Beans, ham, and genuine Goffe bread do you for chow? Tom, get on over to Red Collins' General Store, will you?

Get us a jug of Napa wine, if he's got any. If not, any kind of spirit will do. Here. Here's some money."

Elkins took the folded currency, pulled on his canvas jacket, and made his way out the door, closing it so softly that the cowbell hardly rang at all.

Ben guided Jim Marshall to a chair behind the printing press and then proceeded to stoke the cast-iron stove with chunks of freshly split green cedar.

There was a good bed of coals, and soon the fresh fuel was popping and snapping behind the isinglass window held in place by a polished brass grid.

By noon of the next day, James Marshall was riding northward toward Camptonville and Downieville, and Benjamin Goffe did indeed have a remarkable story.

"He's like the Wandering Jew," Ben thought. "Or like Orestes, pursued by a band of glittering-eyed Furies, each carrying a goldpan. Best thing Jim could do would be to forget about this place and head for Oregon, get him some farmland. Raise cows. . . ."

He sat down at his desk, flipped through the pages of his oversized tablet, used his Green River knife, veteran of the trek westward, to sharpen a stubby pencil, and wrote out a head:

Mrs. Jake's Act of Mercy

He squinted at what he had written, rubbed the end of his nose, and tried again:

Grizzly Cult Rescues Gold Discoverer
Grizzlies Rescue James Marshall
Narrow Escape on the North Fork

Nothing seemed to work, and Ben rose, walked to where Tom was forming furniture around the edges of the already set type, studied the younger man's method, and nodded.

"Thomas," Ben said, "tell you what. Let's knock off for the rest of the day. We'll hit it tomorrow. Think maybe we stayed up talking and drinking a bit too late last night. In any case, we're all ready for our second edition except for the Marshall story, and that's going to take me a while. We'll set type in the morning, proof the galleys, lock up, and start the run. Maybe you could ride out to You Bet and talk to Horace Belcher—he's full of interesting gossip about one thing or another—maybe something for next week's paper. Only that wouldn't exactly be taking the rest of the day off, would it?"

"Sounds good to me," Tom replied. "You mind if I take Old Blue, Mr. Goffe? I have a terrible time with both of the mules. I tell them to go one way, they go the other as sure as anything."

Ben laughed.

"That's the secret, Thomas. Sure, take the big fellow. He gets edgy if he's not had sufficient exercise. I ever tell you about the farmer I bought Blue from? Had a young daughter who used to ride him—a little thing who weighed maybe sixty pounds, soaking wet. She's the one who turned him into a saddle horse, as I gather. Think you can make it out there and back by sundown?"

"Probably not, in fact. But the moon's full, or close to it. We'll make it all right, Mr. Goffe."

Once Tom was out of the office, Ben put the *closed* sign on the door and drew the latch. Then he sat down at the desk once more and began to write.

Stopped.

A half-formed image of the young woman leader of the Maidu band swam before his eyes. She was shaking her head, gesturing with her hands.

"It's crazy," he thought. "She doesn't want me to write this. . . . Or it's my conscience. No, by God! The less known about her, the better. If I tell the world about her, it's just that much more likely she'll be recognized. And if that happens, no matter what I've said, she'll be gunned down or lynched or . . ."

Good Samaritans Rescue James Marshall

"I won't even mention that the rescuers were Indians— that's the way to deal with it. An air of mystery, identities unspecified. The main thing here would seem to be the identification of Lindley as the one who threatened to hang Jim Marshall . . . and the simple truth that Marshall has been a great failure in every mining venture he's attempted since that day at the mill in Coloma. That much of the thing I've got to make clear. Maybe I ought to

challenge Lindley to a wrist-wrestling match—put it right
there in type, for everyone to read. . . ."

*Lindley and Ezra Johnson were ringleaders of the group
that massacred the Maidu village near Coloma, shortly
after the discovery of gold. And this young woman, Mrs.
Jake, wife to Marshall's friend, was one of those Maidus
whose village had been butchered. And now she's the
leader of the Grizzly Cult. It was not merely a rumor or a
wild tale at all. They were real. She was real. And she did
not wish him to write about her. . . .*

Jim Marshall had told him the story, and the man had
spoken the truth. There was no doubt whatsoever in Benjamin Goffe's mind.

10

Rifle Fire in Woodpecker Canyon

February, 1850

*THREE: Thou shalt not go prospecting before thy claim
gives out. Neither shalt thou take thy money, nor thy gold
dust, nor thy good name, to the gaming table in vain; for
monte, twenty-one, roulette, faro, lansquenet and poker
will prove to thee that the more thou puttest down the less
thou shalt take up; and when thou thinkest of thy wife and
children, thou shalt not hold thyself guiltless, but—insane.*
*FOUR: Thou shalt not remember what thy friends do at
home on the Sabbath day, lest the remembrance may not
compare favorably with what thou doest here. Six days
thou mayest dig or pick all that thy body can stand under,
but the other day is Sunday; yet thou washest all thy dirty
shirts, darnest all thy stockings, tap thy boots, mend thy
clothing, chop thy whole week's fire-wood, make up and
bake thy bread and boil thy pork and beans that thou wait
not when thou returnest from thy long-tom weary. For in*

*six days' labor only thou canst not work enough to wear
out thy body in two years; but if thou workest hard on
Sunday also, thou canst do it in six months; and thou and
thy son and thy daughter, thy male and thy female friend,
thy morals and thy conscience be none the less better for
it, but reproach thee shouldst thou ever return to thy
mother's fireside; and thou strive to justify thyself because
the teacher and the blacksmith, the carpenter and the
merchant, the tailors, Jews and Buccaneers defy God and
civilization by keeping not the Sabbath day, nor wish for a
day of rest, such as memory of youth and home made
hallowed.*

*FIVE: Thou shalt not think more of all thy gold, nor
how thou canst make it fastest, than how thou wilt enjoy it
after thou hast ridden rough-shod over thy good old parents' precepts and examples, that thou mayest have nothing to reproach and sting thee when thou art left alone in
the land where thy father's blessing and thy mother's love
hath sent thee.*

The cast-iron stove was growling happily, and the
printshop was comfortably warm, with chunks of uncured
cedar spitting and popping within the belly of black metal.
Ben had settled on a fairly short, to-the-point account of
James Marshall's misadventures, had finished that piece,
and was once more engaged in polishing his *gentlemanly
art of wrist-wrestling* article when the cowbell over the
door clanked and Tom Elkins, white-faced and lips drawn,
entered the building.

"Close the damned door, Thomas," Ben called out.
"There's frost forming on the typecases as it is. You all
right, Tom?"

"Doings in You Bet," Elkins said, striding to the stove
and holding his hands out over it. "Ez Johnson and the
men at Chalk Bluff have gone Injun-hunting, Mr. Goffe.
There was a little village over on Steephollow Creek,
and . . ."

"Was?" Ben asked, sliding back away from his desk.

"Well, there's not one any more. The boys got drunk
after hitting a rich ledge this morning, and after that they

decided to go find Sonny Penryn's mule that got stolen. Apparently they rode in on the village, found everyone half starved to death, and finished the job off. One of the guys came into Belcher's Tavern just as I was getting ready to ride on back to Grass Valley. Mr. Goffe, he had a string of half a dozen clots of hair, and they weren't all scalps. Cunt-scalps, he said. I didn't look close enough to find out if it was true. God save me, I don't understand what gets into the men at times. . . ."

"Mother of God!" Ben said, putting his head into his hands. "That would be the Usto-ma band, I guess. Red Collins told me they used to camp on Wolf Creek, up close to Banner Mountain. Last fall they supposedly moved back, over beyond Greenhorn Creek somewhere—and a few of them set up lodges just past Ophir Hill. Did they kill *all* of them?"

"The guy at Belcher's place thought maybe only half a dozen or so managed to run off into the woods to hide, and a couple of those were wounded. I didn't stick around, Mr. Goffe. Johnson and the rest of his men were supposed to be coming in to celebrate, and I didn't want to be there."

"A good thing you didn't," Ben agreed. "I just hope to heaven the little to-do with Johnson at Rose's place isn't what goaded him into it. If that were true, then . . ."

"You'd be responsible?" Tom asked. "No, Mr. Goffe. A man like Ezra Johnson, he's . . . he's worse than an animal, as I see it. Killing Indians is sport to him. Some of the men down on the Cosumnes were that way, even though they worked all day right alongside Indians. *Wild Injuns is just like bears and mountain panthers.* That's what they kept saying. And they'd clap Mr. Sutter's Indians on the back and ask them if they wanted to go hunting. . . ."

Ben Goffe sat dazed, and the imagined figure of Sacajawea drifted into his mind—an old mental friend, straight out of the Lewis and Clark Journals, wife to Charbonneau the trapper, mother to the younger Charbonneau whom he'd met, Jean Baptiste, the man sent to Europe to receive a civilized education, the man who'd returned to his birthplace only to find that the world he'd remembered vaguely had changed, was still changing, was passing into nonexistence, his father dead and his mother grown old. And so, eventually, he had come west. . . . And then, once again, the imagined figure of Mrs. Jake came to mind, the young woman who was the apparent leader of a small, desperate band of renegade Maidus, pursuing, as Marshall did not fully understand but Goffe intuited, a hopeless path of revenge against the Whites who had slain most of their people.

"What are you thinking, Mr. Goffe?" Tom asked.

"Thinking?" Ben responded. "I'm thinking that something has to be done, though I'm damned if I know what just yet. Get some sleep, Thomas, if you're able. We're going to have to ride up there tomorrow for an inspection of the premises—see if we can get at the cause of the thing. Maybe there's someone that will talk. Might even have been witnesses. We'll report the thing as it happened, insofar as we're able to tell. If it was indeed an unprovoked attack, then there's a possibility some of the men, at least, may be brought to justice. Not mining camp justice, for I'm all too well aware of the nature of that, but the justice of civil order."

"Who'd listen to us? No one in Grass Valley or Deer Creek Dry Diggings or You Bet is going to side with the Indians and against the miners. You know that, Mr. Goffe."

Ben nodded.

"True, true. But there's a provisional legislature meeting, and we've got a provisional civil governor. And the Californians are chewing at the bit to get statehood. News of this matter can find its way clear to Washington, D.C. if we make it happen. Some attempt is better than no attempt. But oil your pistol, Tom, and then get some sleep. It could be you'll need both before tomorrow is over."

After a time, Goffe turned in also, but he was unable to sleep.

He sat up and dangled his legs over the side of the bed, fumbled for his glasses, lit a kerosene lamp, pulled on his heavy coat, and made his way back to his writing desk. After a time he dipped his pen into the ink bottle and began to write:

Grass Valley, California
February 14, 1850 (Day of St. Valentine)

Territorial Governor,
General Bennett Riley, United States Army
The Presidio of Monterey
Monterey, California

My Dearest General Riley:

This day I have received a report of a most bloody massacre of unoffending Maidu Indigenes, to wit the Usto-ma village, whose former encampment was near the mines at Chalk Bluff, to the east of here. I say *former*, because the account I have, while as yet unauthenticated, comes from a wholly reliable source, given at second hand and taken from the words of one of the apparent perpetrators, for the Indian village has been, according to my report, annihilated. The Usto-mas, half-starved and apparently unable to defend themselves, have been cruelly butchered, and not even the women and children spared.

Knowing of your profound interest in seeing to it that California is fully admitted to the Federal Union, it is my belief that you will wish to take some action in this matter. News of such a thing can not avoid finding its way to the eyes of the highest Federal authorities if it is reported via a responsible paper, and I will see to it that this happens. In my capacity as editor of the *Del Oro Star*, I will personally visit the site of the massacre tomorrow and will report all as responsibly and fairly as I am able. Having gotten at the facts to the best of my ability, I will then devote the better portion of an edition of my paper to it, with copies dispatched in all directions.

I realize how busy you must be, particularly now that the civil legislature is in session, but I most humbly request an audience with you. I believe I will be able to supply names of all or nearly all of the perpetrators.

It is for the good of California's future, I believe,

that some sort of governmental action should be quickly forthcoming.

Please advise.

Your Most Humble and Obedient Servant,
Benjamin Goffe, Editor, *Del Oro Star*

Ben read over what he had written, shook his head, and then proceeded to make two additional copies, one for Peter Burnett, the Provisional Governor in San Jose, and the other for John Sutter, himself a representative and meeting with the legislature in San Jose as time and the demands of his various business interests permitted.

February 15 dawned clear and cold. Ben was up quickly, rekindling the fire in the cast-iron stove and preparing a breakfast of bacon strips, oatmeal, and sugar, as well as coffee. When all was ready, he woke Tom Elkins.

The two men ate in near silence, consumed an entire pot of coffee, and prepared for the long ride to Chalk Bluff and the butchered village at Steephollow.

At the livery, Ben was able to procure a courier to deliver a bound packet to John Sutter in Sacramento City. From there, Goffe was certain, Sutter would see to it that the missives to Riley and Burnett reached their appointed destinations.

The rider was a Mexican youth called Jesus. He spoke very sparse English, but he was highly recommended by Red Collins and was generally thought well of about the town.

Ben paid Jesus in advance and handed him the packet containing the letters.

"News for Captain Sutter," he said. "Nothing of value. *Comprende, amigo?*"

Jesus nodded, mounted his pony, and rode slowly away, heading southward.

With that detail attended to, Ben and Tom mounted their own animals, Ben on Old Blue, and Tom on one of the balky mules, and rode eastward, on past the Rose's Ophir Hill Palace and on to the mining camp at the fork of

Greenhorn Creek, thence upcountry to the sprawling tent city of You Bet.

It was shortly before noon when they reached Belcher's Tavern. Here they tethered their mounts and went inside the big wooden-walled tent.

"Ben Goffe and Limping Tom!" Belcher called out as they entered the empty tavern. "I read your paper—it's a good one, by the wing feathers of Gawd. How long we goin' to have to wait for another?"

"Good to see you, Horace," Ben answered. "Not long, I hope. That's why we're out here, in fact. Want to take a look at what's left of that Indian village."

"And you need directions. Always could read an *hombre*'s mind. Guess the boys did a real good job on 'er, Ben. That's one bunch of thievin' Diggers as won't be stealin' no more mules or anything else. God rest 'em, but we're better off for it. Sure, I'll tell you. Ain't been out there myself, but it shouldn't be hard to find. Ought to be plenty of buzzards circlin' around. You boys want somethin' to wet your whistles? Might be you'll need it. Old Ez and the lads fairly well chewed 'em up, I guess. That was their story, anyhow. Gold strike before noon and an Injun party before dark—it's good for business, I'll tell you."

"Many thanks," Ben said, "but it's a little early for Tom and me. Newspaper men have got to keep clear heads, you know. Where is it from here, old friend?"

Belcher pulled a rolled-up, hand-drawn map from under the bar and spread the paper out.

"Okay," he said. "Here's where we be. You ride in the Grass Valley road? Then you saw a sign pointing to Lowell Hill just about a hundred yards back. Take that trail an' just follow your nose. Two miles down an' you'll come to Steephollow Crick. Cross over an' go on up another mile or so. Then take the left branch mebbe another two, three miles. Sonny Penryn told me the village was down at the bottom of the hole, I don't know where. But like I say, follow your nose an' watch for buzzards."

No vultures.
Smoke coiling up from the canyon bottom.

"Good name for a creek, isn't it, Mr. Goffe? Almost straight down, I should say."

"Steep, it is. Best we lead the animals, Tom. Down through that tangle, if one of them slips, we lose Old Blue or the mule and maybe break our necks into the bargain. . . ."

Halfway down the canyon they came to a nearly level bench—a spring, with a small amount of green grass growing about it. Here Ben and Tom decided to leave their mounts. The Percheron and the mule consented without a fuss, and the two men, working their way down the precipitous slope and clinging to wild lilac and manzanita brush, at length made it to the canyon bottom, a small meadow encircled by dense fir forest through which the stream ran, lined by alders on either side.

There were no bodies of mutilated dead lying about, and the scene was one of stillness and calm. A number of brush lodges remained, most of them small, two larger ones. And in the center of the meadow smoke was coiling up from the remains of what had apparently been a gigantic bonfire.

"It's deserted," Tom said. "I don't understand, Mr. Goffe. It's like the men came back and cleaned everything up and . . ."

"Burned the bodies?" Ben asked. "Yes, I'd say that's what happened, all right. If we could sift through the ashes, I suspect we'd find a quantity of ribs and leg bones and so forth, skulls, perhaps even portions of unburned flesh."

Tom Elkins shook his head.

"I don't get it. And what's that god-awful smell? Jesus, I just got a whiff of it."

"Roast of *homo sapiens*, I'd guess. I don't have much experience in these matters, but I'd be willing to bet that's what it is."

"Maybe the men started feeling bad about what they did and came back to make some kind of burial," Tom suggested.

"Or to get rid of the evidence," Ben said, walking about the edges of what had obviously been a great circular inferno just a few hours earlier.

"Look!" Tom called out. "There's been a bear here, Mr. Goffe—hell, there's been two bears, maybe more. Tracks all over the place."

Ben studied the marks—and found others as well, some human tracks, moccasins, the prints clearly visible in an area where the creek had recently overflowed its banks and had left a smooth siltslick.

Half-grown grizzlies, two of them, just as Marshall had said. Indians, not Whites, built this fire—a mass burial pyre. Here this morning and now gone—or watching, up on the canyonside somewhere, waiting for the return of Ez Johnson and his comrades. Maybe waiting for whatever Whitemen might chance to show up. . . .

Goffe felt sweat break out suddenly on his forehead, and he instinctively felt for his pistol, stood back, surveyed the forested walls that rose to either side of them.

"Thomas," he said, fighting to keep his voice calm, "I think we've just stumbled onto a mystery. Indians have come to bury their own, but not just any Indians. The Grizzly Cult has been here, I'd bet almost anything on it. Marshall said that Mrs. Jake had a pair of tame, half-grown bears. And that, by God, is what you've just found—their tracks. My young friend, I have the feeling we're not wanted here."

"You think they're still around somewhere, Mr. Goffe? All of a sudden I'm feeling just a little uneasy."

"That's two of us, Tom. But the chances are we'd be dead already if the Grizzlies were near. We're trampling on sacred ground, so to speak. Let's get back up the mountainside before Old Blue and the mule decide to go on home by themselves. There's nothing more to look at anyway."

The two men turned and began to walk toward the edge of the forest, and a soft wind, drawing downcanyon, brought them again the heavy, acrid odor of death.

Del Oro Star
Grass Valley, California Territory
Eighteenth of February, 1850

Dear Thomas and Elizabeth,
    Whatever insane thoughts I may have had con-

cerning the discovery of Paradise Regained in the wild, free, and beautiful land whose mountains tower into the clouds and upon whose shores the Peaceful Ocean beats have at this juncture vanished utterly. Into whatever Eden our Creator places us or allows us to place ourselves, we human creatures invariably introduce the Satanic Principle symbolized in the body of the Serpent. It is not just the gold and its impact upon the minds and spirits of the men who pursue it that is substantially responsible—no, I wish the matter were that easily explained. I think, rather, it is something inherent in human nature, something analogous to the principle of Sin Original, that, undisciplined, works its fatal will.

Where there is no well-established law, and men are allowed to govern themselves solely according to the dictates of personal morality or codes derived merely from experience and not from a traditionally imposed order of things, chaos and anarchy must invariably emerge.

Lest I turn this epistle into a protracted statement on the natural *condition of humanity*, let me explain that I have just now returned from a burial—that of my faithful and innocent assistant printer, Thomas Elkins, known here in the mining areas as Limping Tom, owing to an unfortunate accident that produced in the man a somewhat ungainly gait. I could find no one willing to dig poor Tom's grave, and so I have been obliged to dig it myself. I was able to procure a rough pine coffin, and therein I have placed him and so interred him. A good Mormon named Red Collins, proprietor of a general store in town, arrived in time to assist me in shoveling the wet earth back into the pit, and thereafter he read a passage or two both from the *New Testament* and from the *Book* of his own faith.

We two comprised the total number of those in attendance, though as we were leaving the cemetery, which I almost believe is growing faster than the town itself, we encountered Miss Anastasia Atwood, the gun-toting owner of one of the local bordellos, in the company of two of her female employees. These three, whose acquaintance with Limping Tom was but slight, had felt at least a twinge of conscience and so had come to pay their last respects.

Let me summarize what has transpired since I wrote to you last, since all things invariably follow, one from another, with cause and effect inextricably intertwined, whether or not we are aware of the correspondence until after the fact.

Limping Tom had come into my employ with the full recommendation of Captain John Sutter, and together he and I managed to master the press sufficient to have produced two editions of the *Star*, copies enclosed. The first of these was a major success, having sold out immediately. And thereafter the sequence of cause and effect came into play that resulted in Tom's death—and which, incidentally, has transformed Benjamin Goffe into the most hated man in the Northern Mines. Perhaps this latter will pass when the men begin to come to their senses, I do not know.

We were visited by James Marshall, the initial discoverer of gold in this region, and from his lips we gained the story entitled "Good Samaritans," p. one. The man seems fated, though I do not say so in the paper, to wander forever like Ahasuerus, the Cursed Jew who declined, out of fear, to provide water to the Savior as He bore the Cross of all our salvations. In a metaphorical way, I can almost see a certain justice in this curse of Marshall's, for in his casual act of discovery, the Satanic Serpent was most certainly unloosed in this land. And yet I know the man and find him to be honest, kind, and patient, very sympathetic to the needs and desires of his fellow humans. So the curse has been laid upon one who most certainly does not in any way deserve it—unless he is being punished for sins committed long before he came to this land, and that I find to be beyond belief.

The "good Samaritans," whom I did not identify, were none other than those Indian vigilantes I wrote you of earlier. It is not a wild rumor but a thing based on fact, and the leader is indeed the Maidu woman Marshall calls "Mrs. Jake," the wife to a halfbreed Coloma Maidu who was Marshall's friend and employee before the massacre, two years since, of the Indian village wherein he lived. This Mrs. Jake, whose tribal name is apparently Woman of the Acorns, appears not only to be leading her band but also engaged upon a vendetta against those who murdered her kinsmen. Marshall did not *know* this, and neither do I; but my powers of intuition tell me that I am correct in my assessment of the matter. Several of the men who participated in that reprehensible massacre are now dead, and the coincidence is simply too great. These men, I have learned, have all been found with their features slashed horribly, as though a grizzly had taken part. This, I have learned, is the mark of the Grizzly Shaman of the primitive religion practiced by the Indians, a thing called simply *Kuksu*, a word whose meaning I have not been able to discover.

Shortly following Marshall's departure from Grass Valley, another massacre occurred—an Indian village close by the mining area of Red Dog and You Bet. And the ringleader, whom I have had the small pleasure of meeting, and the butt of my article about wrist-wrestling in the *Star's* second edition, was apparently also the leader of the mob that massacred Mrs. Jake's village two years ago. That coincidence is not so startling as you might think, however, for as the parable reads, the leopard does not change his spots. In any case, these are hardly the only two massacres that have occurred, for as I think I told you earlier, *wild Injuns* are fair game and are dealt with as such, trophies to be taken on occasional Sabbath Day outings by miners with real or imagined grudges against the natives.

Limping Tom and I visited the site of this latest massacre and found that the bodies had all been placed in a huge pyre and thus had been consumed by flames. And I have reason to believe that the act was performed by Mrs. Jake's wandering band of vengeance-seekers. I knew her group to be fairly close by, since they rescued Marshall from a lynch party, and I have other, more compelling evidence as well.

So Tom and I printed our account of the massacre, naming a dozen of the men responsible, as our lead story for the second edition of the *Star*.

Again the paper sold out immediately, but the good-will and curiosity which greeted the first edition became suddenly transformed into a species of cold hatred toward myself and, to a lesser extent, toward Tom as well. Those who had acted friendly toward us now turned away, their eyes avoiding ours. Insults were hurled at us from the street outside our offices. One copy of the paper, smeared with the blood of some unfortunate beast (at least I hope that's what it was) someone tacked to the front door.

There was no celebration that evening, as you can imagine. Instead we found it politic to lock and double-bolt our doors. Tom was frightened, I could see that. Nevertheless, he assured me that he intended to stick it out, to stay with me whatever the consequences. Now I curse myself for not giving him a proper bonus, along with my heartfelt thanks, and sending him on his way back to Captain Sutter—for, had I done that, Limping Tom would still be alive.

At some time before midnight, we became aware of the smell of smoke. Having slept fully dressed and with our weapons beside us, we dashed out into the front offices to find fire leaping up the exterior timbers.

Fortunately, we had three oaken barrels full of water, and with a pair of buckets we were somehow able to extinguish the blaze. It was at this point that the vandals, seeing their work come to nothing, emerged, apparently intending to try yet again. The men, five of them as certainly as I was able to determine, were masked—and yet I am positive that one was none other than Ezra Johnson, the architect of the massacres specified above. He, more than anyone else, would have sufficient motive.

Gunfire erupted in the darkness, and Tom and I dived for cover and began to return our assailants what they were giving us, firing at the flashes of their own weapons.

The battle must not have lasted more than a minute, and I doubt that any of the vandals was struck by a pistol ball. But when the sordid little affair was over, I turned to find Limping Tom dead, a ball having entered his head just above the left eye.

The gunfire apparently did not attract the attention of our local sheriff or *alcalde* or whatever he is, for the man, as I learned the following day, was drunkenly snoring at Miss Atwood's whorehouse, two miles away from the scene. That, at least, was the story.

And so this day I have buried Limping Tom Elkins, a loyal, hardworking, and gentle young man—one whose disposition should never have brought him to the Northern Mines of California.

I have earlier endeavored to make contact with the territorial authorities, to wit both the civil and the military governors, and I have received word from Captain Sutter in Sacramento City that General Bennett Riley is expected in that settlement on the twenty-first of the present month.

For this reason, in the hope that the primary official of the Federal Government will wish to exercise some species of control over a situation that has passed beyond anarchy, I will ride southward tomorrow in the hope of gaining an audience.

It is possible, and I do not say this out of a sense of the dramatic, that an attempt may be made on my life—and for that reason I will post this missive before departing. If all goes well, however, I will write you again, immediately upon my arrival at Sacramento. Due to the almost whimsical movement of the mails in this region, it is altogether possible and is even quite likely that you will receive that letter well ahead of this one, if not at the same time. Some mail, as you are no doubt aware, travels shipboard to Panama and thence eastward, while other messages are sometimes dispatched overland, should the military or other "trustworthy" agent be moving in that direction. As I write this, I cannot help wondering if *any* of the letters I have sent you since my arrival in St. Louis last summer have reached you. I have not, as of this date, received any mail from you, though I have hoped for some word.

Say nothing of any of this to Etta, in case she remains in New Haven and has not seen fit to depart for her old stamping grounds in Europe. Whatever I may have said earlier about the possibility of a reconciliation at some indefinite future point, I realize now that it can never be. I am much changed, brother and sister. That is to be expected, however, for this "savage paradise" affects all who come to it, whether to a greater or a lesser extent.

Despite my present difficulties, I have an inclination that I will stay in this region permanently. After what I have said previously in this letter, you will not be able to understand what I am saying now. I do not understand it either, I assure you.

The unholy beauty of this land is so strangely discordant with the petty abominations committed by those who live here. . . .

As I say, I will write again when I have reached the relative safety of Mr. Sutter's.

Your Most Loving Brother,
Ben

The light that filtered in through the printshop window was still a thin grayness, and Benjamin Goffe, working by the glow of his coal-oil lamp, was just fitting the caps to his Colt Walker .44 pistol when he heard a light rapping at the office door.

"Ben!" came the voice. "It's Red Collins an' the Rose. Open up, man!"

Ben unbolted the door.

Anastasia Atwood, he noted, was out of uniform—dressed like a man, in San Francisco blue denim, the storm of her copper hair hidden beneath a wide-brimmed Mexican hat.

"Professor," the Rose of You Bet began, her thin lips pinching off the words, "you've got more troubles than you know—and I'd have, too, if the boys knew I was down here telling you about it."

"It's the God's own truth, Benjamin," Red Collins agreed. "Listen to what the lady's sayin' now."

Miss Atwood glanced sideways at the keeper of the general store, momentarily annoyed at having been interrupted.

"Ez Johnson, Sonny Penryn, and a beardless wonder named Lindley, the same one you identified in the paper, spent most of last night at the Palace. They came in late, their eyes gleaming like they'd just managed to bed a sow grizzly. Four others with them, in fact. Like I say, they were in high spirits and intent on getting even higher. Asked for the best rum in the house and female companionship to go with it. . . ."

"Get to the point, Rose, damn it," Red Collins grumbled.

"Quiet your tongue, you half-deaf bacon pusher. The Professor's got to understand the whole thing. Anyway, I asked the boys what was up, and Ez just laughed and shook his head. That son of a bitch said I couldn't get pregnant if I got had by half the United States Army, the short-peckered dirt-washer!"

Red Collins was rubbing at his eyes.

"So what's the news?" Ben asked.

"I'm getting to it. Just keep hold of the family jewels, Professor. So I brought out the rum, and presently I'd gotten the drift of what was up. Before long they was all either crashed cold from drinking or was sleeping off what my girls did for them. And that's when I slipped away and come down to wake up Red here."

Ben stared at the Rose of You Bet and then turned to Collins.

"Apparently the boys are fixin' to lynch you," the store-keeper said.

"Exactly," the Rose of You Bet agreed. "Just like I already told the Professor."

"They've got wind that you're ridin' out today—down to Sacramento to palaver with the General," Red continued. "Fixin' to bushwhack you or string you up."

"Could be they'll need a strong rope," Ben replied.

"Stay home, Professor," Miss Atwood suggested. "Keep

the door barred, and stay inside. This girl done told Sheriff Fischer I'd cut off his water if he didn't tend to business like he's supposed to—and that means keepin' the peace. We pay the worthless little bastard to maintain order."

"Ain't a sheriff alive can do much when the lead hounds get a hard-on, though," Red put in, shaking his head. "Excuse the language, Rose."

"Might of heard it before," she shrugged. "Look, Professor, there's some that will stand with you if you use your noodle. Don't go riding off today, that's all."

Goffe shook his head.

"My thanks to both of you for putting me on the alert," he said, "but I've got a trip to make, and I'm not going to allow scum like Johnson to get in my way."

"Your hearing's worse than I thought," the Rose insisted. "You go wandering off today, and that's probably the last we'll see of you until someone finds the body."

"Ben," Collins agreed, "the Rose is dead right. I know there's not five men in the town could hold you down if you're determined, but for Christ's sake, *think* before you go tootin' off."

"I have thought," Goffe said, reaching for his fully loaded pistol and thrusting it into his holster. "I've lost one friend already to that bunch of murdering bastards, and something has to be done."

"Your head's made up?" the Rose asked.

"It is."

"Then if a bluejay yells, start kicking the sides of that plowhorse of yours," Collins nodded.

"And stay off the Cherry Crick Trail," the Rose added. "Likely that's where they'll be looking for you. Might be there now, with all the time we've used up talking."

"Here," Ben said, handing the heavy envelope containing his letter to Tom and Elizabeth to Red Collins. "Wait until tomorrow, and then send Jesus off to Marysville with it. A letter to my sister and her husband. And this should cover the courier's wages."

He pressed some money into Red Collins' hand.

The day was completely clear and strangely springlike as Ben guided Old Blue away from town, south along the

Cherry Creek Trail toward LaBarr Meadows. From there he turned the Percheron upslope, angling toward the long ridge of Osborne Hill.

From the crest he looked eastward at the long white line of the Sierra Nevada, the mountains distant and brilliant in full sunlight, the range blending downward to blue-white of forested ridges where snow still lay deep beneath the pines and firs to the gray-green sprawl of foothill canyons and slopes of mixed forest of oak and pine and fir.

"Ungodly beautiful," Ben told Old Blue, slapping the big horse along the side of the neck and then leaning forward to scratch his ears. "Well, my friend, we've come a long way together. Let's get on down now and see if that big fish is still in Woodpecker Creek."

A pair of redtailed hawks drifted through the sky, and squirrels darted away as the horse and its rider descended the slopes to the small meadow where two empty Maidu lodges squatted against the earth. Grazing mule deer looked up at the rider, for a moment uncertain whether to watch or to flee. Then the animals bounded off in long, fluid leaps, and were gone into tangles of fir, wild lilac, and manzanita brush.

Ben and Old Blue passed down through a narrow ravine that led to the creek bottom and the mazes of grapevines that clung tenaciously to alders and cedars beside the roaring water of the stream.

Ben drew his horse to a halt and dismounted, scrambled down to the big flat-topped rock where he had stood nearly two months earlier, and gazed into the rushing blue-gray water.

He had not as yet detected any sign of the big trout when the first of three rifle balls struck him.

11

Now He Is Mine

February-March, 1850

SIX: *Thou shalt not kill thy body by working in the rain, even though thou shalt make enough to buy physic and attendance with. Neither shalt thou kill thy neighbor's body in a duel, for by keeping cool thou canst save his life and thy conscience. Neither shalt thou destroy thyself by getting "tight," nor "stewed," nor "high," nor "corned," nor "half-seas over," nor "three sheets in the wind," by drinking smoothly down "brandy slings," "gin cock-tails," "whiskey punches," "rum toddies," nor "egg-nogs." Neither shalt thou suck "mint juleps" nor "sherry cobblers" through a straw, nor gurgle from a bottle the raw material, nor take it neat from a decanter, for while thou art swallowing down thy purse and thy coat from off thy back, thou art burning the coat from off thy stomach; and if thou couldst see the houses and lands, and gold dust, and home comforts already lying there—a huge pile—thou shouldst feel a choking in thy throat; and when to that thou add'st thy crooked walking and hiccupping; of lodging in the gutter, of broiling in the sun, of prospect holes full of water, and of shafts and ditches from which thou hast emerged like a drowning rat, thou wilt feel disgusted with thyself, and inquire, "Is thy servant a dog that he doeth these things?" Verily, I will say, farewell old bottle; I will kiss thy gurgling lips no more; and thou, slings, cock-tails, punches, smashes, cobblers, nogs, toddies, sangarees and juleps, forever, farewell. Thy remembrance shames me; henceforth I will cut thy acquaintance; and headaches, tremblings, heart-burnings, blue-devils, and all the unholy catalogue of evils which follow in thy train.*

My wife's smiles and my children's merry-hearted laugh
shall charm and reward me for having the manly firmness
and courage to say: "No! I wish thee an eternal farewell!"

The Pano Maidus had adopted the expedient of travel-
ing by night when they were in the vicinity of *Wawlem*
settlements, as they were now within the watershed of
Bear River, and particularly when the weather was fine
and the chances of coming upon groups of prospectors out
along the streams was increased. Acorn Girl had made a
point of establishing contact with whatever Nishinam villages existed in the areas through which they wandered
but seldom stayed very long or very close. However sympathetic the people might be to their cause, the Panos did
not relish the danger this contact might put the villagers
into. But Ooti's people nonetheless stopped to trade for
whatever provisions they might find, as well as for
intelligence.

Thus it was that, having traversed the ridge and come
into the long, narrow canyon of the smaller north branch
of the river at dawn, smoke from still-burning lodges
at Usto-ma village drifted up the canyon to them, an odor
distinctly different from the normal smoke of cooking fires
and one that they all recognized instinctively, so that the
whole group stopped as if on a signal that had not, in fact,
been given. The Panos stood or sat their mounts for a
moment as if all simultaneously paralyzed.

"It has happened again," Hurt Eagle said at last, voicing
the thought that none of the rest of them had the courage
to utter. "I am very old, and I had hoped that I would be
in Valley Above before I saw another thing such as this
must be."

A faint sigh passed through the entire band, and Small
Ears, clutching the little girl that had been born to her
and Tied-wing before the last Burning season, began to
weep softly. Tied-wing took her into his arms, but his eyes
remained on Acorn Girl, waiting for some signal. Ooti's
face was hard as ice, and her whole body felt to her again
as if it had been turned to stone. For the second time she
seemed to have become two separate beings, the one

frozen with horror, the other, far back and distant from
her, moving at remarkable speed, making judgments, commenting upon courses of action.

She found Tied-wing's eyes upon her, and she nodded
to him and then to the other young men in the group. She
asked these to come with her to see what they could do for
the burned village, sending the rest to make camp upon
a ridge high above the stream and well back into the
trees, so as to prevent discovery.

She and the young men set out downstream, leading
one horse apiece, but Hurt Eagle insisted on coming along
this time, explaining that he might be needed to treat any
wounded. The grizzlies also wanted to follow, and Ooti's
best efforts to persuade them to stay with Crane were of
no avail. Knowingly disobeying, Before and After trailed
behind, keeping clear of possible discipline.

The winter sun was not up yet, but morning was advancing and the light was bright enough for colors to be
visible by the time they reached the site of the ruined
village. They approached cautiously, although there was
no sound from the encampment to suggest that any of the
destroyers remained, nor any other life for that matter.
The stench of burning flesh was intense, drifting up to
them on the morning breeze. Acorn Girl had to retreat as
far as she could into the stony silence within her to avoid
gagging or screaming.

The visual horror was even worse—bodies lying in every possible position, old people and women and children
in postures of arrested flight. Young men, fighting back as
well as they could without benefit of Whiteman's weapons, had been cut down in their tracks. A woman lay
curled on her side, clutching an infant as if both had fallen
asleep, except that the back of the woman's head was
gone, and the infant's throat had been slit. And many of
the bodies mutilated in unthinkable ways—both men and
women with genitals cut out, breasts gone, one completely headless body, its sex and age no longer distin-
guishable.

The embers of burned huts still glowed, and in these
were charred bodies and smoldering heaps of blankets and
clothing. Other lodges remained untouched, incongruously

empty, as though their owners had simply walked away from them, intending to return at any moment.

Acorn Girl instinctively turned away from the scene, her eyes searching the perimeters of the village.

Hurt Eagle moved among the bodies, now and again bending over to see if life yet remained in one or another.

Now Acorn Girl began to take notice of a faint sound she had been vaguely aware of for some time, a tiny, barely audible wailing which stopped and started. She followed the noise away from the center of the village, pushed her way into a dense tangle of brush, and found a boy of perhaps thirteen winters crouched as far back into his burrow as he was capable of going, staring at her with the round, shiny eyes of a trapped animal. He flinched away from her, and she saw then that he held a baby no more than a month old, his hand across its mouth and nose as the tiny face reddened with rage at having its cry stifled.

"I am Ooti," she said softly. "You are safe now."

The boy did not speak, and she repeated her words soothingly.

"I am Acorn Girl. We are the same people, you and I. We will care for you now."

She held out her hand to him, coaxed him forward, and finally took the infant from him.

"She is my sister," the boy said without tonal modulation, as if speaking from a dream. "I have tried to keep her quiet, but I have nothing to feed her, and she has been crying all night."

"We will help her. The *Wawlems* are gone now, and you can come out. Are you hurt? Is the little one?"

The boy shook his head slowly.

Acorn Girl continued to speak calmly, amazed at her gentle voice when inside her skull and behind her eyes flames leaped, and something was screaming and screaming.

She backed out of the brush, holding the tiny infant, which now wailed uncontrollably. With her other hand she led forth the boy—not back to the village, but rather to a tree out of sight of the massacre scene, to where the Pano Maidu horses were tied. Here she told him to wait for her, repeating the instruction until she was certain it had penetrated the daze that still seemed to block the child's consciousness.

She went quickly to find Hurt Eagle and send him to watch the young ones, but the ancient shaman and the others were already returning to the horses. Elk's Tooth carried a woman who was unconscious but whom Hurt Eagle had determined still to have a flicker of life in her body.

The Panos conferred briefly and decided that Acorn Girl and Hurt Eagle should return to the rest of the band, taking with them the three Usto-mas. Elk's Tooth, Crooked Knee, Tied-wing, and Kingfisher would remain behind to build a funeral pyre to dispose decently of the maimed corpses of what had been, the day before, a living village. When the *Ustu* time came in the autumn, if the Panos themselves had managed to survive that long, they would mourn these strangers properly, along with their own dead.

Ooti lay awake long that night, staring up into the darkness of her lean-to shelter. The band had decided to remain in their present encampment for a few days, for that morning, as the thick cloud of smoke from the funeral pyre rolled up into the sky, three additional survivors, two young men and a girl, had straggled into the area, and Hurt Eagle thought it possible that yet a few more might remain in the vicinity.

The Pano camp, halfway between Steephollow Creek and the snow-blanketed crest of Chalk Bluff Ridge, was hidden in an offshoot ravine, a small, amphitheater-like area surrounded by huge sugarpines and dotted with clumps of leafless azalea and wild lilac. Several springs gathered at this point, and from where the creek they formed dropped out and down over the canyon wall, the Panos were afforded a clear view of much of the surrounding welter of forested ridge and ravine. Miners were all about them, working the lower portion of Steephollow and Bear River, and along the western faces of the bluffs a large settlement of Whites existed, much like Coloma after the discovery of the gold. But for the moment, away from the stream bottoms and the gravel deposits above them, and away from the ridgecrests as well, where mule and wagon trails ran, they were relatively safe from discovery.

No fires could be lighted during the day, however, and only the smallest possible cooking fires were allowed to burn after dark.

The two bears, Before and After, shared Acorn Girl's shelter, one lying to either side of her, and Hurt Eagle snored from beyond Bear-who-comes-after, for he and Crane slept here as well. The boy from the Usto-ma village lay between Hurt Eagle and the grizzly, and Acorn Girl could see, in the faint sheen of reflected moonlight, that he had turned in his sleep and had thrown his arms over the bear's shoulders, at the same time burying his face in the rough fur.

Acorn Girl had not questioned him very much, thinking it best for him to recall only as much as he was capable of dealing with for the time being, but she had found out that his name was Raccoon and that the infant girl, whom Small Ears had immediately upon their arrival in camp taken to nurse beside her own child, was called Little Basket. Of his other relatives, Raccoon had chosen not to speak at all, and when Ooti had tried to probe into the events of the day of the massacre, he had only been able to shudder, and speech had seemed beyond him.

From the others who drifted into the Pano camp later, however, Acorn Girl learned enough for her to be sure that one of the leaders of the raid had been Ezra Johnson, for the Usto-ma girl, Kauda the Snakebite Dancer, particularly remembered the strange, seemingly lidless honey-colored eyes of the man who had dragged her from hiding and had made a brief attempt to rape her before she had clawed at his face and made an escape into the twilit forest.

The two young Usto-ma men, Slow Rabbit and Grass-hopper Man, had spoken at length of the massacre, their words streaming out in a torrent of horror and confusion and hatred. From their descriptions of the *Wawlem* Devils, Acorn Girl became fairly well convinced that the younger Penryn, as well, was among the murderers.

"It is a nightmare," she thought now in the darkness, "and I am dreaming it again. Must I dream it over and over?"

But now, at least, she was certain that all three Whitemen

whom she most certainly intended to kill were close about her—Lindley somewhere along the North Fork of the American River and Johnson and the younger Penryn near at hand. Her enemies were about her, but they did not know either of her presence or her purpose. Not even Lindley, at the time of Marshall's rescue, would have been able to recognize her. Indeed, perhaps none of the three remembered her at all.

But she remembered them and would never rest easily until she had seen their death throes.

Kill all Wawlems. That is the only way we can have back our sanity, our life.

The voice in her head. . . . She lay with her fists clenched into balls and ached with hatred. And hard upon the words that had come to her out of the darkness within emerged the image of Jim Marshall's kind solemn face, or Sutter's beaming round one. She had no anger for such as these. They were White, but they were also human. And even Pine-nut-eater had been half *Wawlem.*

The instinctive, simple solution, then, was not possible—and the numbers of Whitemen had increased so enormously that there seemed to be no end to them. The Nishinam world was becoming ever smaller, more closed off. The sun was dying in their skies.

But the path to revenge was still open, and that was her path.

Some are only fools, and some are vicious. It's important to know the difference.

"Why do I bother about the difference?" she thought again.

Tears of rage, of frustration, of grief and weariness squeezed painfully from between her eyelids. Out of the darkness the boy, Raccoon, moaned and then subsided back into sleep.

You may think the world is becoming very bad, Ooti, but it is only what Olelbis dreams.

The words of Pano, spoken in another lifetime—the night before her infant sons had been named in honor of the Spirit Bear.

The force of her rage turned now upon Him Who Sits Above as well as upon *Wawlems,* and she wished insanely that she had World Maker close beside her so that she might kill him.

"Why do you make us live in this evil dream of yours?" she whispered.

No answer to her question came forth from the darkness, and when at last she slept, exhausted, toward dawn, she did not dream at all, but only remembered hearing the voice of the wind, the timeless, inhuman, infinitely sad notes of the pine boughs responding to the rush of air.

During the next few days the young men seethed with anger and spoke of making a revenge raid upon one or another of the little settlements of miners downstream along the river, but Ooti did not join into the discussions. Instead, she helped Hurt Eagle with the wounded. One of the young men, Ene, Grasshopper Man, had taken a ball in the thigh, an injury not serious in itself but needing to be guarded from infection, and the woman they had carried from the village did not regain consciousness until the second day, at which time she began a thin wailing, her eyes staring off at nothing anyone else could see. This keening continued until Acorn Girl feared her own mind would shatter from the sound.

In addition to the wounded, the remaining survivors were emaciated, for all the game in the area had disappeared with the heavy influx of miners, and the Usto-ma people had been hampered in their acorn harvest by the presence of the *Wawlems* as well.

Hurt Eagle performed the best healing ceremony he could manage under the circumstances, and Acorn Girl packed Ene's wound with herbs. The old shaman tried many methods to bring the wailing woman back from wherever she wandered, both sucking out various evil objects, her pains, *omeya*, and sending his own spirit in search of hers while in a trance, but nothing seemed to change her condition. At last, exhausted, he gave up, speaking to Ooti of what he had discovered in his wanderings upon awaking from his dreams.

"Her heart is already gone," he said solemnly. "I do not know what she saw on that day, but she does not wish to return to life, and so she will not."

The thin wailing went on as before, the eyes staring into nothingness, and Acorn Girl bent her head in acknowledgement of Hurt Eagle's words. She had spoken to the woman, calling her by the name supplied by Kauda, the young girl. "Wawim," Acorn Girl called out repeatedly, coaxing the spirit to return, but that had done no more than Hurt Eagle's attempts. Ooti recognized the truth of what the ancient doctor said now, that the woman did not wish to live, and so would die no matter what they did.

"And yet I wished to die," Acorn Girl whispered, her head still bent. "You called my heart back to my body, Hurt Eagle, but I did not wish to return after . . ."

"Yes," Hurt Eagle agreed, "but you were returned to us for a reason. It was the will of Pano and Oleli."

Acorn Girl nodded, but the explanation did not suffice. For a moment she felt utterly lost, utterly helpless. At length she walked away from the camp to escape the sound of the unfortunate woman's dumb misery, heading toward a clearing on top of the ridge, from which the surrounding country was visible for miles. The sun dropped into a cloudbank that was growing in the west, and the whole flared briefly with red and gold before sinking into the dull purple of winter sunsets and fading to gray twilight. In the canyons below, here and there Ooti could see the red eye of a campfire where prospectors were settled on the streams.

"They multiply like maggots in rotten meat," said a voice at her shoulder, and Acorn Girl turned, startled, to find Crooked Knee standing beside her.

"They will not stop until they have destroyed everything," he continued, his eyes fixed on the spots of fire in the canyons. "That is what all the young men are saying, Ooti. We are saying, also, that we must drive all of them out of our land now, before there is nothing left. Tied-wing and the others, as well as the Usto-mas, want to know what you say about this."

"I say that Tied-wing and the others are fools, and you as well, Crooked Knee," Acorn Girl snapped, turning away, surprised at the vehemence of her own anger.

"We want you to lead us against the *Wawlem* settlements," said a different voice, and Acorn Girl saw what she hadn't noticed before, the figure of Raccoon standing a few feet behind Crooked Knee. "I want to kill every Whiteman in the world," the boy added, his voice shaking with anger. "Your people say you are a great leader, Ooti, and that you have already killed many of them."

"I have killed those who deserved killing. If you and Crooked Knee and the other young men wish to go against the settlements and kill whatever *Wawlems* you happen to find, then I will have to continue alone to find those who need to die—because the rest of you won't be alive to help me," Acorn Girl said, her own rage still rising. "You will be in Valley Above, licking your wounds. Go away from me now. I don't have time to talk to insane people."

The warrior and the boy withdrew, obviously crestfallen at Acorn Girl's sharp response, and she sat alone for a time, gazing out over the land that was infested, just as Crooked Knee had said, with the strange and seemingly mindlessly destructive race. She had not known until the moment Crooked Knee spoke how she would respond to the request that she had known was coming, and she was still surprised at the way she had, in fact, reacted. Her words made sense—a group of seven warriors could do nothing except commit suicide by going against the White settlements, and the move was certain to bring further massacres upon innocent villages of her people. But the strength and immediacy of her fury puzzled and troubled her.

Acorn Girl heard a heavy crashing through the under-brush and turned to see both her half-grown grizzlies charging through the twilight toward her. The first to reach her reared up onto its hind legs and put its huge paws against her shoulders, nearly pushing her over. The second groaned and shoved at her with its head.

Ooti laughed.

"My two strange sons," she said, stroking both shaggy heads at once. "You must remember that you now weigh four times as much as I do. You keep thinking that you are still little cubs, but you can't get into my lap any more. Now you must be still and help me think out things."

*   *   *

When Acorn Girl returned to the camp long after dark, the woman was no longer keening. Hurt Eagle, who with Crane still sat beside the body, glanced up when Ooti approached.

"Her heart has gone away now forever," the shaman said. "She is on her way to *Hipining Kawyaw* to be with her family."

Acorn Girl nodded, feeling a sense of relief more than anything else.

Tied-wing and Kingfisher accompanied the Usto-mas, Snakebite Dancer and Slow Rabbit, back to the remains of the village, bearing the woman's body with them, and buried it among the ashes of her people.

Acorn Girl dreamed that night of Pano, the first such dream she had had in a long time.

The Bear Spirit sat by a fire and smoked a pipe, and didn't seem to notice her standing before him for some time. When he did look up, though, his expression was both stern and terribly sad.

Pano gestured behind him, and Ooti saw, for the first time, Pine-nut-eater, who seemed to be a long way off at the top of a mountain, even though she could see him clearly, could see that he looked back at her with eyes that appeared to be full of night and pain at the same time that he struggled to step away from her, off the top of the mountain.

She saw, then, why he couldn't move further, for there were cords binding his ankles, cords like silvery skeins of moonlight, and these led toward her. Looking down, she perceived that the same bindings encircled her own feet.

"You see?" asked Pano. "You have kept him here with you for far too long. He should have gone to the Upper Meadow, but you won't free him, and that is bad—because there isn't much for a dead person to do in this world."

The Grizzly Spirit now handed her a knife, and she understood what she was to do. She leaned down to sever the tie, but then she looked up and saw Pine-nut-eater so far away from her already, and she couldn't bring herself to perform the act that would allow him to go off forever. She was filled with grief and a new sense of aloneness, and she began to weep.

"Oh well," growled Pano, *"I see that you are not strong enough right now. Never mind. I will send you something. You must keep your eyes open for it. Then, after a while, you will let your husband go as you should."*

"How will I know what it is?" Ooti asked.

"You will know. It will have my mark."

Pano yawned enormously, then, his mouth opening like a chasm, and Acorn Girl awoke, her cheeks still damp with tears from the dream.

They were moving again, westward now, in the general direction of the sacred mountains of *Estawm Yan,* for Acorn Girl, listening to the counsel of Hurt Eagle, had concluded that her band might best find refuge among the last low hills at the verge of the great *koyo,* the Sacramento Valley, in the general vicinity of the Taisida, Kulkumish, and Tonimbutuk villages. And further, by means of passing through the Tsekankan, Pan-pakan, and Yamaku villages as they journeyed, beyond the White mining town of Grass Valley and on down the Yuba River, Acorn Girl reasoned that she would be able to acquire considerable information as to the locations most likely free of the ever-increasing populations of *Wawlems.*

Elk's Tooth, scouting ahead, returned with word that the Grass Valley settlement was far larger than they had supposed, complete with permanent wooden buildings and a number made of brick. It was considerably larger than the White settlements of Chalk Bluff or Red Dog, and there were other, smaller villages round about, including another large town with permanent buildings, just to the north, on Deer Creek.

With this unwelcome news in mind, the Pano Maidus and their new Usto-ma friends moved southward, over a low ridge and down into a system of thickly wooded canyons, following a rivulet that within two or three miles, by virtue of other rivulets springs emptying into it, had grown into a considerable creek that rushed along through a bedrock ravine and lined with alders and firs that were tangled with mats of climbing grapevines.

Perhaps they would be able to visit the Tsekankan and

the two Yuba River villages at another time—when she and Tied-wing would be able to ride back, just the two of them, and so make their inquiries without arousing the suspicions of the White miners.

In any case, Acorn Girl concluded, the edge of the great *koyo* would provide the best place to spend the remainder of the rainy season. During the Big Summer Moon of *Nem-diyoko* would come the time when she would hunt down Johnson and Lindley and Penryn's brother. And when that was finished, perhaps she would indeed listen to the words of Crooked Knee and the others and make a final attack against the White settlement at Chalk Bluff. Had Hurt Eagle not said the sun was dying in Maidu skies? If annihilation were to be the ultimate lot of her people in any case, what better way into Valley Above than to die in battle against terrific odds?

They found the huge horse before they discovered its rider, for as the band moved downstream, seeking a hidden and abundant place to rest for the remainder of the day before resuming their journey toward nightfall, they came upon the beast as large as two normal horses—one such as Marshall had used at the Kolo-ma sawmill, the animals in harness to draw heavy loads. But this horse, though riderless, was saddled and bridled. He came trotting forward to greet the others of his own kind until, catching sight of the two grizzlies lumbering along beside Acorn Girl, he shied back and cantered downstream and out of sight.

What could this mean?

The band halted to discuss the development, Acorn Girl consulting with Hurt Eagle and Tied-wing.

"His rider is nearby, or else the horse wouldn't be here fitted out the way he is," Tied-wing concluded.

Acorn Girl agreed, adding her own guess that the rider must be unaccompanied, since it was the nature of horses to stay close to one another.

"The rider is nearby," Hurt Eagle said as a statement of fact rather than as conjecture. "He is injured and needs help."

"Even if this person is injured, we know that any *Wawlem* might be dangerous," Crooked Knee put in.

"Hurt Eagle and I will search for this *Wawlem* alone," Ooti decided. "He is only one, and it is easier for two people to remain invisible than it is for all of us."

Once again it was necessary to persuade the two grizzlies to stay behind, much to their displeasure. But Crane undertook to pet them and to bribe them with small portions of fresh venison, thus transferring their loyalties momentarily from Acorn Girl to herself.

Ooti and Hurt Eagle, proceeding cautiously, did not have any difficulty in discovering the injured man. Just beyond a bend in the creek, at a place where the canyon was narrow and came down steeply to the streambed, they again saw the big horse standing with his head down and pulling at a clump of bunchgrass that grew next to the water. The horse raised his head to look at the girl and the old man and then, not seeing the grizzlies, went back to his grazing.

Close to where the horse stood was the form of a man, sprawled face-down on the bank, motionless beside a big boulder, one hand dragging in the current. Ooti and Hurt Eagle watched from the cover of a screen of brush for a time, even though the old shaman insisted that there was no danger. At length, satisfied that the man was either dead or unconscious, Acorn Girl moved forward, Hurt Eagle beside her.

At that moment something flashed by her out of the brush, the small, thin form of Raccoon driving in upon the inert figure beside the creek. Before Acorn Girl or Hurt Eagle could react, the boy had reached the man and was dragging at his clothing in an attempt to turn him over.

Ooti sprang toward the boy as Raccoon, giving up the attempt to turn the body onto its back, pulled the head up by its hair and raised a knife, drawing it back preparatory to plunging the blade into the exposed throat.

The Pano leader cried out, a wordless scream, and the boy looked up, hesitating for the moment Acorn Girl needed to spring upon him and roll him back and away from the unconscious man. Raccoon struggled fiercely, silently, his teeth clenched and his face contorted with rage and frustration, but Ooti held his knife hand and pinned him to the ground until his body suddenly relaxed under her and convulsed into sobs, his head turning to one side and tears forming in his eyes.

Acorn Girl eased her grip then, and the boy rolled onto his belly, crouched, gasped.

"Why did you not let me kill him, Ooti?" he cried out in jerky tones. "He is *Wawlem*. I want to kill them all!"

"I don't know, Raccoon, I don't know," she answered—and realized that it was the truth she had spoken. Something instinctive had moved her to save the stranger's life, what remained of it, and she did not know what it was.

Hurt Eagle was already examining the man, and he and Acorn Girl then combined their efforts to roll him onto his back, for he was the largest person that either had ever encountered.

"Three bullets have entered him," Hurt Eagle said, half talking to himself. "One in his shoulder and two in his back."

They unbuttoned the man's jacket and his shirt to expose the chest, which was covered with thick, curly, silver-brown hair.

Acorn Girl drew in her breath in surprise.

"He is like a bear!" she said. "He is as big as one, almost, and he also has fur."

Hurt Eagle grunted, not nearly so impressed as Acorn Girl.

Raccoon turned away and stared into the moving water of the stream, refusing to look at the Whiteman.

"Here is where one bullet came out," Hurt Eagle muttered, finding the wound at the side of the ribcage. "That one must have traveled along a bone. That wound has not hurt him too much, but he has bled a great deal."

The fur of the chest was, in fact, matted with blood, something which had not been evident against the dark fabric of the clothing. There was another exit wound near the clavicle, but neither Hurt Eagle nor Acorn Girl could find the third.

"This man still has a bullet inside him," Hurt Eagle said. "If we wish to save him, we will have to find that third ball of lead and take it out. Do we wish to save his life, Ooti?"

As he asked this question, the shaman looked directly into Acorn Girl's eyes, and she sensed uncomfortably that he saw something inside her head that even she was not aware of. She looked once more at the faintly breathing Whiteman, examining the face for the first time. The eyes were closed, slack, and the mouth was slightly open. There was something reassuring, she thought, in the lines of the face, something gentle about the mouth and eyes, even something about the beard around his mouth and chin. . . .

She glanced back down at the chest. Where the skin showed between the silver-brown wool and the dried blood, the flesh was very pale and looked as soft as a young girl's. Ooti chided herself for being foolish, but in this helpless state there was something about the big *Wawlem* that aroused a peculiar urge to protect him.

"Yes," she said slowly. "I don't know why, but I think we should save this bear-man if it is possible."

Hurt Eagle nodded, hiding a faint smile, and Acorn Girl suddenly remembered the dream of Pano. What had the Bear Spirit said?

I will send you something. It will have my mark. . . .

Had Pano sent her an injured Whiteman who looked like a cross between a human being and a grizzly? She let the question go for a moment, her attention caught by an object whose rim was sticking up from a tangle of flood debris beside the tumbling creek. She reached over, extricated the object, and held it up.

A thin metal frame with two round pieces of glass in it.

"*Spectacles,*" Hurt Eagle remarked. "Some Whitemen must wear them in order to see. They are half-blind without them, like old men and women. If I live long enough, Granddaughter, I may have to go to the store your friend Sutter owns and buy some."

Ooti glanced at Hurt Eagle and then turned to Raccoon.

"You go up and bring the others," she said. "Tell them what we have found and that there is no danger. We will need help to move this one."

Raccoon stared back at her resentfully, his dark eyes still burning with frustration and puzzlement, but after a moment he went to do as he was told.

When the remainder of the troupe came downcanyon, there was considerable disagreement as to what should be done with the stranger. Most of the young men were in favor of disposing of him at once so as not to be encumbered, but some were inclined toward bringing him along in the hope that he might recover sufficiently that they torture him. When they realized that Acorn Girl and might torture him. When they realized that Acorn Girl and Hurt Eagle proposed to save the Whiteman's life, disapproval. The scattered and mutilated bodies that had lain at Usto-ma village were quite vivid in the minds of the Nishinam people. Mercy toward any whites seemed almost beyond comprehension.

At last Acorn Girl drew both her pistol and her knife, taking a stance between the half-dead *Wawlem* and the Panos. She stood tall and set her face into lines of grim determination.

"You are my own people," Acorn Girl said, "but if anyone wishes to fight me over this man, then I will fight!"

A moment of stunned silence followed the assertion, and no one stepped forward to accept the leader's challenge.

Before and After came waddling up now, stopped, wagged their heads back and forth as they studied the form of the unconscious man. Then, moving forward almost like cautious and yet curious coyotes, they both nuzzled at the body. And Bear-who-comes-after began to lick at the dried blood on the Whiteman's chest.

Snakebite Dancer, the Usto-ma girl, laughed and pointed, and then several of the others began to chuckle.

Into the restored calm, Acorn Girl lowered her voice somewhat and said, "I too, Panos, have lost those I loved to the murdering *Wawlems*. But the Bear Spirit has sent this man to me for some purpose—I am certain that is the meaning of the vision I had just recently. Hurt Eagle, is it not so? I sought your counsel and told you what I had dreamed."

The elder shaman nodded three times.

"Now," Acorn Girl concluded, "since the Whites have taken away my husband and my babies, I declare this *Wawlem* who resembles Pano himself to be mine. I will own him for as long as he lives."

12

Where Is This Gold?

March, 1850

SEVEN: *Thou shalt not grow discouraged, nor think of going home before thou hast made thy "pile," because thou hast not "struck a lead" nor found a rich "crevice" nor sunk a hole upon a "pocket," lest in going home thou leave four dollars a day and go to work ashamed at fifty cents a day, and serve thee right; for thou knowest by staying here thou mightest strike a lead and fifty dollars a day, and keep thy manly self-respect, and then go home with enough to make thyself and others happy.*

EIGHT: *Thou shalt not steal a pick, or a pan, or a shovel, from thy fellow miner, nor take away his tools without his leave; nor borrow those he cannot spare; nor return them broken; nor trouble him to fetch them back again; nor talk with him while his water rent is running on; nor remove his stake to enlarge thy claim; nor undermine his claim in following a lead; nor pan out gold from his riffle-box; nor wash the tailings from the mouth of his sluices. Neither shalt thou pick out specimens from the company's pan to put in thy mouth or in thy purse; nor cheat thy partner of his share; nor steal from thy cabin-mate his gold dust to add to thine, for he will be sure to discover what thou hast done, and will straightway call his fellow miners together, and if the law hinder them not they will hang thee, or give thee fifty lashes, or shave thy head and brand thee like a horse thief with "R" upon thy cheek, to be known and of all men Californians in particular.*

NINE: *Thou shalt not tell any false tales about "good diggings in the mountains" to thy neighbor, that thou*

mayest benefit a friend who hath mules, and provisions,
and tools, and blankets he cannot sell; lest in deceiving thy
neighbor when he returns through the snow, with naught
but his rifle, he present thee with the contents thereof,
and like a dog thou shalt fall down and die.

The big *Wawlem* did not regain full consciousness for
many days, remaining in a state of largely incoherent
delirium even after the Panos had made their way down to
the low, rolling oak country on the edge of the valley of
Nem Seyoo, the Sacramento River, and within sight of the
sacred mountains of *Estawm Yan*, the strange, abrupt
formation that rose out of the flatness of the valley floor,
the mountains where Ootimtsaa, the father of acorn trees,
was believed to grow, hills that were as well the stepping-
off place for spirits bound for Valley Above.

The Panos, at Hurt Eagle's direction, had rigged a
stretcher of saplings and blankets for the stranger and
fastened it to drag behind Ranger, the gentlest and most
predictable of the horses. They had hastened away from
the scene of the violence, not knowing for certain that the
assailants would not return, but they halted in a hidden
side ravine a few miles downstream, and Hurt Eagle operated, finding and digging out the remaining chunk of lead,
one that had lodged below the Whiteman's shoulder blade.
The shaman examined the wounds, packed and bound
them carefully to prevent further bleeding, and said a
hurried prayer, waiting until the group reached their destination before embarking upon a full healing ceremony.

"No one of these wounds should cause death or even
serious impairment," the ancient one told Ooti. "I think
he was standing on top of that boulder when he was shot,
and he must have hit his head very hard when he fell. You
see the gash there, just above his ear? But it should be all
right, because the *Wawlems* have very thick skulls. If he
comes back after losing so much blood, and if none of his
wounds go bad, there is no reason why he won't recover.
You heard him groan when I cut him to remove the lead.
He was not awake, but he was alive enough to protest.
That is a good sign, I think."

Acorn Girl listened impassively, nodded when Hurt Eagle had finished.

"That is good," she said, keeping her voice neutral. "He will be a useful slave if he regains his strength. He is not a young man, but he is very strong. Pano has sent me a good gift."

Although the tribe had to exercise considerable caution to avoid the White settlements that seemed to be everywhere, they reached their lowland destination the following afternoon. As they traveled, Acorn Girl led Ranger with the Whiteman carried along on his travois. The huge horse that belonged to the man trailed disconsolately, wanting to stay close to his human but hampered by the bears, particularly After, who had developed a great interest in the stranger and spent much of his time walking along beside the litter, staring and nosing at the man's face and making curious whining noises.

The Panos found a suitable place to set up a semipermanent village, a large swale hidden between folds of oak-studded ridges and watered by several springs which joined to form a tule swamp below the site, an area where ducks and mud hens, egrets, and an occasional blue heron could still be found despite the encroachment of the Whites a few miles away. Here the group erected several *hubos* of brush and tule mats, the first to go up being the one where Acorn Girl would dwell with Hurt Eagle and Crane and with the injured *Wawlem* whom Crane had already designated as *Bear-Whiteman*. There he would have to remain, it was decided, until he was sufficiently recovered to be able to dwell elsewhere.

A problem of no small dimensions, Ooti soon discovered, lay in convincing the two grizzlies that they should sleep outside rather than inside the lodge, for the beasts had initially gained the idea, in the way of grizzly reasoning, that the lodge was primarily their own.

Hurt Eagle began the healing ceremony immediately, preparing his magic regalia, his objects of power positioned properly in their designated leather pouch, his cocoon rattles and his magic *huku* cape all being brought out and prayed over. He and Ooti and Wakwak undertook a fast, though the plump old woman was, in truth, less than totally enthusiastic.

Then began the chanting and the praying, the ancient shaman sometimes sitting by the head of his patient, at other times rising to shuffle in a slow dance around him. Acorn Girl and Crane kept time and saw to the fire and the pipe, joined at intervals by such of the other people as could get away from the task of putting up the *k-umu-ng hubo*, all of the houses, or of hunting. Hurt Eagle sucked out a variety of *itu*, pains, and at last, after several days, went into a trance to call back Bear-Whiteman's heart.

During this period the stranger would rouse from time to time, sometimes muttering incoherently without opening his eyes, but now and again opening his eyes to stare blankly around and speaking clear words. He spoke of someone named *Etta*, at other times called out for *Tom* or *Liz*. And once, rearing up onto an elbow and staring fiercely at nothingness cried out, "Ez Johnson, you scoundrel, I'll see you in hell. And if I don't, then Bully will. *Wagh!* Wrist-wrastlin', now there's a sport for gentlemen. . . ."

Acorn Girl, hearing the name *Johnson*, glanced to Hurt Eagle, startled, but the shaman went on with his chanting as if nothing had happened. She turned to Tied-wing, who was in the lodge at the time, observing the ceremonies although he did not take part in them. He motioned with his head for Acorn Girl to accompany him outside, and she, noting the fire in his eyes, went with him.

"What does that mean—what he said?" Acorn Girl asked her friend when they were a short distance away from the lodge.

"Your big *Wawlem* knows Ezra Johnson," Tied-wing answered. "Now—do you still wish to keep him?"

Acorn Girl studied the young man's face, saw that the mouth was twisted with bitterness as he spoke.

"It does not mean he is also bad," she said slowly. "He did not sound as if he likes Johnson. Our friend Marshall knows all the men for whom we search, but he is not one of them. I don't know what most of this man's words mean, but he called Johnson a *scoundrel*. I think that is like *Sydney Duck*, a bad name among the Whites. I never heard Pine-nut-eater use the word, but that is what the Bear-Whiteman's voice sounded like."

Tied-wing spat on the ground away from her.

"You became foolish when you first saw this *Wawlem*, Ooti. You will make anything about him seem virtuous."

"I am not being foolish, Tied-wing," she said, half-pleading. "It is you who wish to believe this man to be evil. I remember now that *hell* is the place where the Whites think they go after they die. There are two places, actually, one for good people and one for bad people. *Hell* is the one for those who are evil, and that's where he said Johnson would go."

"I don't think you're sure of that," Tied-wing challenged. "But even if you're right, didn't he say he'd *see* Johnson there? That must mean they will both go there."

"No," Acorn Girl said. "Can you not see from his face that he is gentle—like Ranger the horse?"

"I see a Whiteman who looks like a bear, and I see a woman who wishes to keep him for a pet. You should be named *Woman-who-loves-bears*."

"I must do as my visions tell me," Ooti snapped, suddenly growing impatient. "Now I must go into the *hubo* and help Hurt Eagle, who shares my belief. He is trying to sing this *pet* back into the world."

She turned abruptly, but Tied-wing caught her arm. She spun back, glaring at him, but his expression had changed to one of entreaty.

"Don't be angry with me, Ooti. I never could bear you to be angry with me. Even when we were little children, you would lose your temper, and I would be devastated for days. Come walk away from the village with me—for a little way. There are some things I need to speak with you about."

Acorn Girl stared at Tied-wing for a moment, seeing that his eyes were fixed on hers, that his expression was both intense and slightly fearful.

Now he wishes to ask me to marry him, this time in person. . . .

"Not now, Tied-wing," she said, her voice growing more

gentle. "I must go back inside—Hurt Eagle expects me to help him with the healing ceremony. We can talk later of this matter, can we not? We are friends, even though we grow angry with one another at times, and you are the husband of my closest friend. Now you have two little ones to be responsible for, both *Choopim Sawka*, Willow Meadow, your own daughter and now the Usto-ma child, Little Basket, as well. Too much has happened to us too quickly, Tied-wing. Our minds are troubled now, and we are not able to think clearly."

At the end of the long ceremony, when Hurt Eagle had determined that it was time to go into a full trance, he asked both Acorn Girl and Crane also to seek the *Wawlem*'s spirit, his *kakini*, in their dreams. Acorn Girl had long since mastered the art of self-induced vision-states, and with the help of the monotonous chanting and the dim light of the fire, it became even easier to let perception fade until there was only a single bright point in front of her eyes, and then to expand that point into a dream.

In her vision she sought the Bear-Whiteman first near the village, but he wasn't there. A scrub jay told her to seek higher up into the hills, along a stream, and she followed his directions, finding help from other Animal Spirits along the way until she came to the place on the creek where she and Hurt Eagle had first discovered his unconscious form. The Whiteman was sitting there on the big, flat-topped boulder above the water, and the stream seemed to be uttering words that she was unable to understand. Next to the Whiteman sat Pano, and the two of them were playing the guessing game with the marked and the unmarked bones, Peheipe Oleli watching carefully and grinning with some excitement as the sulu *or the* hinduku *was uncovered and the expressions* tep *and* we *were uttered.*

When Acorn Girl approached, Pano broke off the game and gestured to the Whiteman. Then the Grizzly Spirit clambered down from the rock and waddled away, Coyote leaping after him. The big Wawlem rose and looked at Ooti as if confused, and something strange happened. When she saw his face, the lined, pale face with its brush of silver-brown fur around the lips and chin, one that she had studied so often while the man had continued in his long sleep, seeing him awake like this for the first time, she knew absolutely that her judgment had been right, that this was a good man, but more than that it was as if she had always known him, as if she had known him so long ago that she couldn't remember when but that she had been seeking him for years without knowing it. She felt a great and inexplicable joy in finding him, as if he had been away for a very long time and she had missed him terribly.

She wanted to run up to him and throw her arms around him, but she knew that it would not be proper, and so she simply said, "We have been looking for you in the village. Come back with me now."

He still appeared as though he didn't understand, so Ooti took his hand and led him away from the great boulder and walked with him back to the new village.

Darkness.

Shapes of dreams.

Half-visions from time to time of flickering firelight and chanting in a strange tongue, nightmare visions half-man, half-monster dancing around him.

Darkness.

At last a long rise out of the darkness, an upward motion like surfacing from great depths of currentless water.

He woke into silence that he gradually came to realize was filled with the sounds of several people breathing, a reddish light from a dying fire.

Is not this world peopled with demons writhing in strange dances? Perhaps great Satan and his hordes sleep too. . . .

One of the sleepers rose, sighing as if having a difficult time dispatching dreams, came to look down at him. A young woman, the fine lines of her face highlighted by the dull glow of the fire.

"Did I not see you before?" Ben asked.

Sometime in the demon dance, dark angel. Benny, ye iggerant dunghead, ye ain't dead and wound up in one of yore confounded books, no sir. This hyar's a Injun lodge, plain and simple.

The young woman appeared to be smiling at him, but he wasn't sure. The light was bad, and things were blurry in a strangely familiar way.

My glasses. Jesus, I've lost them for good and I'm going to be blind in a savage land. . . .

The woman turned away and was adding sticks to the fire, light flaring up immediately brighter, and then she turned back, studied his face intently.

"My glasses . . . ," Ben managed.

The woman did not respond, but she was definitely smiling at him and continuing to search his face as if there were something important to be learned.

Probably doesn't speak English.

Ben made a circle of the first finger and thumb of both hands and held them up before his eyes in a pantomime that he really didn't suppose would communicate anything.

The woman laughed then and reached into a container at the head of Ben's nest of blankets, pulling back a moment later and holding up the gold-rimmed spectacles, firelight flashing orange off the glass. She put them in front of her own eyes and peered comically through them, teasing, and then handed them to Ben.

"Bear-who-cannot-see-well. I am glad that you have come back," she said in perfectly clear English.

At that moment one of the shadowy shapes in the room seemed to grow and detach itself from the ground, and as it moved massively toward them, Ben stifled a cry of terror. The shape came relentlessly toward him, head swinging, and just as it reached him, the great mouth of the grizzly gaped open, teeth glinting, and Ben could smell the carnivore's rank breath.

I'm still dreaming after all. . . .

The woman was laughing once again. The bear finished its yawn and then thrust its nose against Ben's face, pushed at him with its head.

"Bear-who-comes-after, this is . . . Bear-who-cannot-see-well," the woman said, as if introducing equals, and then added, "After has been very fond of you since we first found you. That is because he understands that you are from Pano. Bear-who-comes-before also likes you, but he is lazy."

"Bears?" Ben asked. "You have two bears?"

"That is true," the woman replied.

"You're Mrs. Jake," he whispered, the memory returning to him.

"How do you know that name?" the woman asked in reply. "I am Ooti, Acorn Girl."

She tilted her head to one side and studied him again.

Now others were stirring inside the low, smoke-smelling room, so that Ben did not have a chance to answer or to press the questions that had begun to surface like bubbles of swamp gas.

Ooti rode away from the village, alone, thinking to wander further up into the hills and ridges. The day was overcast, and all the newly forming leaves of buckeye and willow dripped water. But heavy rains of the past several days had ceased, and she thought that perhaps up in the canyons she could find deer. But more important than the excuse of hunting was simply a need to be alone, to think through the confusing welter of events of the past few days.

She had not spoken to anyone, not even to Hurt Eagle, of the strange dream she had when she went out to seek the heart of the man who called himself Benjamin Goffe.

"Sometimes dreams mean nothing, or something very different than what they seem," she told herself. "And yet Bear-who-cannot-see-well came back to himself and woke up just a little while after I had that dream. . . ."

Although she had not spoken of the vision, yet everything was colored by it—so that when the *Wawlem* had actually awakened, she had still felt its influence and had experienced the same sense of renewed friendship—no, more than friendship, to speak truthfully—for the man, just as in the dream. Despite all her cautions to herself, she could not help responding to Ben Goffe with that sense of pleasure, that sense of familiarity, and this troubled her, both because the man was *Wawlem* and because she didn't yet know him well.

"Perhaps there is something wrong with me, so that I am always falling in love with *Wawlems*. Pine-nut-eater was half *Wawlem*. . . ."

She cried out at this disturbing thought that crept into her mind.

"No," she said, panicky as she remembered the word she had used, "I don't love the stranger. I love my husband. That dream has made me crazy, *wut-a*."

She recalled another dream, the one in which Pine-nut-eater looked at her from the top of the mountain and begged her silently to let him go on to *Hipining Kawyaw*, and that she hadn't been able to cut the moon-silver cord that held him.

The sun broke suddenly through the thinning clouds above, and the vividly green grass and the bare branches of oak, everything around her came alive with light, dazzling with multicolored beads of water. Ranger snorted and threw up his head as if the sunshine aroused some long-smoldering instinct of playfulness in his old frame, and he even increased his pace to a jarring trot for a few steps before he relapsed into his usual plodding walk.

Ooti turned her face up to the sun, felt its fragile warmth against her skin, shut her eyes momentarily and watched the vivid red that the light made through her lids. Suddenly, for no reason, she was filled with an excess of joy, an impulse to wild laughter, or perhaps to get down and run through the wet grass for the sheer pleasure of feeling her body move.

Instead she gave a whoop that made Ranger skip ahead, startled, once again.

"Maybe it is good to be alive after all, horse," she said aloud. "Maybe we do not need to think up reasons, but simply take joy in what Olelbis has chosen to give us."

"Now that our leader has gone mad and talks to her horse, what hope is there for any of us?" called a voice from behind.

Acorn Girl turned, startled, saw Tied-wing come cantering up on the gray horse with half of one ear gone, a horse that she had acquired cheaply because of the injury.

"Tied-wing," Ooti said, trying to keep the annoyance she felt at his interruption out of her voice. "What are you doing here? And why didn't I hear you coming?"

"Probably because you were making so much noise yourself," he laughed, obviously pleased with himself at having taken her unaware. "I saw you set out hunting, and I thought I would come along. I think it's going to be a fine day."

Acorn Girl said nothing, and Tied-wing rode beside her in silence for a time. The sun rose higher, and at last Tied-wing spoke again.

"Let us stop over there, where that little stream comes down. I've brought something to eat. Ooti, you never remember to eat anymore. You're getting skinny."

"I am not very hungry, Tied-wing. I'll go on and see what I can find."

"Ooti. . . ."

She knew from the tone of his voice, then, that she would have to stop, that the conversation which she had been conscientiously avoiding for months could no longer be put off. She drew a breath, turned up the draw.

The two of them dismounted, and Tied-wing brought out some dried fish and water biscuits from a pouch. The clouds had begun building again, and in the distance an indistinct muttering of thunder.

To forestall Tied-wing's inevitable proposal, Acorn Girl began talking nervously.

"Do you remember," she asked, "when you and I and Small Ears got caught in the downpour, and you had to come into our shelter? You were both shy as young deer, and I practically had to push you into each other's arms. And yet any fool could see how crazy with love you both were."

Acorn Girl laughed, and Tied-wing patiently chewed on a strip of salmon.

"That seems like a very long time ago," he said.

"But you are still crazy in love," Ooti went on, not waiting for the man to agree or disagree. "Your wife is still young and beautiful, and now you have two fine daughters. I think it must be that a person can only be mad with love once. Don't you believe that's true?"

Am I telling him or myself?

She thought again of the big stranger, Ben Goffe, Bear-who-cannot-see-well, who had been recovering rapidly in the days since he emerged from unconsciousness.

"I don't know, Acorn Girl," Tied-wing replied, looking at her carefully and smiling a small, noncommittal smile.

Ooti felt at a loss for words.

I wonder if he and Hurt Eagle are telling each other outrageous stories right now? Or perhaps he is teasing Crane about her flirtatious eyes. He is learning our language very quickly, he is a very intelligent man. . . .

"I know what you are doing, Ooti," Tied-wing burst out suddenly, so that she was startled into drawing her gaze back from the distant view of the tops of *Estawm Yan.* "You do not want me to ask you to move into our lodge. What you say about being in love—I don't know. Perhaps it can happen many times. I do not expect that you will ever feel for me as you did for Pine-nut-eater, but you need a husband. And Small Ears will welcome you. She loves you as a sister. And now there is a man living in the lodge with you. . . ."

"Ben Goffe sleeps with Crooked Knee and Raccoon now," Ooti said quickly.

"Then he is spending the rest of his time in your lodge," Tied-wing snapped. "You should be married, so the people won't talk about you. You are our leader, and I would not ask anything of you."

Acorn Girl noticed the emphasis, understood that he was excusing her from sexual relations if she wished.

"I will not even ask that you give up being leader, though the other men will make fun of me. I will not mind that. Ooti, I ask this thing because I care about you. We grew up together. I always thought when we were children that you would one day be my wife, and then Pine-nut-eater came, and we both loved him, and I didn't mind that you were crazy for him, although he was half *Wawlem.* But now. . . ."

Tied-wing abruptly stopped talking, his mouth set as if to keep back words that he didn't wish to say. Ooti moved quickly to cover the pause, for she knew that what Tied-wing had not said had something to do with Bear-who-cannot-see-well.

"I am honored by your offer, Tied-wing," she said. "You are like a brother, and I love you for that. But as I have said before, I will probably never marry again. I must lead the people, and I can do that best by having no mate. It would not be right for you to be ridiculed for having a wife who is leader, and I cannot give up my purpose until the Whitemen who killed our loved ones are dead themselves."

"Yet there is one *Wawlem* you are happy enough to have alive," Tied-wing retorted, his face growing dark as the words were uttered.

"I am certain you do not mean what it sounds like you are saying," Ooti shrugged, surprised at the ice in her tone when she had been so utterly taken off guard.

Tied-wing did not respond for some time, but instead he set the muscles of his jaw and stared off into the distance.

"I think it is time for me to go back to the village," he said at last.

"No. . . ."

But he mounted then, and sat the gray horse for a moment, staring down at her. Then he reached over and touched the side of her face in a caress.

"I wonder if it is true, little Ooti, that you will never marry. This time you said *probably*. Did you notice?"

Acorn Girl did not reply, instead placing a hand on top of his. She felt vaguely ashamed, as if she had told a lie and both of them knew it.

"You are a beautiful woman," Tied-wing continued. "It would be sad if you don't marry someday, even if it is not me you choose."

His tone was very gentle now, and for some reason Ooti felt tears rising to her eyes.

"We will always be friends," she answered, "you and I and Small Ears."

But it was more in the way of seeking a confirmation than a statement.

"That is true," Tied-wing agreed. "We will always be friends—yes, for as long as we are still alive. After that, we do not know. . . ."

With these words he turned the one-eared gray and applied his heels to its ribs and trotted off in the direction of the village. Acorn Girl waited by the stream for a time, and then she turned Ranger in the same direction, her appetite for hunting suddenly gone, and rain beginning to threaten once again.

*   *   *

By the time she reached the shelter of Hurt Eagle's *hubo*, large drops of rain were falling, mixed with hail, and she was thoroughly wet.

Ben Goffe was telling another of his stories, this one once more about the hero called Odysseus and concerning an escape from being eaten by a one-eyed giant—by getting the monster drunk and then blinding him and then clinging to the wool of some huge sheep. Ben spoke in English, and Hurt Eagle was translating certain phrases for Crane, who certainly knew English as well as the shaman did, but also for Crooked Knee and Raccoon. Small Ears and the two infant girls were also crowded into the small space, while the two grizzlies, whining and generally feeling sorry for themselves, were outside, attempting to shelter themselves beneath a spreading liveoak.

Ooti settled near the fire to dry her hair and listened along with the rest of them, shaking her hair over the flames to dry it as she did so. She thought that Bear-who-cannot-see-well had a beautiful voice. It was obvious that he enjoyed telling stories, and through this method had managed to win the general goodwill of most of the band. Raccoon was still slightly hostile but was growing more tolerant, and a few of the other Panos were less than completely trusting of the big Whiteman.

It was a fine talent, this gift for telling stories—strange stories from the land of the Whites, different in many ways from the Maidu creation tales or the stories of Loon Woman or Butterfly Man. Ooti closed her eyes so that she would be better able to hear the musical tones of the speaker.

When the tale of Odysseus was finished, no one spoke for several minutes—until Hurt Eagle began commenting.

"I have seen sheep," he remarked. "At first I did not know what animals you were speaking of, but at one of the places where Sutter's men are, there are also sheep. The Miwok people who work for him drive the animals up into the high country in the summer—to a place not far from Chikimisi village. But sheep are not so intelligent as our own animals, for those live on their own and have to tend to themselves."

"Doubtless that is true," Bear-who-cannot-see-well replied, smiling. "I think the same case could be made for people, Hurt Eagle."

"Perhaps," the shaman nodded. "I am not sure."

"We also have stories like some of those you tell about Odysseus," Ooti said. "Grandfather Hurt Eagle tells them very well. He has many stories about Peheipe Oleli, the Coyote. Poor Coyote! We always make fun of him."

The remark was meant to give the ancient shaman his opening, for of course Ben Goffe had already heard a number of the tales.

"Yes," Hurt Eagle nodded. "But all our stories took place a long time ago. We no longer have monsters around here the way the Elder People did. No, that was way back, even before I was born. Did you know this Odysseus, Bear-who-cannot-see-well?"

Hurt Eagle had also asked this same question a number of times, but it pleased him to ask it again as a mild form of baiting the stranger.

Goffe grinned at the old man, and although he answered politely, Acorn Girl could tell by the deepening of the humor lines around his eyes that he understood the game.

"Yes," the big *Wawlem* said gravely. "He was a close friend of mine—before he returned to Ithaca, at least."

Hurt Eagle translated this without comment, but Crooked Knee took the bait.

"What?" he cried out. "That is not what you said before!"

"Isn't it?" Ben asked innocently, and everyone in the *hubo* broke into laughter.

When the merriment had subsided, Hurt Eagle began to speak.

"Well," the shaman said, "I didn't quite tell the truth, either, for not all the monsters were dead before I was born. Now I will tell you something that happened to me ages and ages ago, for this was when I was still a young man, if it is possible for any of you to imagine such a thing."

Ben smiled, and his eyes came to rest on Acorn Girl. At first he looked steadily into her eyes and then dropped his gaze involuntarily to her naked breasts. And for what must have been the first time in her life, she felt self-conscious and found herself fighting impulses first to cover her chest with her hands and then to sit straighter so that he would admire her more. Instead she looked at the ground near the fire and felt the blood coming into her face.

I am acting like a silly young virgin, she thought, *like a girl who has just completed her dong-kato singing time and has not yet lain with any man.*

She wished it were possible to slip out of the lodge unnoticed. She did not look up to see if the Whiteman were still watching her.

I am the leader of the Pano Maidus. I should not feel this way. I must speak to Hurt Eagle or perhaps to Crane— she is a woman and seems to understand everything, while I am still too young. If I keep this to myself, it may grow into something I cannot control.

Acorn Girl felt somewhat better in having made the resolution, and she carefully refrained from considering the possibility that the matter might already be beyond her control.

The following evening, Elk's Tooth and Kingfisher, who had been out gathering information from the nearby villages, came back to report that they had seen Milton Lindley with a sizable party of miners, apparently heading upstream on the Yuba River. Talk quickly turned to speculation about the possibility of making a raid on Lindley's encampment, but both Hurt Eagle and Acorn Girl counseled against the move, since Lindley's party, according to the report, numbered perhaps thirty men, and the Panos only had seven of their members able to make war, including Acorn Girl herself.

Although they spoke rapidly in their own tongue, Goffe was able to follow more of the conversation than they imagined. At length, looking directly at Ooti, he said, "Mrs. Jake? Might I offer a suggestion?"

Ooti met the Whiteman's gaze steadily now, and her mind quickly turned over the possibilities. Bear-who-cannot-see-well had called her by that name before, and she had chosen to ignore it. But if he had talked with Marshall, and if Marshall had guessed the nature of her little band of vengeance-seekers, then Ben Goffe almost certainly also knew. With each Whiteman they had slain, their fame had spread among the Nishinam villages and no doubt among the White settlements as well.

"Jim Marshall called me Mrs. Jake," Acorn Girl said. "Why do you use it?"

"Yes," Ben answered. "I've met the gentleman, as I've told you before, and I count him as a friend."

Then Bear-who-cannot-see-well changed and began to speak combining English and Nishinam phrasings:

"Acorn Girl, Panos," he said slowly, "I know who you are. Not even Marshall was certain, but I am. I understand your purpose. I wholeheartedly approve, for there is no law to protect you, and the men you seek are worse than wild beasts. In the same way I am certain that Ezra Johnson and his friends, those who committed the massacre of the village near Chalk Bluff, were the ones who shot me and left me where you found me. I have, then, a kind of personal grievance."

He gestured to the wounds in his back and side, the red scar near his clavicle.

"It is far better," he continued, "if you kill them than if they succeed in wiping out what's left of your people. But it is also true that there are many more men like Johnson. I have heard the stories, I have heard the talk of some of the miners. For this reason I think what we need is a long-range plan. First of all, we need more weapons and ammunition, more horses. It would be good if we could find more men, as well. I can help with the guns and mounts, since I am White and can buy such items without arousing suspicion."

Goffe's voice grew more enthusiastic as he spoke of details, how these purchases could be managed, and behind the shiny spectacles his eyes gleamed.

"You have gold to buy these things from the Whites?" Tied-wing asked, glancing with a silent frown at Acorn Girl, whose eyes were fixed on the big Whiteman.

"Well, no. Not much," Ben admitted, the light dimming in his face. "But I can get money if I can find my way to Sacramento City. The bank . . . Sutter . . . has my money. I'll find a way. Maybe I'll have to work in one of the stores or sawmills. I hear wages are high. I could go back to my newspaper in Grass Valley, but I'm not certain just how long I'd last there, since . . ."

"They shot you," Acorn Girl said, finishing his sentence for him.

Now she moved quickly to the small pouch that she kept among her belongings next to her sleeping place, opened it, and pulled out the egg-sized nugget with which Crooked Knee had lured Lindley's men away from Jim Marshall, held it up triumphantly.

Ben's mouth fell open, and he stared without speaking for a moment.

"Where did you find that?" he asked.

"There are many such under the ledge where we stayed last summer, above the big canyon of the Middle Fork of the river the Whites call the American. None of the *Wawlems* has thought to look there yet—it is hard to get to."

"For God's sake," Bear-who-cannot-see-well whispered. "By the balls of the Sweet Blue Jesus, as my friend Farnsworth might say. How much gold is there?"

Acorn Girl shrugged.

"Plenty of gold."

"Then that's what we'll do first," Goffe said. "Now we have a plan."

The Panos looked puzzled, all except Hurt Eagle, who nodded.

Ben continued talking, and it wasn't until later, after he had returned to his sleeping place in the lodge with Crooked Knee and Raccoon, the former talking happily of the plans to return to the high plateau as soon as the weather turned warm enough, and of what the Panos could do with all the new horses and guns, the boy in his usual grim silence. Only at this point did it occur to Ben to wonder at his continual use of the term *we* and his apparent expectation to continue as one of the pathetically small band of so-called *Digger* Indians in their insane quest for revenge against overwhelming odds.

"You had best pull yourself together, my friend, and get your big carcass back to civilization before it's too late," he told himself in a moment of half-panic—not at the danger of the projected undertaking but at the quickness and completeness with which he had apparently identified with these savage people.

Savage, hell. Ain't nothin' more savage than a White-woman who's got her man's bone between her teeth. Hitch up with a good squaw, that's this nigger's advice.

"Bully, you unregenerate old reprobate," Ben whispered.

He tried to imagine himself returning to Etta, top hat in gloved hand, and found that he couldn't quite remember the contours of her face.

Ooti dreamed again of Pine-nut-eater, once again at the summit of Onolaitotl the Sacred Hills. She opened her mouth to cry out to him, but he smiled, and then stepped off the top of the mountain and climbed into the sky, disappearing with a last, sad smile. She looked down, saw that the thread of moonlight still trailed from her ankles, but that it did not go all the way to the top of the Sacred Place. She felt devastated, terribly alone, until she turned and realized that Bear-who-cannot-see-well was standing near. And then she felt as if she were no longer alone, the sense of having known this man forever returning to her. She almost fell into his arms in her gladness—until she remembered, and then she held herself formally back. But the sense of gladness remained.

Beneath a tree nearby sat Pano the Bear and Oleli the Coyote. They were playing the guessing game with the marked and unmarked counters of bone, and Pano looked directly at her. She saw that he was letting her know that he approved, that he wished her to take this man.

In the morning she spoke to Hurt Eagle and told him of her latest vision, as well as of the earlier one concerning Ben Goffe. The shaman listened patiently, and when she finished, she asked him what she should do.

"What does your heart say you should do?" he replied, smiling strangely.

"My heart says I should marry Bear-who-cannot-see-well," she answered, the words emerging before she had thought what she would say.

Hurt Eagle nodded and went back to carving the pipe-stem that he was at work on.

13

A Marriage of Renegades

April, 1850

TEN: Thou shalt not commit unsuitable matrimony, nor covet "single blessedness," nor forget absent maidens, nor neglect thy first love; but thou shalt consider how faithfully and patiently she waiteth thy return; yea, and covereth each epistle that thou sendeth with kisses of kindly welcome until she hath thyself. Neither shalt thou covet thy neighbor's wife, nor trifle with the affections of his daughter; yet, if thy heart be free, and thou love and covet each other, thou shalt "pop the question" like a man, lest another more manly than thou art should step in before thee, and thou lovest her in vain, and, in the anguish of thy heart's disappointment, thou shalt quote the language of the great, and say, "such is life"; and thy future lot be that of a poor, lonely, despised and comfortless bachelor.

A new commandment give I unto you. If thou hast a wife and little ones, that thou lovest dearer than thy life, that thou keep them continually before you to cheer and urge thee onward until thou canst say, "I have enough; God bless them; I will return." Then as thou journiest toward thy much loved home, with open arms, shall they come forth to welcome thee, and falling on thy neck, weep tears of unutterable joy that thou art come; then in the fullness of thy heart's gratitude thou shalt kneel before the Heavenly Father together, to thank Him for thy safe return. Amen. So mote it be.

*   *   *

The time of *Lai-la* had arrived and, despite frequent and heavy rains, the weather turned warm. The low hills abutting the Great Valley were rich with grass, and the *tsakawm tsaa* and the *lawm tsaa*, whiteoak and wateroak, were coming into leaf. Higher up in the hills, where the Pano hunters often ranged, the acorn flour bread trees were already in new leaf, the blackoaks or *hamsum tsaa*, their finger-length loops of flowers and pollen hanging everywhere. It was the good time, *win-uti*, when the blackoaks tassel.

The young men, wearing their ritual deer-head masks, stalked all manner of game—black-tailed deer, tule elk, water birds, squirrels, jackrabbits, the smaller creatures driven ahead into nets that entangled them so that they might be clubbed to death.

The women wove baskets of various sorts out of green willow and tule and cured and prepared the hides of the animals the men had taken in the hunt, forming these into blankets, robes, and garments of various kinds.

To the north, however, along the Yuba River, where that stream debouched out into the valley, a thousand or more *Wawlems* were at work in the extensive deposits of gravel which lay along and about the river's floodplain, the so-called Yuba Goldfields. And the presence of so many miners, no more than a dozen miles distant, posed a very real danger—for sometimes bands of White hunters would wander south in search of game, coming on several occasions within a mile or less of the Pano encampment.

"The *Wawlems* are everywhere in our lands now," Acorn Girl said to Hurt Eagle. "Wherever we go, we find the Whitemen close about us. I think it is time for someone to awaken Olelbis before he has ruined everything."

"Perhaps when they have dug up all the gold, then they will go away," the Man of Many Winters nodded. "For myself, even though *Wakwak*, takes very good care of me and pretends we are still young enough to make babies, I cannot live much longer. Then I will go into *Estawm Yan*, the mountains of *Onolaitotl*, and from there on into Valley Above. That is why I like it where we are now, Ooti. It is

good to look across and be able to see the mountains that
rise from the center of things, the place where the *Ootimtsaa*
tree is said to grow. The *Wawlems* have not cut it down,
no matter what some say, because the Great Tree is only
there when one has entered into the realm of the spirits,
as in a dream when the heart wanders about. Then, once I
have fully passed over, I will not have to worry about the
Whitemen any more."

"I think maybe they are digging up gold even in Valley
Above, Grandfather. They are everywhere else now."

Hurt Eagle glared at Acorn Girl, offended by the thought
she had presented him.

"Yes," he said at length, "these are truly bad times for
the Nishinam. And yet is it not strange? Whatever happens to the people, still the oaks come into leaf, and the
flowers bloom on the hillside, little splashes of yellow and
blue and violet. The Skunk People still raise their tails
toward us when we approach them, reminding us of their
powerful smell. World-Maker dreams many things at the
same time. You are the leader of our people, Ooti. Will
we stay here in the low hills long enough to celebrate the
Hesi and then the *Luyi* and the *Lili* and the *Toto*, our
great sacred dance and the profane dances that come
after? It is now two years since we have been able to make
this celebration."

"I do not think so, Grandfather. Soon the rains will
cease altogether, and we must make our journey to the
toommin before the Whitemen move out away from the
rivers to search for more places to dig the gold. No, I
think we must go very soon. These are new times, and
everything is different from what it was. Bear-who-comes-
before and Bear-who-comes-after are not even able to
make their long sleep. They hibernate only for a short
time, now and again, and when we have to awaken them,
they become very cross.. But that is the way it must be."

Hurt Eagle nodded and gazed out across the low rim to
the west of the Pano encampment to where the ragged
summits of *Estawm Yan* were visible.

"Perhaps you think only of your third bear now," he
said. "I do not know what to make of such a man—one
who must always wear his *glasses* so that he does not

trample upon people or knock down *hubos* with his great size. How will you ever be able to make love with such a man, unless you ride him as you ride a horse?"

Acorn Girl blushed furiously, stamped her foot on the ground, and placed her hands on her hips.

"Crane has put many bad thoughts into your mind," she said.

"But how can you do it?" Hurt Eagle persisted.

"Do you believe that is why I am fond of Bear-who-cannot-see-well?" she demanded. "No, I have not done anything of the kind. And perhaps I never will. Perhaps we do not truly wish to marry each other. He has a wife among the *Wawlems*, even though she is very far away."

The old man's eyes were twinkling with mirth now, and he made the hand gesture indicating that Acorn Girl did not mean what she was saying.

It was her turn to glare at him.

"If I wished to lie with . . . Ben," she said, "I could do it. I would not have any trouble at all."

Hurt Eagle laughed.

"Perhaps part of Bear-who-cannot-see-well is very small," the old man shrugged. "But he weighs so much that he would press all the breath out of your body, and then I would have to go into a trance so that I could wander about in the Spirit Place in order to bring your heart back to you."

The Panos, Benjamin Goffe with them, made their trek eastward toward the high plateau where they had spent the months of the preceding autumn and early winter until the snows had driven them down from their place beyond the formation the Whites called End of the World. Kingfisher and Elk's Tooth were given the task of moving always some distance ahead, on foot, so that the camps of the *Wawlem* miners might be avoided, something that was becoming ever more difficult, for if a stream had gravels along its course, it was now certain a number of Whitemen would be there, panning, digging, running a riffles or even a long-tom if the current were sufficient, the men hunched forward and standing knee-deep in water, their eyes intent upon the motions of current-carried sand. New arrivals to the mining camps, finding the likely claims already occupied, hired themselves out to those with established rights. Many of the newcomers did not even bother to erect shelters sufficient to protect them from the rains, drenching at times, that continued to fall.

The *Wawlems* were so intent upon their work that the Panos concluded it was easier to travel during the hours of daylight—for the Whites seemed oblivious to everything except the lure of gold, working ceaselessly, like those afflicted by *wut-a*, craziness, from first light until sunset.

Nevertheless, discovery and confrontation were not to be desired, and Kingfisher and Elk's Tooth, at Acorn Girl's direction, scouted ahead for ways that kept to brushy hillsides and lateral ravines, a winding and tortuous route but one that provided the greatest possible degree of safety.

Despite all this, the Panos moved ahead with good rapidity, and the morning of the third day of their journey brought them down into Green Valley, the place where they had saved Marshall from a lynch rope. The meadows at the bottom of the jagged canyon were empty now, though there was ample evidence of recent digging among the gravel banks close by the hissing green flood of the river, the stream moving rapidly and heavy with snowmelt at the high elevations.

Ranger nearly foundered during the crossing, and Ben, riding his much larger horse, reached across and grasped the reins of Acorn Girl's mount, twisting the horse's head upward and out of the powerful current.

"You didn't need to do that," she told Ben when all had managed to ford the flooding stream. "Ranger knows what to do—he wouldn't have gone under."

"I wasn't worried about the horse," Ben replied. "I was worried that he might pitch you into the current. Since you *own* me, I have to watch out for you. If you drowned, Mrs. Jake, Tied-wing and his friends would slit my throat in no time. Let's just say I've got a vested interest here."

"I do not understand your meaning, Bear-who-cannot-see-well. And why do you continue to call me by that *Wawlem* name?"

"In Jim Marshall's mind," Ben nodded, "your husband was named Jake, and so you became Mrs. Jake. As a matter of fact, your friend Marshall told me quite a bit about you, Acorn Girl. He even asked me to tell the story of how you rescued him—wanted me to put it into my newspaper."

Ooti stared out over the singing river, watched as King-fisher and Crooked Knee assisted Hurt Eagle and Crane across the glittering green-white torrent.

"You . . . made a newspaper?" she asked. "I know about those. You put words onto sheets of paper and send them all over. Then you told the other *Wawlems* how we chased away the men who were going to kill Marshall?"

"Yes. I didn't say anything about the Panos, though. I'd only heard rumors at the time, and Jim didn't tell me much about what you and your people are doing. Either he actually didn't know or else he thought it best not to share the information with me. So I wrote the story—put the words into the newspaper. But I didn't mention the Nishinams at all. Figured it would be better for you and your people, Ooti, if the miners didn't know you were close by."

"You are a strange man, Bear-who-cannot-see-well. You spend much time with your own thoughts, and you are always very careful about what you say. I think you are a very good—slave."

With that she turned Ranger about and rode back to where Kingfisher and Elk's Tooth were just emerging from the water.

The journey continued, and the Panos made their way upward along Humbug Canyon to the high ridgeback. They encountered no snows—for, indeed, springtime was in full rage here as well, the firs tasseled with new green needles and the lilac brush flaring its clusters of small white flowers. The sunlight was warm with the first hints of the summer to come, and manzanitas were hung with bunches of tiny bell-like blooms, honey-smelling and at-tracting bees and other flying insects.

Ben, in high spirits and feeling healthy once again, his gunshot wounds nearly healed, with only the left shoulder

giving him twinges of pain when he made too-quick movements, rode along on Old Blue. He felt the sunlight on his
face and soaking through the buckskin coat that Crane had
made for him, and he breathed the sweet, rank air of
springtime in the high ridge country intersected by steep,
narrow lateral ravines that lay to the southeast of the
North Fork Canyon.

Acorn Girl, astride the somewhat irascible old horse
that Ben knew once belonged to her husband, a halfbreed
named Jake, rode on ahead, leading the Panos now that
they had passed beyond the last of the mining areas. Ben
watched her carefully, concluding for the first time that
she was, in fact, a genuinely beautiful young woman—
strange, sometimes withdrawn, sometimes vexingly mysterious, and always seemingly in complete control of
whatever situation presented itself. Sunlight glinted from
her long black hair, and when she spoke, her almost
musical voice was nonetheless rich with the tones of
authority.

How had it happened—that she had been chosen leader
of this band of Indians who, against all odds, managed
somehow both to survive and to pursue their course of
vengeance upon those Whitemen who had been responsible for the near annihilation of their village?

In his mind's eye, Ben contrasted Acorn Girl with the
lovely but spoiled, self-obsessed Etta, his wife, perhaps a
dozen years Acorn Girl's senior and yet infinitely more
childlike, despite her civilized sophistication, worldly in-
clinations, and finishing school education. Put Etta in
Acorn Girl's situation, Ben concluded, and she'd die of
starvation because either her pride or her incompetence
in all matters practical or a combination of those traits
would conspire against her, even if game were abundant
and she'd been given the weapons necessary to hunting.
Or perhaps she'd just sit down, refuse to move, and so
pass away through sheer willfulness.

But Ooti—she was the unquestioned leader of her people, and however much they argued among themselves,
they looked to her for the making of decisions that would
affect all of them. Even Hurt Eagle, his face wrinkled into
a map of his life and his old eyes gleaming with accumu-

lated wisdom, though he was obviously the young woman's mentor and occasional guide, he too waited upon her decisions and accepted them with graceful confidence.

What elements had molded themselves together in her being? Ben had gathered that she'd always been a tomboy, as that term might be made to apply to the world of the Maidus, adept from an early age at the skills of running, rock-throwing, spear-hurling, bow and arrow use, and eager to go on the hunt. It was not, apparently, simply a matter of her preferring the life of a male to that of a female, for she had married Jake, Pine-nut-eater, and had borne him twin sons. That Acorn Girl had been a good mother Ben had no doubt. Had she, in fact, not nursed him back from the very edge of death? Her care for all around her was evident—reaching its extreme, perhaps, in her relationship with the two great hulking, if only half-grown, grizzlies, animals that she had found alongside their dead mother and had taken almost as though they were somehow replacements for her own two children, slain at the hands of the Whites, along with husband and mother and father.

She has lived in fire and has become a part of the fire, it has burned her pure and rendered her whole in a way that I will never forget and will probably never understand at more than a merely surface level. She is fire. The flames are all about her if one looks carefully. Heroine, saint, unbelievably complex puzzle, damnably attractive, sensuous—beautiful, beautiful. . . .

Ben leaned forward, felt again the stab of pain in his left shoulder, grumbled, and rubbed his hand alongside Old Blue's rough cut mane.

The two grizzlies, locked in one another's embrace as if in some sort of childhood contest, came tumbling down the brushy slope at whose base the Panos rode, momentarily startling the horses—growling, coughing, and yelping—batting at one another with broad, lethal paws and yet seemingly harming one another not at all.

If she marries again, the buck is going to have to fight off those monstrous bears to lie beside her. . . .

For the moment, Benjamin Goffe concluded, he also felt whole—vital and alive and free as perhaps he had

never felt before in his life. What would Tom and Elizabeth think if they could have seen him at the present
moment? Astride a huge horse, a man dressed in deerskin, a mountaineer's Hawken rifle slung in a scabbard
next to his knee, a Colt Walker revolver in a holster at his
side, and himself a provisionally accepted member of a
band of renegade Indians who seemed bent, against all
odds, upon conducting a kind of covert warfare against an
entire population of White miners.

The Panos, Ben was certain, were fated to tragedy, to
ultimate and absolute destruction and death. But for the
moment they were riding through clear, bright air on the
backs of the mountains, and their grim determination to
avenge their honor as a people made such a desperate
course of action seem complete and compelling and utterly right.

And he was one of them!

They had found him nearly dead and, even though he
was a Whiteman and hence one of their enemies, they had
nursed him back to life—they had considered him as an
individual and not simply as a *Wawlem*—they had granted
him a degree of respect—they had been, so to speak,
fascinated by him, curious about him—and finally they
had accepted him, governed by the iron will of the Joan of
Arc who led them. And so he, in turn, had begun to
identify with them and to sympathize with them. Had his
response to their reality, in fact, not perfectly grown out of
what he had earlier imagined them to be—Mrs. Jake and
her Grizzly Cult, stalking down those who had murdered
her people?

"Farnsworth O'Bragh," Ben whispered, "where the hell
are ye, old coon? Ye ought to be with this child now—ye'd
be in your own element, flat out. . . ."

Once back to the plateau beyond the grove of sequoias,
parklike area of huge sugarpines and Douglas firs and
ponderosas, the Pano Maidus set immediately to the task
of repairing their *hubos*, for the snows had lain heavy,
apparently to the depth of several feet, and the heaped
boughs over the dwelling pits had been in many cases

completely crushed. Ben took up residence with Crooked
Knee and Raccoon, at Acorn Girl's direction. The Usto-ma
boy had remained thus far somewhat frightened of and
hostile toward the big Whiteman who wore the strange
little metal-rimmed mask, though Acorn Girl's apparent
fondness for the giant had encouraged him to grant at least
a provisional degree of acceptance for Ben. The Whiteman
had already learned enough of the Nishinam tongue to
allow him to communicate about basic things, and now, as
the three worked at the task of constructing a new *hubo*,
Bear-who-cannot-see-well suggested placing a large cooking basket beneath one of the ridgepoles, causing Crooked
Knee to shake his head and laugh. In a moment Raccoon
realized the meaning of the strange assertion, and he too
began to laugh delightedly.

"Aw, that is rock," Crooked Knee grinned, pointing and
at the same time using his own limited English. "*Awntee*,
that is cooking basket."

Ben nodded, properly corrected.

"*Aw*, rock," he repeated.

And once again Raccoon burst into laughter.

"*Tep . . . we*," Ben said, raising his arms and mimicking
one of the grizzlies, "this . . . that."

And somehow the reserve the boy had felt toward the
man was broken—as though Raccoon had now decided
that Bear-who-cannot-see-well was, after all, at least mar-
ginally human.

And before the day was over, Hurt Eagle, Acorn Girl,
Tied-wing, and the other Panos observed as Ben hoisted
the lad to his shoulders and went parading about the area
with him, slouching and growling and snorting in bearlike
fashion, Raccoon looking both pleased and foolish, as though
he had now learned how to ride a horse, just like Acorn
Girl.

Then the leader of the Panos herself joined the strange
dance, and old Hurt Eagle, not to be outdone, did likewise. Slow Rabbit and Grasshopper Man, supposing the
gyrations to be part of some ritual unknown to the Usto-
mas, entered the frolic as well. Soon nearly everyone was
dancing, with Crane standing to one side, rhythmically
shaking a cocoon rattle in either hand.

Only Tied-wing and Small Ears and her two little ones remained apart, the husband's eyes narrowed as though he were in the process of making some kind of judgment.

The springs and gravel banks below the rim of the plateau and high above the churning green-blue waters of the Middle Fork proved to be extremely rich in gold, with many nuggets the size of the tip of a man's thumb. A small stream, bursting out through a thicket of azaleas on the canyon's rim and cascading downward in a long band of white spray, rushed past the gravel deposits and provided a means of washing the auriferous sands.

Goffe and Ooti and the other Panos worked together, digging and scraping with sharpened sticks and hand-carved wooden paddles and the one short-handled *Wawlem* shovel that the group possessed. After a time Ben constructed a makeshift riffles by means of excavating a smooth channel through a clay bank, placing split sections of alder across it at right angles to the smooth-bottomed channel, and diverting a portion of the stream into this new course. The Panos watched curiously as Bear-who-cannot-see-well worked at his device, immediately perceived its purpose, and began to carry woven baskets full of gold-bearing sand and gravel to it.

Hurt Eagle himself, heretofore willing merely to observe the mining operations, now rose from where he sat and came to the riffles, grinning widely when he was able to pluck a nugget out of the swirling water and sand in the channel.

A week went by, and the Indians continued with their mining operations—delighted as children, Ben observed, and suddenly obsessed with this new game. Perhaps it was true, as Acorn Girl had explained to him, that her people had always known of the gold but had considered it the "worthless yellow metal," but now the same compulsive, self-generated fever that characterized the miners along the Yuba and Bear Rivers, men whom Ben had observed and spoken with, took hold of the minds of the Pano Maidus.

And the quantity of gold they managed to extract from

the cinnamon-colored deposits of sand and pebbles was quite significant, perhaps as much as fifty pounds of dust and nuggets combined.

Ten dollars to the ounce at Sutter's Fort or Red Collins' store alike times sixteen ounces to the pound times fifty pounds, more or less—that's somewhere near eight thousand dollars. And that, in turn, to be converted into horses, weapons, ammunition, necessary implements. . . .

Ben shook his head.

If the thing could be pulled off, this was one band of Maidus that no group of Whitemen was likely to take advantage of. Even, and here Ben found himself envisioning the thing with a kind of insane glee, an attack upon Johnson and his men at Chalk Bluff was not out of the question.

But where would it lead from there? Had he himself not written to both governors in a plea for the rule of law, of the need for some species of sufficient judicial order? And now he found himself whimsically transported to the other side of things—out of the objective middle defined by the *Del Oro Star* and into a sphere of loyalties defined by the remnants of two Maidu villages, the Tumelis and the Usto-mas, peoples, he had already concluded, for whom there could be no real future and who now, in what they planned, were certainly doing no more than hastening their own end.

"A tragically fated world," he thought, "a world that is ending, and a band of people who will go down in mute glory, in a blaze of gunfire, their motives and their deeds forever untold, anonymous. . . ."

Lines from *Maldon* came to him:

> *Likewise the child of Aethelgar cheered them all,*
> *spurred them to battle. Oft a spear he let fly,*
> *the good Godric, against the Vikings;*
> *so he led that army, went out in front,*
> *cut down and felled till he was fallen in combat.*

"The time of endings," Ben thought, "the time of heroism, the undiminished human will pitching itself forward into the teeth of overwhelming odds, the point at which Saint and Satan are most nearly one and the same. . . ."

Then Acorn Girl, squatting beside the gravel bank above where Ben stood and using a wooden paddle to fill her *daw* winnowing basket with sand to be brought to the riffles and washed, stood up, laughing delightedly. In her hand she held a lump the size of her own closed fist.

"What have you found?" Bear-who-cannot-see-well called out.

"Moloko the condor has left a yellow egg for me to dig up!" she laughed.

The Pano leader scrambled down the bank, a great nugget in her hand, and held it out for Ben to see.

Both began to laugh now and suddenly, at some signal that neither consciously recognized, they fell into one another's arms, clung desperately to one another.

Acorn Girl was sobbing, burying her head against Ben's shoulder, and he, astounded, found it difficult to swallow and could feel incipient tears blurring his vision, tears that had been unknown to him for a long, long while, since the death first of his father and then of his mother.

He kissed at the shining black hair, he pressed his cheek against her ear. He wanted to say something, but his mind had gone completely blank, as though reason itself had deserted him.

Acorn Girl clung to the huge Whiteman whom she pretended to own, felt the great strength of the male body, found her thoughts tumbled backward to a time when she had lain with Pine-nut-eater.

And a great hunger came over her now, a need so intense that she could only struggle to suppress it.

When at length she and Bear-who-cannot-see-well untangled themselves from their standing embrace, and the two of them looked around, they realized that all mining activity had come to a halt. The Panos were standing about, watching them, the facial expressions tolerantly amused.

Only Tied-wing, Acorn Girl realized, was not pleased. His eyes were hard as he stared first at Ben and then at her.

"Look at the size of this nugget Ooti has found!" Ben called out, waving the others forward.

The silence was broken.

* * *

Following the spontaneous embrace by the riffles channel, Acorn Girl placed the large gold nugget into Ben's hands and without further communication turned abruptly and walked away, not back to where she had been scooping sand into her big basket but on over the rim and toward the lacelike waterfall that spilled out from the ridge crest through a tangle of newly leafed azaleas, the flower clusters not yet in evidence. Ben looked from one Nishinam to another, but the eyes upon him seemed detached, almost as though the people were standing about, wide-eyed but nonetheless asleep.

A shiver went up Ben's spine, and he wondered if he had somehow, without knowing it, infringed the Pano leader's medicine or had ignorantly violated some taboo or another.

Not knowing what else to do, he deposited the big nugget into a deerhide pouch and once more knelt beside his riffle channel, used his thumb and forefinger to pick at some birdshot-sized bits of gold that had collected.

When he looked up once more, everyone was back at work, and Kingfisher and Slow Rabbit, in apparent good spirits, were scrambling downslope with full baskets of auriferous sand to deposit at the head of the sluiceway.

But Tied-wing was nowhere in sight.

This warrior, Bear-who-cannot-see-well had gathered, had definite eyes for Acorn Girl, though he himself was already married to Ooti's friend Small Ears, the father to her infant girl—and now, as well, to the Usto-ma child.

But a man might well have more than one wife among these people—something Crooked Knee had told him a few days earlier and Hurt Eagle had confirmed when Ben made inquiry later.

The afternoon waned, and yet neither Acorn Girl nor Tied-wing had returned to the mining site. At length Ben diverted the full flow of the little stream back into its normal channel and, using a wide-bladed knife, removed the accumulations of black sand and fine gold from behind each of the baffles he had set into the thick yellow-white clay of the trough. This mixture, composed primarily of flakes of iron sulphide, heavy like gold and so caught by the baffles as the water spilled over them, Ben scooped into a separate pouch, to be dried and separated later.

"Magnets," he thought. "What we need is a couple of good horseshoe magnets—yes, and one or two other civilized implements, like shovels, for instance."

Ben lifted the two pouches from the little shelf in the claybank he had cut to accommodate them, rose, and turned to start the climb to the canyon rim two hundred feet or more above. He glanced about, surprised—for the Maidus had already gone, were out of sight, had left him behind as he was engaged in collecting the black sand from the riffles.

Wagh! Somethin' afoot, ye blue-balled idjit. Ain't none but a dumbass Connecticut nigger wouldn't have figgered it out hours ago. . . .

"Thanks, Farnsworth old friend," Ben muttered.

Name's Bully, ye stubborn warthog.

Ben climbed to the rim, kneeled to drink from his cupped hands just where the little stream poured over the stone rim, savored the clean, cold taste, and rose again—finding himself face to face with Tied-wing.

Without thinking, Ben went for his revolver, but Tied-wing, his handsome bronze face without expression, shook his head.

"I do not come to fight you, Bear-who-cannot-see-well," he said. "That could happen at some other time, but not now."

"What's going on?" Ben asked, drawing his hand away from the still-holstered weapon. "You startled me, Tied-wing, and I . . ."

"You are a *Wawlem*, and that is reason enough for me to dislike you. And yet the best friend I ever had was half *Wawlem* in his blood, and so I know it is wrong for me to feel as I do."

"Pine-nut-eater, Acorn Girl's husband?" Ben asked, intuiting the matter.

"Yes," Tied-wing said. "You know about that—then Ooti has told you. Now there is something that I must tell you, Bear-who-cannot-see-well. Perhaps you are one of us now, and perhaps not. You have had many chances to leave us, but you have stayed. And yet I think that eventually you will return to your own people. Listen to me now. I think you will marry Acorn Girl, for it is right that she should have a man. She cannot be with Pine-nut-eater again until they are both in *Hipining Kawyaw*. I would gladly have taken her into my own lodge, for Ooti has always been like a sister to me, and it would be good to be married to two women who are already very close friends. Yes, that would have been good. But now our leader has decided to make you her husband."

"I've never so much as . . .," Ben started to say.

"That is what I fear most," Tied-wing replied. "Hurt Eagle says you have a wife among your own people. I think it would be good if you returned to her, Bear-who-cannot-see-well. That is what I think, and so I have said it. But Ooti wishes to have you, not me, for a husband."

Ben held out his hands in a gesture of ignorance.

"She has made her decision," Tied-wing continued, "and I love her too much not to respect it. If you are her husband for a time and then go away, it will be for the better. But if you give her a child and then leave her, I will hunt for you until I find you—and then I will kill you, no matter how strong you are. Now that I have a pistol, just as you have, I do not think you are any stronger than I am."

With these words, and not waiting for any kind of an answer from Ben, Tied-wing turned and strode away into the approaching darkness.

Ben was stunned, shaken. Acorn Girl, who had saved his life and in some way or another *owned* him, now wished to marry him?

It was true. He had already come to feel closer to this woman than to any he had ever known. At some level or another he had loved her long before the Panos had found him, half-dead, by the big rock in Woodpecker Canyon—had loved the *idea* of her, Mrs. Jake, leader of a band of infinitely courageous but utterly doomed renegade Indians, the little band systematically tracking down precisely those men who had destroyed their village.

Ooti, Ooti-du, Acorn Girl—who was she?

Gudrun, Joan of Arc, Pallas Athena, Sacajawea, the

*Massasoit woman old Judge Goffe married, Betsy Ross,
Persephone, Helen, Io, Bathsheba, Cleopatra, Mountain
Lamb who had married Carson's friend, Joe Meek, an
avenging Eve cast out of the Garden and her Adam
slain. . . .*

No.

*Acorn Girl, neither myth nor specter from history.
Acorn Girl, hoyden, tomboy, mystic dreamer, leader of
her people, avenging angel.*

*Beautiful, innocent, savage, tamer of grizzly bears, un-
daunted and sensuous, childlike in a wisdom as old as the
human race itself, owner of Benjamin Goffe, former professor of literary Puritanism and presently known as
Bear-who-cannot-see-well.*

Goffe's laughter rang out through the great standing pines
and firs whose boles seemed almost to support the heavens
themselves. He held his sides and shook his head, wiped
at the tears of mirth that had started to his eyes.

Then he was calm again and stood, silently, watching
the immense flood of crimson that flared across the western sky beyond the End of the World and the seemingly
endless shadowed canyons and ridges.

The moon, past full, would not rise for another hour or
more, and Ben turned and walked back under the darkness of the giant trees.

When Bear-who-cannot-see-well reached the Pano encampment, the people were already engaged in eating
their evening meal, a roast of venison along with water
biscuit and portions of *awmpes*, an acorn mush that had
been cooked on hot rocks and then flaked off into segments that resembled fried pork rinds.

Crane rose from Hurt Eagle's side at Ben's approach,
filled a woven basket with food, and brought it to the
Whiteman.

"This is your supper," she said, grinning almost foolishly, Ben thought.

"Thank you, Wakwak."

"You are to eat here, away from the others," the old
woman said. "Then you must go directly to your lodge."

"I don't understand. . . ."

"It is best not to question good fortune," Crane laughed—
and then turned and walked back toward Hurt Eagle, a
springiness in her gait that Ben was certain he'd not
noticed before.

He squatted down, his back against a fir, and ate alone,
as he had been bidden to do.

The Maidu band, only a few yards from the fir he
leaned against, seemed utterly oblivious to his presence.
Even young Raccoon, stealing a glance at him, turned
away quickly as their eyes met.

Ben was confused, but at the same time he was beginning to understand that he was being required to partake
of some kind of ritual, and his intuition was sufficient to
tell him what it was.

After a time Crane returned with a leather water pouch,
and Ben drank, thanked the woman.

"Now go to your lodge," she said, her face expression-
less but her old eyes twinkling.

Ben rose and walked to the *hubo* he shared with Crooked
Knee and Raccoon. But when he entered he discovered
that neither of those two was inside.

Acorn Girl sat cross-legged on a new, larger bed covered with a fine rabbitskin blanket, her figure almost
dreamlike in the half light of the lodge and illumined only
by the flames of crossed staves of pitchpine.

Upon his entry, Acorn Girl pulled open the deerskin
cloak she had worn, placed it on the bed beside her, and
stood up. She was completely unclothed.

Involuntarily Ben stepped back, but Acorn Girl shook
her head.

"I have made this fine bed to honor my husband," she
said in a quiet voice. "I have chosen you, Bear-who-
cannot-see-well, and now you must be my husband for as
long as you remain with me and my people. When it is
time for you to return to your own people, then I will be
sad—but not until that time. Take off your clothing now
and we will lie down together in the way of a man and a
woman."

Whatever it was that Benjamin Goffe had thought might
happen, this was not it. But now, in a flash of understand-

ing, he realized that in the manner of the Maidu people, he was already married to Acorn Girl. In another time and in another place and in another world he might have brought presents to her father until one evening he would have perceived a new bed in the lodge. And he would have lain down upon it and waited, possibly for a long while, until the mother and father and other children had retired and after that for whatever length of time it took the woman to lie down beside him—or, had she not wished to be his wife and had wished to terminate his courtship, she might have remained sitting up throughout the night, and he would have been obliged to slip away before the dawn.

Did he desire this woman?

Yes.

Was he afraid of her, of her power, of her female presence?

Yes.

"Take off your clothing, Bear-who-cannot-see-well," Acorn Girl repeated, "and then lie down with me. I will prepare you to make love to me. I have been married before, and I know what to do."

Ben felt foolish and excited at the same instant. But if he was uncertain what he should do, he did what the Pano leader told him.

"Take off your glasses also," she said when he stood unclothed before her and feeling embarrassed, too large, too clumsy, his hands and his entire body trembling with uncertainty.

Then she began to laugh, and Ben realized that he himself was beginning to laugh as well.

He laid his glasses on top of his folded clothing and then kneeled beside her, reached out toward her.

"I will make you very excited first," she said, "and then maybe I will make you wait for a long time. . . ."

III

Pano-ng-kasi
The Grizzly Dance

They, looking back, all the eastern side beheld
Of Paradise, so late their happy seat,
Waved over by that flaming brand; the gate
With dreadful faces thronged and fiery arms.
Some natural tears they dropped, but wiped them soon;
The world was all before them, where to choose
Their place of rest, and Providence their guide.
They, hand in hand, with wandering steps and slow,
Through Eden took their solitary way.

—John Milton,
Paradise Lost

14

Ye Ain't Dead, Are Ye?

May, 1850

Kuksu, First Man, discovered fire, and immediately he saw how to use it. He brought it to Morning Star Woman, his wife, and she placed it in a pit and laid dried grass and twigs upon it so it flared up and gave off heat.

"Use this fire to cook our meat with," Kuksu said, and Morning Star Woman did as her husband told her.

But then Thunder came and saw what was happening. He did not want the people to have fire, so he took it away from them. If the people could not have fire, he reasoned, then they would all die.

Thunder took the fire home with him to where he lived with his three beautiful daughters, and he gave Loon the task of guarding it so that the people or the other animals could not steal it back.

But the people did not die. They found ways of getting along, either eating their food raw or asking the Red Dog Salamanders to sleep next to their meat, for their orange-red color was able to cook the meat nearly as well as fire itself.

At that time all the people lived together in a big sweat lodge that was as large as a mountain.

In the mornings the Salamanders were always the first to go out. They would climb to the roof of the sweat lodge to warm themselves in the sunlight. And one morning as they were looking across the valley and toward the Coast Range, they saw smoke.

"Fire," one said. "We must tell the people."

* * *

A time of rains set in following the marriage of Acorn Girl and Bear-who-cannot-see-well, bringing a virtual end to the mining activities of the Panos and doubling the difficulty of the task of hunting. The meagre supply of acorn flour taken the preceding autumn was now exhausted also, and suddenly it was *ka-awk*, the hard times, with gray squirrels, ground squirrels, and wood rats being taken for food. When Grasshopper Man discovered a winter nest of lethargic rattlesnakes, more than thirty in all, it was a matter for rejoicing.

Whatever gustatory revulsion Benjamin Goffe might have experienced, he had been with the Panos long enough by this time to adapt, through necessity to the diversity of their dietary scheme of things. And to a man with an empty belly, he reflected, roasted snake flesh was palatable indeed.

At length the rain changed to snow, and for several hours the soft whiteness sifted down upon the forested extent of the *toommin*, draping the boughs of the giant trees and causing the branches of lilac and azalea, already in leaf, to sag under the weight.

When the snowfall ceased, long blue streaks appeared in the sky as the clouds split apart, allowing a glorious warmth of sunlight to spill down over the snow-draped highland.

Suddenly Maidu faces were cheerful, the talk animated. Crooked Knee and Ben set out hunting, the Indian with his bow and the Whiteman with his Hawken percussion rifle, and just beyond the sequoia grove, the two men came upon a band of mule deer, the animals huddled together under the protection of one of the big red-barked trees, shivering and wet in the new sunlight, their breaths drifting up in wisps of steam.

Ben sighted in on a young buck, antlers emergent and covered with velvet, while Crooked Knee sent an arrow into the throat of a doe that had no little ones.

In a moment the remainder of the mule deer were gone, but Ben and Crooked Knee clapped one another on the back, exhilarated by their good fortune.

Ben stayed with the game they had killed, not wishing to have the prizes taken over by wolves or coyotes or one of the mountain lions whose tracks the Panos had seen and whose voices, those almost human screams and wailings during the nights, they had heard. The big cats themselves had stayed away from the Pano encampment, being cautiously shy by nature and no doubt not wishing to enter into any disputes with Before and After, though in such a conflict, Acorn Girl had told Ben, the cougars would have been quite capable of holding their own.

Crooked Knee sprinted all the way back to the Pano encampment and returned in short order with Acorn Girl and Ranger and one of the other horses.

"My husband and Crooked Knee have been lucky at hunting," the Pano leader laughed. "Tonight we will all eat well, but I think Kauda will be served the choicest portion of the doe Crooked Knee has killed. Will she accept your gift, Crooked Knee?"

The young warrior pretended ignorance with regard to Ooti's meaning, but he could not suppress a slight smile.

A big firepit was prepared, and soon portions of venison were spitted and roasting over the bed of coals, droplets of fat flaring and giving off a maddeningly delicious odor.

The Panos gorged themselves on their first fresh meat in more than a week, and a warm wind flowed up over the plateau. The last of the clouds had vanished, and the night sky was strewn with countless stars.

Yo-meni now, the time of flowers resplendent across the mountains, springtime. The days were utterly clear, and the temperature rose quickly in apparent anticipation of the coming summer. The *Tem-diyoko* moon controlled the night sky, and Acorn Girl, the strength of her purpose renewed, spoke first to Hurt Eagle and then to her people.

"It is time to leave this place now," she said. "We have taken much gold, and Bear-who-cannot-see-well says that we will be able to buy horses and guns from the *Wawlems* if we are careful in the way we go about it. My husband is a Whiteman in his blood, even though I think his heart is now with us. And with the gold that we have taken from the gravel in the canyonside, he will have no trouble in buying the things we need to help us destroy our ene-

mies. Then we will go after the *Wawlem* named Johnson
and those others who work for him, for those men are
hated both by Panos who used to be the Tumeli and those
who used to be the Usto-ma. What Pano has told me to do
is well known to all of you, even if it may not be possible
to kill all of the *Wawlems* who have slain our people—for
the Whites come and go. They do not live in tribes, the
way we do. Most of them do not even have their women
with them. No, they wander from place to place, always
seeking for more of the gold. But Johnson and his men
will probably still be at the place called You Bet, not far
from where the Usto-ma village once was. If those men
are there, then we will find them and kill them. If they
have gone elsewhere during the time we have been away,
then we will continue to search for them. That is all,
hammu."

Ooti instructed Tied-wing, in accord with the judgments of Hurt Eagle, to lead the Panos westward, to a
small meadow near the stream beside which they had
found the unconscious Ben Goffe, a meadow that lay behind an unusual formation of pointed rock. He was to
avoid all contact with the Whites, staying well away from
such mining camps as Michigan Bluff and Illinois Town—
for the attack at You Bet, when it came, had to be executed with a maximum element of surprise.

Tied-wing, eager as he was to strike at the *Wawlems*,
listened to the words of his leader and agreed with her,
however reluctantly.

"Hurt Eagle's *kuksu* medicine," Acorn Girl said, "will
tell us when the proper time has come."

A greater problem lay in convincing Bear-who-comes-
before and Bear-who-comes-after that they, indeed, should
follow Hurt Eagle and Crane rather than herself and her
husband. The two grizzlies, in fact, had been somewhat
temperamental and cross ever since they had been ex-
cluded temporarily from Ooti's marriage lodge, acting rather
like two huge, overgrown children who were being de-
prived of their mother's attentions. Now she was obliged
to speak at great length to her adopted children, and they

stared at her with puzzled expressions, occasionally grunting or grooming one another as she spoke.

"Do they actually understand what you're saying?" Ben asked.

"Perhaps," Acorn Girl answered. "It is hard to tell with bears, even if one is their mother."

"Or one's wife?" Ben asked.

"That too, my husband. But soon you will return to your own people, and then I will not have to worry about the problem any more."

Goffe placed the tips of his fingers to Acorn Girl's lips, stared into her searching, dark brown eyes.

"You speak foolishly, Ooti," he said softly. "But right now I want to see if your . . . our sons are going to obey you."

"Go with Hurt Eagle!" Acorn Girl said for perhaps the tenth time.

Finally Bear-who-comes-after, whimpering and wrinkling back his lips to display his teeth, scrambled to his feet and lumbered off toward Hurt Eagle, Tied-wing, and the others. After an indecisive moment, his brother followed.

Crooked Knee, who had been designated as the one who was to accompany Ben and Ooti on their procurement mission, waved to Snakebite Dancer and grinned broadly when the young Usto-ma woman waved back.

Then, all three of them mounted on horseback, with three additional horses trailing behind, to be utilized as pack animals, the Pano leader and her husband and the young man she had allowed to come back into her group, turned eastward, intending to circle the maze of canyons further upcountry and then to make their way to the mining towns of Greenwood, Hangtown, and Placer Dry Diggings.

"Old Blue is happy to be moving again," Bear-who-cannot-see-well said to his companions. "This beast and I have come a long way together, about two thousand miles all told, from far beyond these mountains."

"That is where the Whitemen come from?" Crooked Knee asked. "From out in the deserts that lie beyond the mountains? I thought only the *Baawmkawle*, the red-faced wild people lived there. But they are not the same as the *Wawlems*, are they?"

"Tell us about the land you came from as we ride, my husband," Acorn Girl said. "And also about the lands you crossed through on your way here. You have told me before, I know, but I like to listen to the stories. Perhaps when you have finished, if there is still time and we have not already grown old, I will tell you the story about the girl who married her brother and then he married another and killed her. You like to write things down in your book full of blank pages. Maybe you will wish to write down this story also."

"The tale of Loon Woman," Crooked Knee said, his voice trailing off. "Yes, that is a beautiful story, but it is frightening."

"She married her brother?" Ben asked.

"Yes, she did that," Acorn Girl replied. "Her name was Ishanihura, and she lived a long time ago. But right now I wish to hear about the lands you say lie beyond even the deserts."

In Greenwood Ben had hoped to make contact with the son of the old mountain man, Caleb Greenwood, who had been a friend of O'Bragh. He'd met John months earlier, at Sutter's Fort, and with that brief encounter as a basis for trust, Ben hoped to be able to procure both White clothing for his Pano companions and a quantity of caps, powder, and lead as well—two objectives, he reasoned, that he would easily be able to accomplish without arousing suspicion of any kind. In truth, he had no way of knowing where young Greenwood's sympathies might lie. But back in Grass Valley Ben had heard the rumor of a thousand-dollar reward being posted for the head of the female leader of the Grizzly Cult.

Whiteman with a squaw, her brother riding with them? Should be nothing unusual in that. It's knowing the reality of a situation that makes the would-be criminal wary. And that's what I am, isn't it? A Yale professor turned White renegade, intent upon procuring arms for hostile Indians—a hanging offense, and no need for judge or jury, if such things even existed in California. For all I know, we've been admitted to the Federal Union since the boys up in Grass Valley put lead into my backside. . . .

Ben glanced over at Acorn Girl, riding beside him, studied the fine features of her face, thought beyond those to the dark kernel of hatred and need for revenge that lived inside her. Was it there, the darkness of the human heart? Was she in fact, for all her good nature and amorous abandon, not a variant of Medea, the witch whose jealous hatred drove her to destroy her own children as a means of gaining revenge upon the faithless Jason?

Don't know what ye'd do, ye oversized ox, if ye couldn't be comparin' every damned thing as happens to ye to some foolishness or other that ye've read in a book. Look around ye, man! Look straight at things for a change. Wagh!

Were the words, Ben wondered, something that Farnsworth O'Bragh had actually said—or were they something he'd imagined O'Bragh might have said?

No cure for ye, ye dunghead idjit. . . .

They reached Greenwood's post after a ride of two days, but the owner was not there, the little mercantile store being tended to by an Indian woman who identified herself as Greenwood's wife, a Miwok who had apparently adapted quite well, as Ben concluded, to the role of a White storekeeper's mate.

There were a number of Whites living in the area around the post, and several of the men, whether engaged in mining or some other activity, had wives—White women—with them.

Civilization's coming to the goldfields, no doubt about it.

In exchange for the proper amount of gold dust, Ben was able to acquire a calico dress for Ooti as well as a red bandana to wear as a kerchief, and for Crooked Knee some denim trousers and a blue-checked flannel shirt.

"He need a belt to go with them?" the Indian woman asked, jotting marks on a piece of brown wrapping paper.

"Yes, a belt," Ben nodded. "And we need a small keg of

black powder, percussion caps, and lead shot—fifties, forty-fives, and thirty-fours."

Greenwood's wife weighed out the amount Ben asked for, put everything into a burlap sack, and took Ben's gold in exchange.

Once back outside and mounted, Acorn Girl began to laugh.

"Now we will look like *Wawlems*," she said, "and you will still look like a Maidu. You bought us clothing, but nothing for yourself."

"Hadn't thought of it," Ben admitted. "Well, I'm dressed like a mountain man, a White Indian. It's probably the best disguise I could have."

"Do the *mountain men* wear deerskins and glasses?" Crooked Knee asked.

Ben shrugged.

"The small *Wawlem* who was standing outside the store," Acorn Girl noted, "he was also wearing spectacles. Do you remember the men at Kolo-ma, Crooked Knee? Two or three of those Mormons did also. Now we must stop up ahead, Bear-who-cannot-see-well, so that Crooked Knee and I can put on our disguises. It will be better if the clothes do not appear to be too new when we reach the larger *Wawlem* villages. Many of the Maidus work for the Whites, and most of them wear *Wawlem* clothing. You worry too much . . . Ben."

After some discussion, Acorn Girl and her husband decided against making the venture south to Hangtown—a journey that would require the backtracking of some twenty miles or more through an area nearly overrun by miners and various small tent settlements along the South Fork of the American River. Rather, they proceeded to Coloma, where a town, complete with wooden-frame buildings, had grown up and where Marshall's mill, in the absence of its founder, was busy—the big circular blade humming and groaning as it cut through logs of ponderosa and digger pine and fir, the smell of pitch and sawdust heavy in the air.

Acorn Girl was fearful of being recognized, though Ben

assured her that it was highly unlikely any of the men from that earlier time would be still in the area.

"The Kolo-mas themselves may recognize me," she said. "My husband who is dead was one of them before he came to live with my people, and for a time he and I lived together in a square lodge made of planks, just as the *Wawlems* do. I would feel better if Marshall were here. He is my friend."

"So he told me," Bear-who-cannot-see-well nodded. "It's just as well that he's not here, in fact. A man can let word slip out, even when he doesn't intend to. Stay close to me, both of you. First thing we have to do is to acquire a few horses, pack animals or otherwise."

After making a few preliminary inquiries, Ben found himself at O'Kelley's Pens, a small stockyard of sorts, the corrals containing twenty or more cows and half a dozen mules.

"Those are the ugly, bad-natured horses," Crooked Knee said softly when Ben began to take an interest in the creatures.

"That they are," he replied, "but very intelligent. I have it on the best of authority. Better for pack animals than horses, and willing to be ridden as well. Almost indestructible, in fact."

"You are certain of this?" Acorn Girl asked, the tone of her voice somewhat skeptical. "The ones we already have are stubborn."

"I had two of my own in Grass Valley," Ben said. "Maybe I ought to go back for them. Those mules came clear across the mountains and deserts with me and Old Blue."

Acorn Girl and Crooked Knee exchanged glances, and then Acorn Girl nodded to Ben.

Chip Randall, the present owner of O'Kelley's Pens, was asking seventy dollars apiece for the mules, and Ben shook his head, started to turn away.

"Sixty each," Randall asked. "Them's good mules."

"Deal," Ben agreed, turning back to face the man. "Need pack saddles as well. Can you fix me up with them?"

"How you payin', Mister?"

"Dust."

"Packs is twenty each."

"I'm paying fifteen, no more."

"Let's see yore dust, Goliath."

With their mules and pack horses in tow, it was now more convenient to stay on the rutted wagon road that twisted and turned its way from Coloma to Placer Dry Diggings to the north. From the canyon rim, Ben and Ooti and Crooked Knee could look down to where the North Fork and the Middle Fork of the American joined, smoke rising from a number of campfires and various tents and shanties standing close along both sides of the streams.

"Placer Dry Diggings should be just beyond," Ben said, pointing toward the opposite rim of the canyon. "And it looks like the boys have even slung up a bridge across the river for us. Mules appreciate bridges. . . ."

As they began their descent of the canyon, a cloud of vultures, a dozen or more of the big birds, rose up from a rocky outcropping, their wings beating at the air. Ben nudged Old Blue's sides and guided the Percheron away from the main trail, curiosity having gotten the better of him.

Two human forms, or what was left of them, were lying spread-eagled beside the outcropping of limestone, the eyes already gouged out and the belly of one laid open.

"What in God's name?" Ben gasped as he stared down at the two dead men.

Both had been riddled with bullets, and oak staves had been driven through their chests, fixing the bodies in place. A short section of planking had been attached to yet another stake and implanted into the rocky ground.

Ben dismounted and walked close to where the dead men lay, kneeled, and read the words that had been hastily inscribed in charcoal upon the section of board:

Hardt & Hawley, blood-suckers to the last, shot & buried this way because they cleaned out a honest man's riffles. Done by the Vigilance Committee, 7th of May, '50.

"I have seen that one before," Acorn Girl said, pointing to the corpse on the left. "I don't know about the other one—his face is too torn apart. The vultures have done a good job. Who killed these men, my husband?"

"Vigilantes," Ben said. "A kind of Whiteman's justice. You mean that one was . . ."

"I do not know whether he came to the village with Johnson and the others that night, but he was there at Kolo-ma. He worked for Marshall, just as my husband did. Why were they killed in this way?"

"Stealing another man's gold," Ben shrugged. "Caught in the act, most likely—or else just rounded up and done away with. Not all *Wawlems* are like Johnson and Sonny Penryn and the others. Some actually believe in the law. Your people would never think to steal from one another, but sometimes Whitemen do, and then . . ."

"This was a *Wawlem* revenge-taking?" Acorn Girl asked, apparently satisfied with the idea.

"Yes, I guess so," Ben said.

"Let us go," Crooked Knee complained. "These dead men stink very badly. We must allow the big birds to finish what they have begun. Vultures will eat anything."

Benjamin Goffe, his two apparently tame Indians with him, made the rounds of general stores, hardwares, and gunsmiths in Placer Dry Diggings and with the expenditure of some three thousand dollars in gold managed to purchase a number of pistols, rifles, knives, additional quantities of percussion caps, powder, and lead, along with five saddle horses.

The purchases made by the big man in buckskins did not go unnoticed, however, and by the time Ben had found his way to the livery to acquire the horses and to load everything for the ride northward, several townsmen gathered about outside the stables.

"Quite an outfit you're fittin' up, stranger," the red-faced, nearly bald proprietor remarked as he weighed out the nuggets and dust. "If a man didn't know better, he'd figger you was outfittin' a band of desperadoes or some like."

"North Fork Mining Company," Ben said, feigning in-
difference to the man's curiosity. "Dan Cummings' bunch,
he's the foreman of the outfit. High water this spring took
out our main storage building, truth to say."

"Where'd you say you was mining?"

"Don't remember mentioning it," Ben replied.

"North Fork of the American—that where you be?"

"Hell no," Ben laughed. "Cummings, he sent me and
my squaw and her brother down to Sacramento City—
little business with Sam Brannan. You've heard of him?
We went down the Yuba to Marysville and then south,
decided to come back this way. How much for that silver-
dollar bridle hanging from the rack?"

"Not for sale," the red-faced man answered. "Yore operation's up Downieville way, then?"

Ben glanced at Acorn Girl and Crooked Knee, then
back at the proprietor.

"You've got it figured," he confided. "Old Dan and the
bunch of us have got the richest damned lead in the
mountains, by God. There's twenty-two of us all together,
counting our Miwoks, and we're set up to run off anybody
that gets near. We've laid six men under already this
spring—that's just between you and me, friend."

"That a fact?" the red-faced man said.

Ben shrugged.

"We've got to protect what's ours," he said.

The final transaction was quickly completed, and Ben,
Acorn Girl, and Crooked Knee rode northeastward, following the Illinois Town road for a mile or two and then,
suspecting that they might be followed, diverged from the
main trail and made their way along the rim of the American River Canyon.

Acorn Girl told Crooked Knee to turn his horse and
swing back down the way they had come, to keep out of
sight.

The young warrior returned within just a few minutes,
an uneasy expression on his face.

"Seven *Wawlems* on horseback," he said. "They're after
us, Ooti. Do we try to outrun them? How can we do that
with these animals all loaded down?"

Acorn Girl stared at her husband, and Ben knew the

meaning of the question that was in her eyes. If it came to a conflict with the Whites, what would he do?

"Down into the ravine ahead," she ordered. "We cannot get away from these men, so we will have to wait for them."

Ben laughed and urged Old Blue ahead. The tone of Ooti's voice was so utterly calm, he reflected, that only a fool would question her.

There's trouble coming. A time of choice is upon you, Benjamin Goffe. A man signs his name to a document and then he may live to regret it. I left my family and crossed an ocean. . . .

Ben recognized the voice that played through his mind, but the present moment, he concluded, was hardly an appropriate time to conduct any sort of dialogue.

Acorn Girl, amazingly adroit on the back of the forlorn horse called Ranger, quickly maneuvered the pack animals to the crest of an oak thicket beyond the shallow ravine, a spot from which the open fields through which they had been riding were completely visible.

"Now we will watch the men Crooked Knee discovered," she said. "Bear-who-cannot-see-well, maybe this is not your fight? There is still time for you to get away. . . ."

Ben slapped the stock of his Hawken rifle and grinned.

"You talk nonsense," he replied. "I've got a score to settle too, some scars I didn't have a while back."

"You are with us then?" she asked.

"You own me, Ooti. Haven't forgotten that, have you?"

Acorn Girl laughed.

"No," she said. "I haven't forgotten. Look, Ben—they're coming."

"Seven," Crooked Knee muttered, "just as I reported."

Goffe raised his Colt Walker revolver and sent a single shot singing over the swale, the sound echoing with surprising loudness from a low rise beyond the open meadow. Bluejays began to scream in outrage, and the seven Whitemen drew to a sudden halt.

"What do you thieves want?" Ben roared.

A volley of pistol fire came in answer, and then the apparent leader of the group began to curse.

"Hold fire, damn it! You, up on the hill—this is Deputy

Sheriff Boggs! No point in anyone getting galena in his hide—come on down from there, I want to talk is all!"

Ben glanced at Acorn Girl, and the Pano leader nodded.

Goffe stood up and took half a dozen steps forward, still unwilling to move directly out into the open.

Another sudden volley of pistol fire, one ball thudding into the bole of a bush-shaped oak that was just coming into leaf, the shot spitting bark.

Ben dived for cover, uncertain for a moment whether he had actually been hit. Then he leveled his own pistol and fired back.

More gunshots from behind him—Acorn Girl and Crooked Knee now beginning to fire. And the men below, dismounting hurriedly, were beginning to make their way, dodging from tree to tree, toward the oak-covered knoll.

Then, from the low rise beyond the meadow, the heavy crack of what Ben took to be some sort of plains rifle, and one of the men below seemed to jerk in midstride, took another step or two, and fell sideways, all without making a sound.

A screeching half-yell, half-yodel from the rim beyond and then another echoing boom of rifle fire.

Acorn Girl and Crooked Knee were continuing their barrage at the men below, and Ben now quickly emptied his revolver, reached for his Hawken and fired that, and then reloaded the revolver, his hands trembling as he set the caps.

Again a rifle blast from the far rise, and three of the seven men below were lying stretched out amidst clumps of thick spring grass, tangles of sweetpea vines, and occasional clusters of bright yellow poppies. Horses were screaming and rearing, and one of the men, attempting to mount, was thrown hard to the ground. As he struggled to rise, another precisely aimed rifle ball from the low rim struck him in the head, tearing away his nose and one cheek. The wounded man screamed out, clasped his hands to what was left of his face, and then jackknifed backward as a second shot hit him.

Four men lay dead, and the other three, successful in mounting their horses, had ridden wildly away, leaning low against the necks of their animals.

After a moment a thrush began to sing, and once more a bluejay cried out. Ben wiped the sweat from under his eyes and readjusted his glasses, smelled the distinctive odor of the thin grass where he had lain. He turned about, started to crawl toward where Acorn Girl and Crooked Knee were waiting behind the screen of liveoaks.

"Ben Goffe, ye damned fool!" a male voice drifted up to him. "This hyar's the Irish Vulture. I been lookin' for ye, lad!"

Two riders came down from the low rise, a man and a woman, both on muleback—and following behind them came two more pack animals.

This is all a dream, a crazy dream. I must still be lying unconscious beside the creek where I saw the big fish. . . .

"Basic problem is," Bully O'Bragh said after a break-neck ride of several miles and a nearly disastrous fording of the narrow but torrential Bear River, "yore husband, Miss Acorn Girl, he's already married to some no-account, high-class Eastern female. Done told me so hisself. An' second, Big Ben hyar's already dead, gone under more'n two, two an' a half months ago. Fact is, the boys in Grass Valley already done lynched a Peruvian for 'er, an' that's the truth, by the blue balls o' the Virgin Mary."

Goffe burst out laughing, and O'Bragh chuckled at his own incongruous mixture of figures. Acorn Girl and Crooked Knee merely looked puzzled, and Rabbit-chaser shrugged.

"Well, I'm not dead as it turns out. Ooti and her people found me and pulled me through. Perhaps Connecticut Yankees are a bit tougher than they're generally given credit for. You were in Grass Valley, as I take it, old friend?"

"Been thar," O'Bragh said, patting Porcupine the mule across the rump. "Yore newspaper es-tablishment's been burned to the ground, for a fact. Ain't nothin' left there, Benny me lad. I come lookin' for ye—thought ye might be of a mind to head back to St. Louis or summat, an' what did this nigger find? A pile o' charcoal, that's what. *Wagh!* For all this child knew, ye was a part of it. But yore other girlfriend told me different."

"He has more than one wife already?" Acorn Girl asked.

"What are you talking about, O'Bragh?" Ben demanded.

"Not one as he was married to," Bully said, winking at Acorn Girl. "Jest kind of an occasional companion, ye might say. Lady by the name o' the Rose of You Bet, as it turns out. An' she said ye had writ to the gawddamned gov'ner an' had rode off to meet with 'im down to Sutter's Fort. When ye never arrived, old General Riley an' some of his soldier boys rode up to find ye out, an' that's when the whole thing got kind of put together. An' when they was no word of ye for a couple of weeks, the General done writ a letter to yore wife, sayin' she ought to think about finding a new husband or some such—that ye was dead, without question. An' that was when that dumbass Fischer arrested Lupe Velasquez, the Peruvian card thief—on suspicion, mostly. But the boys busted into the jail an' took old Lupe out to Hill's Flat an' strung him up."

Goffe shook his head.

"Things happen quickly in the California goldfields, as I gather."

"Do that," O'Bragh agreed. "Tell me for true now, Benny. Ye ain't really dead, are ye?"

"Do I look dead?"

"Hard to tell sometimes. Me, I been dead for ten, twelve years myself—got tore up by the Rees when I was comin' back down river with Lewis and Clark, Gawd rest their souls an' may they have plenty o' hump rib in the Spirit World."

Acorn Girl had been studying the old man in the tattered buckskins and beaver cap for some minutes, trying to intuit what lay behind the wrinkled lines of the face, and not failing to take note of the strings of scalps, both Indian and White, that Bully had fastened to either side of his mule's packsacks. Here by the river, gabbling away, he appeared harmless enough. And yet Ooti was just now putting fully together what had happened in the meadow where the poppies had been in bloom. Four men were dead, and it was nearly certain that none of her own pistol fire or Crooked Knee's or that of Bear-who-cannot-see-well had been responsible. No, this old man, this friend of her husband's, had very accurately and casually slain four of his own kind.

"Can he be trusted?" she asked Ben. "This friend of yours who led you into our lands?"

"Aw, missy, o' course ye can trust Farnsworth O'Bragh. Jest don't use that handle to call me by, is all. Name's Bully. Done got yore fat out o' the fire, din't I? Shore I did."

"No," Rabbit-chaser said, speaking directly to Acorn Girl, "you can never trust this one. He is very crazy in the head, but he has been a good husband to me."

"Damned right," O'Bragh grinned.

"So how did the general know my wife's—Etta's—name and address?" Ben asked.

O'Bragh shrugged, grunted.

"Mebbe Sutter told 'im," Bully suggested.

Nightfall found the party reunited with the Pano Maidus, who had made camp, as agreed, in a small meadow that lay behind a jagged upthrust of rock, high in the hills above Woodpecker Ravine and the tumbling creek beside which Goffe had been left for dead.

Ooti conferred immediately with Hurt Eagle and Tied-wing, and meanwhile the other Panos were inspecting the new mules and horses as well as the arsenal of rifles and pistols and knives.

When the ancient shaman and the most powerful of the Pano warriors rejoined the others and were introduced to Bully O'Bragh and had listened to the story of how the mountain man had saved Acorn Girl, Bear-who-cannot-see-well, and Crooked Knee from the possibility of being captured or of having their animals and guns taken from them, Acorn Girl proceeded to assign either horse or mule to each of the young men and to hand out the weapons. All now possessed either a pistol or a rifle, and several had both, men and women alike.

"It is not long," she said, "before we will conduct a different kind of *Pano-ng-kasi* for the gold miners at Chalk Bluff, Johnson and Penryn and the others, and Lindley too, if he is there. The Spirit Bear will be proud of the grizzly-bear dance we will hold. The gold that brought the *Wawlem* curse into our lands has now for the first time been good to us—it has given us many weapons and horses to ride. We will be able to move quickly once you have all practiced riding the horses and mules. We have enough guns to defend ourselves against anyone. We are not many, but we have now grown very strong. Those who have murdered our people and burned our villages will soon discover how strong we are! *Hammu*, this is all I have to say. Now we must wait for Pano himself."

Loud murmurs of approval went through the group as Acorn Girl turned to the *kuksu* master, Hurt Eagle, and embraced him.

"Ye've hitched up with a real hellcat, ain't ye?" O'Bragh whispered to Ben. "But are ye sure for certain that ye wants to be tied up in all this? I take it she's fixin' to take on a whole damned town. Benny, the odds is jest powerful as hell that Ooti an' all her Red Divvels is goin' to end up deader'n yore fundamental mackerel. An' that means you an' me too an' Rabbit-chaser if we string along. Sonny, ye ought to think the matter through. Don't all them books ye read tell ye nothin'?"

That night, with the coyotes yelling back and forth across the canyon, Bear-who-cannot-see-well and Acorn Girl lay in each other's arms, a half-grown grizzly to either side of them, the bears sighing and coughing and grunting in their sleep. The man and the woman clung tightly to each other, and Ben became aware, as if for the first time, of how small and how soft Ooti was. True, she was taller than any of the other Maidu women, and true, the muscles in her arms and legs were tensile, powerful for a woman. But in his embrace she was small, and here under the oak trees and the warm, cloudless sky above, she was cuddled to his chest and was pressing her lips to the recently healed wound in his shoulder.

Then with one hand she reached down to grasp his manhood, and he groaned softly, in pleasure.

"I am already all wet between my legs," she whispered.

"Put your male thing into me, or I will squeeze it so hard that it falls off."

"Well," Bear-who-cannot-see-well said, "since you put it that way."

"Roll over on top of me," she insisted. "I will not be able to breathe until you are through, but that is all right. I cannot wait any longer, my husband."

But instead Ben slid down the length of her and touched his lips to the wet place, thrust his tongue into her and moved it back and forth.

"You must not do that," she whispered, pulling at his hair.

"Lie still," he growled, "and see what happens."

She did not resist, attempted to relax. And after a moment she said, between shallow breaths, "I think I know . . . Ben . . . I can hardly stand this. . . ."

He fell into sleep with the yelpings of coyotes in his ears and the warm odor of grizzly bears in his nostrils. But in his mouth was the taste of Ooti, and the taste played like fire about his half-numb mouth.

A small child now, hiding, hiding behind two large rose bushes in the garden, watching what was happening in the open space beyond him, the smell of bruised grass, the discordant cries of bluejays.

Etta, her primly small mouth, the thin-plucked eyebrows, violet eyes and the abundant storm of blonde hair, the curls, each precisely set, looping down about her face, the painfully thin waist and large breasts, the woman who kept herself cinched in and had an entire closet full of underthings and who at first refused ever to make love with a lantern burning and then later did not wish to make love at all, not with him.

There she was. And he saw her stripping her clothing away in wild abandon, saw her pulling at the gown of a young Catholic priest, saw her pressing her mouth down to his middle.

And his face—a skull, fleshless, the hollow eyesockets dark, the teeth clicking together, clicking. . . .

He tried to cry out, but no words would form—only an

*inchoate growling, great effort to make any sound whatso-
ever.*

Intense light then, and when it had diminished once
more, Etta and the priest were both gone.

A gallows to one side of the yard, a great fire on the
other. A witch being hung. Another screaming out from
a halo of flames. And British soldiers in full uniform—
they were dragging a half-rotted corpse about and singing:

> Cromwell's mad
> And we're glad
> And we know what will please him. . . .

Then corpse and soldiers and gallows and fire were all
gone, and a tall, gaunt figure emerged, a man in officer's
garb, a broadsword in his hand. Yet another man emerged
from the shadows beyond the rosebushes, challenged the
man to a duel.

The combatants hurled themselves at one another, and
the fight went on without a discernible advantage to either
until the challenger stepped back and cried out, "You're
either the Devil in disguise or General Goffe, for no one
else could fight so well!"

At those words, Ben struggled forward, the thorns of
the rose tearing at his clothing. He was a full-grown man
once more, and now he faced his great-great-great grandfather.

"I'm Benjamin," he said, his voice shaking. "I'm one of
your descendants."

"You know me?" the elder Goffe asked.

"Yes. Yes. I've studied about you, I've thought about
you often, talked with you often. Don't you remember?"

"You're no doubt one of the new king's men," the elder
Goffe said, offering to strike with the broadsword.

"No!" Ben cried out. "You are my grandpa, don't you
understand? You're General William Goffe, Major General of the Commonwealth of England. You signed the
death warrant of King Charley. Don't you remember me,
Grandfather?"

"I was looking for that damned Whalley," the elder
Goffe said. "Have you seen him, son?"

"You are my . . . forebear. You are Judge Goffe, and you fled to New England and hid in caves and cellars. You married an Indian woman, and your blood still lives in me!"

The elder Goffe laid the sword aside and sat down on the grass, withdrew two cigars from his coat pocket, and handed one to Ben, lit the other, and blew smoke into the air.

"I remember you now, Benny," he said. "It's harder and harder for me to recall things. Yes, her name was Loon-cry, and I insisted on calling her Agatha. But the marriage was not legally binding, you understand that. I already had a family in . . ."

"I know that, Grandfather," Ben said. "And I too have left a wife behind me. I've married an Indian girl, and I've been declared legally dead."

"You're fortunate, Benny. I could never escape my own identity, and yet I had not sinned. The king was already dead—we only executed the man who had falsely worn the crown and had claimed infinite power."

"Tell me what I am to do, Grandfather. I need your help. . . ."

General William Goffe puffed on his cigar and once again blew smoke up into the air.

"Your name's Benny?" he asked. "Yes. Well. Tell me, lad, is she . . . well, is she good in bed? By God! I'd say change your name and go out into the wilderness. New Haven Colony, Hartford, Boston—these are not places for men of vision. And as to guilt—why, it's the most unproductive thing on Earth. Live well, and be true to your sense of honor. . . ."

Bear-who-cannot-see-well came half awake, put out an arm, and touched rough fur. In a moment he realized his mistake and turned back to where Acorn Girl was lying beside him.

15

Bully and Ben Have Fun

May, 1850

The people heard the cries of the Salamanders and came running out of the sweat lodge—but then, when they realized the Red Dogs were talking about fire, they believed a trick was being played upon them, and they lost interest.

"Look for yourself!" one of the Salamanders called out. "Do you not see the smoke over in the west?"

But before the people could look, Peheipe Oleli the Coyote leaped up onto the roof of the sweat lodge and began to throw dirt on top of the Salamanders, and the people down below started to laugh and cheer.

Then Kuksu emerged from the lodge, and he called out to Coyote and told him to stop.

"You foolish Coyote," he said, "why do you always cause trouble? You like to start fights, and then you run away, howling and laughing. The Salamanders are right, and you are wrong, as usual. We should never listen to you at all."

Then Peheipe Oleli and all the people looked to where the Salamanders had been pointing, and they saw the smoke that was rising above the Coast Range.

"How shall we steal the fire back from Thunder?" Morning Star Woman asked. "He is a bad man, and he is very powerful. I don't know whether we should try to get it or not."

"I have an idea," Coyote said, "but no one ever listens to me. Kuksu says I'm a troublemaker, so perhaps I'd better go look for an old bone to chew on."

*   *   *

Tem-diyoko, the moon of fawns, would soon reach its full, rising just as the sun flamed crimson across the long ridges to the west of the temporary encampment, and the fully armed Pano Maidus made their preparations for the move eastward, to the drainage of Steephollow Creek, where the Usto-ma village had once stood. Acorn Girl announced that the group would once again move by cover of night, for the area into which they were entering was populated by numerous small *Wawlem* camps, to say nothing of the larger settlements at Sandy Bar, You Bet, and Red Dog. A band of Nishinams, whether leading or riding horses and carrying weapons would, if observed, not only rouse suspicion but almost certainly encourage an organized attack by the Whites.

"The woods are dense," Acorn Girl said, "and it is possible for us to slip through by daylight, spreading out as we move and using great care. But this way is better, for the Whitemen will be sleeping. After working in the mud all day, they are too tired to do anything else."

By late afternoon all was ready, and the Panos ate a cold meal, unwilling to risk the danger of even a few small cooking fires. And afterward, to while away the remaining time until their departure, they gathered around as Slow Rabbit engaged in a mock wrestling match with Bear-who-comes-after, the young grizzly growling and snarling with proper histrionic vigor but at the same time being careful not to harm his human playmate.

When Slow Rabbit managed to slip away from the somewhat clumsy bear, the Panos applauded, and Before rolled over on his back and seemed to clap his forepaws together in the air. Slow Rabbit danced about his opponent and then, as Before scrambled to his feet, leaped onto his back, hugged him about the neck, and was given a fast, short, and suddenly terminated ride, the grizzly setting his feet and lowering his head so that Slow Rabbit was pitched off almost at Acorn Girl's feet.

Now After wanted to enter into the game, but Slow Rabbit had had enough. The two bears, not to be discouraged, took a few playful swats at one another and then went nuzzling up to Crane to see if the portly old woman had anything else for them to eat.

The group was just disbanding, each to see to weapons, supplies, and horse or mule—when After stood up on his hind legs, growled and whined, and shook his head back and forth, peering downslope to where the springs gathered to form a little stream.

O'Bragh's Hawken was suddenly in his hands, and the mountain man was gesturing wordlessly toward Ben and Acorn Girl.

"We seek your help!" a voice cried out from below, the words in Nishinam, not English. "We have not eaten for two days, and our old people and little ones cannot go any further. I am Goose Leader, Huku of the Kulkumish Maidus. I have people from the Hembem village with me also. Do you have anything for us to eat?"

Acorn Girl glanced at Hurt Eagle and then at Tied-wing, nodded, and called out: "Stay where you are, Goose Leader! If you are the person you claim to be, then we will give you what we have. Are there truly children and old people with you?"

"I will come up to you alone," Goose Leader answered. "You will see that I mean you no harm. . . ."

The solitary figure appeared from out of the draw, a man of perhaps sixty winters. He used a long stick to walk with, and one leg was loosely bandaged with a pad of grass fastened on by bands of deerhide.

"You walk with a stick," Acorn Girl called to him, stepping forward from the others and at the same time signaling for Tied-wing, Crooked Knee, and Grasshopper Man to fan out along the edges of the draw so as to make a quick count of the number of people hidden there. "What has happened to you? What kind of wound do you have?"

The Kulkumish leader hobbled on up the grassy slope, the corded muscles of his arms gleaming in the late sunlight as he utilized his tall cane as an aid to the one leg he half-dragged along.

He stopped, took a deep breath, and said, "We are not enemies. You can see now that I am unarmed. I could not even protect myself if I wished to do so. Seven days ago the miners destroyed Hembem, down on the river. Those who escaped the *Wawlem* rifles came to me for assistance, and I took them in. But then the *Wawlems* struck at us also. They came into our village from Illinois Town, just as they had done many times before. They seemed very happy, but then they began to shoot at us. They have slain all who did not manage to run away from them. So now we are searching for a new place to live, but we have found nothing to eat, only one dead deer that vultures were crowded about. . . . Hurt Eagle, is that you, my old friend? Do you not recognize me? I came to you many years ago as a student."

"I recognize you, Goose Leader, even though you are much changed. This man speaks only the truth, Acorn Girl," Hurt Eagle declared.

"Tell your people to come into our camp," Acorn Girl said, her voice hardly above a whisper. "We will share all that we have with you."

She felt pain in her chest, terrible pain beneath her breasts. She looked up and saw the sun flaring westward, a glorious explosion of gold and silver and crimson that burned in the bandings of cloud. And for an instant it seemed to her that the Maidu sun was indeed dying, would never rise again.

"How many times—how many times will it happen to us?" she whispered into the gentle wind that moved about her.

The horror of Kolo-ma, the deaths of those she had loved, the violation, repeated violation at the hands of the miners—and the strewn bodies at Usto-ma, heads hacked off, sexes cut out, skulls split open, the horrible odor of burned human flesh, splatches of black, half-dried blood on the earth. . . .

She watched the people, the remnants of Kulkumish and Hembem villages, file up the hill, their eyes all but dead, old women with infants in their arms, not their own, young men dazed and beaten, old men who had seen their world vanish.

There were no young mothers among these people, no girls of marriageable age, not even girls of twelve or thirteen or fourteen. And Acorn Girl knew why, knew without question that they had been raped and killed or taken as slaves by the Whites, to be fed and used for so long as they were able to satisfy their masters.

Bear-who-cannot-see-well, Benjamin Goffe, was now standing beside her, her husband, her huge husband who was also a Whiteman—and she wanted to turn to him, wanted him to hold her in his great arms, even to make her feel like a small, secure child again. No, he was not a part of this, he was not a Lindley or a Penryn. But he was *Wawlem*, and for the moment she knew she was unable to look at him. It was not his fault, but she could not do it.

And so she willed the heart that was broken within her to heal itself, to burn and to fuse the fragments into one. Her mind grew hard and strong, and the mind willed the heart together. The mind glowed with hatred and a need to strike back—not just a need any more, an unslakable desire. Perhaps, after all, Tied-wing had been right. If one could not determine the exact identities of those responsible, then others would suffice— their blood would have to suffice.

How could this be the dream of Olelbis? Or, if Pano was indeed right, then perhaps the dream, without knowledge or permission of the dreamer, had turned itself into a nightmare, a nightmare that would eventually destroy everything.

Bear-who-cannot-see-well touched his hand to her shoulder, and she willed herself not to flinch away from her husband.

"Extermination," he said.

Acorn Girl had not heard this English word before, but even so she knew exactly what it meant.

They remained yet another day, and Acorn Girl, incandescent with the fires that now burned within her, insisted that all the newcomers who were able should be given a weapon and instructed in its use. No practice shots were fired, for the sound of gunshots would echo across the canyons and could, in all likelihood, draw the curious. While the Panos were now sufficiently armed and numerous enough to fend off any but a concerted effort against them, the time and the place were not yet right. No, Ezra Johnson and his company of miners were probably still where they had been, near You Bet. And that settlement lay just a few miles to the northeast, close by the ridge known as Chalk Bluff.

O'Bragh, who had picked up the Nishinam language from the Silong-koyo villagers at Quincy and American Valley, was everywhere, giving instruction in the use of the various assortment of weapons that Ooti and Ben had managed to procure. Ben and Ooti and Tied-wing and everyone else who had become adept in the use of fire-arms did likewise, explaining matters of loading, tamping, the use of wadding with the rifles, how to tap the priming pans with the several old flintlocks, how to set the caps, how to sight and squeeze off the rounds, to anticipate impact against shoulder or palm. For hours the instruction went on, and all without the triggering of so much as a round.

Only when the darkness was near did Acorn Girl instruct all to whom the use of pistol or rifle was new to fire off a single shot at the fallen trunk of a big liveoak that had apparently gone over in some storm of the preceding winter.

Streak after streak of blue-white flame leaped out, and the sounds echoed off across the maze of hill and canyon.

Then the Panos began their move northeastward, toward the White settlements in and around You Bet.

When dawn came, the Panos had reached their old encampment above the creek called Steephollow, and for several hours the people slept, exhausted after the night's ride, slow-going over a circuitous route determined by the presence of clusters of miners' tents and shanties that were nearly everywhere along Bear River and Greenhorn Creek and the lower reaches of Steephollow itself, below the falls.

Hurt Eagle elected to stand watch, insisting that Acorn Girl herself sleep for a time and that, in any case, at his age he no longer needed sleep.

The sun was well up into a flawlessly blue sky when Ben awoke, realizing that the terrific pressure of After had numbed his legs.

Ooti stirred also then and sat up. Bear-who-cannot-see-well leaned over, kissed his wife on the forehead, and ran his fingers over her long black hair.

"What I need," he said, "is some coffee. Think I'll raid O'Bragh's saddlebags—he's always got a bag of beans somewhere."

"No fire today," Acorn Girl said, shaking her head. "We must not let the *Wawlems* know we're here. They will have coffee in You Bet, though, won't they?"

"Of course," Ben said, standing up and stretching and then, observing that both grizzlies were now sitting about on their haunches like gigantic dogs, stroked their muzzles and roughed their fur. After decided that this was an invitation to sport and proceeded to tug at Ben's leathers, pulling him backward a step or two before Ooti reprimanded her ungainly pet.

"Ben," Acorn Girl said, "I will lead an attack this night. It is possible that we will all be killed, if that is the will of Pano. My people and I are bound to do this thing, no matter what comes of it, but the Bear Spirit has placed no obligation upon you. If you wish to return to your own people now, my husband, I will understand. You have given me love when I believed I would never love again, and it has been good, very good. I must make this attack because of things that happened long before you came to me, and it is not right that you should die because I am *moka*, insane for revenge. Now I think that you and your strange friend should leave us so that we may do what we must."

Bear-who-cannot-see-well stared at the woman he loved, grinned, and shook his head.

"You really think you're going to cheat me out of all the fun?" he asked.

Ooti studied his face, said nothing.

"Acorn Girl, Ooti-du, I have made a long journey to find love. I have made a long swim. Forty-eight winters have passed over my head—I am not a young man, beautiful one. How then could I ever live again if I thought you had died and I was not with you? If Pano requires that you pass into the Upper Meadow, Ooti, then I will go with you. Consider this—I did not force you to marry me, and I did not even court you in the way of your people. No, I was a stranger. You saved my life when your people wished to leave me there by the stream—that or put another bullet into me. Yes, I've learned about how it happened. But you saved my life, and I became yours. Then you had me sent to your bed and forced me to make love to you. That's how it happened, and you can't deny it. You were shameless, and you took my virginity, so to speak. Now you have grown tired of Bear-who-cannot-see-well, and yet he refuses to leave you. Even if you should decide to divorce me in the way of your people, I will not go away. I will sit around with your other bears, outside your lodge, and whine all night long."

Acorn Girl smiled then, but there was a kind of distant sadness in her eyes.

"I do not want you to go, my husband," she said. "I wish . . . I wish there were somewhere we could live, somewhere my people could live and hunt and fish and gather the acorns, the gifts of *Ootimtsaa*, the oak tree. Even now, part of me does not really hate these Whitemen, no matter what they have done. But another part of me, that part hates them and can never rest until it has destroyed as many of them as it can. Do you understand my words, Bear-who-cannot-see-well?"

"Yes," Ben answered, "I understand perfectly."

"You will not go?"

"No, Ooti. We will fight together, and if your gods or mine will allow it, we will find a way to pass beyond what happens tonight. Bully and I went through some lands where no Whiteman will ever wish to live, places where there is no gold. There are no oaks either, but there is game. And the people who live there gather nuts from the pinyon pines. It is a land that will not change much, no matter what happens here."

Ooti touched her fingertips to her lips and gazed up into the cloudless sky, watched a pair of great-winged *molokos*, condors, flying away southward.

"Even the birds leave now," she said. "This place you are talking of—is that where the Paiutes and Shoshones live, for that is what I have heard. Do you think oaks would grow there if we took acorns with us and planted them?"

But it was not the season for acorns, and both knew it. It was not *Se-meni*, the seed-bearing time.

The sun was at mid-sky when Benjamin Goffe and Bully O'Bragh left the Pano encampment and began the five-mile ride that would take them over the big ridge and away from Steephollow and down to the tent cities of You Bet and Red Dog, both of which lay close to Greenhorn Creek, their object that of determining the exact location of the Chalk Bluff Mining Company, Ezra Johnson, foreman. In the interval since he had been wounded and left for dead, Ben was well aware, the operation could have folded or relocated elsewhere. During his brief stint as editor of the *Del Oro Star*, Goffe had come to realize that a week never passed without a rumor or two circulating of immensely rich new strikes being made beyond Downieville, east of Camptonville, on Bear Gulch above the Middle Fork of the Feather, at Crystal Caves on the Cosumnes, and the like. And each time the news spread, usually founded on no more than hearsay or simply wishful thinking and a need to move on, a certain number of miners pulled up stakes and headed out in favor of this new hint of Eldorado.

His task now was to gain whatever information he could. But whether Johnson and his sidekick Sonny Penryn were in the area or not, he had come to realize, Acorn Girl meant to attack anyway. In her mind, as well as in the minds of all the others, the idea of precisely who was guilty among the Whites had become somewhat diffuse— and for good reason. And for the new members of the group, Goose Leader and those he had brought with him, the specific identities of Johnson or Penryn or Lindley, the third of the targeted Whites and the one who did not seem to act in concert with Ez Johnson, were meaningless. The Kulkumish and Hembem villages had been situated, it was true, no more than ten miles as the crow flew from You Bet and Red Dog, though the distance by trail was considerably greater. But Johnson was hardly the only Whiteman who took sport in killing Indians. No, indeed, for the practice, as Ben had gathered, existed up and down the mining regions, from the Klamath River far to the north of Mt. Shasta to Murphys, Sonora, and Coulterville at the southern terminus of the Mother Lode, as the region of auriferous gravels had come to be called.

Acorn Girl and her Panos would strike now, whether Johnson and the others were in the vicinity or not. The honor of the remnants of these four Maidu villages, Tumeli, Usto-ma, Kulkumish, and Hembem, required it. Extinction or near extinction, it seemed to Goffe, now hung like the sword of Damocles above the heads of all the Maidus— and the Miwoks and the Yokuts and the Yanas and the Wintuns as well. The same was probably true for all the native peoples of California, whether within or outside the mining regions. So the essential choice lay either in waiting for starvation or smallpox, the disease that had decimated the Plains people, or tuberculosis or the ravages of syphilis and rotgut whiskey—or, as Acorn Girl had decided to do, strike back against unsurmountable odds, killing whatever Whites she could, and going down to death under a riddle of rifle and pistol fire or being taken captive and tortured and hung, but nonetheless dying with a clear sense of purpose, dying honorably, dying in hopeless and unequal battle, like Homer's Patroclus or even, yes, like Milton's Satan.

A time of epic struggle, a fatal clash of civilizations— but here with the odds so utterly against these wild children of the forests who would now strike back albeit blindly against an inchoate enemy, gold-crazed, to whom they, the Maidus, were no more than an annoyance and a sport, hardly regarded as human at all. These Whitemen had stolen their lands, destroyed the fishing in their rivers, slaughtered their game, driven them back and away from areas in which they might reasonably be able to survive, and massacred and brutalized their people—all heedlessly and without even granting them the status of fully human creatures. The Whites did not even hate them. They despised them. And when accounts of this time were ultimately written, the Maidus would be mentioned only briefly, if at all, perhaps relegated to a few insubstantial footnotes. And people in the civilized East would never conjecture for a moment the richness that had been destroyed so totally, so brutally, and so utterly without thought. The Maidu sun was indeed, just as Hurt Eagle had said, dying in the skies. Where the Indians of America had fought back before being subdued, they came to be thought of as worthy if barbarous opponents to the Jehovah-favored Chosen Ones of this nation of theoretically free and equal men, the new Israelites systematically conquering their Promised Land. But where the Indians did not resist and perhaps did not even understand that it was possible to resist, they passed away into darkness, into oblivion, unsung and unrecorded.

Yes, but Acorn Girl would strike back—and be crushed. And to the moment of her death she would believe that the One Who Sits Above, Olelbis, had merely chosen to dream a different kind of dream for a time. . . .

Surely this mission of reconnaissance to You Bet and the area around was not merely a ploy to put him, Benjamin Goffe, at a safe distance from the fighting? Surely Acorn Girl would not make her attack during his absence?

No.

At least such a possibility had not occurred to O'Bragh, for the old mountaineer had left Rabbit-chaser with the Panos.

Words drifted into his mind then, bits and pieces at first, and then the entire passage, one of a thousand or more that he had set formally to memory during the course of a lifetime spent at his studies, some lines from Francis Bacon: *When I found however that my zeal was mistaken for ambition, and my life had already reached the turning-point, and my breaking health reminded me how ill I could afford to be so slow, and I reflected moreover that in leaving undone the good that I could do by myself alone, and applying myself to that which could not be done without the help and consent of others, I was by no means discharging the duty that lay upon me,—I put all those thoughts aside, and (in pursuance of my old determination) betook myself wholly to this work. . . .*

The passage was strangely out of context with either his previous reflections or with the reality of the present moment—or was it?

A different time, a different place, a different course of action to follow. . . .

"She's like to get hot an' heavy tonight, Benny me lad," O'Bragh said, his voice almost dreamlike. "Ain't nothin' new to this child, an' that's why I figger I'll string along. I know I've always chided ye about yore books an' all, Bear-who-cannot-see-well, but now I'm thinkin' as to how this hyar ain't yore piece of cake, no sir. Ye've changed a mite since I first took hold of ye, Ben, an' that's the truth. But this nigger's havin' a hard time thinkin' of ye in the middle of a firefight. That woman of yores, she's somethin', a real hellcat. Tougher'n nails, an' I don't think ye even realize it. But she loves ye, lad. She does. Wanted me to get ye drunk in a tavern an' then whop ye over the head with a pistol butt—so's ye wouldn't come to until the business was done."

"She what?" Ben demanded.

"Truth. Told 'er I didn't figger it'd work, an' I don't know how for-serious she were anyhow."

"So that was the little bitch's scheme. Well, O'Bragh, don't get behind me. I can handle myself, don't you worry. I've had good teachers, and I've got a reason or two of my own to take on this fight."

"Guess ye have," O'Bragh agreed. "Wal, we got to do us some *researchin'* first. Ain't that what you pro-fessors call it?"

Bully drew up on Porcupine's reins, pulled the mule to a halt. Ben drew Old Blue alongside, and the two of them gazed down from the rim toward the mining settlement below.

"You Bet," Ben said. "But where the hell's Belcher's saloon?"

"Don't know nothin' about it," Bully mumbled, shaking his head. "That a place ye been to before?"

"Couple of times. Belcher's the man I bought my printshop from. That's where it was, over there."

"Looks like they might of been a leetle fire," Bully said. "Happens all the time. Half of American Valley done burned to the ground a week or so before me an' Rabbit-chaser left our fixin's. Fire ain't got much respect for boards an' canvas, as it turns out."

Ben whistled through his teeth and reached forward to stroke Old Blue's neck.

"Bully," he said, "there's something I should have asked you a long while back."

"An' what might that be, lad?"

"How'd you know who I was—that time back in St. Louis? You know I ended up with a whore afterward, and in the morning I woke up hung over and a hundred dollars poorer. And the sad thing is I can't even remember whether I actually bedded her or not. Anyway, after that I'd half convinced myself that you were nothing more than a figment of my somewhat overactive imagination—part of a drunken dream I'd had after I passed out in the Mulatto girl's room."

O'Bragh sucked in his lips and nodded.

"Now yore startin' to get smart, lad. I wondered how long it was goin' to take."

"You *are* an illusion, then?"

"Lad, I'll let ye in on a secret. Fact is, you be at home in Connecticut, sound asleep. Ain't none of this ever happened. *Wagh!* Ye're one hopeless dunghead idjit, Benny."

Early afternoon on a Sunday in You Bet, California. A preacher in ill-fitting and somewhat ragged clothes was standing in front of the two-story frame rooming house, the single permanent structure in the disorganized village of two thousand souls, more than nineteen hundred of whom were men, the remainder, all but half a dozen, professional ladies—some Indian, some Mexican, some White. A small throng of men stood before him, listening and heckling as the man of the ragged cloth held forth on the dangers, both moral and physical, of venal sin, backing his assertions and cautionary parables with garbled phrases attributed to *Saaaint Paul* and to *Jesus H. Christ*.

Ben and Bully tied their mounts to a hitching rail and walked across the already dusty interval that served as a main street to *The Big Nugget Tavern*, whose entryway was graced with a pair of unpainted and apparently recently installed swinging half-doors.

Across the canvas-sheltered room, as they entered, they noted a tightly grouped circle of men apparently observing with great interest something that was being performed on the plank floor in front of them.

"What's going on?" Ben asked the barkeep.

"That?" the man asked, squinting. "Little contest is all. The boys like to see who can stay in the saddle with Maggie the longest. Tall fella, he's got a damned stopwatch. Whoever wins, Mag ends up with their dust, so it's all right. What'll you fellas be having?"

"Give us a bottle," Bully laughed. "Ben hyar's payin'."

The barkeep obliged, and Ben measured out the required number of pinches of gold dust.

"We're looking for the Chalk Bluff Mining Company," he said. "Can you tell us where it is?"

"Johnson an' Penryn an' Milt Lindley's bunch? They're working gravel over on Steepholler, just down from the falls, where the road crosses. Lowell Hill road, left as you're heading south from town. Don't think Ez is looking to take on any new hands, though. Ed Harper, other side of Red Dog, he's looking for a crew. He's the one I'd try if I was you, gents."

"Lindley's with Johnson?" Ben asked.

"You know old Milt? That smooth-talking Virginian, yeah, he blew in here about a month ago—had a couple dozen men with him. That's why I don't figure Johnson's looking to put on anybody else."

"Never met the man," Ben said. "Just know about his work is all."

Ben swigged from the bottle, shut his eyes, swallowed, and shook his head. Then he handed the flask to O'Bragh, who tilted it to his lips and drank contentedly.

"Powerful dry, powerful dry," Bully said, handing the bottle back to Goffe.

"Well," Ben went on, "I guess we'll mosey out to see old Ez, all the same."

"Save yourself some time," the barkeep suggested. "That's Sonny Penryn, Johnson's sidekick, over there next to Tall Joe, the one with the stopwatch. He'll know what the chances are."

"That a fact?" O'Bragh said. "Sonny Penryn hisself?

Ben, keep yore hand away from that pistol, don't be a damned fool now. This hyar ain't the place. We've done found out what we was sent to find out, now let's get on back to . . ."

But Goffe had already shrugged Bully's restraining hand away and was striding across the saloon to where the young, yellow-haired Penryn was standing next to the miner known as Tall Joe.

The man and the woman had gotten up off the floor, and the man was tucking himself in and buttoning his pants. The woman was attempting to straighten her thick brown hair, readjusting the blue ribbon that held it.

"Three minutes an' forty-seven seconds. You lose, Tennessee. Vollmer, he's got you beat by almost a full minute."

The man called Tennessee shook his head.

"Harder'n it looks," he admitted.

"Not after you're through, it ain't," someone said.

"By God, I want to try that," another blurted, pushing forward.

The woman named Maggie held up her hands and shook her head.

"No more, boys, not today. A lady's cunt gets sore after a certain amount of pounding, you know. Joe, you got my money there?"

Penryn was laughing, his hand to his forehead, when Ben grasped him by the arm and spun him around.

And then *The Big Nugget Tavern* went suddenly and strangely silent.

"Let go my arm or I'll put lead in your belly, mister."

"Aren't you the Penryn who was down at Coloma a couple of years back?" Ben asked, grinning.

"Might be. Let go my arm, I'm warning you, *El Gordo*, I ain't one with a lot of patience."

Hardly more than a kid—like one of my Yale students. Yet this is the one who murdered Ooti's child, one of the men who raped her and left her for dead, one of the ones who butchered her people and the Usto-mas as well. Not even really able to grow a proper beard yet. A young rattlesnake, the most deadly kind. . . .

"Thought you might be, young fellow," Ben said.

And then he drove his fist, the full force of his massive

body behind it, into Penryn's face. The blow lifted the
man off his feet and sent him hurtling sideways, into the
arms of his startled companions.

*Much shouting. Maggie screaming and laughing at the
same time. The barkeep yelling his lungs out.*

"Try somebody your own size!" Tall Joe yelled, leaping
at Ben.

But Ben came around with another looping punch, this
one to the tall man's belly, doubling him over and sending
him to the floor.

Several grabbed at Ben at once, but he pushed them
aside and went for Penryn, who was still struggling to rise
to his feet. With a roar that might have frightened off a
mountain lion, Goffe grasped hold of Penryn with both
hands, lifted him over his head, and hurled him to the
planking. Penryn struck the boards face down, and even
in the midst of the melee those present could hear the
neck snap.

Sonny Penryn was dead.

The men stood back, suddenly silent, and stared at the
twisted body. Even Maggie pushed forward to take a look.

"He was no good, this one," she said, one hand going
nervously to check the ribbon in her hair. "He made me
do things I didn't want to do."

"Time for a necktie party," Vollmer drawled. "Let's take
him, boys. . . ."

Then it was on again, and Ben started hurling men
about like so many tenpins.

Guns began to go off.

O'Bragh was whaling away with the stock of his Hawken
rifle, and some of the men, half-drunk and blissfully unconcerned as to whom the actual enemy might be, began
to pitch into one another.

The barkeep fired off a blast from the shotgun he kept
behind the oaken counter, the pellets tearing a jagged
hole in the canvas ceiling. And then a pistol ball hit him in
the throat, blood spraying out over the neatly stacked
bottles behind him, and the shotgun fell from his hands
as he sank to his knees, gasping for air that would not
come.

A fist clipped Ben alongside the forehead, and his glasses

went flying. But he was roaring with laughter now, grabbing two men at a time and thumping their heads together.

"Head for the doorway, ye dunghead idjit!" O'Bragh called out. "We got to make tracks, lad."

Brought to his senses by Bully's voice, Ben pushed through the blur of men before him, knocking them down and trampling on them, and lunged toward the oblong of daylight. O'Bragh was beside him, rifle still in hand, and together they were running for the rail where Old Blue and Porcupine were tied.

Men were pouring out of the *Big Nugget* behind them, and O'Bragh, now mounted on his mule, the animal spinning about, fired off the Hawken without even aiming, and the blast sent miners diving for cover.

"Ride, damn it!" Bully yelled, "an' keep low!"

Mule and Percheron pounded down the dusty track of the main street through a hail of wild pistol fire, and Ben and Bully emerged at the end of the business section of You Bet unscathed.

Ben turned, looked back, things at a distance clear to him, however blurred objects close about him might be. And he noted that a plume of gray-black smoke was rising from the general vicinity of where they had just been.

"Rule number one," O'Bragh yelled, thumping his knees to Porcupine's sides, "always leave the boys a leetle present if ye're tryin' to get away from 'em. Sort of distracts their minds."

"You set the fire?" Ben asked, slapping Old Blue's neck and urging him into the best run the big horse was capable of.

"O' course, ye thick-headed Connecticut lunk! Didn't I jest say that was rule number one? Ye got to learn how to listen, lad. . . ."

Then they were back to the dome of the ridge and under the cover of a thick stand of firs and pines.

The men drew their mounts to a momentary halt and stared at one another, shook their heads.

"*Wagh!* This child ain't had so much fun since we lynched Aunt Martha. But ye done jumped the gun, Benny. Should ought to have waited for the moon-ball to come up. The one ye kilt sort of belonged to Acorn Girl, as I see 'er."

"I lost my temper," Ben admitted.

"Sure ye did. Problem is, ye ain't experienced enough. Didn't I ever tell ye about the old bull an' the young bull?"

"Farnsworth, my friend, not that I recall."

Bully squinted one eye, grinned, and pretended to reach for his pistol.

"All right then, lad, listen now. They was a bunch of fat young cow bufflers down in a leetle valley, an' up on a rimrock was a old bull an' a young bull. Youngun says *Let's run down an' hump one of 'em*. But the old bull, he says *Lad, let's walk down an' hump all of 'em.*"

"Take your time, conserve your strength, and do the job properly," Ben nodded.

"Couldn't of said 'er better myself."

"And you're right, of course. Damn it, Bully, I've lost my glasses. Eight, ten hours until the world ends—I guess I can make do without them for that long."

"Ain't no reason for the world to be endin', jest because we're fixin' to put the Chalk Bluff Mining Company under, is they? Like I keep sayin', lad, yore heart's in the right place, but ye lack experience. What Acorn Girl's got planned, it's goin' to be tough, but it ain't impossible. I figger we'll be seein' the sun come up tomorrow."

Ben shrugged.

"In that case," he said, "then I'll be needing to get some new glasses. I left my extras back in Grass Valley, and you tell me my place burned to the ground."

O'Bragh chuckled, whistled, and gave a little yipping sound.

"These what ye be worryin' about, lad?" he asked, holding out Ben's spectacles. "I spend my life lookin' out for ye, this old coon does."

"How in the bloody hell . . . ?"

"Let's jest say I've got me ways," Bully grinned. "They don't call me the Irish Vulture for nothin', no sir. *Wagh!*"

With that he slapped his knees to Porcupine's sides, and the two compañeros resumed their ride back to the encampment where Acorn Girl and the others were waiting.

16

The Revenge of the Grizzlies

May, 1850

*Kuksu shook his head and stamped his foot, and Peheipe
Oleli sat back on his haunches and grinned, just as though
he had been caught eating excrement.*

*"The best one of us had better try to get that fire,"
Kuksu said, and Coyote wagged his bushy tail.*

*"I am smarter than anyone else," he said. "I will do it
for you. Mouse, Deer, and Dog must come with me,
though, for I will need some help."*

*"Should we trust him?" Mouse cried out, turning to
Kuksu.*

*Kuksu, the First Man, thought about it for a long while,
and then he said, "I guess so. Thunder is powerful, but
Peheipe Oleli is much more clever. I think it is safe to trust
him this time."*

*Coyote danced about, jumping into the air and yip-yip-
ping. Then he stood on his hind legs and pointed to Deer.*

*"Go get a flute," he said. "Get Kuksu's flute from inside
the sweat lodge. We will need that."*

"Why do you want my flute?" Kuksu asked.

*"That is how we are going to carry the fire," Coyote
answered. "Fire is very hot, and we have to put it into
something. I will take very good care of it, Kuksu, for I
know it is important to you. There's no need for you to
worry. Just tell the women to gather twigs and dry grass.
I am hungry already."*

After Bear-who-cannot-see-well and his friend the Irish
Vulture left the encampment, Ooti called together the

warriors and those who would stay behind as well and discussed details of the planned attack, saw to it that final preparations were well underway. That done, she moved away from the others, for she felt a need for silence and solitude so that she might order her own thoughts.

Small Ears approached her then, obviously wishing to talk, and Acorn Girl had to repress a flicker of annoyance as she listened to her friend. She loved Small Ears, and yet her friend's nervous excitement made conversation a chore.

"I want to come with you and the others tonight. I wish to be with my husband and my closest friend. I do not know how to shoot straight, but I can reload the rifles," Small Ears said, almost timidly.

Acorn Girl looked intently at her, felt ashamed of her own impatience when she saw both the fear and the determined courage in the steady eyes, the slightly quaking upper lip. Then suddenly she embraced Small Ears, and the two of them clung together for a long moment.

Ooti stepped back, still holding her hands on Small Ears' shoulders, and said, "I would be glad of your offer, my friend, for any help is welcome, and I know your heart is good. But you have two little ones to care for, the Usto-ma child and Choopim Sawka, Willow Meadow, your own infant girl. They must not be left without a mother."

"Wakwak will take care of them. Even if I don't come back, Crane will see that they grow up."

The trembling of the upper lip increased, and the round eyes began to gleam with water which Small Ears blinked back.

"I cannot bear to sit here in camp," she went on, "and not know whether my husband is . . . and you, my best friend since we were tiny, even if you are the leader and a *kuksu huku* now."

Ooti embraced her again, then stepped away and spoke firmly.

"Small Ears, you know that your place is with your babies. Crane cannot nurse them, and it would be hard for the little ones. Tied-wing is the wisest and most skilled and courageous of all the young men. You should not fear for him."

Unless we all . . .

The thought came, but Acorn Girl did not put it into words.

"No," she said, "I forbid you to come with us. Some of the other women will come—Snakebite Dancer can handle weapons as well as most of the men, and her heart is burning to kill the *Wawlems*. But she has no little ones. Please understand this, Small Ears."

Her friend turned away without speaking further, but not before Ooti detected the glint of tears.

I would willingly have gone with Pine-nut-eater to Valley Above if I could have. . . .

Acorn Girl watched her friend walk away and wondered if she had done the right thing.

The leader of the Pano Maidus wandered among the groves of sugarpines and ponderosas, thinking to find a place to sit and to be alone with her thoughts, but she couldn't seem to remain still and continued to walk restlessly. In a clearing where a spring seeped from the side of a steep rise, a cluster of azaleas was beginning to bloom, the odor sweet, intoxicating. Idly she picked a few blossoms, worked them into a strand to put into her hair, and then wondered at the impulse that had caused her to adorn herself like a young bride when, in fact, she would be going into bloody combat within a short time.

Acorn Girl wandered on, the sunshine filtering in bright single rays through the branches of the great pines, the air utterly still among the columns of the trunks. Here and there remnants of the late snow gleamed from dense shade, but in other places the patches of sun lighted brown needles and fallen cones, the ground already dry beneath them. The silence, the oblivious serenity of Olelbis' dream in this quiet, sun-dappled place soothed her, almost lulled her into a dream-state of her own, but she found no coherent thoughts forming beyond the constant and wordless awareness that before another day came, her revenge would be accomplished—or she would be dead.

A sound of blows, and a huffing and grunting accompanying them. Acorn Girl paused, listened.

The sound came from a clearing ahead of her.

She approached cautiously, stared into the clearing from behind the trunk of a great pine.

A grizzly, a full-grown, golden-brown monster, was tearing up a rotten log, the massive claws ripping apart the soft wood. He sat on his haunches, absorbed in his labor, whuffling and snorting from time to time as if talking to himself. When he had ripped open a fresh section of wood, he paused and licked at it with his tongue, and Ooti knew he was getting white woodworms from the log.

Impulsively she stepped into the clearing and addressed the bear in bold tones.

"Greetings, Pano," she said. "I am sorry to interrupt your meal."

The huge head came up, the eyes squinted nearsightedly in her direction.

"You are my tribe's totem," she said. "I hoped you might have something for us."

Pano snorted, rocked his head back, and then returned to his work as if she weren't even there. He continued tearing up the log, exposing the white worms and licking them up with obvious pleasure. At last, apparently satisfied that he had gotten the last bit of good from the log, he turned away, rolled over onto his back, and squirmed about happily. Then he climbed to his feet and, with a last glance at Acorn Girl, the huge bear jogged off into the darkness of the trees.

"Is this a sign, Pano?" she asked the silence after the grizzly's branch-breaking passage had subsided. "Does this mean the Pano Maidus will devour the *Wawlems*?"

No answer, nothing but silence and the sunlight pouring down into the empty clearing. Somewhere a jay squawked derisively, a woodpecker drummed a few notes against a tree trunk.

"Or perhaps it is just that a bear was eating grubworms," she whispered, discouraged, and turned to leave the clearing.

At that moment three distinct visions flashed across her mind, simultaneously and instantaneously, in a way that she would never be able to describe or understand afterward.

One vision of fire, of red flames leaping at the sky all around, the cries of men dying, confusion, bodies milling hopelessly, a writhing and demonic death dance among the flames.

One vision of peace, cattle grazing green hills, river-bottoms planted in rows, the strange plants of the Wawlems, and people going about their business, laughing, eating, working, playing, and among them not a single face that could belong to a Nishinam.

One vision of herself as an old woman, the skin drawn tight about the bones of her face, the hands delicate, dry, and around her where she sat in the grass several children, their faces not distinct, but she knew that these were her grandchildren, and that the place where they were was peaceful.

Ooti staggered under the impact of the sudden flash of overlaid and intertwined pictures, feeling almost as she had felt on the day on the mountaintop when she dreamed of being struck by lightning.

She thought of the vision of herself as a grandmother, remembered her *Wawlem* husband, Ben, speaking of a place they might go to, a place where they could live in peace. Was she being offered choices? If the vision of fire and death were fulfilled, then the other vision, the vision of the end of a long and prosperous life, perhaps that would vanish. And the middle vision, in which the *Wawlems* owned this world. It was only a picture of what she knew was inevitable, despite her actions to counter the invaders. And there were no Nishinam people in that world.

"Or perhaps all three things will come to pass," she thought. "It is true, we cannot save our beautiful land. That is part of the dream of Olelbis. Even what happens this night is part of his dream."

She began walking slowly back through the forest, heading toward the encampment, pondering.

"The Spirits send puzzles," she concluded, again impatient and annoyed. "We read the message one way, and it turns out to be right, but there is no way of knowing in advance. It doesn't matter, for there is only one thing I can do, and that is what I have sworn to do all along. If I do not live to have grandchildren, or even to see the sun

another day, then that is what will happen. I wish the
Spirits would not toy with us. Perhaps that is Peheipe
Oleli the Coyote who sends such dreams. The bear in the
clearing devoured the worms."

The sun was low in the west by this time, the rays of
light long and golden. Acorn Girl suddenly stopped, seeing
something gleaming in the soft earth ahead of her.

It was the footprint of the grizzly, the track filled up
with water from the damp earth, and gleaming like gold,
or fire, in the late sun, the track pointing southwest, along
the ridge and downstream, pointing toward the encamp-
ments of the miners.

Ooti caught her breath, knelt to examine the footprint
more closely, and embedded within the footprint an oddly
shaped stone, oblong, rounded and bulging at one end,
tapering almost to a point at the other, a stone shaped like
an acorn.

"I thank you, Pano," Ooti whispered, picking up the
pebble that she knew was a powerful gift of the Bear
Spirit.

A wave of exultation swelled the region of her heart,
and she began to sing a fierce song that Hurt Eagle had
taught her. She was glad for the warlike song, since most
of the chants of her people were peaceful, prayers of
thanksgiving or requests for blessings, and these would
not fit her mood right now.

"Perhaps I will die, and that is all right. Pano himself
has directed me," she thought.

By the time Acorn Girl reached the encampment, Ben
Goffe and Bully O'Bragh had returned from their nearly
disastrous foray into the town of You Bet, and Ooti listened to their report in silence. When Ben told of the
death of Sonny Penryn, her eyes narrowed fiercely.

"He was mine," she said.

"Don't be too hard on yore man," Bully interceded.
"*Wagh!* Leastways the varmint's dead, an' that's what
counts, ain't it?"

Acorn Girl turned her gaze to the old mountain man,

held his eyes for a moment, as if struggling with something, and at last nodded.

Bear-who-cannot-see-well told her of the location and setup of the mining camp, and again she nodded, murmuring to herself, "That is just where Pano said it would be."

"What did you say?" Ben asked.

But she only shook her head.

"Should of seen old Ben, Ooti. Lifted Penryn over his head an' then set 'im down on the floor. Busted his neck, lass. Aye, an' I'm telling the Gawd's truth, too."

O'Bragh tilted back his head and began to laugh.

"This one is a *Wawlem* version of Peheipe Oleli," Acorn Girl said, placing her hand on her husband's forearm.

The sun sank behind the western ridges, the clear sky flaring out into a great fan of golden light before fading to the silver-blue of twilight. Venus hung like a syllable of the Divine tongue, great and lustrous and shining before any other star was visible. Ooti listened to the rest of what Ben and Bully had to report, occasionally interjecting a question but otherwise not commenting, and when they were done, she turned away to see that all was indeed ready for the battle ahead.

"Seems a mite distracted," O'Bragh commented as the young woman walked away. "I suppose it's nateral, come to think of 'er. Sort of reminds me of the time back in '13 when I was guidin' Colonel Scott up to Fort George. Me an' Andy Jackson together must of kilt us about two hundred British."

"Andrew Jackson?" Ben asked, raising one eyebrow. "If I'm not mistaken, that worthy gentleman was down in Mississippi at the time."

O'Bragh winked.

"Jest testin' ye, lad. Jest testin' ye."

Ben shrugged.

"I don't know, my vulturine compañero," he said. "Ooti's head is full of ghosts and demons. The gods are not a reliable source of aid in battle from what I've read. And I'm not sure her mind is working clearly."

"Still," O'Bragh huffed, "it don't hurt none to get a

leetle extry help. Don't think ye needs to worry about that one's mind, Benny me lad, no sir."

"Maybe. But she's not getting out of my sight tonight, I know that."

"Good luck to ye, then," Bully commented, looking blandly into the distance. "I wonder if Rabbit-chaser's got anything fixed for supper. Cain't go into battle with an empty meatbag."

They moved out near midnight, a full moon sailing high in a clear sky and penetrating even the bottom of Steep-hollow Canyon. All afternoon the Panos had been engaged in the manufacture of fire-arrows, each shaft collared with a handful of dry pine needles and dipped into hot pitch. Each warrior armed himself with a quiver full of these and another quiver of regular arrows, as well as being fully supplied with firearms, lead, powder, and caps.

The Panos chose to lead their horses down to the min-ing camp below where the Whiteman's road crossed the creek at the head of the falls—the animals to be kept close for quick escape, should that prove necessary. The two hulking, half-grown bears could not be cajoled into staying behind by means of any form of trickery that either Acorn Girl or Crane could devise, the animals sensing the excite-ment of their human friends, and so Acorn Girl bound them to trees with lashings of thick rope, leaving them whimpering and moaning and hauling against their bonds. Crane spoke soothingly to them and fed them bits of honeycomb, but they refused to be comforted.

The attack force was greatly enlarged by the addition of men and adolescent boys from Kulkumish and Hembem villages as well as by a few of the childless women, includ-ing Snakebite Dancer, toward whom Crooked Knee felt extremely protective, staying close by her side.

Small Ears did not weep when her husband left, but she stared at him as if she could not bear to release him from her vision.

Parting words were exchanged all around, and the Panos, with Acorn Girl in the lead and Bear-who-cannot-see-well and Bully O'Bragh with her, set off, the band of warriors picking their way down through the undergrowth and along the slope of the ridge that protected the encampment.

The location of the Chalk Bluff Mining Company's diggings was in a small valley along the creek, a level area surrounded by wooded and bushy benches and ridges. Acorn Girl was pleased with the arrangement, and the fighters spread out to these elevated and well-concealed areas after securing the horses in a hidden ravine a short distance upstream.

The camp lay mostly in moonlight, the village of tents reflecting white, but a number of fires still glowed, and the watchers could hear the sounds of drunken voices raised in heated debate or complaint. A figure stumbled, reeling, from one lighted tent, stood unsteadily a short distance away, caught in moonglow, and urinated, then staggered back toward the tent.

Suddenly he fell with no sound that was audible from where Bear-who-cannot-see-well lay concealed, not far from Bully O'Bragh, who was sitting below a rock outcropping close to Crooked Knee and Snakebite Dancer. No, not soundless, for Ben realized that he had heard a sharp whirring sound in the air near his head, turned, saw that Ooti had risen to her knees and that her bow was still raised, the string vibrating. Her eyes gleamed with bluish fire in the moonlight, and her teeth gleamed from the shadows of her face.

Bully gave a soft snort of laughter, but Bear-who-cannot-see-well couldn't help feeling momentary horror.

"What are you doing?" he whispered. "I thought first the fire-arrows and then . . ."

The insanity of his comment, generated by civilized and rational training so inbred that it operated like impulse when dealing with all actions but his own, struck him. He began to laugh deep in his throat, absurd whispers of laughter that shook his frame and threatened to break through the barrier of his lips.

What is she, this woman who has saved my life and seduced me and married me and has gotten hold of me to such an extent that I could never stand to be apart from her again?

Down below someone had come to the door of the tent

and called out, presumably to the man who lay dead, shrugged, and returned after a moment.

And that was when Ooti gave the signal, lighting a fire-arrow, the pitchy needles instantly flaring into smoky yellow flames. She stood, held the brand above her head, and circled it several times so that the others watching would see her move. Then she fit the shaft to her bow and launched it down into the mining camp, the arrow lodging into an oiled canvas roof, where it continued to burn. Immediately lights sprang up from all sides, and more fire-arrows sailed down into the encampment. The material of the first tent began to flare up, and a figure stumbled outside, shouting and cursing—then standing stock-still in confusion as he observed little blazes springing up in numerous places. Fire seemed to be raining from the moonlit sky.

The miners were slow to comprehend what was happening, even slower to gather themselves into any sort of defensive posture, and a number of the men had fallen to arrows or rifle balls before the rest even turned out of their tents.

Acorn Girl gave a sudden, blood-curdling shriek as she rammed home a ball into her old flintlock rifle and readied the priming pan.

Ben had his own rifle sighted down on a man he thought he recognized from the saloon, but Ooti's cry just at the instant of firing caused his shot to jerk wild. Acorn Girl raised her own weapon, drew down carefully as the moonlight would allow, slowly squeezed off the round.

Ben methodically measured powder into his barrel, cursed the dim light, and pushed down wadding and ball. Answering cries echoed from the slopes on all sides, and more fire-arrows hurtled into the camp. Fires blazed happily now in a number of places.

Ooti gave a small grunt of satisfaction as the man she had sighted in on fell, the butt of her rifle kicking powerfully against her shoulder. But inside her heart a wild exultance was building, boiling, expanding her chest. Smoke from the fires rolled up into dreamlike clouds, and she thought for a moment she saw the figure of a great bear, and the bear was dancing.

"*Pano-ng-kasi*," she whispered. "*Pano-ng-kasi* the Great
Bear is dancing now, yes, and he is also *Meta*, the coach of
the dancers. . . ."

She laughed, reloaded.

From Bully's rock formation the sharp report of the old
Hawken, then the mountain man's own whoop of celebration.

Ben sighted in on another man, a dark outline now
against the blaze of a tent, squeezed, watched the figure
crumple, try to rise, stumble, and fall again.

*I didn't even have the excuse of supposing I recognized
that one. . . .*

He reloaded mechanically, seized with a sense of utter
unreality.

*Now I am a murderer, I guess, even if, one way or
another, I wasn't before. Penryn needed killing. But this
doesn't seem any more significant than picking off ducks
on a pond.*

Ooti gripped his arm, her face almost glittering with
excitement in the cool glow of the moon, its pale light in
insane contrast to the orange inferno below.

"Now I know you are my husband, Bear-who-cannot-
see-well," she said. "I think we will live through this night
after all. These *Wawlems* are not much."

Ben raised his rifle to his shoulder, aimed, fired again.

"What was it, Farnsworth," he called out, "about being
a *figment*? If everyone around me is a figment, does that
mean I've become God?"

"*Wagh!*" Bully called back. "Jest means ye're snorin'
away in some Gawd-forsaken jungle called Con-nettycut.
Quit yore jawin' an' aim lively, or ye might not wake up
from this one, lad. Ooti—take one of yore fire-arrows an'
stick it in the roof of that leetle board shanty close by the
crick. A firebug on that shake roof, an' mebbe we'll have
us some entertainment."

The miners were beginning to think about defense now,
and while some returned fire from the meager shelter of
whatever rocks or bushes they could find, a large number
made for a willow thicket downstream. One man seemed
to be directing things, standing near the frame building

O'Bragh had spoken of and shouting out orders and curses. With a shock, Ooti recognized him as Ezra Johnson— something about the stance and outline of the man making her certain of his identity although she couldn't see his features clearly.

With a high humming in her ears, she raised her rifle, sighted in upon the figure. She was having trouble controlling a trembling in her hands, and she drew a deep breath, held it until the shaking had subsided. She opened her eyes, sighted again, carefully, carefully. Her heart was pounding in her ears as she began to squeeze the trigger, and then Ben cried out beside her, began to rise, gripping her arm.

She turned, looked to where he was pointing, saw that one of her own people had come into view, running down a slope nearby, bent low. She saw at the same instant that one of the miners had a pistol drawn and was pointing it at the Pano's midsection at close range. Acorn Girl moaned as she recognized Tied-wing, raised her rifle, and fired without bothering to aim, heard the crack of Bully's weapon an instant before her own recoiled into her shoulder, and saw the Whiteman fall, his pistol discharging as he went.

"He has missed Tied-wing," she thought—but watched with helpless horror as the young warrior stumbled, pitched forward.

A small knot of miners had noticed the intrusion of the Maidu, and as this group moved toward the stricken man, Ooti and Ben and Bully fired almost simultaneously into their midst. One man fell forward, another grasped at a shoulder, the arm suddenly hanging lifeless. The miners scattered, rushing first one direction, then another, and the one who had fallen staggered to his feet and also attempted to lurch away.

By this time Tied-wing had pulled himself up onto one knee and was struggling to rise. And at that moment, running heedlessly, without the slightest show of caution, a woman came into view.

"Small Ears!" Acorn Girl cried in anguish. "I told her to stay with her little ones. . . ."

Ben was already on his feet.

"Keep shooting," he shouted. "Don't let up, don't let them have a chance . . . I'm going down."

The woman below was drawing attention from various quarters, and Ooti and Crooked Knee and Bully O'Bragh struggled to fire and reload and fire again as Ben worked his way toward the wounded Tied-wing and his wife.

Small Ears now knelt beside her husband, holding him and tugging at him, trying to help him to his feet. Ooti could see that the warrior was attempting to motion her back, but she wouldn't go.

Then the massive figure of Bear-who-cannot-see-well appeared, knelt, lifted the wounded warrior into his arms as he might have carried a child, and herded the frantic woman before him.

A pair of miners, hiding behind some rocks close by and seemingly wishing to keep out of harm's way, suddenly emerged and began dragging at Ben's back, pulling him off balance, one of them speaking urgent words to him as the other grabbed at Small Ears, who had refused to go ahead without her husband.

Those watching above were helpless, since to shoot at either of the assailants risked killing their friends.

It was then that Ooti heard the heavy crashing of brush, sensed massive bodies hurtling past her from upslope. In a moment, roaring and swinging, Bear-who-comes-after seized upon the man who was clinging to Ben's arm. In the next instant Before appeared, swinging a massively clawed paw in assistance to his brother, who now had the miner's head partly in his jaws.

The *Wawlem* who had held Small Ears now released her and screamed, began to run. But After keyed on the movement and bounded toward the man, knocking him to the ground with a single blow to the head. The Whiteman did not rise, and with a few sniffs and chews, After left him and rejoined Before.

Goffe glanced down at the mutilated miner who was, half dead, still attempting to shield his face with his arms, picked up Tied-wing once more, and dashed toward the undergrowth.

A band of men was converging upon the spot where all this drama had taken place, their weapons aimed at the two grizzlies, and Ooti and her companions fired into the group, reloaded, fired again.

The two bears moved quickly after Ben.

Then they were beside her, groaning and whuffing and licking at her face. Ben, bearing Tied-wing and herding the frantic Small Ears before him, stumbled onto the shelf where Ooti and Bully O'Bragh stood.

Acorn Girl pushed the grizzlies off, scolding them briefly for disobeying her and chewing through their ropes. Then she knelt by Tied-wing to ascertain the location and severity of his wound.

"I will live," he gasped impatiently. "I have not been struck in a vital place, a bullet in the thigh. . . . I was a fool, Ooti, but as soon as I can stand, I am going to beat my wife for not listening to what I have told her."

But the look in his eyes and the caressing hand he placed on Small Ears' hair belied his words.

Ooti saw that his wound was bleeding, but not badly enough to indicate damage to any major blood vessels. She left Small Ears behind to bind the wound and resumed her position overlooking the mining camp. The bears fell to wrestling and tumbling about the ledge, apparently taking the whole adventure as a great lark, and Ooti had to scold them severely to get them to lie down quietly.

By this time the miners were in full rout, those trying to escape in almost any direction being cut off and turned back in upon themselves. They were firing their own weapons wildly, aiming sometimes at the general area of their attackers, but at least twice Acorn Girl saw one miner's shot cut down another of his own kind.

"I tell ye," Bully fussed again, "if ye want some fun, ye got to put one of them fire-arrers into the roof of the shanty."

Acorn Girl complied, lighting and firing the last of the missiles she had into the designated structure.

Cedar shingles began to burn, the flames growing higher and beginning to eat through, but Ooti could see nothing of great interest in the sight. She turned her attention to the milling figures of the demoralized *Wawlems* who remained alive, aimed, fired, reloaded, fired again. She could not see Johnson now, and the thought that she might not have another opportunity to kill the man nearly brought tears of frustration to her eyes, but she took out her anger on the other dancing, churning figures set off against the firelight below.

Could Johnson be hidden in the willow thicket? An occasional pistol shot still came from there, sometimes several at once. Perhaps several men . . .

Acorn Girl fired off a few rounds into the blind, but quickly gave up the effort as futile.

"Have you caught sight of the round-faced *Wawlem*, the one called Milton Lindley?" she asked Ben.

"I saw that man," called Tied-wing. "I think he got away down the creek already. Several got away. I was going to head them off when I got hit."

"I know I've told the Panos to stay back and protect themselves," Ooti said, "but I'm going to get those men out of the willows. That must be where Johnson is. I cannot let him escape also."

"Hold off for a second," O'Bragh called, "I think ye'll save yourself some trouble."

Ooti glanced at Irish Vulture, puzzled, but Ben Goffe was grinning.

The frame building, portions of its roof having already collapsed and the walls beginning to blaze up, seemed suddenly to shudder, the entire structure expanding, and the next instant the shock wave and the roar of an explosion hit the watchers on the hillside. Those miners who were near the building were flung to the earth, some unmoving, some trying to pick themselves up when the next explosion went off, knocking them flat again and hurling flaming debris high into the air.

"Figgered the boys might be storin' a few kegs of powder inside!" Bully shouted over the noise. "Hurrah for the mountains!"

A whole series of ear-splitting roars succeeded one another, and what was left of the building seemed to jerk and then rend itself into fragments, the flaming wreckage falling in all directions.

The men below scrambled frantically, and those se-creted in the willows emerged as a large portion of roof, still blazing, landed in their midst. Ooti watched these men intently, ignoring the confusion, the screams and wild running of the other trapped miners. But Johnson was not among them.

Explosions continued to resound, flaring fountains of fire and noise still going off—although the building was completely flattened now.

"By the purple toenails of Gawd," Bully exulted, "ain't never seed one purtier. Not since me an' Fiddlehead rousted that Hudson Bay post over on Fraser River. . . ."

Those miners who were still mobile were now scattering in absolute panic, running directly at their attackers in a frantic attempt to flee the inferno. Most were cut down as they ran, although some few managed to escape in the confusion.

One young man, barely old enough to have a beard, ran up the draw directly toward Acorn Girl and the others. Startled, both Ooti and Crooked Knee fired off shots at him, missing. Ben, seeing the boy's youth, could not bring himself to shoot, moved by something he told himself later was not racial loyalty but common compassion. But like a flash, Snakebite Dancer launched herself at the adolescent, knife in hand. The boy spun, pistol drawn, and fired a wild shot in her direction.

Crooked Knee, with a cry of anguish, leaped forward to block the girl from the young *Wawlem*, and the Whiteman's revolver barked again, this shot taking Crooked Knee in the leg. The Pano went down, his leg crumpling beneath him, and the White boy aimed with both hands at the fallen Maidu, forgetting Snakebite Dancer for an instant.

Then she was upon him, leaping onto his back and plunging the knife into his chest.

The youth gave a gasp, blood pumping from his wound, stared blankly at the other Panos who had by now con-verged upon him, and collapsed. Yet Snakebite Dancer was not through. With her knife she had ripped open the front of his trousers, and the others saw that she was mutilating him in the manner that the *Wawlems* had prac-ticed upon so many of her own people. Kauda held up the bleeding parts before the face of the White boy, his eyes already glazing with failing consciousness, and was rewarded with just a flicker of expression, enough to tell her that he saw what she held. Then his eyes went fixed, blank, and his head lolled to one side.

Snakebite Dancer turned to the others, her face fierce, other-worldly, her breath coming in quick gasps.

"I remembered this one from before," she said—and then flung the severed genitals into the dead boy's face.

Dawn came dull red through a thick haze of smoke that filled the flat beside Steephollow Creek. Nothing had stirred below for several hours; and with the coming of light, the Pano Maidus moved down to investigate the scene of the battle. Embers still smouldered in the remains of the demolished building and among the wooden frames of some of the tents. The Panos probed the little valley and surrounding slopes carefully, but none of the inert figures remained alive. In all, they counted thirty-one dead, and although several of the bodies were charred beyond recognition, Acorn Girl thought it unlikely that any belonged either to Ezra Johnson or Milton Lindley. None of the warriors reported having killed either of these men, and none had seen either go down. It appeared that the two men whom Ooti most passionately wanted dead had somehow managed to escape.

She expressed her anger and frustration, her face blackened with smoke and soot from probing every possible area for her primary enemies, her features drawn with exhaustion.

Ben tried to take her into his arms, her agitation making him fear for her sanity, but she struggled loose and went again among the warriors, questioning each closely, trying to elicit the reply that she wanted to hear.

At last Bully O'Bragh, who had been watching silently, spoke to her.

"Sometimes Old Man Coyote, Oleli ye call 'im, don't give ye everything ye wants. But this child would reckon ye could count yourself among the favored, Ooti. Damned if it ain't been a *shinin'* revenge-taking."

Acorn Girl looked at him sharply, her eyes still gleaming with the unnatural light that had seemed to burn in them since the previous night.

"What Bully says is true, Beloved One," Bear-who-cannot-see-well added, speaking quickly and with compelling gentleness—and noting a slight alteration in the determined set of her features. "We were not sure that any of us would be alive to see this dawn, and yet we haven't lost a single person. Tied-wing is wounded in the thigh, and Crooked Knee has a ball through his calf. No one else is even very seriously injured."

Acorn Girl's drawn, blackened face softened, and at length she nodded wearily. Now she stepped into Ben's embrace, throwing her arms tightly around his middle and leaning her face against his shoulder.

"Bear-who-cannot-see-well speaks true," she murmured. "Hurt Eagle will lead a dance of thanksgiving when we have reached a good place to camp. As for me, my husband, I will do whatever penance you think is proper."

With this last, she turned her face up to him and smiled a small, mischievous grin, the effect in her smeared and weary mask so incongruous that Ben laughed aloud.

"I will think of something, wife," Bear-who-cannot-see-well said. "For now, I think we would be well-advised to put some distance between this place and ourselves, and after that perhaps we should sleep for a month or so."

The two half-grown grizzlies, having followed Acorn Girl about through the ruined camp, now wrestled with one another, rolling and tumbling boisterously through the ashes. When Ooti called to them, Before and After stood up, completely pale-gray, like ghost-bears, snorting clouds of ash from their noses and sneezing and shaking.

Acorn Girl looked at them, looked at Ben, who was still grinning at her, his own face streaked with soot and sweat, and suddenly she broke into laughter also, laughing and laughing as she stood among the smouldering ruins, laughing into the smoky dawn.

17

A Knack for Catchin' Lead

May, 1850

Coyote, Dog, Deer, and Mouse set out toward the place where the thin column of smoke was rising, and many other people followed along behind them. They journeyed for a long while, but finally they reached Thunder's lodge.

Coyote stopped, lifted his leg, and made water upon a bush.

"We have to have a plan," he said.

Just then Loon, who was supposed to guard Thunder's fire, began to sing out from his place by the lodge's smoke-hole: "I am the one who never sleeps. I scream and yodel all night long, and Thunder pays me for my work. He gives me beads that I wear about my neck and my waist!"

Peheipe Oleli grinned and made his muzzle whiskers twitch.

"Thunder's daughters are very good looking," he said, "but they are also very modest. They would hate for anyone to see them naked. This is what you must do, Mouse. You are small. And Thunder's daughters are all asleep right now. Wait until Loon closes his eyes, and then climb in through the smoke-hole. Go to where the girls are lying and untie the waist-string on each one's skirt of woven grass. After you have done that, then fill up Kuksu's flute with fire."

"Then what should I do?" Mouse asked.

Coyote gaped and wagged his head back and forth.

"Well," he said, "if you stay there, Thunder will wake up and step on you. So probably it would be a good idea to bring the flute full of fire back out here. After that we will all run away."

*   *   *

Acorn Girl's Panos returned to their encampment in the bench above the deep portion of Steephollow Canyon by midmorning, elated with their easy success. Whatever they might secretly have believed before, they knew now that the *Wawlems* were far, far from invincible. The same tactic that had been employed with such devastating effect on their own villages worked equally well against the Whites themselves. And if perhaps it was true that the Whitemen were by now infinitely too numerous ever to be driven from the mountains, even if all the Nishinam villages were somehow magically united in purpose and armed with sufficient numbers of weapons, it was nonetheless true that thirty-one of the enemy lay dead, scattered about a burned-out camp, below the falls on Steephollow Creek.

Pursuit by other Whites was no doubt inevitable and the ultimate fate of the Panos highly uncertain, but had they not, some of them at least, managed to avoid the *Wawlems* and moved about undetected for the passage of two winters? Had they not been able to strike again and again, culminating in the present brilliant accomplishment?

In two years, only Tied-wing and Crooked Knee had ever been wounded in the course of their sustained revenge-taking against the Whites, and neither man was fatally injured, Crooked Knee not seriously at all.

With the continued help of Bear-who-cannot-see-well and his strange friend who never seemed to miss with his rifle, the Panos concluded, they were well able to protect themselves and to strike back when the moment was right.

But for now the men had had enough of battle. Thoughts of hunting and fishing and the gathering of acorns began to fill their minds, some way of returning to the way things had been only a few short years earlier. But where could they do this? Some talked of returning to the *toommin*, the big sugarpine hill high above the Middle Fork of the American River, while others thought of the swale at the edge of the Big Valley, a place from which they could look across and see the sacred hills of *Estawm Yan*, a place where oaks grew in profusion and where they would be able to take an abundant harvest of acorns during the *Se-meni* season.

And one day they hoped, but without believing it, the *Wawlems* would at last have found all the soft yellow metal and would have returned to their own lands.

Clearly, it was a time for celebration.

Ooti could sense the mood of her people, the women elated that no one had been killed, the men proud with their victory. But for Acorn Girl, the revenge-taking was far from finished. Of the three men she had sought, only Sonny Penryn was dead, and not by her hand but by the hand of Bear-who-cannot-see-well. No, her obligation to Pano and to those she had loved in what now seemed like an earlier lifetime would not be fulfilled so long as the *Wawlems* named Ezra Johnson and Milton Lindley remained alive.

So close! My victory was within my reach—Johnson and Lindley were both there in the camp, I know they were there, and yet I allowed them to slip away during the night. Why could those two not have been among the dead? Why could I not have killed them with my own weapons? And now the Panos have had enough of fighting, enough of killing. They will still mourn their own dead during the Ustu time, and they will heap woven baskets upon the fires, they will tie long strings of baskets to the poles and light them aflame in the night. Perhaps it is I alone who cannot forget, cannot rest until . . .

She approached Hurt Eagle, embraced him, held tightly to the thin old man, found herself trembling uncontrollably as he held her.

She was sobbing. She was sobbing like a young child.

"My beautiful Ooti," Hurt Eagle said, "Granddaughter. You have done what no leader of the Nishinam people has ever done before. Always we have cowered before the *Wawlems* and sought to avoid them, we feared them because we could not fight them with our spears and bows and arrows. But you have led us to a great victory. You have followed the words of Pano, and I know he is pleased with you, just as this Old One is. Perhaps I will die soon, I do not know. But in Valley Above I will be able to say that

I have followed a great leader, one who was stronger than any man, even though she was a lovely young woman. Not even your father, Kuksu Man, could have done what you have done, Ooti."

She gained strength from the ancient shaman's words, pulled back from him, and wiped the offending tears away from her eyes.

"But the revenge is not finished," she said. "The two leaders that night at Kolo-ma are still alive. They were there, and yet I allowed them to escape."

"It is enough, Ooti. What you have done is more than enough. The people will never forget that you led them, and when it is time for them too to go to Upper Meadow, they will still be proud. They will be able to hold their heads high."

Crane came to her then and hugged her tightly. But Acorn Girl saw there were questions in the old woman's eyes.

"My grandfather is right," she said at last. "Our people have had enough of killing now. We must think about where we will go next."

But the *kakina* within her was not satisfied, and she resolved to continue with her revenge-taking, even if it were necessary to do so alone.

Ez Johnson and Milt Lindley and seven of their men had indeed managed to slip away from the gutted Chalk Bluff Mining Company camp shortly before sunrise and, driving themselves along at a forced run, they had escaped the deathtrap the Indians had caught them in.

The village of You Bet was still asleep when they reached it, with only half a dozen souls up and about and wandering around. The nine men made their way to the Greenhorn Rooming House, demanded coffee, and began to unfold their tale of the massacre.

Seminole John, a big Indian who had been fired from Ed Harper's river-turning operation on Greenhorn Creek a few days earlier and who had remained drunk most of the time since then, and Tall Joe as well listened with genuine interest, cursed the damned Diggers, and made pointed suggestion that a bunch of the boys had best get together and go wipe the Injuns out.

"Exactly my thoughts, exactly my thoughts," Milt Lindley said. "The heathen indigenes are troublesome enough when they're merely thieving mules and the like, but this—this was God-awful, cold-blooded murder."

"By the red eyeballs of Jesus," Ez insisted, "I'll kill every damned Injun I see for the next ten years, I swear it. No offense, John, you ain't one of them murdering bastards. I lost more than thirty men, damned good men, an' before this week's out, I aim to see to it they ain't a live Digger within ten miles of here. I'm going to have to build my whole damned camp over again. Jesus, Joe, they just poured burnin' arrows down onto us, and everything went up like haystacks in August. The boys had come in late after chasin' them two that murdered Sonny, an' we just wasn't expecting nothing. We must of let some of them Diggers from up the crick get away when . . ."

"It's more than that, Ezra my friend," Lindley put in. "Joseph, John, I tell you the Diggers were armed to the teeth. The flaming arrows started it, but there was rifle and pistol fire from all sides. Our lads came out half asleep and right into an unbelievable skirl of it. Peculiar, peculiar— only one heathen ever came out into the open—came running right at us, pistol in one hand and a knife in the other, like a rabid wolf, I'd say. I put a bullet in him, and after that another one of them came down to drag the dead man away. But that's just not the way Indian savages fight. I've been through a number of scrapes, and I've never seen anything like it. Ez, as I told you before, I'll lay money that those Diggers had been trained and paid to do what they did—if they were Diggers at all. I'd not be surprised if . . ."

"White coons from down country was wantin' to run us off the creek?"

"Exactly," Milton Lindley said.

"It was fuckin' Injuns, I tell you. I've had nothin' but trouble with them bastards ever since me an' Sonny come up here. Well, by the time I get done with 'em, there's not going to be no more trouble. Look, Milt, when that one Red Devil come running an' got hit, the one that

come next an' tried to drag him away—that was a female
Injun, probably the buck's squaw. An' that's why I'm
telling you it was a damned tribe of 'em."

"Your imagination's enflamed, my friend," Lindley said.
"I didn't see any squaw."

"By God, I guess I can smell an Injun split when one's
near, an' that was a squaw. I've stuck enough of 'em so's I
ought to know by now."

"That you have, Ezra, and so have we all. But with rifle
fire eating us alive and the entire camp engulfed with
flames, I just think . . ."

"Damned right," Johnson said, pounding his fist on the
table. "An' they're better'n sheep, particularly when there's
no sheep in the mountains."

"A colorful way of putting the matter," Lindley hummed,
shaking his head. "Look, given the circumstances, this is a
very foolish argument. If you wish to believe in rumors
about a Grizzly Cult . . ."

"Mr. Johnson . . . ," Seminole John started to say.

But Ez Johnson wasn't listening.

"All right, Milt, have it your Goddamned way. But what
about them bears? I seen *bears*, I tell you."

"Get hold of yourself, Ezra my friend. We've got dead
men lying all over camp out there, and unless we intend
to take this thing lying down, we've got to do something—
and we've got to do it now."

"You going to need a new crew, Mr. Johnson?" Seminole John asked. "I'm a good worker. Any of the boys'll
tell you."

Johnson squinted at the Indian.

"So why'd Harper fire you, then?"

"I guess he figured I was the one who strangled Prigley."

"An' of course you didn't."

"Of course not."

"How you for trackin' down murderin' Diggers?"

Seminole John grinned, pleased with the knowledge
that he'd just been hired on.

"Very good at that," he said. "Heap smart Injun. Follow
trail in dark, by God."

"What about you, Tall Joe?" Milt Lindley asked.

"Count me in, boys. I ain't been hunting in a week or
two."

"Hey, cook!" Johnson yelled. "Bring out the fixin's. Me an' the boys want something to eat. Five minutes more and by God I'll burn this rat trap down."

"Ezra," Milt Lindley said, "I believe I'll go ring the town bell. The gents may be somewhat less than enthusiastic after they've heard what's happened, but we need some more men if we're going to take care of this business. Will your friend at the livery give us horses on short-term credit?"

"Vollmer and Tennessee Tom'll hire on, Ez," Tall Joe said. "That'll make, what? Thirteen of us. Good horses and enough guns and ammo, and we'll smear those damned Diggers into the mud for you."

"If they *were* Indians," Lindley said as he strode toward the door.

With the ringing of the bell, a goodly number of men assembled, and all listened with great interest to the tale of what had happened over on Steephollow Creek during the night. And when Ez Johnson vowed to wipe out every Digger within ten miles, the men shouted their encouragement.

But when Lindley asked for volunteers to ride with them as a *posse comitatus*, the men began to shrug and move away, each to his own claim or hired-on employment.

Johnson and Lindley ended up with precisely the thirteen men that Tall Joe had judged would be sufficient to get the job done.

Once back at the remains of the Chalk Bluff Mining Company works, Seminole John surveyed the bodies, shook his head, and felt the urge to vomit. But at Lindley's urging, he set about trying to find *sign* of which way the massacre party had gone. And since the forest floor was still damp in many places, John was able to discover what he was looking for.

At length he yelled out, "Up country!" and the search was on.

With a minimum of dead ends and sidetracks, the posse moved forward, up and away from the creek and on toward a saddle in a lateral ridge of the main bluff itself.

"Several of the horses are shod," John said, nodding.

"Of course," Lindley agreed. "But what does that mean? If these are indeed Indians, then the horses are stolen. The native savages do not raise horses of their own—and that leads me to believe . . ."

"Whitemen," Johnson said.

"Some of them, at least. This was a very well planned operation, Ezra my friend. There's no question about it."

"One of these horses is very big," Seminole John remarked. "It has bigger hooves than any I have ever seen."

Johnson studied the tracks.

"Plough horse," he said.

"And there'll be at least one mule," Lindley added. "The two that killed Sonny—one's supposed to have been riding a plough horse, the other a mule."

"So why in the hell couldn't the boys track them down?" Ez Johnson demanded.

Goose Leader, the Kulkumish *yomi*, a man who in his youth had been accepted as *yombasi* by Hurt Eagle and had studied the *kuksu* under his direction, now stood watch at the high saddle of the ridge beneath which the Panos were encamped, the people in high spirits after their victory of the preceding night. K-aima Huku surveyed the wooded drainage beyond him, saw nothing, sensed nothing, and thereupon turned his attentions to the bullet wound in his lower thigh, repacking it with bracken frond and once more drawing the deerhide bindings tight. The lead ball had passed cleanly through the flesh, with much bleeding at first. But now the perforation, though still painful, was healing nicely, and Goose Leader was quietly pleased that his always strong body, though he was now more than sixty winters of age, still had the capacity to mend easily.

The sound came to him.

From the ridgeside across the drainage below where he stood a pair of bluejays had begun to chatter.

A mountain lion possibly or a family of coyotes?

Goose Leader squinted, using his hand to shield his eyes against afternoon sunlight. The mischievous blue birds, he knew well, were fond of following predators about, warning potential prey of danger.

Then the sound of a horse whinnying.

A group of *Wawlems*, mounted, emerged into an open area just down from a huge, newly leafed *hamsum tsaa*, a blackoak. One man dismounted, and the others drew their horses into a half-circle about him.

"Thirteen *Wawlems*," Goose Leader whispered.

Then, after waiting a moment to see if any more would emerge from the dark forest beyond the flour-bread tree, Goose Leader grasped his walking stick and moved with surprising agility back downslope toward the Pano encampment.

The unwelcome news galvanized the Panos into activity, a momentary seizure of near hysteria, but Hurt Eagle called out to them, his old voice booming, and the people grew silent.

"Now then," he said, "hear what your leader will tell you. How can she speak when all of you are running about like frightened children?"

The eyes turned to Acorn Girl, who stood in their midst, rifle in hand.

"We must act quickly," she said. "Listen carefully. Goose Leader tells us that there are only thirteen of them. Why should the Panos fear a group of this size? These men present no real danger, but now I am worried that others, many more *Wawlems*, may be following some distance behind. Bear-who-cannot-see-well and I will take our weapons back to the saddle above and hold off these Whitemen. The rest of you must leave at once. Those who cannot walk are to ride, but the men will follow behind the others in order to kill any Whitemen who may be able to get beyond the ridge—but I do not think any will be able to do so. Hurt Eagle has told me of a big valley in the mountains to the north of here, not far from the last high, snowy mountain. He will lead you to that place, and my husband and I will meet you there. You must go now and not wait. Help Tied-wing and Crooked Knee to their horses, old Goose Leader also. Hurt Eagle and Crane must ride. Go now and do not think to discuss this thing. Follow Hurt Eagle."

"Rabbit-chaser," O'Bragh said, "foller the shaman. Don't worry none about me. This Irish nigger's got more lives than a big tree full of rackety-coons. My head's made up, Ooti. Might be I can help some."

"Go!" Ben yelled. "Kingfisher! Help Crane and Hurt Eagle to get those two grizzlies moving. No point in having one of them shot up."

The directions had been given in a properly decisive manner, and the Panos began to move, on horse and muleback and on foot, Before and After herded along with them, away from the encampment.

Acorn Girl and Ben and Bully, mounting and checking their weapons, urged their animals toward the low spot in the westward crest, tethered the mule and two horses at a grove of young firs, and scrambled quickly to the rim.

The miners, their horses trailed out in a line, worked their way slowly upslope.

"Ez Johnson," Ben whispered. "That's him, third horse back. Didn't get enough last night, I guess."

"Milton Lindley," Acorn Girl said, her voice low and cold. "They are both here, then."

"Shouldn't be much trouble," O'Bragh chuckled as he tapped the priming pan on his Hawken. "Tell ye what. This old montan-yard ought to be able to handle the problem first-rate. You younguns get on back to yore varmints an' catch up with the rest. Benny, look out for Rabbit-chaser for me, will ye? Woman's got rovin' eyes, she has. Git now. This child'll be along after a spell."

"O'Bragh, you damned old fool," Ben hissed. "Planning to martyr yourself, are you?"

"Got to speak English, lad, if ye want me to understand ye. Git movin', I say."

"Ooti," Ben said, "you go. The Panos can't lead themselves—they need you."

Acorn Girl laughed.

"Then you would go find that *girlfriend* of yours, the Whitewoman Bully told me about. You belong to me, Bear-who-cannot-see-well. I must stay to take care of my slave."

"Damn fool kids," O'Bragh snorted. "No more brains than a Kain-tuck punkin'. *Wagh!* Wal, this hyar ain't no time for a confab."

Ooti leveled her rifle and fired, the shot echoing across the forest, and one of the Whitemen turned suddenly in his saddle, put both hands to his throat, and slowly tilted sideways and fell to the ground.

O'Bragh's Hawken boomed, and another man pitched from his horse.

The *Wawlems* were leaping down now, scattering, searching for protection behind boulder or tree or thicket of lilac.

"Fan out now," O'Bragh said. "Ooti, ye stay hyar. Ben down there. I'll set up shop yonder."

Johnson and Lindley and their men worked their way toward the saddle, crawling, then moving in bursts from tree to tree.

Ooti and Ben and Bully, now spread about fifty yards apart, controlled the heights, however, firing and loading again and firing once more. Pistol fire sang up from below, and all over the slope little puffs of blue-gray smoke went up and trailed on the air.

More bluejays had joined the two that Goose Leader had originally heard, and now, in the brief intervals between gunshots, they sent up a raucous chorus of gleeful protest and warning, their cries like bright, invisible exclamation points.

Another of the miners lay dead on the slope. Yet another, caught in midstride between one pine and a second, doubled over at the waist and fell, tumbling a few yards down the incline and coming to sudden arrest against the bole of a big sugarpine.

Ben watched the man's death with a kind of grim fascination and then shifted his glance back to the group of four he'd been waiting upon. In a moment they'd have to make a break for it across an open space just about a hundred feet down from the rim.

But they were gone. Nowhere in sight.

"Goddamn it!" he muttered. "Farnsworth, your student hasn't learned his lessons yet. . . ."

He scrambled forward, not wanting to get too far from his appointed position but feeling the need to assure himself as to the whereabouts of the four men.

He made it to a big rock that projected at an angle from the mat of pine needles and resinous tarweed, scanned everything below him. Could see no one.

A shot missed his head by inches, spitting off fragments of stone from the boulder.

You damned fool, you damned fool, you've let them get behind you. . . .

He turned, rose to one knee, and began to squeeze off shots from his revolver.

A bullet caught him just above the knee, passing cleanly through the flesh.

No pain.

He stood, stumbled forward.

And another shot hit him, this one in the chest, close to the heart, driving him backward and over the top of the angular sheaf of stone.

I ought to be dead—but I'm not—there's still life in me. I can still get them before the lamp's blown out. . . .

He stood, pistol in hand, and fired from behind the rock. One of the four was already sprawled on the thick duff of pine needles and dry oak leaves, and now his shots took down two more.

Pistol's empty.

The last of the four, leaping wildly, hurtled over the edge of the boulder, and Ben lunged for the man's arm, had it, pulled, and twisted—hurling his assailant to the earth. Then he dropped his full weight upon the stunned man, gripped the pistol, twisted it loose from his grasp, and then placed his hands upon the man's throat and squeezed, felt the bones snap.

Bear-who-cannot-see-well rose then, steadied himself against the boulder, unconsciously pushed his glasses back against the bridge of his nose, and pulled his leather shirt open to see where the bullet had entered.

Losing blood, but by God I'm still on my feet. Pano the

Bear-God, are you looking out for me too? Where's that girl? I've got to get to her, got to protect her from . . .

With shaking hands Ben loaded his revolver. Then he retrieved his rifle and, hobbling about, picked up the weapons of the men he had killed, thrust them under his belt.

Blood all over my hands . . . my God, there's blood everywhere. . . .

Reeling and stumbling, Bear-who-cannot-see-well made his way back along the crest of the saddle to where he prayed he would find Ooti unharmed.

"Turn around real slow, big man. Took some lead, did you? I guess you don't kill easy, but this time I'll be damned if I don't finish the job. From the description the boys give me, I knew it had to be you, Professor."

Goffe considered hurling himself flat, drawing in one motion, turning, firing.

Leg won't work. Pain in my chest . . . hard to breathe. I know that voice, it's Ez Johnson. Can't do it. Got to edge up to him, then I've got a chance . . . to get my hands on him, kill him. I've taken two slugs and I'm still walking. One more, two more before I can grab him, then . . .

"That's it, turn around. Go for one of them popguns and I'll nail you right in them specs."

"I'm hurt, dying," Ben said. "Don't waste your time on me, Johnson. I've got a friend who's looking for you. An old friend of yours too, from what I'm told. Sorry we didn't get you last night, Wrist-wrestler. Well, your operation's going to be somewhat shorthanded for a time. Thirty-one dead, that's what we counted. You been back there to look things over?"

"Seems like we're always seein' things from different angles," Johnson grinned. "Where's all your Injuns, Goffe? Looks to me like they've run off an' left you. Don't know how you came back to life that other time. Guess I should have invested one more round in your ugly carcass. Injuns found you, huh? That's the way I figger it. An' you got guns for 'em an' come looking for me. You're worse than the lot of 'em, a damned gun-runner. You know that you're already dead, *official*? I even helped string up your murderer, a dumbass card sharpie. Ain't that ironic, by God? So you see, Professor, they ain't no way I can take you in an' have you hung proper, wisht they was. Damned if everybody in You Bet wouldn't turn out for it. Maybe we'd even have some music an' let you give a speech or somethin' before we stretched your overgrown hide. But I guess it ain't going to turn out that way. Can't hang somebody who's already dead *official*."

Bear-who-cannot-see-well slouched forward, collapsed to his knees, coughed. But the pain was too great for him to continue.

"Weak in the knees, are you? Sure you don't want to try the arm-twisting again? I guess you're not up to it, Professor. That right now?"

A lunge, grab the knees, head's spinning, getting dark, got to fight it off, one more thing to do. . . .

He willed away the nausea, fought away the whirling grayness, gathered what strength remained.

The sound of the pistol crashed in his ears as he threw himself toward Johnson's feet, and Bear-who-cannot-see-well knew he was hit again, both legs now, but he grasped forward, his hands finding nothing but tarweed and winter-flattened pine needles.

Someone screaming, Ooti's voice? Another yelp—a man's voice, wounded, in pain . . . Johnson?

Two figures locked in embrace.

Glasses gone—where are they?

His fingers fumbled over the ground, found what they sought. He rolled to one side, pressed the spectacles back onto his face.

Johnson's pistol went off again, but the man was staggering about, the handle of a knife projecting from his stomach, just below the breastbone.

Acorn Girl clinging to him from behind, one hand clawing at his face.

Johnson spun, hurled her from his back, reached for the knife in his belly, and pulled it out. He groaned in agony as he did so, his mouth open, his lungs heaving, sucking at the air.

"Murdering bitch, I'll . . ."

But then his face caved in, and the rear of his head simultaneously exploded outward, blood and brains spewing into the air.

Ez Johnson fell over backward, arms out in cruciform position, and lay utterly still amidst the deep green of the tarweed.

Bear-who-cannot-see-well struggled to his knees, and Acorn Girl was there, kneeling beside him, her face pressed against his hair, her arms draped about him.

"Ooti," he managed, "my beautiful Ooti-du. It's all right, little girl, it's all right. . . ."

Bully O'Bragh came skipping down the hillside, half a dozen new scalps trailing from a rawhide cord about his neck.

"This child thought ye was gone beaver, Benny me lad," the mountain man laughed, "but Acorn Girl hyar saved the bacon for ye. Wearin' some lead, are ye? Sure got a knack for catchin' lead with that big body of yores, Sonny. Mebbeso ye should lose some weight. Make a smaller target that way, so to speak."

"Goddamn you, Farnsworth," Ben coughed.

"This isn't a time to be funny," Acorn Girl said. "He's hurt, he's hurt."

"This old nigger ain't blind," O'Bragh nodded. "But it don't look to me like he's headin' off to no Spirit World as yet. Bleedin' like a stuck pig, though. Pull back his shirt thar, Ooti. Let's have a look-see."

Acorn Girl cut the leathers away and immediately placed her hands over the ragged flesh of the chest wound.

"Can ye breathe all right, Benny?"

"Hurts," Ben managed.

O'Bragh knelt, pulled Acorn Girl's hands away from Ben's chest, and squinted, nodded his head.

"Don't look good," he concluded, "but ain't nothin' punctured I'm thinkin'. These big New England coons, they don't die all that easy, no sir. *Wagh!* I remember once when me an' ol' Termite Joe was up on the Wind River, an' Joe he . . ."

*   *   *

Acorn Girl and O'Bragh made a quick count of the dead who lay along the slope, as well as the scalps Bully had taken and the number killed by Ben and by Ooti herself.

"Four of the *Wawlems* are still alive," Ooti said.

"Probably run for cover by now," O'Bragh suggested. "Ain't nothin' quickens a man's feet more'n seein' his compañeros lyin' scattered about."

"Did you kill Lindley?" the Pano leader demanded.

"Wouldn't rightly know. He look like one o' these hyar?" Bully asked, stretching out the string of scalps.

Then rifle fire erupted from above, the ball striking Ben low in the back. With a groan he twisted sideways, twitching and then lay still.

Acorn Girl screamed and then began to fire off repeated shots from her revolver as Tennessee Tom and Tall Joe came running downslope, yelling and firing their own weapons.

O'Bragh raised his horse pistol and squeezed the trigger, his shot striking Tall Joe in the face, and Tennessee went down with three shots in close pattern in his chest.

"By the dung o' Saint Paul," Bully said, "we damned well didn't need that to happen. Got flustered, this child did—countin' skulps an' all. Ben still alive, Ooti?"

She put her hands to his face, nodded.

"He's still breathing, there is still a small flame of life in him."

"I am Indian!" a voice rang out from the hillside above. "Now I have changed sides. I know who you are, Irish Vulture. I recognize you. I will not fight against you any more. I do not like this man anyway, so I will give him to you to do with as you wish!"

It was Seminole John, his left arm locked about Milton Lindley's throat.

When he finished speaking, Seminole John thrust a knife into the Whiteman's back and, giving him a hard shove, sent him sprawling down the steep slope. With that he leaped back out of the way and, head down, began to run.

O'Bragh lifted his Hawken, took aim, and then lowered his old buffalo gun.

"Guess he done us a favor," Bully shrugged.

Acorn Girl rose, walked slowly to where her enemy was lying, helpless. O'Bragh followed a pace or two behind.

Milton Lindley was obviously having a great deal of trouble breathing.

"Help me, for the love of God!" Lindley begged. "You—you're a Whiteman, just as I am. Keep the Red Devil away from me. I'll pay you whatever you ask—get the knife out of me and help me back to town."

Lindley coughed, grimaced, spat up some blood, the flecked spittle drooling from the corner of his mouth.

"Lung's bust," O'Bragh said. "Guess ye'll drown in yore own juices, me lad."

"I'll be all right. Help me back to You Bet, for the love of Christ!"

"Do with 'im what ye want, Ooti," Bully shrugged, turning and striding to where Benjamin Goffe was lying.

"Do you remember me, Milton Lindley?" Acorn Girl asked. "No? But I remember you very well. I remember that you killed my husband, you and your friends. I remember that many of you raped me. Do you know me now?"

Lindley's eyes were wide with fear but not with recognition.

"It is sad that you do not remember me. But perhaps you remember Jake—Jake at Kolo-ma two winters ago? I wish you would remember, Milton Lindley. Your friends always admired you for the skill with which you talked. They all wished they could be like you. And yet now you have nothing at all to say. Tell me that you remember what you did to Jake and to my babies—maybe I will even let you live then. Do you have nothing to say?"

Milt Lindley coughed again, gagged, spat up more blood this time. And then, though he was dying, he lunged toward her, sprawling to one side, and screaming out as the weight of his body pressed the knife in his back yet further into his flesh.

"It is a shame you will not remember," Acorn Girl said.

She checked the load in her pistol, thrust the barrel into Milton Lindley's gaping mouth, and squeezed the trigger.

18

Dan Fischer's Posse

May, 1850

When Loon closed his eyes, Mouse slipped into Thunder's lodge. He was frightened, and for a moment he couldn't seem to remember what Peheipe Oleli had told him to do.

But then he remembered.

He crept over to where Thunder's daughters were sleeping and used his sharp little teeth to untie the waist strings of the skirts. One of the girls rolled over in her sleep and nearly crushed him, but Mouse scurried out of the way and dragged the flute over to the fireplace. Within a moment he had managed to fill the flute with fire, and then he crept out, past the dozing Loon, to where his friends were waiting for him.

"We must hurry," Coyote said.

He took some of the fire and put it into Dog's ear. He put another portion of the fire onto the hock of Deer's leg, and even today Deer has a reddish spot there. Then he took the flute with the rest of the fire in it into his mouth, and motioned for Mouse to hold onto his bushy tail.

Then they all began to run as fast as they could toward a mountain-sized sweat lodge where the people lived.

At about that time, Thunder woke up, suspecting something was wrong.

"What has happened to my fire?" he called out in a voice that sounded like great boulders crashing together. "Wake up, Daughters! That thieving Coyote has robbed us!"

* * *

334

As Acorn Girl and Bully O'Bragh were in the process of constructing a travois rig to bear Ben's weight behind Old Blue the Percheron, Before and After came loping up the heavily forested slope, and Ooti rose from what she was doing to make a halfhearted attempt at chastising them for not having remained with Hurt Eagle and the others. The grizzlies paid her scant attention, however, instead becoming suddenly stiff-legged as they now cautiously approached the unconscious Ben. After licked gently at the big Whiteman's face, whimpering, looking puzzled.

Then Kingfisher, Elk's Tooth, and Slow Rabbit appeared, urging the mules they rode upslope.

"We decided that we were not tired of fighting after all," Kingfisher said. "That is why we have come back. Is it all over, then?"

"Bear-who-cannot-see-well is still alive?" Elk's Tooth asked. "How badly has he been wounded?"

"Ain't no time for jawin'," O'Bragh said. "Benny's hurt some, but he'll pull through. Git down off yore varmints an' give us some help. Best if we all make tracks before more company shows up. We already took care o' the ones Goose Leader caught sight of."

Acorn Girl nodded.

"Johnson and Lindley are dead."

Her voice was subdued, almost noncommittal.

"Then it is over now?" Kingfisher asked.

"It is over. Slow Rabbit, go catch up with Hurt Eagle. Tell him to wait—that my husband needs his help. We will be there as quickly as we are able."

"I will tell the shaman all that I have learned," Slow Rabbit said, turning his mule, and riding off in the direction from which he had come.

"Let's get old Blind Bear onto his travelin' cot," Bully said. "Grab hold of his legs, Elk's Tooth. *Wagh!* Takes six men an' a boy jest to lift 'im, an' we ain't got but three of us."

"Will he live?" Elk's Tooth asked, his voice half a whisper out of deference to Acorn Girl.

"Hell yes, ye iggerant savage. Don't think we'd be totin' him along if he was gone beaver, do ye?"

Elk's Tooth shook his head, not half understanding what O'Bragh was saying.

"If he lives until we reach Hurt Eagle," Acorn Girl insisted, "then he will live. Hurt Eagle has brought him back before. He will be able to do so this time as well."

Once Goffe had been secured to the litter and the travois fastened to either side of Old Blue's saddle, the little group moved out, downslope toward the former encampment. Here Bully shielded his eyes and gazed momentarily toward the afternoon sun, its silver disc gliding westward across a cloudless blue sky.

"Downright warm today," the mountain man said to Ooti, wiping at his brow and then removing the battered old beaver cap he'd been wearing. "Duff's dried out enough these past couple o' days so that things might even burn if they was lit."

Acorn Girl stared at him.

"What do you mean?" she asked.

"Could be we ought to leave a leetle diversion, lass. I'll be damned surprised if we ain't got more company on the way—by tomorrow if they ain't ridin' right now. Like I'm always tellin' Benny, if ye're tryin' to get clear o' something, it's best to leave a present or summat. To occupy their minds, so to speak."

"Set the woods on fire?"

"Me very thought, gal. Shame yore bedmate don't savvy as quick as ye do. Keep on ridin'. This coon'll catch up with ye in a bit. Old Porcupine gets real fast when thar's smoke behind."

With that O'Bragh dismounted, waved the others onward, and began to scoop up armfuls of the most likely-looking pine needles. These he heaped at the foot of the slope, just below where the growth of tarweed was thickest.

In a moment blue-white smoke was coiling upward and small orange-colored blossoms of flame were hissing and snapping.

O'Bragh mounted, crossed the cathedral-like swale, and continued yet a few more yards up the opposite slope before he drew Porcupine to a halt.

With great interest he watched the fire struggle to make headway into the knee-deep tarweed and for a time was half afraid the little blaze would die and he would be obliged to make a second attempt at arson.

But then the fire was moving, eating its way upslope through good fuel, the flames dancing brightly.

"Wonder if manzanita brush burns this time o' year?" Bully mused, shielding his eyes and again gazing off toward the sun. "Wal, even a Gawdawful beautiful woman can only give ye what she's got, an' that's gospel. What we need hyar's a good suck o' wind."

Lilac brush wilting in the heat, leaves turning brown and then igniting. Dead portions of manzanita taking flame. Tarweed hissing and pouring blue smoke into the air.

A mule deer, coming downslope, sensing the danger and fleeing, the brown form in fluid motion, the animal leaping in long, quick bounds.

A young oak, its leaves a fragile new green-yellow just moments before, suddenly torching and throwing off sparks into the thick mats of pine needle and dead leaf further up the hill, the duff taking hold and blazing also.

O'Bragh grinned, patted his mule on the shoulder.

"Better day for a bonfire than a man might of figgered," he said. "*Wagh!*"

By noon, word of the massacre of the Chalk Bluff Mining Company camp had reached Grass Valley, the news being brought by a rider from You Bet.

Sheriff Daniel Fischer listened to the tale, cursed, and shook his head. Rumors of a so-called Grizzly Cult of Maidus had been current for some time, but Fischer assumed all along that the entire thing was essentially a figment of the miners' imaginations—a quick explanation for every dead man found out in the woods, whether put under by an angry partner, sluice thieves, some band of vigilantes, or a damned bear. Even the reported deaths of Hardt and Hawley had, by first accounts, been laid at the feet of these mythical Grizzlies—it being only later confirmed that vigilantes left a printed sign claiming responsibility for the bizarre deaths of the two alleged claim-jumpers, the bodies found with oaken stakes driven through their hearts.

Though some of the local citizenry complained of his
drinking, had in fact ever since he accepted the ill-paying
post of sheriff a year earlier, Dan Fischer was a man of
considerable experience in California, possessing an excellent knowledge of the lay of the land, and both his prowess with a revolver and his bulldoglike tenacity once he
had set out to track someone down were admired, even by
his detractors. He'd been in California nearly nine years
now, having come overland with the Bartleson-Bidwell
group and having ridden with such men as Father De
Smet and the redoubtable Thomas Fitzpatrick, the latter
having guided the Bidwell expedition as far as Fort Hall,
Idaho. Fischer well recalled the party's passage over the
Sierra, a fortunate crossing, late in October of that year,
and yet no snow. But they'd resorted to eating their oxen
and mules and, at last finding their way down into the
salvation of the San Joaquin valley, had been well pleased
with a roast of fat coyote. But at length they reached John
Marsh's ranch near Mt. Diablo and had been afforded
warm hospitality, though some of the party deemed Marsh
a skinflint of the first water.

Fischer grinned, recalling that Marsh had charged Bidwell
what later were discovered to be standard California prices
for a bullock and a small hog, and that the emigrants had
been obliged to pay Marsh in lead, powder, and knives.

Then, of course, there was the matter of Marsh charging
them three dollars apiece for interceding in their behalf
and obtaining for them the required passports from pro-
vincial authorities.

Well, that was a good while back now, and much water
had flowed under the proverbial bridge. With the discovery of gold, the world had changed—with thousands upon
thousands of men pouring into California. And now actual
statehood was at hand, and he was making do on short
wages, with only two deputies for assistance, in an area in
which constant turmoil and general lawlessness were the
rule.

"Grizzly Cult or not," Fischer reflected, "there are dead
men scattered all over Steephollow Creek. Guess we got
to do something."

When his informant left the tiny office at the front of the

jail, Fischer took a long swig from the bottle he kept in his
desk drawer, slipped the flask into the inner pocket of his
jacket, and strapped on his Colt revolver.

"Be good to know where my deputies are," he thought,
"Jackson and Bates. Maybe the boys are out keeping the
peace at Ophir Hill Palace. Most likely place to look,
anyhow. . . ."

*A flood of images, a cascading torrent like a river in
flood. Faces. Names. A long, straight road leading somewhere undefined, leading to something permanent but
without form. And then a branch, a pair of wagon-ruts,
twisting away from the main track and following along a
broad, shallow river on the other side of which yet other
pilgrims were plodding along—and he wondered if, indeed, he should not be one of them.*

*Major General William Goffe, an ax in his hand and a
Mexican sombrero upon his head—and his eyes a strange
kind of flaming violet color, almost as though fires were
burning within them.*

*Judge Goffe, one and the same, somberly affixing his
signature to some document of unspecified importance.*

The Elder Goffe, playing a banjo and singing:

> *O, I hain't got no home*
>   *Nor anything else, I s'pose,*
> *Misfurtune seems to follow me*
>   *Wherever I goes;*
> *I come to Californy*
>   *With a heart both stout and bold,*
> *And have been to the diggin's,*
>   *There to get some lumps of gold.*
> *But I'm a used-up man,*
>   *A perfect used-up man,*
> *And if I ever get home again,*
>   *I'll stay there if I can.*

*Major General William Goffe, paying court to a faceless
Indian woman, disappearing into a brush-covered lodge
with her, the two of them emerging moments later surrounded by several half-breed children.*

"Are you telling me that I am to go home again, Great-great-great-Grandfather?" Ben called out.

Judge Goffe turned, scratched his head, looked about as if attempting to discover the source of some irritating sound.

"I was buried with my broadsword beside me," he said. "I did what I believed had to be done, and then I did what I had to do to save my own hide. What are you doing here, Bernard?"

"My name's Benjamin. Have you forgotten me, Grandfather?"

"Oh yes, Ben, Benny, little Benny. Come out from behind that tree, then. Yes, I have something to tell you."

Ben stepped forward, aware that he was dressed in Indian leathers and wondering if the Elder Goffe would even recognize him.

"Now then," Judge Goffe said, "listen to my words. Oft at each daybreak I am doomed alone to bewail my cares. Not one now is alive that I to him openly dare to say my mind. For sooth I know that is a worthy wont in a kemp that fast he bind his breast and keep his thoughts to himself, think as he will."

Ben stared at the other man as if not believing what he had heard.

"A translation of lines from The Wanderer," he said. "I don't understand your meaning, Grandfather."

"Here kine are fleeting, here kin are fleeting, here men are fleeting, here mates are fleeting, all this earthly frame grows idle at last."

"I don't understand you," Ben complained.

"Always was slow, Sonny," the Elder Goffe laughed. "I'll put 'er in by-Gawd simple English for ye then. 'Thrice have I left this cursed spot, but mine it was to learn the fatal truth, that dust we are, to dust we shall return!' "

"You're making me angry, Grandfather. I am not Benjamin Goffe any longer. I am Bear-who-cannot-see-well."

"The very son of Cain, then."

"Yes," Ben agreed, "of the Clan of Cain. I'm not sure now why I ever spent my time worrying about you or listening to the things you told me."

"I never told you anything," Judge Goffe said, slicing

*through the air with his broadsword. "You have invented
the whole thing, Benjamin. Is it not possible for you to
distinguish between dreams and realities?"*

*"I also have an Indian wife," Ben confided. "Just like
you, Grandfather."*

*"Had one perhaps, had one. Not any longer, Benjamin
the Pedant."*

"You're wrong," Ben insisted. "Ooti is waiting for me."

Major General William Goffe roared with laughter.

*"Best get back then, young man. Unless, that is, you
wish to accompany me on my eternal voyage into nothingness. But, after all, your time will come soon enough . . . ."*

*Then he was running through flames, fire that did not
consume him, did not burn him at all. Nor did he have
even the slightest idea as to how long he had been running—
only that he could not stop, that he would surely die if he
dared to stop.*

*A blue-white glow before him, and he ran toward it.
Pains in his chest, pains from the long run. But his will
was absolute, and he had no intention of wavering. Somewhere ahead she was waiting for him. . . .*

O'Bragh had overtaken Ooti and the Panos about noon
the following day, just as the Indians were completing a
difficult crossing of the churning South Fork of the Yuba, a
few miles upstream from the mining town called Washington.

"Bridge down yonder," Bully laughed when he too had
managed to ford the racing green water. "Could of mo-
seyed right on across, as it turns out. Town's damned near
deserted—big gold strike ten miles downstream."

"Then why did you not cross on the bridge?" Ooti asked.

"How in hell did I know whar ye was? Answer me that."

"You were not following our trail, then?"

" 'Course not. Layin' false trail, that's what I was doin'.
We got more company back thar, as it turns out. Wal, best
we not set hyar jabberin'. Is Ben . . . ?"

"Still alive," Acorn Girl said, answering the unfinished
question. "But he is in the dream world. Sometimes he is
very quiet, and at other times he says things that I do not
understand."

"*Wagh!*" Bully laughed. "I knew 'er. Jest no way that big nigger's goin' to die. Yore husband's jest too damned stubborn to give up easy. Did Hurt Eagle dig the lead out of his hindside?"

"Yes. Crane and I helped him to do that last night. The ball was flattened against the hip girdle, very close to the base of his spine. We have prayed for him, but there has been no time. . . ."

"Aye, aye. An' ain't no time now, nuther. Point yore leetle parade up that crick canyon ahead. Me an' Rabbit-chaser rode this trail when we come lookin' for Ben in the first place. What ye done with my woman, Acorn Girl?"

"Rabbit-chaser? Oh, she wandered off with another Whiteman, I don't remember his name."

"Like hell she done that!"

"If you don't believe what I say, then catch up with Hurt Eagle. Perhaps your wife has come back by now and is riding with him, alongside of Bear-who-cannot-see-well."

"Damned pore time to be jokin', if ye ast me," O'Bragh growled.

The Panos moved ahead up the steep-walled canyon through which a big creek roared and cascaded, the white water hissing and spraying up from one fall after another. Snow lay deep on the mountainsides above them now, and O'Bragh predicted that they would encounter several miles of snow at the head of the canyon, which widened out the further up it they traveled.

The prediction proved accurate, and the going became very slow, very difficult.

When they finally reached a point beyond which the terrain dropped away to lower elevations along the bottom of the canyon of the Middle Fork, they left the snow behind. But now precipitous slopes proved an equal hindrance.

Sundown found them along the turbulent river, the stream high with snowmelt from the peaks to the east, but nonetheless Acorn Girl directed her people to cross over to the northern bank of the river, thus providing at least this margin of safety should any pursuing group of *Wawlems* attempt to catch up to them by means of riding through the night.

The Panos were on the verge of exhaustion, some with feet still half-numb from the traverse across snowfields above, but the crossing, difficult against the current of the river, was made without the loss of a single horse or mule. Ranger had stumbled, nearly being taken by the current, and Ben with him, for the trailing edge of the travois had been secured to the forequarters of Acorn Girl's horse, but the immense strength of Old Blue, pulling on ahead, allowed the venerable saddle horse to right himself.

The evening meal consisted of strips of dried venison and *oosaw*, acorn mush, the last of this foodstuff. After eating, the people turned immediately to their blankets of deerhide or woven rabbit skins and slept.

Ooti, however, though she as well as the others had been without sleep for the preceding two nights, sat doggedly awake by her husband's side, sometimes singing softly to him, sometimes talking to him in the light of the moon now beginning to wane.

She had all but fallen asleep in a sitting position when she heard him speak.

"Roast beef, if you don't mind. . . ."

"Ben?" she said, starting fully awake.

"Hungry," he answered. "Ooti? Is there anything to eat, Ooti? And coffee—I want coffee. Bully's got some, I know he has."

Acorn Girl bit off a portion of the dried venison that she had not eaten and placed it into Ben's mouth, watched him chew for a moment and then swallow. She gave him another morsel, and he chewed once again.

"I need some coffee," he complained. "Will you get some for me, Ooti? Where are we? Did we get them all?"

"Johnson and Lindley and the others? Yes, they have all entered into the darkness, my husband. And we are a long way from there now. Hurt Eagle is leading us to the north, to Oidoing-koyo village, close by the mountain that blew up long ago. Grasshopper Man has relatives there, an aunt and an uncle as well. But it is still a long way, many days' journey."

"I knew you were waiting for me," Bear-who-cannot-

see-well said. "Am I shot up as badly as last time? I have
had strange dreams that seemed to go on for a very long
time. You had not come to find me, Ooti, so I had to find
my way back to you. Ooti, Goddamn it, I love you. Do
you understand me? I couldn't . . . not without seeing you
again."

"You talk too much," Acorn Girl replied, pressing her
lips to Ben's forehead and wiping at her eyes. "I would
have come. I was going to come. We had to flee . . .
O'Bragh says more *Wawlems* are following us."

"O'Bragh," Ben said, his smile faintly discernible in the
thin moonlight, "that old pack rat's got coffee beans. He's
even got *ground* coffee. I saw it in his saddlebag the
night Goose Leader led his band up out of the draw.
Everyone's sleeping? Wake him up, Ooti, and tell him the
Connecticut Vulture wants coffee. Tell him to come drink
some with us."

"All right," she said. "I will get coffee. But you must
promise not to go away again while I go to get it."

"I promise you that," Ben said. "Wake the old bastard
up and tell him I want to wrist-wrestle."

Then she was gone from beside him, but only a minute
or two passed before she returned, Bully O'Bragh with
her.

"Farnsworth?" Ben managed. "Where's my coffee, you
miser I knew you were hoarding it all along."

"Name's Bully, an' ye know it well enough, ye overgrown ox. Damn, lad, it's good to have ye back among the
livin'. Can ye breathe all right now?"

"As long as I don't try to laugh," Ben said—groaning as
he chuckled to himself.

"I should not light even a little fire," Acorn Girl said,
"but we are well armed in case the Whitemen find us. I
will stretch out a deerhide and tie it to the bushes. That
way the light will not be visible from over there."

She gestured toward the south bank of the river.

In a short time the coffee was boiling in O'Bragh's
battered old pot, and Bully poured a tin cup full of the hot
liquid and held it for Ben to sip.

"Not too fast now, ye damned fool. No point in blisterin'
yore mouth, ye big lug."

Ben sipped, savored the taste, swallowed, and then demanded some more.

"Do only the young ones get to drink the coffee?" a tall, thin, shadowy figure asked. "I could not sleep any more because of all this talking, so I woke up. I see that the dead man has now become a live man once again. It is easier when I do not have to go searching for him."

"Grandfather!" Ooti said, rising and embracing the ancient one. "Bear-who-cannot-see-well has decided to live."

"Yes," the old shaman said, "I can see that he has."

By noon of the following day the band of Panos and their horses and mules had managed to work their way up out of the steep, rocky-sided canyon and were making good time through a series of meadows that drained northward toward a precipitous drop-off into the much larger canyon of the North Fork of the Yuba. And riding before them, like a massive dome of summer thunderheads, was the big white mountain of spires, the final major peak in the Sierra Nevada, a mountain the *Wawlems* called simply Sierra Buttes. To either side of the meadows the land slanted upward to the crowns of lesser mountains, these nonetheless mantled in deep snows. But along the northward-flowing creek, spring grasses were abundant, and the mountain cornflowers were unfolding themselves as the drifts receded.

Elk's Tooth came pounding down the meadow, his horse at a full run. Assigned the position of rear watch, he now drew up alongside Acorn Girl and used his hands to make the gesture of hopelessness.

"The *Wawlems* are nearly to the top of the canyon wall," he said. "I think there must be fifty of them."

"Yep," O'Bragh said. "Them's the ones, all right, jest like I told ye. Ooti, ye an' Ben an' the troops head up that next draw an' make for the slot between them high rocks. We still got a full powder keg?"

"Yes, yes, we do. We will fight the *Wawlems* again. You are right, that is a good place to do it."

"Listen to me, ye leetle hellcat. Take Benny an' yore gang an' keep on goin'—to Oidoing-koyo, or whatever ye call 'er. This hyar's goin' to be my party, mine an' Rabbit-chaser's. Don't by Gawd argue with the Irish Vulture. Ye an' yore Red Divvels would only be crampin' me style. Give me the keg an' four, five more rifles an' get gone the hell out of hyar. Could be we'll catch up with ye later."

Bully and Rabbit-chaser positioned themselves among a group of pinnacle-like granite boulders and, working from the bottom of a sand-filled trench behind a lichen-crusted rim, set half a dozen rifles in place. This done, they sat back, side by side, and chewed on strips of venison jerky, waited.

"Point is," Bully said, "the lads have got to think you an' me has got a leetle army up hyar. Cain't come up more'n two at a time through the draw, but she's best if we can keep 'em back jest a mite. If the Gawd-dog's with us, mebbe we can discourage 'em enough so they'll decide they wanted to swing off over toward Downieville all along."

"Do you think there are as many as Elk's Tooth said, husband?"

"More than like, more than like. It's probably Dan Fischer an' as many o' the louts from Grass Valley, Red Dog, an' You Bet as didn't have nothin' better to do for two, three days. Any coon with a long-tom or a good sandbar to attend to wouldn't of been willing to waste his time on no goose-chase. This child has seen posses before. Sometimes the boys gets tired o' riding an' makes their way to some leetle town or another. Get drunk, raise hell, sometimes half of 'em ends up in jail. Or else they jest take off prospectin' an' forget about the whole keeboodle."

"But if there are fifty, as Elk's Tooth said, won't they be able to climb up here and kill both of us, no matter what we do?"

"It's a damned possibility all right."

"You are a crazy Whiteman," Rabbit-chaser said. "I do not know why I ever listened to all those things you told me that cold day when you came to my lodge. I was not waiting to die, no matter what you thought. When spring had come, I would have gone north to where my relatives live. They would have taken me in."

"Who'd of wanted a homely old woman like ye?"

"That is not the way you talked when you asked me to be your woman, Irish Vulture. No, you did not talk that way at all. You said you could still see the beautiful young woman I once was, even though my face had grown wrinkled and I had lost some of my teeth. That is what you said, O'Bragh."

Bully grinned.

"An' I meant 'er, too. Sorry now that ye listened to this child?"

Rabbit-chaser pursed her lips and exhaled through her nostrils.

"Maybe not," she replied. "We still have time to slip away, Vulture. We do not have to stay here and allow the miners to kill us both."

"Jest two of us," Bully replied, "an' we're old ones. Mebbeso it won't be no great loss. Hell, Rabbit, we'll jest wander on up into the Spirit World together, singin' an' dancin' like children. Don't that appeal to ye none?"

"Here they come, O'Bragh," she said, pointing.

Bully squinted, nodded his head.

"Fifty o' the niggers at least. Mebbe a thousand or more. Get ready, Rabbit old gal."

Rabbit-chaser moved quickly to one of the loaded rifles, took up firing position.

"It's a good day to die," she said, looking back hopefully at her husband.

"Good as any, by the green bung o' Jesus. Keep down now, an' don't go shootin' until this hyar Irish nigger does."

"Should we kill all of them, Crazy Man?"

Bully pondered the matter for a moment.

"Do seem like a good idee, don't it now?"

O'Bragh settled behind his own rifle, crouched low, and studied the posse that was moving upslope toward the defile between heaped granite boulders. The trail wound up, passed through a small open area at the foot of a scree beneath a broken-off rim and then came ahead, so that the men would be obliged to pass either one or two at a time directly beneath where he had placed the rifles.

"Got a new plan, by Gawd!" Bully whispered. "Gal, I'll

be right back. Listen now. When the boys get to the leetle
opening down thar, fire off one, mebbe two shots into the
midst of 'em."

"It's too far to aim very well," Rabbit-chaser protested.
"Where are you going?"

"Don't worry none. This child'll be back directly. Jest a
leetle adjustment is all. Minor elaboration of the thesis,
that's what Benny said one time. Remember now, soon as
they get into the hollow, crack off a couple. Give 'em
something to think on. *Wagh!* This hyar's goin' to be more
fun than skulpin' bald men."

*Be careful, my husband. I do not wish to die alone, and
if you die, then I do not wish to live any more. Why did I
ever listen to the pretty words you put in my ears?*

When the party of Whitemen reached the place Bully
had pointed to, Rabbit-chaser fired—then scrambled over
to a second rifle and fired again, set immediately to
reloading.

She heard the commotion she had created, the men
cursing and the horses whinnying, but she concentrated
on what she was doing, did not look up until the rifle was
loaded and ready once more. Then, scrambling back to
the first of the guns, she looked down, saw that one of the
horses was down, the men seeking what cover they could
find among the larger boulders at the foot of the scree.

Then Bully was back beside her.

"Ye done good, Rabbit," he grinned. "Winged one of
the coons an' took down a pony. Them shots come so fast
the boys probably didn't even see whar they come from.
That's how come they ain't shootin' back yet."

"What do we do now?" Rabbit-chaser asked. "I'm frightened, O'Bragh."

" 'Course ye are, 'course ye are. Leetle secret, gal. The
Irish Vulture, he's scared shitless. Always am, any time
the guns start poppin'. Mebbe that's the reason I've gotten
out o' so many scrapes in me time. It's natural, that's all.
Nothin' to worry about."

"Are we going to get out of this . . . *scrape?*"

O'Bragh shrugged.

"Hard to tell yet," he said. "Mebbe. Let's give the boys
a few more rounds. Tell ye what. Shoot for the horses.

That always gets 'em flustered—the lads start thinking about how they's goin' to have to walk home, by Gawd."

Crazy Whiteman. I have lived a good life, it is all right to die now. It is a good day to die. . . .

Now both of them were firing, moving from gun to gun, shooting again.

"Start reloadin', Rabbit."

If we die together and go into the Spirit World, then I do not wish to go back to my other husband. No, I will stay with this one. But probably he will find trouble to get into even there. . . . I wonder if we will be young again when we get to that place? It is far away, across the long hazy band of stars.

Sheriff Daniel Fischer stared up over the rim of the boulder he was crouched behind, studied the high tower of granite from which rifle fire was coming.

"The bastards are pegging our horses," he said. "How many you figure are up there, Bates?"

"Not more than five or six I don't think. Or else they're just saving ammunition," the deputy suggested.

"Doesn't make sense, damn it," Fischer said. "They've fired maybe a dozen shots so far. Two men wounded, and six horses crippled or dead. We're outside their range, and they've got to realize it."

"I don't think our shots are doing any good at all," Bates said. "It's too far, and they're up too high. I haven't seen anyone up there yet."

"Guns don't fire themselves," Fischer drawled. "We can either back off, or we can try to get some of the boys around behind them."

"Who'd go?" Bates asked.

"You and Jackson, naturally. Take that big Indian, John, and four or five of the others. If you can make it up the slope right above us, you can work your way along that rim—maybe without even being seen. From up there, the damned Injuns or whoever's shootin' at us should be sitting ducks. You can come down behind them just over that crest—you see where I'm talking about?"

Bates looked doubtful.

At that moment one of the You Bet men came running toward where the sheriff and his deputy were crouched. In midstride his joints appeared to go loose and, with what looked like a wide grin on his face, he spun around, threw one arm up, and flopped onto his back.

"Guess they're not quite as far out of range as we thought," Fischer said. "One man dead and two wounded. Things are startin' to get serious."

He drew out his flask, yanked the cork with his teeth, and took a long pull, squinted, and coughed. Then he offered the bottle to Bates.

"Go ahead, finish 'er. Then we got to get down to business."

Fischer signaled and then, the deputy following him, he moved forward another twenty yards before taking cover once more. A dozen of his men moved up as well, and yet even then, Fischer noted, the rhythm of rifle fire from the rim did not increase. He could see the white puffs of smoke from among the rocks, now here, now there, and he began to wonder if there might be only two or three men in the fortress of granite, two or three men fighting a kind of delaying action.

He signaled again, and another cluster of men ran forward, dodging from side to side.

"Jackson's down, Sheriff! I'm going back and pull him in."

"Don't be a damned fool. . . ."

But the deputy was already gone, had made it to where his fallen friend lay, grabbed the man by his arms and had pulled him, heels dragging, toward a big juniper that grew from a split in the granite.

Then Bates too was lying dead in the open.

"Goddamned fool! I tried to tell you. . . ."

Now the posse began to open up at the area from which the rifle fire was coming, and for a few moments everyone was firing off shots as rapidly as possible.

"Hold it! Hold it!" Fischer yelled out. "We're not doing any good yet. Got to get some men upslope and around over the rim. . . ."

An hour or more passed, and each of the three attempts to get a group up the scree and onto the crest ended in failure. Three more men were dead, and half a dozen others were crouched amidst the jumble of boulders and pinned down.

"Seminole John, damn it!" Fischer yelled. "Get your red ass over here."

John came scrambling, his face covered with perspiration and dust.

"You and me, Big John—let's see if we can get up there."

The Indian shook his head.

"Me dumbass Injun," he said, "but not that dumb. Always heard that Whitemen were better at climbing rocks than anybody else. You go, Sheriff. I'll stay here and cover you."

"Not up to it, ehh?"

"Hell no. But I'll tell you who's up there. It's Irish Vulture and that Grizzly Woman. They're the ones that killed Ezra and Lindley. Only the big dumb Injun, I got away."

"And you're certain it was O'Bragh, the one that used to trap for Fitzpatrick and Sublette?"

"He was at Bent's Fort a dozen years ago," Seminole John said, "I know that much. And I saw him cut a man's throat without even thinking twice. Had a hat made out of scalps, by God. Sheriff, I think we ought to go home. I should have known better than to come along in the first place. A man gets things figured out after awhile."

"Bully O'Bragh," Fischer mused. "The old bastard must be sixty-five, seventy years old by now. One of the legends of the mountains. What in the hell are we doing then? You're *positive* you saw O'Bragh over on Steephollow Creek?"

"Would I lie to you?" Seminole John asked.

"Yeah, well. There's not going to be much honor in bringing him in—if it is him. And a good bit less honor if the old coot manages to poke lead into my hide. Whoever's up in them rocks, it sure ain't no Injun, not the way he shoots. No offense, Big John."

"Maybe I kill you if he doesn't."

"Fair enough. I'm going up the slope—are you with me or not?"

"Me dumbass Injun. Okay, let's go. . . ."

But at that moment the side of the mountain appeared to lift outward in one place, a cluster of boulders forgetting suddenly about the ties of gravity. And everything seemed to slip and give as a torrent of rock came spilling down.

Men cursing, yelling, running heedlessly in all directions with another and yet another falling to the deadly gunfire from the rim above.

An avalanche of stone, granite hissing and cracking in its descent, a rush of sound gaining and then subsiding and ending with a few last fist-sized rocks dancing downward, striking larger masses of rock, popping and leaping up into the air and then settling.

A swirling column of dust drifted in the suddenly still air, hanging there and then losing form.

The narrow defile ahead was blocked, and some of the men had vanished—buried, Fischer realized, by the rubble of stone.

The tattoo of rifle fire from above had ceased. A tall, gaunt figure in buckskins was standing on the rim now, waving a rifle over his head. And the figure of a woman beside him.

Then both forms disappeared from sight, and Dan Fischer, solemn-faced, gazed about at the shattered posse. The men, returning to their horses, were already beginning to ride away. Some, however, stood in stunned silence, and others, those whose horses had been slain, were vying for the animals belonging to those who lay dead or were buried beneath slide rock.

"Mr. Fischer," Seminole John queried, "you going to need a new deputy now, ain't you? I'm a real hard worker. Ask anyone."

19

White Rock All Fall To Pieces

September, 1850

Thunder's Daughters jumped up at once, and their skirts of woven grass fell off. Thunder grew angry, but the girls refused to go anywhere until they had tied their skirts back on.

Then all four of them gave chase, and even though Peheipe Oleli and his friends had a great lead, Thunder and his daughters were catching up with them. There was a heavy wind and terrible rain and a hailstorm as well—and that might have put out the stolen fire, but Coyote had hidden the flames carefully.

Peheipe Oleli and his friends were nearly to the great sweat lodge now, with Thunder and his Daughters close behind them.

"Keep running!" Coyote shouted. "You're almost to safety!"

Then he stopped suddenly, so suddenly that Mouse fell from his tail and had to scurry away into the tall grass. Coyote himself was very frightened, for he had seen Thunder hurl his lightning bolts many times before. He had seen the lightning knock over great pines and oaks.

But he stood his ground and carefully drew his bow and launched an arrow that flew straight into Thunder's throat and killed him, so that he had no choice and had to go up into the sky, halfway to the Spirit World.

"Now you have to stay in the sky!" Coyote called out. "Now you will not be able to follow people and try to kill them!"

Seeing what had happened to their father, Thunder's Daughters fell down onto their backs, and their grass skirts came up over their faces so that they could not see.

Coyote wagged his tail and then copulated several times with each of them.

After that he was very tired, but he picked up the flute full of fire once more and carried it back to where Kuksu was waiting.

"For once you have done well," Kuksu said. "I will take the fire, but I will let you keep the flute, Peheipe Oleli. Yet now you have married Thunder's Daughters, and I think you are going to have to live with them."

Upper Eden
Headwaters of the North Branch of Rio de las Plumas
California, U.S.A.
September 21st, 1850, Equinox

Dear Liz & Tom,
   No, this is not a late-arriving letter from a dead man. Whatever communication you may have received from official sources concerning my unfortunate death, I hasten to assure you that I am once more in sound health and indeed have not suffered a single hay fever attack since my departure from New Haven some fifteen months since. The only ills I have had to endure have been inflicted by my fellow human beings via gunshot. You will be pleased (or horrified, as the case may be) to hear that I am now almost completely healed and walk with only a slight limp, and that problem seems to be improving with each day. Since I last wrote you, I have been shot some seven times. The first three of these wounds I received on my way to confer with the governor. Left for dead, I was discovered by a band of friendly Maidu Indians, and through the offices of their shaman, a man whose age must be well in excess of a hundred years, I was brought back to life.
   What has happened to me since that time will eventually provide the basis for the book I intend to author—concerning life in the goldfields, as I have told you before. But the tale is too long and involved for me to attempt here, even in the most summary

fashion. When I am able to find the requisite leisure, I will, however, write more fully on the matter.

It will probably shock you to learn that, yes, I have been living among the savages, so-called, and continue to do so. And I may as well tell you something you may perhaps find most offensive. I have taken a wife among them, a girl of less than half my own age but far wiser than I in countless ways, faultlessly brave and courageous, and most loving. Her name, in their language, is *Ooti-du*, the translation of which is Acorn Girl.

Do not censure me too severely, Liz and Tom. You must remember that I am, as it were, a man returned from the dead—and like Lazarus himself, no doubt, I am somewhat befuddled and finding it difficult if not impossible to value those things I formerly held true and dear and certain with the same reverence I once did.

Try to remember that our esteemed forebear, General Goffe, cast up upon the shores of a New World, found love in the arms of an Indian woman. Do you recall, Liz, the rapt attention we paid as young children when Grandpa told us those stories?

For all practical purposes I am dead—legally dead. I pledge you to the utmost secrecy in this matter. Whether Etta has remarried by now or not, she is never to know. My will has by now certainly been executed, and so I consider myself fully quits with the former Mrs. Ben Goffe.

As to those properties I left to you in the will, rest assured that having once died and granted them to you, I will not now emerge from my grave in any attempt to retrieve them.

The letters of credit which you dispatched in my behalf to San Francisco will not, however, return to Connecticut—inasmuch as, being once more alive, I had need of them and so have redeemed them. You must not begrudge these to your dead brother.

I should not jest in this fashion. You are both dear to me and have been faithful to me in all matters. Captain Sutter, I know, has returned three of your letters, to you. He also, at the time, believed me dead, though he is now aware of my continued temporal existence.

California, as you well know, is officially a member of the Federal Union, having been admitted as a State, fully and equally, on the 13th of last month. The news has just reached us here at Upper Eden within the past several days—and at the same time I learned the sad news that President Taylor had succumbed to the cholera, just as had so many in St. Louis and as have so many here in the mining regions. The disease, apparently, is a catholic democrat, treating all equally. But Fillmore will do well enough in the great man's stead, particularly with Daniel Webster to assist him in the capacity of Secretary of State.

You will not find Upper Eden on any map, for indeed I have coined the name myself. I have homesteaded an extensive piece of land, some by claim, some by purchase, perhaps ten miles to the south of a mountain, quite lofty, called by the nearby *Oidoingkoyo Maidu* Indians *Wahgalu* or *Little Tehama*, but known to the Whites as Lassen's Butte, after the trailblazer, Peter Lassen (Larsson) whose rancho lies at the foot of the mountains, some miles to the west of Upper Eden. The mountain is a volcano, still active judging by the numbers of boiling springs, sulfur jets, and so forth that play about its sides. A much larger mountain, according to the *Oidoingkoyos*, once rose where Lassen's Butte now stands, a great volcanic peak that blew up and so destroyed itself, with the present mountain forming as something of an afterthought. The whole thing is most likely a wild tale, and yet, having been several times up on the slopes of the *Present Tehama*, I have seen much evidence suggesting that something of the sort happened.

Suffice it to say that this land is exceedingly beautiful, and I cannot believe that Milton's Eden, envisioned in the darkness of that towering mind, could have been more lovely, more wild, more grand. In fact, I have now come to see our sedate English cousins as relatively innocent, relatively naive. Yet how can I say this of a people whose own history is so clotted with intrigue and violence and bravery and madness?

I have written enough for now, but promise to write more fully at a later date.

Know then that I am well (though I have not explained about my four most recent gunshot wounds), I am happy, I am outrageously in love with a woman who is like Eve (though more knowledgeable of life, braver, keener of intellect, and altogether kinder and more loving), and I have—we have our own tribe of Indians, the *Panos*, who live here on our ranch with us (though some have drifted off and are now keeping house in *Oidoing-koyo* village, not far away), and with the assistance of these *Panos* and a few of Lassen's men and my dear friend Farnsworth O'Bragh, of whom I have spoken before, Acorn Girl and I have now built a house, half log cabin and half *Maidu* lodge, thereby establishing an entirely new mode of frontier architecture. And finally: I am happy, Tom and Liz, more contented than I have ever been before in the course of this restless life of mine. And so I hope to continue for so long as the *Great Gawd Coyote* will allow it.

I had intended to close, but see how I run on?

There is one further bit of conspiracy I must ask you to enter into. As befits a man formerly dead, I have found it politic and wise to assume a new identity. By this name I am now known here in California, a name I consider as my own by right of having earned it. When you write, then, I must insist that you address your missive to Benjamin McCain, Gent.

And if our old New England forebear, Bill Goffe, comes wandering about as ghosts sometimes do, tell him that Little Ben challenges him to a wrist-wrestling match. In this part of the world, at least, I am considered essentially invincible.

Your Most Loving Brother,
Ben

*   *   *

Ooti lay stretched on a boulder at the margin of a small
pool, one hand trailing in water that was lukewarm. Her
eyes were closed, and the sunlight made a tracery of red
and black through the eyelids. She felt the warmth like a
weight on her body, almost like a hand touching breasts
and belly and thighs. She could hear the rushing of the
stream that tumbled down the sheer mountainside before
leveling out somewhat across the bench where she lay,
slowing enough to form a pool. She could hear the occasional callings of birds. She could smell the rotten-egg
odor of sulfur, a smell similar to the smoke of black powder from guns, for part of the water in the stream came
from hot springs higher up. At first the smell had repelled
her, but she had grown used to it, had almost come to
enjoy it when she noticed, for it was associated with this
great mountain with its wonderful warm waters, this magical place called Wahgalu.

She put her hands to her abdomen, as yet firm and flat,
pressed gently, and her face, eyes still squeezed shut,
tautened into a smile. She hugged her secret within herself.

"This is the dream of Olelbis," she thought in her
half-slumber. "Everything is different, everything is turned
inside out, and yet everything seems the same."

The season drew close to the Ustu, Burning Time, and
her people in the meadow down at the base of the great
peak, the mountain still white in places despite the advanced season, were preparing for the celebration. In a
way that a few months ago had seemed impossible, life
had become good once more for the small band, remnants
of Tumeli, Usto-ma, Kulkumish, and Hebem villages. They
had come to the beautiful land where there were no gold
miners, a valley watered by a wandering stream at the foot
of Wahgalu, upstream from an existing village of her own
people, the Oidoing-koyo. The Panos had been received
with warmth and welcome. Game was plentiful, and in the
canyons that drained to the southwestward, not too far
down, there were extensive stands of oaks that provided
an abundant acorn harvest.

Bear-who-cannot-see-well, now healthy once more, had

signed some papers in Sacramento, using a different *Wawlem* name that he said was now *ours*, and this signing, he claimed, would ensure that no one could ever take the land away from them. Acorn Girl did not entirely trust this particular magic, but for the time she would believe her husband's words. And since they had come to this place, it was true, the only Whitemen who had visited them were those whom a man called Lassen had sent to help them build their house. Yes, in the meadow above the stream Bear-who-cannot-see-well insisted that a house be built, the Panos assisting, and in turn he offered to help with the construction of a similar lodge for any of the others who desired such a dwelling, but no one took him up on the offer, preferring to erect the familiar brush-and-thatch *hubos*. Construction of an earth lodge, a great *k-um* for dancing, had also been started, but it seemed unlikely that this structure would be completed during the present season.

There will be other seasons. . . .

Somehow, from their uncertain life of flight and battle, of moving from place to place and never being sure even of the next day, they had all come to believe in the inevitability of their own final destruction. But now, suddenly, they found themselves able to contemplate an unbroken string of seasons when the old and blissfully peaceful way of reckoning time reasserted itself, the times when flowers bloomed, the time of oak-flowering, the season of acorn harvest, the time of cold when people stayed warm around fires and told tales.

A time of new life.

Ooti touched her abdomen again, then turned in the sunlight. When the moment came, the right moment, she would tell Bear-who-cannot-see-well the result of the peaceful summer spent building, the warm nights spent making love, taking joy in each others' bodies.

A clumsy splashing, and then a spray of water dappled the warmth of her skin, shockingly cold. Ooti sucked in her breath, startled into full waking, and sat up, opening her eyes.

Bear-who-comes-before was standing in the edge of the water, shaking, his hide seeming to flop back and forth

independent of his growing body, droplets still spraying
from him, catching the light of afternoon sun so that he
appeared to be surrounded in a halo.

"You!" Acorn Girl said. "I thought you went hunting
with my husband and my grandfather."

The grizzlies were approaching their third year now,
massive animals, and to Ooti it seemed that they had been
growing increasingly restless as the season progressed.
Before now groaned and wagged his heavy head back and
forth, settling down near Ooti and sighing. But within
moments he rose again and walked about the bench, at
last standing at the edge and looking intently down into
the great tumble of canyons and stone faces that composed
the southern slopes of Wahgalu. He stood so for a while,
and then came back to her, lying down once more.

"Perhaps it is the time for you to go away from your
mother and seek a family of your own," she said to him.
"You are nearly a grown man-bear now, and I think you
are tired of living in your mother's lodge."

The grizzly placed its head down upon its forearms, the
small eyes still fixed on Ooti, and sighed again. She reached
out, stroked at the damp fur of the forehead. Before closed
his eyes, snuffling contentedly.

Acorn Girl slipped into the tepid water then, swam a
few lazy strokes, and returned to her sun-warmed boulder. A great lethargy seemed to have seized her these
past few months, but an immensely sweet languor. For
the time being, she wished neither to act nor to think very
hard. She had become, she thought, almost totally a creature of the physical rather than of the spiritual realm,
almost as one who is recovering from a long illness.

"Olelbis has changed his dream. I know everything is
different, and yet it is as if, in this one valley, in this
northern land, there is a small place left that remains
hidden from the new dreaming. Yet Bear-who-cannot-see-
well says that change will come even here, that our children will live more like the *Wawlems* than like the
Nishinams, and that we must be prepared for it. If that is
the way the world must be, then that is what we must live
with."

Ben had begun teaching her to read the marks on

paper, having managed to procure a *Bible* and a small volume of what he called *fairy tales*. He spent hours, also, carving each of the separate marks onto a plank of sugarpine wood and teaching her what each *letter* stood for. Once she had gotten the idea that these marks stood for sounds rather than for ideas, the whole process seemed fairly simple. Acorn Girl was impressed with the cleverness of the idea, and quickly she made the deduction that Nishinam as well as English words could be put down in the same manner.

When the others learned what was happening, several, including Tied-wing and Small Ears, also asked to be taught the magic. More trailed in as well, at last even Snakebite Dancer and Raccoon, and for a time each day at first the shade of a large maple and later the unfinished front room of the cabin became a classroom. Even Crane decided she wished to know what this new witchery was all about, although Hurt Eagle declined, insisting that he would have no use for such paraphernalia in Valley Above.

When the old shaman made his assertion, Ooti remembered with a smile that Bully O'Bragh (still with them at the time) had asked, "How ye know ye ain't already in Valley Above, ye iggerant Red Divvel? This hyar place looks like the right one to me."

"Perhaps it is so," Hurt Eagle mused. "Perhaps the foolish, drunken miners killed all of us. But if that is truly so, then I am content."

"Reckon ye're about the only nigger I cain't never get a rise from," Bully grumbled, spitting on the ground and winking at Acorn Girl.

Now Ooti wished that Bully and his Paiute wife, Rabbit-chaser of the Te-moas, had not left. She had grown particularly fond of the eccentric old *montan-yard* and thought of him as she thought of Peheipe the Clown in the Kuksu dances—so funny he could make one's sides hurt with laughing, and yet serving a serious, even a sacred purpose. Bully O'Bragh, she mused, was almost a living *Wawlem* version of Old Coyote Man. Yes, she missed the Irish Vulture—that was perhaps the one sad thing, and yet she had known always that Bully was not the sort to stay in one place for very long, if there were no battles brewing or other excitement to be had.

The sun had gone behind a shoulder of the mountain now, and the air was growing chilly. Acorn Girl rose, drew her cloak around herself, and began to gather dry wood for a fire. Ben and Hurt Eagle should be back soon, whether or not they had had any luck with hunting. It would be good to have a fire to welcome them.

Bear-who-comes-before sat up, stretched, lumbered after her, keeping close to her heels and getting underfoot every step that she took, several times nearly knocking her to the ground out of sheer clumsiness and size and strength.

Although her belly was not yet in the slightest rounded, she fancied that she could feel the life growing in there. She spoke to the unborn child as she worked.

"True Bear," she greeted it. "How is it with you today? Soon we will tell your father about you. Perhaps not tonight, but soon. I do not know if he will wish True Bear to be your only name. That will be all right, for he should have a choice. But to me this will be one of your names, little one."

Ooti was convinced, but not as a matter of reason, that the child could hear her words and understand them. She thought she sensed a response, a tiny flicker of consciousness deep within. And from the beginning, as well, she was certain that the small consciousness was masculine— that the dim, tiny entity was content, knew he was already loved.

My son. . . .

Acorn Girl began to sing as she carried the armful of fir knots back to the place beside the pool.

It had been dark for a long time before Bear-who-cannot-see-well returned to her. The half moon had risen well above the eastern ridges, and the fire had burned down to embers despite Ooti's best efforts to keep the flames blazing. She was not really worried yet, even though the men assured her they would return before nightfall, for it was in the nature of men to make such promises with the best of intentions and then to get so interested in what they were doing that they forgot what they had said. Still, she stayed awake, drinking the coffee that Ben always kept in supply now and that she, herself, had grown fond of. But at last she became so drowsy that she was unable to remain upright, and so she dozed, curled in her cloak.

She was dreaming of Hurt Eagle, heard him singing one of his songs, when Bear-who-comes-after crashed down the slope to where she lay, dislodging loose stones in a miniature landslide. Ooti jerked upright, looked around. In a few moments Ben followed, moving much more slowly and looking distracted. Acorn Girl put more knotwood onto the fire, warmed the coffee, waiting for her husband to speak. At last she could stand the suspense no longer and prodded him.

"What is it, Ben? Something is wrong. Where is Hurt Eagle? I thought I heard him singing just now."

Ben looked up from the mug of coffee Acorn Girl had poured for him, ran his fingers through his hair and then over his beard, took his glasses off, and unconsciously began to polish the lenses against the cloth of the new red flannel shirt he had purchased at the trading post near Lassen's rancho.

"I don't know where he is, Ooti," Ben answered.

"Do you mean he is lost? That is nothing to worry about. Hurt Eagle will always find his way back eventually. He has probably just gone on down to the village. . . ."

"You don't understand," Ben replied, interrupting her nervous flow of words. "He went up to the top of the mountain. He wanted to go to the very summit and wouldn't let me go with him."

"Hurt Eagle thinks the Wahgalu Mountain is a good place for *Kakini* Spirits. He is *yeponi*, and that gives him strength, but he believes if you were to see a *Sule* Ghost, you might die. Any place where the Spirits live is very dangerous for those who are not shamans."

"No," Ben said, his tone flat. "You must allow me to finish. This is very difficult, and you have to let me tell you. . . ."

Acorn Girl felt something go cold inside her, but she kept silence.

"Hurt Eagle said he wished to see *Estawm Yan*, that he thought the Sacred Hills might be visible from the top of the mountain. He said that he thought it might be possible to step into Valley Above from the summit of Wahgalu, just as it was from *Onolaitotl*, since the old fire-mountain goes far up into the sky. Hurt Eagle said he wished to speak to the Spirits to see about this matter—because he was ready to go. He said, 'My people are at peace, now, and no longer need me, and I have seen a hundred winters. Now that Olelbis has changed his dream, I long for Upper Meadow where things will always be the same.' "

A loon shrieked its long, mad laughter from somewhere, perhaps from one of the small lakes further up the stream, and Ben started involuntarily, then sipped at his coffee to moisten his throat. Ooti sat watching him, her eyes hidden in shadows, so that he could not tell what she was thinking. One hand, he could see, stroked absently at the fur of one of the grizzlies.

"I can't really explain what happened next," Ben continued. "Hurt Eagle told me that I must not follow him. There was something in the way he spoke . . . didn't even occur to me until later that I was perhaps allowing him to go off to his death. But how could I disobey him?"

Acorn Girl nodded calmly. She knew that very powerful shamans such as Hurt Eagle could easily exert such influence over anyone.

"I am a grown man, for God's sake," Ben complained, "an intelligent and highly educated, self-willed being. Yet it didn't occur to me to do other than let the old fool go off to jump from the top of the damned mountain."

"Do you know what he has done?" Ooti asked.

"No. I sat there waiting for him for hours before I began to realize what he had been saying—what he meant. At that point I started looking for him. I climbed all the way to the top, searched everywhere that I could, even after it got dark. He wasn't on top, he wasn't anywhere, so I came creeping back down. . . ."

Bear-who-comes-after took Ben's hand into his mouth, began to chew gently. Ben removed the hand, stroked at After's muzzle.

"You will never forgive me," Ben said, "for letting this

happen—and I don't blame you a bit. I know how you loved that old man. I did too, I guess."

With a little cry Ooti moved to sit close to her strange husband, took his hand in both of hers, and then reached up to caress his face.

"*Wawlems* are very foolish, and your blood is still *Wawlem*, Bear-who-cannot-see-well. Do you not think that Hurt Eagle has the right to leave us if he wishes? We cannot keep him here if his heart longs for Valley Above. That would be selfish. And that is why you could not disobey him, because you knew inside that he was free to do as he wished, and you would have been wrong to stop him."

"Ooti, you're as bad as he is," Ben muttered, shaking his head. "I'm damned if you haven't half-convinced me that this insanity you spout is the truth."

"It is not *wut-a*," she said. "It is the wisdom of *Moki*, just as Hurt Eagle is . . . was *Moki*, the highest rank among *kuksu* Spirit Impersonators."

"I know that's what you believe. I'm sorry, Ooti. But you must understand that I believe something different— and I know in my heart I should not have let the old man wander off up the mountain."

"If Hurt Eagle had been crazy, then that would have been one thing. But he was not crazy. We have had him for a long time, and . . ."

Acorn Girl's voice, which had been strong and clear, suddenly broke, and she didn't speak again for a time.

"I will miss him," she continued at last.

Ben reached for her and hugged her tightly.

"We will go see what has become of him as soon as it grows light," she said, the words muffled against her husband's chest.

Neither of them wished to lie down and sleep, but when the crescendoing chorus of birdsong roused Ben, he opened his eyes to a wash of golden light spreading against the eastern sky—and he knew that he had slept, his back against a young red fir. Ooti lay curled sideways, with her head in his lap.

He wakened her gently, threw some small twigs onto the fire, and heated again the dregs in the coffee pot.

They drank the stale brew and set out, chewing on pieces of dried venison. The air was very cold—the sun had not fully risen as yet. They moved quickly. Before and After followed, complaining loudly about the necessity for travel when it was much more pleasant to curl together and sleep.

The two humans and the two grizzlies climbed, following the deer trails that Ben and Hurt Eagle had used the day before, stopping frequently to draw breath, for not one was accustomed to the thin air of this high altitude.

The sun was up now, and where its rays fell, things quickly grew warm. But when Ben and Acorn Girl moved out of the forests of pine and fir, into an area of great expanses of stone and gnarled, windswept hemlocks, the dark-green, twisted forms looking like grotesque dancers frozen in midmotion, the seemingly gentle wind bit at their faces. Even ground cover was sparse and bent low to the stony earth.

"This is where he left me," Ben said, entering a grove of hemlocks growing up against a buttress of stone. "He went behind that ridge, and I guess he climbed up on the other side. The slope's easy enough—I climbed it later."

They rested briefly and then resumed their climb, now moving up the cracked stone of the peak itself. They emerged quickly above timberline, working their way along the natural declivities that afforded a gradual ascent. In many hollows snow still lingered, large patches of hard-frozen ice that never melted completely away, being buried by a new winter's fall before summer had dissolved it.

Wahgalu itself soared above them, out of their sight so that they saw only the slope rearing upward, the summit hidden.

Perhaps we too shall step into Valley Above. Perhaps my husband only returned to bring me with him. There are stories like that. . . . No, he would not wish to take me to where Pine-nut-eater lives. . . .

Acorn Girl giggled incongruously, and Ben turned to look at her, a question in his eyes. She touched at his arm, reassuringly solid beneath the fabric of his jacket.

"The air is thin," she said. "It makes strange thoughts come into my head."

They climbed onward. The two bears had deserted them in disgust shortly beyond timberline, apparently having determined that the human people were not going to give up on their foolishness and that bears had more sensible ways of spending their time.

Ooti was not concerned over them, certain the grizzlies would find them when they wished to.

The bare rim of the peak gave no sign of Hurt Eagle's passage, lacking soil to imprint a step. And no small plants appeared to be broken or bent.

At last they reached the summit, and here, also, they were greeted by silence and vast spaces and a light wind that seemed somehow to contain a message that they couldn't quite understand.

From the top an immense tangle of ridges and jagged, lesser peaks stretched out below them, deep clefts of canyons that drained from this mountain that harbored fire within itself, volcanic wastes to the north and east, the broken remnants of what Ben surmised to be a blown-out caldera to the south, the greater mountain that had vanished in noise and smoke and fire according to the Oidoing-koyos, the Greater Tehama that no longer existed. And westward, beyond a maze of canyons and ever-diminishing ridges, lay the long, amber-green hollow of the Great Valley, blue-gray haze softening the distance. Far to the west Ben and Ooti could see the Coast Range, and south-westward, rising from the floor of the enclosed plain, were *Onolaitotl, Estawm Yan*, blue in the distance, the Yuba Buttes, where the Spirit Tree *Ootimtsaa* surely still grew and continued to bear all twelve varieties of acorns.

Toward Estawm Yan Ooti directed her gaze, but Ben turned northward, sought out the huge, shining snow-peak of Shasta, its crown obscured by laterally banded windings of circular cloud, lenticular sworls of silver-gray.

"Wahgalu is truly a most sacred place," Ooti whispered.

"Beautiful," Ben agreed. "And you are beautiful also. . . ."

"If this is where my grandfather chose to step off into the Spirit World, then I think he did well. If that is what happened, Ben, then we will never find him, for from this place I shouldn't think it would be necessary to leave a body behind."

Nonetheless, they searched for some trace of the old shaman, traversing from one side of the peak to the other, staring down from cliffs where they could not descend. They found nothing, not the slightest suggestion that anyone had ever been near the summit.

It was well past midday, and seemingly from out of nowhere great thunderheads began to pile up around them, the view into the distances quickly obscured by a heavy blanket of damp gray. Thunder began to mutter at some distance, and both Ben and Ooti thought it wise to climb down to timberline and seek some sort of shelter from the oncoming storm.

As they descended, the thunder grew louder, and they began to see forked streaks of purple light striking out of the clouds. By the time they reached the first ragged growth of timber, lightning was stalking all about them, and the thunder was a series of sharp explosions with a peculiar hollow sound. The air around them became charged, so that they saw flickering veils of light dancing like ghosts in the mists.

Ben felt a strange wave of exuberance and shouted at the thunder, but Acorn Girl quickly put a hand on his arm, her face calm but watchful and sober.

"You must not do that, my husband," she cautioned. "Such noises might attract the Thunder Beings."

Ben laughed but suppressed another shout.

Before and After burst out of a grove of stunted hemlocks just below timberline and rushed for their human friends, bolting again into cover a second later when a crash of thunder boomed over the mountain's back.

"Perhaps they have found as good a place as any to wait out the fireworks," Ben suggested, and the two of them followed the grizzlies into their scant shelter.

Not much rain fell despite the volume of the sustained electrical discharges, a scattering of drops and a burst of small hail, but lightning continued to walk on the back of the mountain. After a few minutes Ben and Ooti decided to continue their descent, hoping to reach, if not their house, at least some better shelter further down before the darkness fell.

As they came into the first stands of heavier timber, a

tremendous crash of thunder resounded—almost simultaneous with the blast of light that had occasioned it, causing the shadows about them to vanish for an instant. Turning, they saw that a juniper had been struck, its top shattered and a black blaze-mark smoking down one side of the trunk. A few of the branches sprouted little nests of flame.

A faint sheen of light continued to dance in the air beneath the trees, and in the shadows something else, something moving between the evergreens.

Then, almost at once, three great, golden-furred grizzlies emerged, spaced as if with geometric precision, moving along at the edge of the forest, perhaps twenty feet separating one from another. A fourth bear stepped out then and walked slowly toward the humans, stopping a few yards distant and rising onto its rear legs, forearms held out toward Ben and Ooti as the creature balanced there, snuffling.

Bear-who-comes-after gave a long groan and then ran toward the standing bear, who dropped to all four feet and seemed to dance back into the trees. Like flames flickering out in a windstorm, the other grizzlies vanished from sight. After ran in the wake of his brother, and both stopped just at the edge of the trees, turned, roared a cry of anguish, and waited.

"Go ahead, my sons," Acorn Girl called out, "if that is what you wish to do. It's time for you to find wives and have families. I give you my permission . . . and blessing!"

Before dropped to his feet and trotted into the shadows, where the grizzly who seemed to be *huku* waited. After continued to stare back at the humans. Then the strange grizzly gave a sharp roar—and After, with a last glance over his shoulder, shambled on behind the others.

Light flickered in the electric air, and as the bears vanished, both Ben and Ooti believed they saw sparks playing about the fur of the creatures.

Then merely a glow in the distance, half-obscured by the trees.

The man and the woman stared for a time and then walked on, neither speaking.

"Perhaps you should try calling them," Ben suggested at last—for it seemed to him that Ooti was sad.

"No," she answered, perhaps too quickly. "They have their lives to live. They would still be children if they were human, but they are bears—and so they are ready to leave. Things change."

"You miss them already."

"I miss them, but that is how life is. We lose some things, we gain others."

And suddenly, with no transition, she was crying, tears streaming from her eyes, sobbing so that she couldn't catch her breath.

"And now I have learned what the old people always told me," she gasped, "that this is what life is. The longer we live, the more things . . . people . . . we lose. Even you, my Bear-who-cannot-see-well, someday, if I live a long time, I will lose you also. We love people, and then they go away."

"I guess that's true," Ben murmured, holding her. "I'm twenty-five years or more older than you are. I will have to live to be as old as Hurt Eagle himself if we are to step into . . . Valley Above . . . together. And it doesn't help at all that our grandparents tell us the truth, does it?"

"I have lost so many people, and I am not even very old," Acorn Girl said. "I thought perhaps it was over for a time, now that we have come to this place. How can I live without Hurt Eagle being here? He carried me when I was nearly dead, he carried me himself, even though he is old. He was both my father and my mother after everyone else was dead. . . ."

She wept as if for the first time for all her losses, for all the loved ones vanished, for her sons and her other husband, her mother and father, for her bears who had been her sons, now gone also, and most of all for Hurt Eagle. It was right, she knew, it was the way of things, that the two young grizzlies should seek their own kind. A new son was growing within her, and now Before and After had left, had gone away. It was right that Hurt Eagle should journey to Valley Above if his heart wished to be there. And yet it was too painful for the ones who remained behind—

all these leavings as though space itself had collapsed and yet an emptiness, a terrible void remained.

At last the tears exhausted themselves, and, feeling numb and a little ashamed, Acorn Girl continued the long walk back to their new home. Bear-who-cannot-see-well was beside her, and for the moment it was all right for her to rely upon his strength.

Night came before they reached the base of the mountain, and they camped again beside the warm pool. Just at sunset the clouds had broken, and the light streamed through, golden and crimson, blazing as if the world were being made anew.

With the first light, they resumed their walk home, reaching the village in the beautiful valley at midmorning. Small Ears, who was pounding acorns by the stream, came running to greet them, the two infant girls stumbling and crawling after her.

Ooti embraced her friend but did not know how to speak to her, did not know how to go about revealing what had happened to Hurt Eagle.

"I am glad you have come back," Small Ears chattered. "The acorns are all in, many more than we need. We took the mules and went far down into the big canyon. Many fine *hamsum tsaa* trees there and huge *babakam tsaa* also. Come look at the big piles of acorns we have made. You were not with us for the end of the harvest, but now it will soon be time to begin the *Ustu*. . . ."

Suddenly she stopped, becoming aware of her friend's expression.

"What is it, Ooti? What is wrong?"

Acorn Girl shook her head, reached down to lift Little Basket up, hugging the child against her neck—and then repeating the ritual with Willow Meadow, Small Ears' own child.

"I will speak to you about everything later. First I must see Crane," she said. "Where is Wakwak?"

"Why, she is in her lodge. Tell me what is wrong. Where are your two bears?"

"Before and After have gone to live as grizzlies," Ooti

replied, walking off in the direction of the *hubo* that Crane and Hurt Eagle had shared, Ben gesturing helplessly to Small Ears and following his young wife.

"I do not know how I will tell Crane," Acorn Girl whispered to Bear-who-cannot-see-well. "I find that this task is beyond my courage."

Ben put an arm about her shoulders, squeezed.

"I can't do much," he said, "but I will help the best I can. You have a warrior's heart, Ooti. Be brave now."

As they approached the *hubo*, Crane stepped outside, humming a song and carrying a tightly woven basket full of *ootim hai*, acorn kernels.

Ooti's heart felt like stone.

"Wakwak!" she called, finding that her voice was firm and clear after all, "I must speak with you."

"Ooti. Good. Go inside. I will be right back as soon as I have placed these where the water can draw the *suk* from them."

"Wait. . . ."

"I will be right back," the old woman insisted, and Acorn Girl saw that it would be better to wait for her inside than to chase after her and to try to tell her the sad news on the run.

Ben entered first, leaning down to pass through the small entryway. As Ooti was still crouched and making her way inside, she heard her husband utter a quick *Wawlem* oath and then burst into booming laughter. She could hardly credit her own hearing.

The next instant she was through, squinting into the half-darkness of the dwelling's interior. Tobacco smoke scented the air, and then she saw, leaning against a headrest and smoking his pipe quite comfortably—Hurt Eagle himself.

She could not speak for a moment, and then she threw herself into the ancient shaman's arms.

Crane entered a moment later, chuckling.

"I cannot leave this man alone at all. I go out on an errand, and when I come back he has a strange woman climbing all over him!"

"What in the hell happened up there, you old coot?" Ben was roaring. "We thought you were . . . we spent all day looking for you, damn your wrinkled hide!"

Hurt Eagle went on smoking as Ooti sat back on her heels to listen.

"What is there to tell? I did not mean to worry you, Ooti. But the Spirits—they said my *kakini busda* was not ready yet. And my heart was not yet pure enough. But I think it may be that Wakwak here has a special hold over Coyote, even though she will not admit it. The woman is insatiable for me, you know."

"Hah!" muttered Crane. "That is not the way it is in the robes at night."

"Perhaps, perhaps," Hurt Eagle mused. "Granddaughter, I think it is you who should tell us something. Up on the mountain of Wahgalu I learned that I should stay here a while longer if I wished to see my new grandchild. The Spirits said it would not be very long at all."

For a moment Acorn Girl stared blankly at the Ancient One. Her secret. She had forgotten, somehow—even Bear-who-cannot-see-well did not know this thing. She blushed, then smiled broadly, then laughed aloud.

"It is true, Ben. I forgot to tell you because of all the excitement. He will be born in the spring. I already call him True Bear, for I am certain I carry a man-child. But you may call him any name you wish."

Ben stared at the woman, his wife in truth. His eyes were wide behind the glitter of his spectacles.

A child!

He tried to comprehend the idea. He was forty-eight years old and had not for years even thought of having children. His chest seemed to expand, as if it were filling with something lighter than air. And when he attempted to speak, he found that all that could come out was a soft laughter.

He threw his arms about Ooti and hugged her until she complained he was breaking her ribs.

"Yes, yes, True Bear is a fine name," he said.

And suddenly the figure of William Goffe appeared in his mind, the old general smiling for once.

"But perhaps," he continued, raising one eyebrow, "our child could have another name, also. I'd like to name him for an ancestor of mine, a crusty old curmudgeon at that. Does *William True Bear* sound right?"

Acorn Girl nodded, still smiling.

"William True Bear Goffe McCain. . . ."

For a moment everyone in the lodge stood about, grinning foolishly at one another.

Then Crane intervened.

"This is all very fine," she said, "but there are things that need to be done now. Ooti, if you are finished wandering around, I think you should find a good Burning Ground for us. After all, you are the leader of these Panos. Do I have to do everything?"

Acorn Girl followed the older woman out of the *hubo*, where Crane winked and embraced her.

"Olelbis dreams," Ooti thought. "He wakes up and thrashes around, and everything gets thrown out of kilter. He dreams again, and everything is changed. But now it is time for the *Ustu*, and the year will come round once more. I do not understand very much, but I understand that we must set up the tall poles now and tie the strings of baskets to them. We must pile food and other things at the bases of the poles, and then, when it is dark, Hurt Eagle must set everything afire. And we must all continue to wail and cry and sing throughout the night of the Burning—for all of those whom we have loved who have gone on ahead to Upper Meadow. I do not know if the dead have any need for the things we burn in their honor, but I know that we must do it nonetheless. For that is the way it has always been. . . ."

Aawpawpawkawm aawm yoo-oolooshkit. White rock all fall to pieces. Hammu! That's all. Yes. Yaaw-huy-eni, don't go away, just circle around. Hammu!

The author wishes to make special acknowledgment to Richard Simpson for his wonderful book, *Ooti: A Maidu Legacy* (Celestial Arts: 1977). This volume combines Simpson's photography and tale-telling, the latter in many places integrated with the words of Lizzie Enos, a Maidu woman whose entire life of 87 years was spent in her ancestral Sierra Nevada foothills, keeping alive both her own language and the traditional practice of harvesting and preparing acorns, the staff of life for her people in the old times, converting the kernels, *ootim hai*, into the finest yellow acorn flour, *ootim bat*. In contemplating one of Simpson's photographic portraits of Lizzie, I found myself re-creating her in the guise of an eighteen-year-old girl. And at that moment *People of the Sacred Oak* was born.

—Bill Hotchkiss

Woodpecker Ravine
Nevada County, California
May 13, 1983

ABOUT THE AUTHOR

BILL HOTCHKISS is a poet, critic, and novelist whose most recent books include *Mountain Lamb*, *Spirit Mountain*, *Ammahabas*, *Soldier Wolf*, *Crow Warriors*, and *The Medicine Calf*. Born in New London, Connecticut, in 1936, Hotchkiss grew up in California's Mother Lode country and was educated at the University of California, San Francisco State University, and the University of Oregon. He's the holder of several graduate degrees, including a Ph.D. The author and his wife, Judith Shears, live in Woodpecker Ravine, near Grass Valley, California. He is currently at work on a new historical novel to be published by Bantam Books in the near future.